About the Authors

USA TODAY bestselling and RITA® Award–nominated author **Caitlin Crews** loves writing romance. She teaches her favourite romance novels in creative writing classes at places like UCLA Extension's prestigious Writers' Program, where she finally gets to utilize the MA and PhD in English Literature she received from the University of York in England. She currently lives in California with her very own hero and too many pets. Visit her at caitlincrews.com.

Sharon Kendrick once won a national writing competition by describing her ideal date: being flown to an exotic island by a gorgeous and powerful man. Little did she realize that she'd just wandered into her dream job! Today she writes for Mills & Boon, featuring often stubborn but always *to die for* heroes and the women who bring them to their knees. She believes that the best books are those you never want to end. Just like life…

After spending three years as a die-hard New Yorker, **Kate Hewitt** now lives in a small village in the English Lake District with her husband, their five children and a golden retriever. In addition to writing intensely emotional stories she loves reading, baking and playing chess with her son—she has yet to win against him, but she continues to try. Learn more about Kate at kate-hewitt.com

Billonaires
COLLECTION

January 2019

February 2019

March 2019

April 2019

May 2019

June 2019

Billionaires: The Rebel

CAITLIN CREWS

SHARON KENDRICK

KATE HEWITT

MILLS & BOON

First Published in Great Britain 2019
By Mills & Boon, an imprint of HarperCollins *Publishers*
1 London Bridge Street, London, SE1 9GF

BILLIONAIRES: THE REBEL © 2019 Harlequin Books S.A.

The Return of the Di Sione Wife © 2016 Harlequin Books S.A.
Di Sione's Virgin Mistress © 2016 Harlequin Books S.A
A Di Sione for the Greek's Pleasure © 2016 Harlequin Books S.A

Special thanks and acknowledgment are given to Caitlin Crews, Sharon Kendrick and Kate Hewitt for their contribution to *The Billionaire's Legacy* series.

ISBN: 978-0-263-27555-1

9-0219

MIX
Paper from
responsible sources
FSC® C007454

This book is produced from independently certified FSC™ paper to ensure responsible forest management.

For more information visit: www.harpercollins.co.uk/green

Printed and bound in Spain
by CPI, Barcelona

THE RETURN
OF THE
DI SIONE WIFE

CAITLIN CREWS

CHAPTER ONE

THE HAWAIIAN ISLAND of Maui was tropical and lush, exactly as advertised, which irritated Dario Di Sione the moment he stepped off his private jet and into its unwelcome embrace.

The press of the island humidity felt intimate, and Dario didn't do *intimate*. The thick air insinuated itself against his skin, making the faded jeans and expertly tailored jacket he'd worn on the long flight from New York City feel limp and too close as he strode across the tiny tarmac toward the Range Rover that waited there for him, as ordered. A gentle breeze carried the exotic scent of the island—deep green things in exultant growth and the rougher, deeper smell of sugarcane production from all those fields they'd flown over on the way in to land—playing across his face like so many unsolicited kisses.

It only annoyed him more. He was trying to conduct a business conversation, not indulge in sensory overload on a damned tarmac.

"Is the car waiting as promised?" his secretary, Marnie, asked through the top-of-the-line, brand-new smartphone he had clamped to his ear. He was a proud user of his company's highly coveted products. "I was very clear

about the need for a sports utility vehicle. The road out
to the Fuginawa estate is very rough, apparently, and—"

"I can handle rough road," Dario told her, trying to
rein in his impatience. He didn't want to be here so soon
after the major product launch his company had pulled
off this past weekend—or at all, for that matter—but that
wasn't his secretary's fault. It was his. He should never
have allowed an old man's sentimentality to win out over
his own hard-won rationality. This was the result. He was
halfway across the planet—when he should have been
in his office—surrounded by lazy palm trees and exotic smells, all to appease an elderly man's whims. "The
Range Rover is fine. And here, as ordered."

Marnie moved on to the long list of calls and messages she'd fielded during his first absence from the office he'd actually been sleeping in these past few months,
a flashback to the kind of stress he'd been under six years
ago when he'd first started with ICE. Dario scowled as
another sultry breeze licked over him. He didn't like
flashbacks and he didn't like that breeze, either. It was
fragrant and sensuous at once, moving through his hair
like a caress and getting beneath the fine linen of the
button-down shirt he wore. Like a woman's fingers trailing down the length of his abdomen, suggestive and
mischievous.

He rolled his eyes at his own flight of fancy, then
scraped a hand over his unshaven jaw, aware that he
looked a little more disreputable than the CEO of a major
computer company, currently the darling of the tech industry and the smitten public, probably should. And he
was about as interested in the intimate touch of Hawaiian breezes as he was in being here in the first place.
Not at all.

This entire trip was a waste of his time, he thought as Marnie kept talking her way through the pile of messages and calls that needed his personal attention immediately, if not sooner. He ought to be back in his office in Manhattan today, handling all of this in person. Instead, he'd flown some ten hours down his grandfather's memory lane to appease the very worst kind of nostalgic sentiment. Giovanni had sold off his collection of beloved trinkets years ago and had talked about them endlessly throughout Dario's youth. Now, ninety-eight years old and facing down his impending death with his usual sense of theater and consequence, the old man wanted them all back.

They remind me of the love of my life, his grandfather had claimed when he'd asked Dario to buy back these earrings for him. From a reclusive Japanese billionaire on his remote estate in Hawaii.

In person.

Dario actually snorted at the memory as he threw his bag into the back of the Range Rover and shrugged out of his jacket, too. He didn't know how he'd managed not to do exactly that to his grandfather's face when the old man had summoned Dario to his side earlier this month and made his outlandish request. But who refused an old man what he'd claimed was his dying wish?

"Email me those specs, Marnie," he told his secretary before she could ask what that noise was. Bless that woman. She was infinitely more dependable than anyone else he knew, including every last member of his overly dramatic and periodically demanding family. He made a mental note to give her another richly deserved bonus, simply because she was *not* one of the pain-in-the-ass Di Siones he shared his blood with, if little else. "Give

me a minute to switch to hands-free and then start rolling the calls."

He didn't wait for Marnie to respond. He rolled his
sleeves up, hoping that would cut some of the tropical
humidity. He dug out his earpiece and activated it, then
climbed behind the wheel of the sparkling, brand-new
Range Rover. He started it up, punching the address he
needed into the GPS and heading out of the small airport
as the first call came in.

But even as he listened to one of his vice presidents
lay out a potentially tricky situation with the brand-new
phone they'd just released over the weekend, he was
thinking about his grandfather and the so-called lost
love of his very long life.

Lost loves, in Dario's experience, were lost for a
damned good reason. Usually because they hadn't been
worthy of all that much love in the first place.

Or possibly—and this was his pet theory—because
love was a great big lie people told themselves and everyone else to justify their own terrible and usually painfully dramatic behavior.

And lost loves certainly didn't need to be found again,
once the truth about them came out the way it always
did. Better to leave the past where it lay, so it could fes-
ter on its own without infecting the present, or so Dario
had always believed.

It had been difficult not to share his thoughts on that
with his grandfather when Giovanni had told Dario that
same old mushy story about love and secrets and blah-
blah-blah. He'd shared it in one form or another all his
life. Then he'd sent Dario off on this idiotic errand that
anyone—literally, anyone, including the overzealous recent college grads working in Dario's mailroom—could

have performed. But then, Dario was used to biting his tongue when it came to the foolish emotions other people liked to pretend were perfectly reasonable. Reasonable and rational and more than that, *necessary*. Whatever.

There was never any point in saying so, he knew. Quite apart from the fact that Dario wasn't about to quarrel with the elderly grandfather who'd taken him and his siblings in after his parents had died, he'd also come to realize that the more he shared his opinion on subjects like these, the more people lined up to tell him how cynical he was. As if that was an indictment of his character, or should allow them to dismiss his opinion out of hand. Or as if it should be a matter of deep concern to him, that weird fetish he had for *realism*.

He'd stopped bothering years ago. Six years ago, in fact.

And the truth was, he cared so little either way that it was easier to simply do as he was asked—in this case, fly across the planet to buy back a pair of earrings that could easily have been sent by courier had there not been so much *sentiment* attached to them, apparently—than to explain why he thought the entire enterprise was ridiculous. He was vaguely aware that the old man had been sending all the Di Sione siblings off on these pointless quests for what he called his Lost Mistresses, but Dario had been far too busy with this latest product launch to pay that much attention to round nine hundred and thirty-seven of the Di Sione family melodrama.

Surely they'd had a lifetime's worth already. He'd been sick of it at eight years old, when his hedonistic and undependable parents had died in a horrible, utterly avoidable car crash and the paparazzi had descended upon them all like a swarm. His feelings on the subject hadn't improved much since.

There was a part of Dario—not hidden very deeply, he could admit—that would have been perfectly happy if he never heard from another one of his relatives again. A part of him that expected that, once the old man passed on, that would happen naturally enough. He was looking forward to it. He would retreat into his work, happily, the way he always did. God knew he had enough to do running ICE, the world's premier computer company if he said so himself, a position he'd won with his own hard work and determination. The way he'd won everything else that was his—everything that had lasted.

Besides, the only member of his family he'd ever truly loved had been his identical twin brother, Dante. Until Dante had smashed that into so much dust and regret, too. He couldn't deny that his brother's betrayal had hurt him—but it had also taught him that he was much better off surrounding himself with people he paid for their loyalty, not people who might or might not give it as it suited them.

Dario *really* didn't want to think about his twin. That was the trouble with any kind of involvement with his family. It led to precisely the thoughts he spent most of his time going out of his way to avoid.

He'd assumed that if he performed this task for his grandfather the way the rest of his brothers and sisters were supposedly doing, they could all stop acting like any of what had happened six years ago and since was Dario's fault. Or as if he shared the blame for what had happened in some way, as he'd been the one to walk away from his marriage as well as his relationship with Dante. He hadn't exactly *asked* his brother to sleep with his wife during what had been one of the most stressful periods of his life. And he refused to accept that there was something wrong with him that he'd never forgiven either his brother or his wife for that, and never would.

They'd let him twist in the wind, the two of them. They'd let them think the tension between them was dislike, and Dario had believed it, too busy trying to sort out what to do with the company he and Dante had started and whether or not to merge with ICE, which Dario had thought was a good idea while Dante had opposed it. All that mess and tension and stress and sleeplessness to discover that the two of them had been betraying him all along...

Here and now, in Hawaii of all places, Dario thought the only thing wrong with him was that he was still paying any kind of attention to anything a member of the Di Sione family said, did or thought. That needed to stop.

"It *will* stop," he promised himself between calls, his voice a rasp in the Range Rover's quiet interior. "As soon as you hand the old man his damned earrings, you're done."

He drove through the business district of Kahului, then followed the calm-voiced GPS's directions away from the bustle of big-box stores and chain restaurants clustered near the airport toward the center of the island. He soon found himself on a highway that wound its way through the lush sugarcane fields, then up into the hills, where views even he had to admit were spectacular spread out before him. The Pacific Ocean gleamed in the summer sun with another island stretched out low in the distant water, green and gold. The old volcanic West Maui Mountains were covered in windmills, palm trees lined the highway and exuberant flowers in shockingly bright colors were everywhere, from the shrubs to the trees to the hedges.

Dario didn't take vacations, but if he did, he supposed this would be a decent place for it. As he waited for another call to connect, he tried to imagine what that would even look like. He'd never lounged anywhere in his life, poolside or beachside or otherwise. The last almost-vacation he'd taken had been an extreme sports weekend with one of Silicon Valley's innumerable millionaire genius types. But since he'd landed that particular genius and his cutting edge technology after they'd skydived down to a killer trail run in Colorado, en route to some class-V rapids, he didn't think that counted.

Even so, he certainly hadn't been lounging around that weekend out west, contemplating the breeze. He'd always worked. Maybe if he hadn't been working so hard six years ago, he'd have seen what was coming. Maybe he'd have seen the warning signs between his brother and his wife for what they were instead of naively assuming that neither one of them would do such a thing to him…

Why are you dwelling on this old, boring nonsense? He shook his head to clear it.

The road headed out along rocky cliffs that flirted with the ocean, then turned to packed red dirt, and Dario slowed down. He was listening to one of his engineers when his cell signal dropped out, and he sighed, scowling at the GPS display that showed he still had quite a distance left to go.

He didn't understand why anyone would live out here, this far from the rest of the world. He knew the current owner of his grandfather's earrings was the kind of wealthy man as well known for his eccentricities as the family fortune he'd augmented considerably throughout his lifetime, but this was taking things a little bit far. Surely a paved road wouldn't have gone amiss.

But then, Dario loved New York City. He liked to be where everything was happening, all the time. Where he could walk down streets as busy at 4:00 a.m. as they were at four in the afternoon. Where he could be anonymous on the street and then recognized instantly when he walked into a favorite restaurant. He didn't understand all this lonely quiet, no matter how pretty it was out here. He didn't get what it was *for*. It appeared to allow entirely too much room for maudlin contemplation.

Then again, his idea of relaxing was closing a new deal and bolstering his stock portfolio. Things he was very, very good at.

Dario passed a tiny little country store that was the only sign of civilization he'd seen in miles and continued down the dusty, winding, rutted track at the base of the looming mountain. There were old, intricate stone walls and stretches of green pasture to his left, climbing up the steep side of the mountain, and wilder-looking fields to his right that gave way to rocky cliffs each time the road wound its way around again.

He felt as if he was on a different planet.

"Only for you, old man," he muttered.

But this was the last time Dario planned to extend himself, even for Giovanni. He'd had enough family for one life.

Without any cell service he was left to his own dark thoughts, which Dario preferred to avoid at the best of times—the way he'd been doing for at least the last six years, thank you. He shut off the AC and lowered his windows, letting that same mysterious breeze fill the car. It smelled like sunshine and unfamiliar flowers. It danced over him, distracting him, seeming to fill him up from the inside.

Dario scowled at that nonsense and focused on the rough, decidedly rural landscape all around him instead. It was hard to believe he was in one of the foremost tourist destinations in all the world. This part of Maui was not the luxury-hotel, world-class golfing mecca he'd been led to expect had taken over the whole island—or hell, the entire state of Hawaii. This was all gnarled trees and wild, untamed countryside. He made his way along the foothills of the mountains toward rocky beaches strewn with smooth pebbles and sharp-edged volcanic rock. A small, proud little church drew itself up at the end of the world as if it alone held back the sea, and then Dario was climbing back up into the hills again to skirt this or that rocky, black stone cove.

Right about the time he ran out of patience, he finally found the gleaming entrance that marked his turn inward to the Fuginawa estate. At last. He had a brief discussion with a disembodied guard over the intercom before the imposing iron gates swung open to admit him. This drive was not paved, either, but it was noticeably better tended than the previous road—which was called a highway even while it was made of little more than reddish dirt and grass. The estate's private lane meandered lazily from the cliff's edge over the water until it delivered him to a sweeping, landscaped circle behind an impressive house that rambled for what seemed like miles in both directions, commanding a stunning view out over the water and on toward the horizon.

Dario climbed out of the Range Rover, unable to keep himself from taking the kind of deep breath that let perhaps too much of all that dizzy sunshine into his lungs. Fog clung to the mountain above him, draping the hills in ribbons of smoke and navy, the mist seeming to dance a bit as he looked at it. It made it hard to keep hold of his impatience, but still, he managed it.

Pretty wasn't going to run his company for him, and no matter that the sun felt good on his face after the mad crush of the past few weeks and a long plane ride. He glanced at his watch to see that it had just come noon here, as his secretary had arranged with Fuginawa's representatives. There was no reason he couldn't get the damned earrings for his grandfather and get right back on his plane. He could be back in New York by the start of the business day tomorrow. He certainly didn't have to stay in this odd place any longer than necessary.

Dario raked a hand through his hair and followed the path down toward the impressive, faintly Asian-inspired front door, his own footsteps seeming unduly loud in all the quiet. Even the door itself opened soundlessly as he approached.

He was beckoned inside by a smiling member of staff, who then led him through the graciously appointed house. It was all high ceilings with silent fans to move the air about, and shockingly expensive, highly recognizable art on the walls. The inside spaces blended seamlessly into outside spaces with walls that rolled back to let in the air and light, making the house wide open to the elements in a manner Dario found...reckless. Very nearly disturbing, especially given the priceless paintings on the walls—but what did he care? It wasn't his art at risk. It was only his time he was wasting here, nothing more. The staff member invited him to sit in one of the outside areas, tucked beneath an overhang wrapped with blooming vines, offering sweeping views out toward the deep blue Pacific Ocean and the winding road he'd just driven up.

It was still so quiet Dario almost thought he could

hear the ocean waves crashing into the rocky black shore down below, when he was sure that couldn't be possible this far up the side of the mountain. He thrust his hands into his pockets. If he'd had to traipse this far off the beaten path into what appeared to be the distant edge of the middle of nowhere, he supposed a view like this made it almost worth it.

Almost.

He heard a step on the stones behind him and turned, itching to get to the actual point of this absurd journey so he could get back to New York as quickly as possible. He wasn't a hobbit en route to Mount Doom, and no matter if that mountain above him was actually the side of a dormant volcanic crater. He was a very busy man who didn't have time to waste gazing at the view on the back end of the world—

But then Dario froze.

For a stunned moment he thought he was imagining her.

Because it couldn't be *her*.

Inky black hair that fell straight to her shoulders, as sleekly perfect as he remembered it. That lithe body, unmistakably gorgeous in the chic black maxidress she wore that nodded to the tropical climate as it poured all the way down her long, long legs to scrape the ground. And her face. *Her face.* That perfect oval with her dark eyes tipped up in the corners, her elegant cheekbones and that lush mouth of hers that still had the power to make his whole body tense in uncontrolled, unreasonable, *unacceptable* reaction.

He stared. He was a grown man, a powerful man by any measure, and he simply stood there and *stared*—as if she was as much a ghost as that damned Hawaiian wind that was still toying with him. As if she might blow away as easily.

But she didn't.

"Hello, Dare," she said with that same self-possessed, infuriating calm of hers he remembered too well, using the name only she had ever called him—the name only she had ever gotten away with calling him.

Only Anais.

His wife.

His treacherous, betraying cheat of a wife, who he'd never planned to lay eyes on again in this lifetime. And who he'd never quite gotten around to divorcing, either, because he'd liked the idea that she had to stay shackled to the man she'd betrayed so hideously six years ago, like he was an albatross wrapped tight around her slim, elegant neck.

Here, now, with her standing right there in front of him like a slap straight from his memory, that seemed less like an unforgivable oversight. And a whole lot more like a terrible mistake.

Anais Kiyoko had been dreading this moment for six years.

Dreading it, dreaming it. Same difference.

And still, nothing could have prepared her for this. For him. For Dario, her Dario, in the flesh.

Nothing ever had. She'd never seen him coming. Not when she'd met him on an otherwise ordinary winter afternoon, not when he'd turned into a stranger in the middle of their marriage, accused her of the worst betrayal and then left her. Never. Today, Anais thought, she'd take control. She wouldn't be blindsided by him again.

She just needed to recover from the sucker punch of seeing him again first. She'd assumed she never would.

"What the hell are you doing here?" he growled at her.

That same voice, rich and low, kicked at her, leaving a shower of sparks behind. It was definitely him. She'd expected him, of course, but some part of her hadn't thought he'd really show after all these years. After the way he'd left things. After all this cruel, deliberate silence.

But it was him. It was really, truly him.

Dario stood there before her on Mr. Fuginawa's lanai, the rolling green pastures of the remote Kaupo district's countryside behind him, the ocean a bright blue far below, like something straight out of her fantasies. And despite her many fervent prayers over the years, time had not smacked him down the way she would have preferred.

The way she'd prayed it would, more than once.

He was not a troll. He was not disfigured by his own cold, black heart and his dark imaginings the way he richly deserved. He was not stooped with loss or rendered appropriately hideous by the things he'd done.

Quite the opposite.

Unfairly, Dario Di Sione was the most beautiful man she'd ever seen in her life. *Still.* He exuded that intense, brooding masculinity of his the way other, much less intriguing men smelled of aftershave or cologne. He wore the kind of seemingly casual jeans only very rich, very powerful men could make look like formal wear, and one of those whisper-soft shirts of his that clung to the glorious planes of his chest, the sleeves rolled up to show off his golden skin and the sheer strength of his forearms. She knew that behind the aviator sunglasses he wore, his eyes would still be blue enough to rival the Hawaiian sky all around him, always such a dizzying contrast with the black hair he wore a touch too long and what looked like a day or two's growth of beard on his perfect jaw.

Damn him.

And damn her for being just as susceptible to him as she'd always been. Despite everything.

"I asked you a question."

Anais blinked, trying to shove aside her wholly unwanted reaction to him. But her fingers dug into the leather folder she carried, and she didn't think she was fooling anyone. Least of all herself.

"I hope you didn't have any trouble finding the place," she said, as if this was a normal business meeting, the kind she carried out as Mr. Fuginawa's lawyer, his first line of defense and his preferred method of communication with the outside world, all the time. "The road is a little bit tricky."

Dario didn't move. And yet she felt as if he'd reached across the distance between them and snatched her up in his fist. She had to force herself to take a breath. To stop holding the last one in as if letting it out might hurt her.

Especially when he slid those sunglasses from his face and focused all that furious blue attention on her.

"Really, Anais?" His voice was as mocking and withering as it was harsh, but she didn't recoil at the sting of it. She was tougher now. She'd had to be, hadn't she? "That's how you want to play this?"

Anais didn't look away. "Should we pick up the conversation where we left off six years ago, Dare? Is that what you want? The fact you cut me off without a word back then suggests not."

"Was that a conversation?" His voice took on that same lethal edge she could see in the tense way he held himself, and it made her stomach ache. "I would have chosen an uglier word to describe the scene I walked in on."

"That's because your mind is a gutter," she replied, still trying to keep her voice cool and professional, despite the topic. "But I'm afraid that has nothing to do with me. It never did."

He laughed. Not the laughter she remembered from when they'd first met, when she'd been a third year at Columbia Law and Dario had been finishing his MBA. The laughter that had made the entire city of Manhattan seem to stand still around him, lost in that rough sound of pure male joy. This was not that. Not even close.

"I don't care enough to ask you what you mean by that." He looked around, his gaze as hard as that set to his jaw. "I came here for a pair of earrings, not to play Ghost of Christmas Past games with you. Can you help with that, Anais, or was this whole thing a setup so you could ambush me?"

By some miracle, her jaw didn't drop at that.

Because she realized he meant what he said. She could read it in every hard, belligerent line of his body and that bright blaze of temper in his gaze.

"You knew this meeting was with me," she managed to make herself say, though she couldn't pretend she still sounded calm or in control. "We've been emailing for weeks."

"My secretary has been emailing for weeks," he corrected her. He shook his head, impatience etched across his features. "I've been busy with things that actually matter to me. And don't flatter yourself, please. If I'd known you were going to be here, I wouldn't be."

And his voice was precisely as cutting as she remembered it from that horrible day when he'd walked out of their marriage, and her life, without warning and without a backward glance.

As if no time had passed. As if nothing had changed.

As if he really did think she was the cheating whore she still couldn't quite believe he'd so easily, so quickly, so *utterly* accepted she was based on one easily explained and wholly innocent moment with his awful brother. Just as she couldn't believe he'd never stuck around for that explanation—or even a fight. He'd simply…left.

Which meant all her silly expectations about this meeting today were nothing more than the same foolish dreams she'd nurtured all this time, all the while pretending she'd gotten over him and his shocking betrayal. That maybe he regretted what he'd done. That maybe he'd finally put aside his pride. That maybe he'd come to his senses at last. It was bad enough that she'd entertained such fantasies. It told her all kinds of uncomfortable things about how pathetic she was, how desperate and sad.

But much worse than her own hurt feelings and obviously messed-up heart, it meant that he still had no idea.

He still didn't know about Damian.

He really had come all the way to this remote corner of Maui for a pair of earrings, not for her.

And certainly not for their son.

CHAPTER TWO

"HAVE YOU LAPSED into a coma?" Dario asked, the silk and menace in his voice hitting her like a lash and cutting deep. "Or is this remorse at last?"

And Anais hadn't entirely realized *how much hope* she'd allowed herself to feel in the weeks leading up to this meeting with him, after all these years of silence, until now. When he took it all away again.

She should have known better.

"Remorse?" she echoed. She moved farther out onto the lanai, dropping the leather folder on the table between them and ordering her legs to stay steady beneath her when they felt like one of the palm trees being buffeted this way and that by the relentless trade winds. "For what, exactly? Your extended temper tantrum six years ago? I have a lot of feelings about that actually, but remorse isn't one of them."

Dario's mouth moved into a hard, cynical sort of smile that made her stomach clutch. She'd had no idea he could look like that. So etched through with bitterness. She told herself he deserved it, but still. It made her ache.

"It's good to know you're as shameless as ever," he said. "But why change? It got you what you wanted."

"Yes. How silly of me. You storming off into the

ether was exactly what I wanted. It's like you read my mind."

"My mistake, of course. Maybe you were angling for a threesome? You must have read too many tabloids. You should have asked, Anais. I would have told you that I don't like sharing anything with anyone, least of all my twin brother."

"I see you're still hell-bent on being as insulting and disgusting as you were back then. What a happy reunion this is. I'm beginning to understand why it took six years."

After the way he'd treated her, after the way he'd acted as if she'd never existed in the first place—refusing all contact with her and barring her from entering his office or apartment building as if she was some kind of deranged stalker—she *couldn't believe* that, deep down, she still expected Dario to be a better man. Even now, some part of her was waiting for him to crack. To see reason. To stop this madness at last.

Anais told herself it was because of Damian. She wanted her son's father to be a good man at heart, even if that took some excavating, like any mother would. She wanted his father to be the man she'd once believed he was, when she'd been foolish enough to fall in love with him. Because that would be a good thing for *her child*, not for herself.

Or not entirely *for yourself*, whispered that voice inside of her that knew exactly how selfish she was.

But life wasn't about what she wanted. She'd learned that as a child in Paris, the pawn of two bitter parents who had never wanted her and had only wanted each other for that one night that had created her and thrown them together, like it or not. Life was about what she had.

Like her cruel, flamboyantly unfaithful French father and the embittered Japanese mother whose name she'd taken when she'd turned eighteen because she'd been the lesser of two evils, those two things had never matched. It was high time she stopped imagining they ever would.

She tapped her fingers on the leather folder. "These are the contracts. Please sign them. Once you do, the earrings are yours, as promised."

"Are we back to doing business, Anais?" he asked softly. She didn't mistake that tone of his. She could hear the steel beneath it. "I might get whiplash."

She allowed herself a careless shrug and wished she actually felt even slightly at her ease. "Business appears to be the only thing you know how to do."

"Unlike all the things you know how to do, I imagine. Or should I ask my brother about that? He was always the more adventurous one."

Anais would never know how she managed to keep from screaming out loud at that—at the unfairness and the cruelty of it, from a man whom she'd once believed would never, ever, say the kinds of things to her that her parents had hurled at each other all her life. She felt a vicious red haze slam down over her, holding her tight, like a terrible fist. But somehow, she beat it back. She thought of Damian, her beautiful little boy, and stayed on her feet. She managed, somehow, to keep herself from screaming like some kind of banshee at this man she couldn't believe she'd married.

Not that he didn't deserve a little bit of banshee, the way he'd acted back then and was still acting now. Still, that didn't mean she had to give him the satisfaction of acting insane.

She met his condemning gaze with her own.

"I have nothing to be ashamed about," she told him. Icily. Distinctly. "I did not sleep with your brother. I don't care if Dante has spent the past six years telling you otherwise. I didn't. He's a liar."

"I wouldn't know what he is," Dario said with cool nonchalance. "I haven't spoken to him since I found him with you in my bedroom. Don't tell me you two lovebirds didn't make it. How heartbreaking for you both."

That shocked Anais in a way she'd have thought was impossible. The Di Sione twins she'd known had been inseparable. *Until you*, she reminded herself. *Dante hated you on sight.* She tried to blink it away.

"The fact you thought anything happened between us—and still think it, all these years later, to such an extent that you feel justified in hurling insults at me—says more about what a vile, dark little man you are than it could ever say about me."

Dario seemed almost amused by that. "I'm sure that's what you tell yourself. It must be comfortable there in your fantasy world. But the truth is the truth, no matter how many lies you pile on top of it. So many it looks like you've convinced yourself. Congratulations on that, but you haven't convinced me."

If he'd been thrown by her appearance here, he was over it now, clearly. This was the Dario she remembered. The stranger who had walked into their home that awful day and had inhabited the body of the husband she'd adored a whole lot more than she should have. This cruel, mocking man who looked at her and saw nothing but the worthless creature her parents had always told her she was. As if that twisted truth had merely been lurking there inside of her, waiting to come out, and after their wild year together, he'd finally seen what they'd always seen when they'd looked at her.

Dario had done a great many unforgivable things, many far worse than how he'd looked at her that day, but that had been the first. The shot over the bow that had changed everything. Anais found she still wasn't over it.

At all.

His lips thinned as he looked at her and he reached for the leather folder, pulling out the stack of documents. Then he acted as if she was another piece of furniture. He ignored her. He pulled out a chair and sat down, then proceeded to read through the dense, legal pages as if he was looking for further evidence of her trickery.

Anais thought sitting down with him at the table as if this was a normal, civilized meeting might actually break something inside of her, so she stood where she was instead. Calmly. Easily. On the outside, anyway. Letting the breeze toy with the ends of her hair as she stared out at the water and pretended she was somewhere else. Or that he was somebody else. Or that his being here didn't present her with a huge ethical dilemma.

She didn't want to tell him.

He didn't deserve to know.

What if he turned this cruelty, this viciousness, on his own son?

But even as she thought it, she knew she was trying to rationalize her dilemma away instead of addressing it head-on, the way she should. Because he kept hurting her feelings all these years later, not because she truly believed Dario would ever do anything to hurt a child.

Not telling him now would change everything. She recognized that. Up until today, the fact that Damian didn't know his father had been entirely Dario's own fault. He'd made sure Anais couldn't contact him, and she hadn't seen how taking out an advertisement in the papers—as her aunt had suggested one night after a few too many of Anais's tears and rants to the heedless walls—could help her child. By feeding Damian to the hungry tabloids? By making his life a circus? No, thank you. And she'd have eaten a burning hot coal before she'd have called Dante for any help, that manipulative bastard.

Dario had maintained his silence ever since that day back in New York. That wasn't her fault.

But letting him leave here today no wiser? That would be.

She felt her hands bunch into fists and couldn't quite make herself smooth them out again, even though she knew he'd see it. He could think what he liked, she told herself stoutly. He would, anyway.

"I have something to tell you," she said woodenly, forcing the words out past lips that felt like ice and keeping her eyes trained on the sea. The beautiful Hawaiian sea that didn't care about her troubles. The sea that washed them all away, or seemed to, if she stared at it long enough. The sea that had saved her once and could again, if she let it. Even from this.

Even from him. Again.

"I'm not interested."

"I don't really care if you're interested or not. This might come as a surprise to you, but there are some things in this world that are more important than your feelings of persecution."

He pushed back in his chair and looked up at her, and because he was Dario, he appeared in no way diminished by the fact that he had to look *up* to meet her gaze. Or by the fact she was standing over him, wearing three-inch wedges that made her nearly six feet tall. If anything, he appeared even more powerful than he had before.

She'd forgotten that. How easily he dominated whole rooms, whole cities, whole swathes of people, without even trying. How that beat in her like her own traitorous heart.

"I don't feel persecuted, Anais. I feel lucky." Dario even smiled, in that same sharp and bitter way that she worried might actually leave scars on both of them. Perhaps it already had. "It wakes me up at night, wondering what my life would be like if I hadn't caught the two of you when I did. How many more ways would you have tricked me while I was so wrapped up in my work? How much more of a fool would you have made of me right under my nose? What if I'd never caught on?" He shook his head and blew out a breath. "I should thank you for being dumb enough to take my own brother into our bed. It saved me a world of hurt."

It shouldn't still cause her pain. None of what he said was a surprise to her. She knew what he thought. What Dante had stood by and let him think. Dario hadn't bothered to ask *her*, his wife, to confirm or deny his suspicions. He'd walked into the house, seen Dante buttoning up a shirt in their bedroom and leaped to the worst possible conclusion. He'd believed the worst, instantly, and that was that.

And still, she felt that heaviness deep inside of her, a little too much like shame. As if she'd actually done something to make him think so little of her. As if she could have done something to prevent it. As if, despite everything, the things he'd done to her and the son he didn't know he had was somehow all her fault.

She didn't think she'd forgive him for that, either.

"I keep waiting for you to come to your senses, but you're not going to, are you?" she asked softly. Rhetorically, she was aware. "This is who you are. The Dario Di Sione I met and married was the make-believe version."

She'd believed in that made-up version, that was the trouble. Why did some part of her still wish that was the real Dario? She should know better by now, surely.

"Whatever you need to tell yourself." He signed the last page of each set of documents and then shoved the stack of them toward her. "Can I have the earrings now? Or are there more hoops to jump through?"

"No hoops." She did her part with the documents, slipping them back into the leather folder when she was finished. Then she reached into one of the deep pockets of her dress and pulled out the small jeweler's box. She cracked it open and set it down on the table between them, watching the way the light danced and gleamed on the precious stones, perfect white diamonds and gorgeous emeralds. "These are the earrings. Note the size of the emeralds and the delicate craftsmanship of the diamonds. They're extraordinary and unusual, and Mr. Fuginawa would not have let them go to anyone save your grandfather. He conveys his deepest respects, of course."

"They're earrings," Dario said bluntly. He snapped the box shut as he surged to his feet, then shoved it in his front pocket. "Whatever tiny bit of sentimentality I had was beaten out of me six years ago, Anais. Old earrings are just old earrings. They don't matter to anyone in the long run. My grandfather is a foolish old man who should be using his money to make his last days easier, not for this kind of nonsense."

Anais straightened her shoulders and told herself to

spit it out. To get it over with. To do what was right because it was right.

Because none of this was about her. It was about Damian.

"I'm delighted to hear you're so unsentimental," she said, and her only possible defense was to keep her voice as ice cold as she could. To act like she was a glacier, the way she had as a girl, because feigned, icy indifference was the only way she could get her parents to leave her out of their daily target practice. So that was exactly what she did now. It was almost alarming, how easy it was to slip back into old patterns. "Maybe this conversation doesn't have to be as unpleasant as I feared it would be."

He didn't actually sneer. Not *quite*. "This conversation is already unpleasant."

"Then what I'm about to tell you is unlikely to improve it."

Anais held that harsh blue gaze of his. She reminded herself this was the right thing to do, no matter how it felt.

Be cold straight through, she told herself. *Feel nothing but ice until you become it.*

She didn't look away. "You have a son."

"I beg your pardon?"

Dario felt bolted to the stones beneath his feet. Pierced straight through. His heart stopped beating, then kicked at him hard, while his entire gut seemed to drop down to the ground and stay there.

And Anais only stood before him, as calm and unbothered and *untouched* as ever, damn her.

"You have a son." She didn't seem surprised she had to repeat that. "We do, I suppose. Biologically speaking. His name is Damian."

He didn't think he could breathe. "Tell me this is one of your jokes."

"Because I'm renowned for my stand-up routine?" she asked tartly, and he recognized that sharp tone. He remembered it. On some level, it was much better than *unbothered*—but he couldn't process that at the moment. "No. I'm not joking about my child."

He continued to stare at her, like an idiot, while his head spun. As if she'd anticipated that reaction—and of course she had, he told himself bitterly, because she'd known he was coming today, hadn't she?—she reached into the other pocket of that long, flowing dress and pulled out something. It took him a moment to understand it was a slightly bent photograph, and then she was sliding it onto the table before him.

Dario didn't want to look. Looking would be admitting…something. But he couldn't help himself.

A small boy with black hair and his mother's eyes laughed in the sunlight. He was kneeling on a beach, his little body sturdy and perfectly formed. Ten fingers covered in sand, stretched toward the camera. And aside from those eyes Dario knew all too well came straight from Anaïs, every other part of his face could have been lifted from the pictures Dario had seen of himself and Dante at the same age.

There had been exactly one other time in his life when he'd wanted to deny the truth in front of him this much. When he'd felt precisely this sleepless and out of his depth and furiously incapable of processing what was happening. And this, six years later, was worse. Much worse. The world went white around the edges. Or maybe he did.

"How?" he heard himself grit out, not looking at her.

He didn't touch that photograph and he didn't trust himself to look at her. Every muscle in his body was so tense he thought he might rupture something where he stood. There was a storm building inside of him and he thought it might simply blow him to pieces right here—a thousand jagged, broken shards of him, until neither one of them was left standing.

It took him a minute to recognize that storm for what it was.

Fury.

Pure and undiluted and directed straight at this woman and her betrayal of him.

Again.

"I'm sure that if you think about it, you can figure out how," Anais was saying. He wouldn't call that tone of hers *amused*, exactly. It was far too crisp and pointed, and she still managed to sound so distant besides. That made it all worse. "I'll give you a hint. It wasn't a stork."

He was still reeling. Dario pushed back in the chair and onto his feet, leaving the photo where it sat as if it was poisonous. He raked his hair back with both hands, and then he got a hold of himself.

It was painful.

"And how," he asked, his voice rough and his gaze probably a lot worse than that as he finally looked at her again, "do I know this is my child and not Dante's? We're identical. I can't even take a DNA test to find out the truth."

She stiffened as if he'd struck her. Then her dark eyes blazed—and damn him, he preferred that over the chilliness.

"Then I suppose it will have to remain a mystery," she threw at him. "What a shame. Damian and I will have to continue doing just fine without you, you incredible jackass."

He didn't process what was happening until she was almost through the great, open doorway that was the length of the pulled-back wall. That she had thrown that bomb at him and was now walking away as if it didn't matter.

"Where the hell are you going?" he demanded. "After dropping that kind of thing on me?"

Anais stopped walking, and the stiffness of her back told him that was a battle. She turned slowly. Very slowly. He thought she looked pale, and her lips were thin, and he didn't understand why he even noticed that. Why he cared at all.

You do not care about her, he snapped at himself. *You care about this lie she's telling.*

"I'm going to carry on with my life," she told him when she faced him fully, in that overly precise way of hers that indicated the raging temper inside of her. He remembered that, too. He could even see the faint hint of it in her eyes. "What did you expect me to do? Stand here and cry? Beg you to believe me? I've already been down that road. I'm well aware it's a dead end."

"Then why bother with this conversation at all?" he gritted out. "Unless you just wanted to throw a few grenades around. For fun."

That smile of hers was much too sharp. One more blade stuck deep in his gut, a match for all the rest.

"The only difference this conversation makes *to me* is that I no longer feel any sense of responsibility about the fact you're too much of a sulking child to have picked up the phone and found this out years ago." She leaned forward slightly, as if some unseen hand was keeping her from hurling herself at him, holding her back from attacking him with those fists he could see bunched up at her sides. "Thank you, Dario. Truly. I needed the reminder that you're absolutely useless. And, worse than that, cruel."

She turned to walk away again, and he should have let her. He should have cheered her on. He couldn't have a child. He *couldn't* have a child. Not him. He'd never wanted one, not after his own disastrous childhood, and he certainly didn't want to test that theory with the woman who had betrayed him so horribly with his own brother.

This can't be happening.

Maybe that was why he found himself across the patio without knowing he meant to move, wrapping his hand around her smooth upper arm to pull her back around to face him.

"Don't walk away from me."

And it was a mistake to have touched her. It was a terrible mistake, because touching her was what had caused all of this in the first place. His uncharacteristic loss of control when he'd first met her. His astonishing decision to marry her—and who cared if he'd lied to himself and told himself it was to secure her a visa to stay in New York? That wild, nearly ungovernable fury when he'd discovered her deceit. He knew better. It had all been about this.

This touch. Her skin. The wildfire he was horrified to realize still raged between them that easily, that unmistakably, even now.

"Take your hand off my arm," she snapped at him, her voice not quite as cool as it had been, and he was the little man she'd called him, wasn't he? Because he derived far more satisfaction from that than he should. "Now."

Dario hated the fact it was hard to let go of her. That he didn't want to do it. But he forced himself to release her and he took a perverse pleasure in the way she rubbed the place he'd touched her with her other hand, as if she could feel the same lick of fire that leaped in him, too.

Chemistry had never been their problem. Never that. It was only honesty and fidelity that had tripped them up, or her stunning lack of both, and he needed to remember that. He needed to remember that no matter what his body agitated for, wild and loud in his blood just now, he knew who she really was.

"You kept my child from me for all these years. *Six years.* Is that really what you're telling me?"

"Please spare me the sob story you're making up in your head," Anais bit out, jutting her chin out as he stood over her, and whatever shoes she was wearing put her almost exactly level with him. That mouth of hers, *right there*, and what the hell was the matter with him that he could think about something like that now?

Especially when she was talking to him as if *he* was the person at fault, when they both knew better.

"You refused to take my calls. You moved all of your things out of our home while I was at work. You barred me from your new apartment building and you instructed the security people in your office to call the police if I tried to get in—which I know, because they did."

He shouldn't have been fascinated by the spots of color that bloomed on her gorgeously high cheekbones, shouting out her temper in unmistakable red. It was as if her betrayal and the six years between them had never happened. The fact his body didn't care about any of that made that fury in him burn brighter. Colder. As if he was complicit in his own betrayal here.

Against his will, he remembered the confusion of those first days after he'd discovered Anais and Dante together. How the stress from the work decisions he'd had to make had fused with the terrible blow he'd suffered and had made him waver. He'd considered going back on his decision. He'd considered a thousand things in the even more sleepless nights that followed, just him and his bitterness and the messages he deleted unread and unheard from both his twin and his wife. There'd been a certain comfort in knowing that nothing could ever hurt him as much as they had then. He'd built his new life out of that certainty.

It had never occurred to him that he could have been wrong about that.

"My emails bounced back and you disconnected your cell phone number," Anais was saying. "I watched you rip up a letter I left on your car, unread, with my own eyes." She lifted her hands and then dropped them again as if what she really wanted was to use him as a punching bag. He almost wished she would. "So what exactly was I supposed to do? How was I supposed to tell you? I tried. But you were too busy licking your wounds and hiding yourself away behind all the wealth and privilege you could stack around you like stone walls. That's not my fault."

Dario concentrated on his temper as if it would save him. He had the sinking feeling it was the only thing here that could.

"You're talking about a child," he said very distinctly. "If you'd really wanted to tell me, you'd have found a way. This is just another game. You never run out of them, do you?"

"I told you today, the very first time I've seen you since you walked out on me," she said icily, but there was nothing cold in that furious gaze of hers. "There's no game." She shook her head when he started to speak. "I don't have to stand here and listen to this. Your feelings about the child you could have known all his life if you hadn't deliberately hidden yourself away aren't my problem. I didn't tell you because I want something from you. I told you because it was the right thing to do."

"Anais…"

"And now I'm leaving," she interrupted him, her dark eyes glittering with emotions he couldn't name. He shouldn't want to name them. He shouldn't believe they existed at all. "I don't really care what you do with this information. Go lick your self-inflicted wounds some more. Pretend you still don't know. Whatever lets you feed that persecution complex of yours, I'm sure you'll do it."

He couldn't bear it. There was that fury in him and something much darker and deeper and worse. Much, much worse. Raw and aching and terrible. She eyed him as if she was looking for something on his face, but then her gaze shuttered and she started to turn away again— and he really couldn't bear *that*.

So he did the only thing he could think of to do.

Maybe he wasn't *thinking* at all.

He reached out, slid his hand over her delicate neck to cup her nape and pull her close and then he took her mouth with his.

It was the same madness he remembered. That same wild burn that sizzled through him, lighting him up and making him crazy, eating him alive. She still tasted sweet and perfect, the way she always had, as if no time at all had passed.

Dario moved closer, slid his hands onto the thick fall of her hair, then tugged her mouth into a better angle beneath his and kissed her deeper, harder.

And she kissed him back, the way he remembered she always, always had.

She met him, a tangle of tongues and need while the fire between them raged, and their whole history seemed to dance between them in the flames. It was as raw as it was hot, as greedy as it was painful, and Dario knew this was the worst idea he'd had in a long, long time.

But still he kissed her, over and over, as if he could glut himself on her. As if he could block out not only what she'd told him and all the accusations she'd thrown at him, but the six years since he'd touched anyone like this or let himself be touched in turn. He hadn't wanted anyone near him. He hadn't wanted anything that resembled intimacy, with anyone.

And yet here, now, with that damned soft breeze still dancing all over him, and Anais's perfect mouth hot and demanding beneath his, he couldn't seem to remember why that was.

She wrenched herself away. He heard the small sound of distress she made and he hated that it lodged itself in his chest, like one more bullet in this strange afternoon bristling with them. She stumbled back a step until her back hit the wall, and she stared at him.

She looked as shaken as he was. He hated that, too—the idea that she could actually be affected, that she might not be acting...

Of course she's acting. Everything about her is an act.

He hated everything about this. This wild, untamed place. That insidious breeze that was messing with his head and making him feel restless and edgy. Anais and her lies and her deception, six years ago and today, and the fact she was still the most beautiful woman he'd ever beheld only made it worse. He hated that he could taste her now. That he could *feel* her again, as if her perfect lips were some kind of brand and she'd marked him. Changed him.

And he hated that she'd made him feel again, when he'd tamped that down and shut it off in those tortured days following the end of their marriage. He hated that most of all.

"While we're on the topic," he said, not even sounding like himself, because that was what she did to him, *still*, "I want a divorce."

Dario wanted nothing more than to make her feel as ripped wide open as he did, to take all the hurt and the fury and that spinning in his head, that unacceptable need that still surged in him, and make her feel it, too.

So he grinned while he said it, to make sure she got his point. To make sure it was painful. And because it was true and there should be a record of it. "On the grounds of your infidelity, of course. With my brother as the named third party."

CHAPTER THREE

THE KNOCK ON the front door of Anais's little house in Kihei, a few blocks up the hill from the ocean in a strictly residential, tourist-free neighborhood, came after nine o'clock that same night.

Anais scowled at the door as if it had transformed into a snarling monster.

Her comfortable two-bedroom house was arranged in a breezy open plan. That meant she didn't have to get up from the living area's couch where she had files spread out on the coffee table before her to see that the figure standing on her front step and visible through the panes of clouded glass in the door could not possibly be her aunt or uncle or any of her friends.

He was too tall. Too solid. Too obviously *him*, and besides, that knock had been brusque and demanding, not anything like friendly.

She gritted her teeth and wished she hadn't changed into her comfortable evening-at-home clothes after she'd put Damian to bed hours ago. Yoga pants and a tank top didn't seem like adequate armor against Dario. Not here in her own home. Not when she could still feel his mouth against hers from earlier, the way he'd tasted her and tempted her and taken her over, leaving her with nothing but that fire she'd convinced herself over the past six years had been entirely in her imagination.

Her imagination was pretty vivid, it turned out. So vivid her breasts seemed to swell at the thought of him now, and she felt that deep, restless ache low in her belly that only Dario had ever brought out in her.

Anais got to her feet reluctantly. She threw a glance over her shoulder toward the half-closed door to Damian's room, but she knew her little boy could sleep through a rock concert. And she also knew enough about Dario to realize that if he'd tracked down her home address and shown up at this hour, he didn't plan to wander off quietly into the night simply because she hadn't answered his first knock.

He knocked again, louder, and she blew out a breath as she crossed the room. She smoothed a hand over her high ponytail and wished she really was the cool, practical woman she'd gotten so good at pretending she was. The kind who could take anything in stride, including the reappearance of her son's father on her doorstep. The kind who wouldn't spare a single thought for how she looked under the circumstances.

That woman does not exist, she told herself staunchly. *That woman is nothing but other women just like me, faking it.*

Then she steeled herself and wrenched open the door.

Dario stood there before her on the lower step, looking edgier and more dangerous than he had out on Mr. Fuginawa's lanai earlier in the day. It was dark now, a thick Hawaiian summer night that seemed to cling to the edges of things. It made Dario look as ruthless as he did powerful, somehow. He stared at her, unsmiling and intense, and she was unreasonably glad his hands were thrust deep in the pockets of his jeans. As if that made him safer when she knew better than that.

He should have looked disreputable, in jeans and an untucked shirt. Instead, he looked like a particularly gorgeous object lesson in wealthy young scions who also happened to be world-famous CEOs of major companies at such a relatively young age. Not that she'd followed his many corporate exploits on the internet, or anything.

Anais folded her arms and stood in her doorway. She did not invite him in. And she didn't particularly care if every last one of her neighbors on the small cul-de-sac was watching this scene from their windows right now. If anything, that gave her the courage she needed to handle this.

Like a glacier, she told herself. *You're cold to the core. Heat can't touch you, even his.*

"I don't recall inviting you over for a nightcap," she said coolly.

She'd invited him to go straight to hell, and she hadn't stuck around to see if he'd taken her up on that. She'd driven so fast down Mr. Fuginawa's drive and then back out the rustic Piilani Highway toward home that her car had bottomed out in the rutted road more than once.

It hadn't slowed her down at all.

"Is this impolite? I'd hate to be *impolite* in a situation like this." His voice was as thick and dark as the night all around him, and seemed to stick to her as if it was barbed. Anais felt goose bumps shiver over her bare arms and had to fight to keep herself from rubbing at them and giving herself away. "Maybe you can explain the etiquette of secret babies and hidden children to me. I'm not as familiar with it as you are. Obviously."

"What do you want?"

"You claimed you had my son. What do you think I want?"

"Damian is in bed, the way small children often are at this time of night." She made a *shooing* motion with one hand. "Go away."

"I want to see him."

Anais had to grit her teeth to keep from shouting loud enough to bring the entire island to her door. "You don't get to decide that, Dario. You can't show up here after being absent his entire life and spring yourself on him in the middle of the night."

"I knew you'd use him as a pawn. Why am I not surprised that you're precisely this shameless?"

"He is *five years old*. He wants a father more than you can possibly imagine. I'm not using him as a pawn. I'm *protecting* him."

"From me?" If possible, his face got even darker. She thought his arms tightened, as if he was clenching his hands into fists in his pockets. "What's that supposed to mean?"

Anais couldn't pretend to keep calm any longer. She couldn't stay cool and smooth and hard. And she didn't much care what he might make of that. She didn't care about *him*, to be honest. Not when it came to Damian's feelings. Not when Dario could crush her little boy so easily. And likely would.

"It means I know what you do to hearts." She hadn't meant to say that. She wished she'd bitten off her tongue instead, especially when he made that derisive sound that might as well have been a punch to the gut, the way it hit her.

"This is exactly the kind of crap I expected you to say and I don't have time for it. I'm not going to participate in whatever great melodrama you have planned here, Anais. I want to see the child." He shifted, as if it hurt him. Or as if maybe he wasn't as hard as he seemed, either—but it was dangerous to imagine such things. She'd already made that mistake six years ago, and look what had happened. "*My* child, or so you claim."

"Listen to me." She stepped forward, out of her doorway and onto the wide top step, not caring that it put her much too close to him again, even raised to his eye level. She shoved her finger in his face and she wished it was something more substantial, like a kitchen knife. "This is not about you. I understand that you must be feeling all kinds of things right now. I'm not particularly sympathetic, but I understand. Still, Damian doesn't know you. You've been missing in action his entire life. It doesn't benefit *him* in any way to be woken from a sound sleep so that a strange man can brood at him. And if it doesn't benefit him, it's not happening."

Her voice had gotten loud there. Or maybe it only felt that way, as if it echoed back from the gentle movement of the palm trees and the thick, dark night pressing in against them. And either way, Dario did nothing but study her, as if he was assessing her weaknesses and looking for evidence to use against her. He probably was. She only acted glacial in short, controlled bursts. She'd long suspected that the truth about Dario was that, deep down, he truly was nothing but a block of ice masquerading as a man.

She didn't know how long they stood there, with nothing but the tropical night between them and all around them, the breeze dancing over them as if it was playing tag with the moonlight.

Dario was the one to break the silence, his voice dark,

yet calm. "Why did you bother to tell me about him if you were only going to keep him from me?"

If he could put on that calm act, she could, too. She made herself do it.

"I'm not keeping him from you. I'm simply choosing not to wake him up so I can parade him in front of you right this very minute. They're not the same thing."

"You planned all of this, didn't you?" He sounded as if he was marveling at the very idea, but his blue gaze was frigid as it held hers. "You want to stab a knife in my ribs any way you can. This is revenge served cold, six years later, because I didn't stick around to play your deceitful little games with you."

Anais made herself breathe, even though her temper and her sense of injustice at the *unfairness* of all this roared inside of her. She didn't know how she kept herself from hauling off and slapping him. Only that whisper of something else deep inside her, that worried what she'd do if she touched him again because she doubted it would be as violent as he deserved, kept her from it.

That and the little boy who slept even now only a few yards behind her, completely unaware that his life had irrevocably changed today. That nothing could ever be the same, because now Dario knew that he existed. His father finally knew about him. That made everything different.

"I'm not going to do this with you," she gritted out when she could trust herself to speak. Not to scream at him as he deserved, but to speak the way *Damian* deserved his parents to speak to each other. If she'd learned nothing else from her own parents, it was that. "You're the one who made yourself unreachable for six years, not me. You don't get to show up here and throw your weight around because you've suddenly decided that there's something worth paying attention to in this life you walked away from so callously."

"So you are planning to use him as bait. There's the calculating, manipulative Anais I know."

"You can see him." And it was for her to know how much she wanted to tell him the opposite, purely out of the kind of spite she knew made her a truly terrible person, down deep inside where she tried hard to hide it. "But it will be on my schedule, not yours. I decide he's ready, not you. Do you understand me?" When he only glared at her, his face like stone, she continued. "This isn't about your pride or your ego or your miserable existence, Dario. This is a little boy's life."

The air between them went flat and taut. Then electric. Temper, history. Fury and need.

It seared through Anais, from her exposed arms all the way down to her bare feet. She saw the way Dario held himself, as if he was *this close* to putting his hands on her again, and what worried her was that she didn't know if she'd push him away or pull him closer. The trouble with Dario was that she didn't know herself at all when she was near him.

But he stepped back instead, and Anais had to confront the fact that she didn't feel any sense of relief at that, the way she should. She felt…disappointed.

You are sick, she told herself in no little despair.

He raked a hand through his black hair, making it look even messier against the jaw he still hadn't bothered to shave. She didn't understand how that could make him look more attractive, not less. Or why she couldn't seem to keep herself from noticing things like that at a time like this.

Or maybe she did understand, and hated herself for that, too.

Dario considered her for what seemed like days, and then he bit out the name of one of the grand luxury resorts further south on this side of the island in exclusive Wailea.

"Do you know it?"

"Of course I know it."

Not that she'd stayed there, of course. The prices were astronomical, even by exalted Maui resort standards. And she'd hardly had a lot of call to stay at luxury resorts in the past few years.

"That's where I'm staying." He studied her for a moment. "I'll expect you tomorrow evening at seven o'clock."

"I'm afraid I have a…"

"Cancel it, whatever it is." His full mouth thinned and the way his blue eyes glittered made her heart leap in her chest. It made her the liar he'd always claimed she was. "Don't make me hunt you down, Anais. You'll like it even less than I will."

And then he melted off into the night. She heard the sound of a car engine turning over in the street, outside her line of sight, but she couldn't seem to move. She stood there on her own front step for much too long, as off balance as if she was out at sea on a rickety boat, trying and failing to handle the swell.

He'd left her with nothing to do but furiously debate whether or not she planned to follow his peremptory orders.

Of course not, she told herself sharply, shaking herself out of whatever daze this was and walking back inside. It took a great deal more strength than it should have to keep from slamming the door shut, loud enough to bring the house down around her ears. *Who does he think he is to issue commands? You don't have to pay that man the slightest bit of attention!*

Anais returned to the couch and tried to get back to the work she'd been doing, the work she needed to get done tonight, but it was no use. She was too…stirred up. Too uncertain and off balance, still.

He's Damian's father, a countering voice reminded her, as if she was likely to forget it. *You owe Damian this, not Dario. Hammering out some kind of solution here helps him, and that's what matters. It's the only thing that matters.*

Anais hardly slept that night.

She couldn't get comfortable in her own bed. She checked on Damian more times in the night than she had since he was a newborn and she'd been terrified he might stop breathing if she relaxed her panicked vigilance even a little bit. He'd been so tiny and fragile for such a massive, lifetime responsibility and the blinding shower of love she felt every time she looked at him. She'd come to the conclusion that maybe she was the one who'd stopped breathing during those first, overwhelming months.

She hadn't been entirely alone, thank God. Her elderly aunt and uncle had been the only bright spot in her family tree her whole life, and nothing had changed when Anais had come here to Maui with the shards of her marriage clinging to her like broken glass. They'd taken her in without question, the way they had back when she'd been a girl, desperate to escape her warring parents for a school holiday here, a summer there. When she'd finally admitted to them that she was pregnant, they'd taken that in stride, too. They'd helped her get on her feet and figure out a way forward as the single mother she'd never planned to become. And they'd been a steadfast, dependable presence in Damian's life since his first breath.

Compared to some women, Anais knew, she had it good.

She reminded herself of that the next morning, when Damian woke up in his holy terror mode, in the full fury of all his five short years. She got his things ready despite his protests, wrestled him into something resembling an appropriate outfit for school, then had to cajole and threaten and bribe him into the car for a miserable ride all the way to drop him off.

She released him to his school with a muttered apology for unleashing a Damian in his most unreasonable and mutinous state upon them. Then she went into her law office where she was a senior associate for the single named partner and disappeared behind the mountain of paperwork on her desk. She told herself that she had no idea if she planned to go and see Dario *as commanded.* She told herself that repeatedly. But when her aunt called in the afternoon and asked if Damian could have one of his sleepovers at their house the way he did from time to time, it seemed like a sign.

"A sign that you should use the night to catch up on work," she muttered to herself, scowling at her cell phone after she tossed it back down on the nearest case file. "Not gallivant about with the dangerous past."

It wasn't until she was back home that evening and finally able to clean up the evidence of Damian's morning tantrum that she started to rethink that stance. She imagined Dario had visions of some appropriate movie child in his head, all serene smiles and quiet playtime with noninvasive toys under someone else's cheerful supervision. That was a lovely daydream of a perfect little angel. She'd shared it herself before she'd become a mother. But it wasn't reality and it definitely wasn't her son.

She found she couldn't wait to tell Dario so—and even a guilty look at the stacks of files waiting for her on her coffee table failed to sway her. The man who she suspected had sheets of ice where his heart should have been couldn't possibly want a child, no matter what he might have said on her doorstep. Hadn't he said so a thousand times when they'd been together? There was no reason that should have changed in all the time since. And Damian deserved more than a father who would, sooner or later, begrudge his very existence.

Anais had lived that bleak, miserable life. She wouldn't condemn her own son to it. *She wouldn't.*

The front desk was expecting her when she finally made it through the last of the summer traffic down through bustling Kihei and into Wailea, then followed the unobtrusive signs into the parking area of the exclusive resort. A staff member announced that Mr. Di Sione was waiting for her in one of the resort's private, waterfront villas and proceeded to lead her there as if one or the other of them was visiting royalty.

Of course. Nothing but the best for Dario.

But if she was honest, wasn't that part of the reason she'd found him so fascinating? He'd been a shot of controlled recklessness. Bright color in the middle of her black-and-white life. He'd been raised wealthy and indulged, and then he and Dante had made their own, personal fortunes while they were still in college. It had meant neither one of them had to pay any attention to the kind of boundaries other people had no choice but to obey.

And Anais had been feral, more or less. She'd raised herself in the crossfire of her parents' endless wars, and she hadn't had the slightest idea how to have fun, or fall in love, or be silly for absolutely no reason—all the things Dario had taught her.

Taught her, then taken away, as if all those things belonged to him and had only ever been on loan to the likes of her.

Anais got more and more furious as she walked, following the diffident staff member across one of the most stunning hotel grounds on Maui as the sun dropped toward the water, all sweeping views juxtaposed with sleek, modern designs that somehow evoked ancient Hawaii in the gathering dark—not that any of it registered. The truth was, she was lucky. She'd been an attorney for years now in one of the most beautiful places in the world. She liked her job, her clients and the life she'd built here. Practicing law was comfortable and it allowed her to take care of Damian and help out her aunt and uncle, too, when she could.

She was damned proud of those things. This was the life she'd built all on her own. Her parents had stopped even the pretense of any obligations to her the day she'd turned eighteen. Her husband had abandoned her seven years later, right after she'd finally learned to trust him. Yes, her aunt and uncle helped her as best they could and that had been everything to her at times, but ultimately Anais had made herself *by* herself.

Anais had never had Dario's kind of money, however, and she never would. She'd spent a long time telling herself she was glad of that—that it was all the money he and Dante had made while they were still in college that had ruined him, in the end. It had made him expect too much from the world and everyone in it, as if he could make everything he looked at what he wanted it to be, simply because he wanted it that way. It had also trained him to see the very worst in people, as they schemed to get close to him and use him for their own ends.

She'd been arrogant enough to think she was the antidote to that, but it had turned out that once a man was poisoned, that was how he stayed. Unless the man in question wanted something different for himself. Dario had pretended he had, but he hadn't.

In the end, he hadn't wanted anything he'd claimed he did. Particularly not Anais.

And for some reason the exquisite four-bedroom villa that would have been more than suitable for a king and the whole of his royal court seemed to press that fact deeper into her as she found herself knocking at his door, the staff member having long since melted away into the exultant, flowered shrubbery festooned with torches and dancing with real flames against the sunset.

She knocked with a wide-open hand, loudly and rudely, and of course Dario didn't rush to answer her. It gave her far too much time to stand there and think better of this. To wonder what she thought she might gain from acquiescing to his demands no matter what her reasons might have been.

And worse, what she stood to lose.

Nothing with Dario had ever been straightforward. They'd skipped regular dating altogether—having fallen hard into something far more intense neither one of them had dared name. Then they'd gotten married much too fast, each telling the other and maybe themselves it was a cool, rational decision based on Anais's immigration status as a French citizen instead of that insane fire that had consumed them both in bed. Dario had told her very little about his family, except that his twin was the only one he truly cared about at all—and yet Dante had been openly suspicious of her from the start. She'd tried to ignore that, too, swept up in her first year of law practice and the head-spinning reality of her first lover who was also the husband she didn't dare admit she'd fallen head over heels in love with.

Maybe it wasn't surprising that it had taken exactly one year for it all to fall apart.

There was nothing good to be gained by poking her fingers into those old wounds, she told herself then, scowling at the villa's front door.

This is for Damian, she reminded herself. She chanted it a few times, just to make sure she was listening to her own words, and knocked again. Louder.

And this time Dario swung the door open and took her breath away.

It only made her that much more furious with him. She kept telling herself *that*, too, with even less success.

Dario wore nothing but a loose pair of linen trousers that hung low—*much too low*—on his lean hips and made it impossible to do anything but gape at that remarkable chest of his. She'd assured herself that he couldn't possibly be as good-looking as she remembered, as perfectly formed, like something that ought to have been carved from marble and propped up in a museum. She'd had six years to decide she'd built him up in her head.

She hadn't.

If anything, he was far, far better than she remembered, all flat planes of muscle and that ridged abdomen, smooth olive skin and a dusting of dark hair that arrowed down beneath those low-hanging, decadent trousers. Even his bare feet were gorgeous, big and inescapably male, and she hated everything about this.

Mostly, she hated that terrible yearning that ripped through her, tearing her wide open and making it impossible to lie to herself about it. She wanted him. She'd always wanted him. That connection between them had been everything to her, for a time.

There had never been anything as huge or powerful or all-consuming in all her life, until she'd held Damian for the first time in the hospital.

She'd been silly enough to think that connection was what had forged the true bond between them, back then. That their marriage had been conducted for all the practical reasons they'd agreed upon in their analytical way— for Anais's green card, because Dario had liked the idea of a lawyer in the immediate family to handle the company he and his brother ran, etc. It had all made such sense on paper.

But the truth of it, the truth of *them*, had been what happened in the fire that raged between them. Always. At the slightest touch. At the ways they tore each other apart and put each other back together, night after night. The things they talked about in the cold light of day were their cover, their pretense. The nights were their truth.

That was what she'd told herself. It was what she'd believed. What she'd *felt*, deep inside, in that cold place no one else had ever touched.

Until he'd smashed it all into a million little pieces when he'd walked away from her without a backward glance.

"I hope you didn't undress just for me," she said, smiling faintly at him as if she found his bare chest—truly, one of the great wonders of the world, to her way of thinking, and she hated that she still thought it—embarrassing. For him. "I wouldn't touch you again with a ten-foot pole covered in all your wealth and status. Look what happened the last time."

CHAPTER FOUR

"STARTING RIGHT IN with the lies?" Dario asked.

And because she hadn't let him into her house last night—which annoyed him a lot more than he cared to admit, and had gotten under his skin the more he'd thought about it—he blocked the doorway to his villa now. She could see how she liked it, and if there was a part of him that was ashamed at his own childishness, he ignored it.

He ignored a whole host of unfortunate truths, many of them making themselves known physically, as he gazed at her. "Touching me was never the issue, as I think we both know."

She looked at him as if she pitied him, which made him want to…do all kinds of things he wouldn't let himself do.

Yet.

"I was foolish and young back then," she said in that prim voice of hers that had always, always, driven him crazy with lust and need. Today was no different, damn her. "I thought the package mattered a lot more than what was inside it. But people change."

"Selective memory isn't change. It's a lie you tell yourself."

"Happily, you don't know me well enough either way."

She shrugged. If it bothered her that he hadn't stepped aside to let her in yet, she didn't show it. That, in turn, cranked up his irritation even higher. "I could have undergone a huge personal transformation. I could be lying through my teeth. Neither one has anything to do with the cold, hard fact of your paternity, does it?"

Dario had woken up at eight in the morning New York time, which was six hours earlier than here in this lost corner of the world. He'd spent a couple of hours on the phone and another hour or so on his laptop, and then he'd dealt with the restless anger beating at him by going for a very long run on a dark island road that wound down to beaches made of hard, black volcanic rock. He'd greeted his first Hawaiian sunrise with a swim in the shockingly warm sea, and then he'd come back to his villa and banged out a hundred furious laps in the significantly cooler pool, just to make sure he had a handle on himself.

Except he hadn't.

He'd spent the day on a series of calls and video chats with employees all over the world, and then he'd gone on a second, much harder run up into the hills, and even that hadn't done a damn thing.

Not when Anais appeared in front of him again.

She looked as effortlessly sexy as she always did, and he bitterly resented it. He resented *her*. She'd been beautiful yesterday on that remote estate. She'd been ridiculously appealing last night in nothing but a tank top and stretchy pants that had clung to every inch of her long, shapely legs. And today it was worse.

Much worse.

She'd put her hair up into one of those complicated, seemingly messy buns that he'd used to love to watch her create with her clever fingers and a series of pins she shoved into the masses of her silken hair seemingly at random. She wore a deceptively simple blouse in a soft cream color that made her skin seem to glow, tucked into a pencil skirt in a warm camel shade that should have been illegal, the way it clung to her lean curves and made her look even more feminine and alluring than she already was. Some animal part of him hated the fact she walked around like this. That anyone could see her. Even the delicate red shoes that clung to her feet and wrapped around her ankles annoyed him, sleek licks of flame that anyone could lust after the way he did—and likely had.

She looked elegant and cool and distressingly, achingly sexy. As untouchable as ever.

And Dario wanted nothing more than to dirty her up, the way he always had. The way he had from the moment he'd first seen her, looking like a faintly irritated librarian, prim and disapproving and ridiculously gorgeous in hushed Butler Library on the Columbia University campus, where he and Dante had been making entirely too much noise one winter afternoon. He couldn't remember what they'd been laughing about, only that someone had shushed them—and when he'd looked up, he'd seen Anais scowling at him from behind a pile of books.

He'd had the sudden and nearly overpowering urge to mess her prim exterior up a little, get under her skin, see how straitlaced she really was. He'd wanted to peel back her winter layers and her offended expression and see what kind of woman lurked beneath.

Something inside him, in that swirl of heat that unfurled in his gut, had whispered he already knew.

He'd wanted to get inside her, badly. Right then and there. That longing hadn't eased any, then or now.

And he was aware that the urge had nothing at all to

do with the child she claimed was his, and everything to do with the madness inside of him that had already claimed him once.

"Be careful, brother," Dante had said with great amusement when Dario had kept staring at Anais in that library, until she blinked and looked away, her cheeks flushing. "She'll eat you alive."

Dario hadn't liked that. His easy relationship with his twin had never been quite the same after an incident with a woman they hadn't known they'd both been sleeping with at the same time when they were younger. They'd forgiven each other, if not the woman in question—but Dario hadn't quite trusted Dante in the same way as he had before. It had bled over into their business. Dario had been overwhelmed back then, fighting to figure out the future of the company in that year before they sold—and he hadn't felt that Dante had been willing to shoulder his half of the responsibility. It had made him want to punch his twin right there in the library for even looking at the same pretty girl in a way Dario didn't like. He'd shoved it aside then, but he hadn't forgotten it.

Later, when Anais had packed up her things and headed out and Dario had made to follow her and chance an "accidental" meeting, his brother had outright laughed at him.

"Don't blame me when she ruins your whole life," Dante had said. "Which I can pretty much guarantee she will."

"You have no idea what you're talking about." Dario had shrugged on his coat. He had *not* punched his twin. "It's like your own, personal perversion."

"A city full of women who would throw their panties at you if you smiled," Dante had murmured, shaking his head. "They have. And yet you want to chase the one who disliked you on sight. Maybe I'm not the perverted one."

Dario blinked now, astounded that the memories he normally kept locked away and inaccessible had taken him over like that. He wanted to think about his brother about as much as he wanted to think about his marriage. Meaning, he didn't. More blame he could lay at her feet, he thought furiously.

He turned back into the villa and walked toward the kitchen area, where the hotel staff had left him a selection of fine wines. He heard her close the door behind her and follow him, those high red heels loud against the smooth floors, and he poured them both a glass. Red for him. White for her. The way it had always been, back then.

And he didn't think he imagined the way she swallowed hard when he handed her glass to her, as if the memories were getting to her, too. He hoped they were as unwelcome as his were, and as uncomfortable.

"What is this?" she asked, but she didn't put her glass back down.

He crooked a brow. "Wine."

"You didn't think to dress, but you had different kinds of wine delivered? What a fascinating approach to a meeting. No wonder ICE is doing so well." She tipped her glass toward his chest. "Do you tantalize your investors and stockholders like this? Maybe put on a little cabaret number to seal the deal? Everything begins to make a lot more sense."

He bit back the insulting words that flooded his mouth, because that was no way to play this game. And Dario had always been very, very good at games. He won them without trying very hard. He'd spent all day in heated conversations with his lawyers discussing the different ways he could win this one, too. Decisively.

But it was amazing how different the game looked to him when it was dressed like this, all womanly curves and that mouth of hers he could still taste against his.

That didn't exactly bode well for what he had to accomplish here. But Dario ignored that with the ruthlessness that had allowed him to come into ICE and change the company from the ground up over the course of the past six years. He'd made it his. That was what he did.

"How does this work?" His voice was low, smooth. Appropriate, for a change. He was trying to make it seem as if he'd had time to calm down. To get his temper and his emotions under control.

To accept that this woman had kept his child a secret from him for five years.

Five years.

He told that tiny voice inside of him that knew he'd blocked her every attempt at contact, that knew he'd made contacting him impossible, to be silent. The point wasn't what he might have done—he hadn't had all the information she had. The point was what she'd done, and hadn't done, when she'd been the only one who knew everything.

She took a sip of her wine, then smiled at him. Almost politely, as if they were cordial strangers at a cocktail party. "Because, presumably, I'm the expert on paternity issues?"

He eyed her a moment and reminded himself this was a game. That he needed to win it—and that meant controlling his temper. "Because you're the lawyer."

"How this works is, we talk," she said. She stood on the other side of the marble bar that separated the sleek kitchen from the expansive teak-and-glass living area and gazed back at him. And if she was even remotely chastened, he couldn't see it. "Rationally and reasonably, if we can manage it. We come to mutually acceptable arrangements."

Dario was contemplating how much he loathed the fact that she still seemed so unaffected by all of this—and particularly by him, if he was brutally honest—when she tilted her head to one side.

"Do you think you can handle that?"

That sweet tone of hers with all that bite beneath it was better. It told him exactly where they stood. On the same uneven ground.

"If he's mine..."

"If you say *if* one more time, this conversation is over. For good."

He wanted to ignore that, but something in the way she watched him just then made him think better of it. Would she really walk out on him? He didn't want to believe she could. And he *really* didn't want to investigate why he thought that.

"I don't know what you want from me, Anais," he said after a moment. "You can claim the moral high ground. You can tell yourself that the fact I blocked your access to me is the issue here. We could argue about that for years."

"I'd rather not."

"It doesn't change what I saw."

He saw something flash in her dark eyes then, he was sure of it.

"You saw a man walk out of your bedroom buttoning up a shirt."

"I saw *my brother* walking out of *my bedroom* with *my wife*," he gritted out. He slammed his wineglass down on the counter, and he'd never know why it didn't shatter and send red wine and glass everywhere. "Shrugging his half-naked body into one of *my shirts*."

It took him a long moment to realize that while she did nothing but glare at him, with that otherwise unreadable expression on her face, she was trembling. Fury? Shame? Anger at being called out on her unfaithful behavior all these years later? Something as complicated as what surged in him—as much desire as what he desperately hoped was distaste? He didn't know.

"Yes," she said, after a minute. "That's what you saw. You didn't see Dante and me naked and writhing around. You didn't even see us touching. You saw your brother changing his shirt, and you ended our marriage on the spot."

But Dario had been angrier with Dante by the day back then. Dario had walked in and seen what he'd seen and it had all made so much sense. That tension between Dante and Anais that Anais had assured him was *dislike*. The distance between the twins where their business was concerned, that Dante had claimed was about *different philosophies*. All such lies and misdirection. *This is the truth*, he'd thought then, like a death knell inside of him. All his late hours, all his work, all the responsibility he'd been carrying—it had all been a ruse, to keep him out of the way, so these two people who supposedly loved him and hated each other could meet. In his bedroom.

It still made him furious, as a matter of fact, when he should have been over it years ago.

He thought she could hear it in his voice when he spoke again. "Is this where you think I'm going to beg you to tell me what was really going on that day? So you can spin some fairy tale for me?"

"Or tell you the truth."

He didn't quite laugh. "That's never going to happen. Don't be so naive, Anais. Or do I mean self-absorbed?" Dario shook his head. And though it wasn't an entirely fair representation of what had happened, he continued. "Do you really believe you're the first woman Dante poached from me?"

She swallowed hard enough that he could see it, and it didn't help matters to focus on the delicate line of her throat and the sheer perfection of that collarbone he'd spent many a night exploring with his own mouth. It didn't help at all.

"Damian is your son," she said after a moment. "I'm not going to argue about it. You either believe that or you don't, and if you don't, there's no reason for us to bother talking to each other."

"Then what we need to talk about is what any parents in these situations talk about," he said casually, as if this was an academic discussion with no painful personal history behind it. And as if he hadn't spent entirely too long today on the phone with his own lawyers, running through various scenarios. "Visitation. Custody. Child support. The usual things."

He thought she stiffened at that, or her dark gaze sharpened, but she only placed her wineglass back on the counter with a sharp *clink* and then folded her hands in front of her.

"Before you go too far down any kind of legal road, you should probably know that your name isn't on Damian's birth certificate."

He hadn't known he had a son a day ago, and yet hearing her say that made Dario want to howl at the sky. Break his glass and every other one in the villa. He didn't know how he managed to keep himself from doing all of those things at once. How he sucked it all back in and tucked it away and managed to sound nothing but faintly icy when he responded.

"I beg your pardon?"

"If you'd like to claim paternity," she said calmly, though her gaze was hard, "you'll have to first prove it, and then, of course, pay all the back child support you owe me since his birth."

"How mercenary."

"Not at all. If you want to claim your son, you need to do something to make up for the fact you've ignored five years of his life. You can't go back in time and be less horrible to his mother, more's the pity, but you can pay. Maybe that's all you're good for, and that's okay." She smiled at him. It was not a nice smile. "Damian deserves a robust college fund out of this, if nothing else. It's not mercenary. It's an insurance policy."

"Other terms come to mind."

"You're filled with all kinds of unpleasant terms, aren't you?" She shrugged again. Dario was beginning to think that shrug might be the most infuriating gesture he'd ever seen. "That's not exactly a surprise."

"I never called you names, Anais, and I could have."

Her dark eyes glinted. "Don't sell yourself short, Dario. Your nonverbal communication was deafening."

"To be clear," he said when he could speak in an even tone, "you claim you're not using the child as a pawn, but you are perfectly prepared to hold him for ransom. Am I getting that right?"

"He's just a concept to you, Dare," she said after a moment, and he wondered if she knew she'd reverted to that nickname only she had ever used. He didn't let himself think too much about why *he'd* noticed. Especially when she was looking at him as if it hurt her to do so. "But to me? Damian is everything."

She shook her head at him as if she found him deeply lacking, and there wasn't a single reason in the world he should care what this woman thought of him. What her opinion of him was. Not a single, solitary reason.

More than that, he wasn't doing this to hash out things between them. He told himself he didn't care. This was about the child she'd hidden from him. That was the only reason he hadn't flown back to New York the moment he'd had those damned earrings in his possession.

He'd made a plan and he had every intention of carrying it out to the letter, and it didn't make one bit of difference what she thought of him or what she called him or anything of the sort. None of that mattered at all.

Why was he finding it so hard to remember?

Anais couldn't handle the way he looked at her then, so she turned away and walked toward the open doors that led out to his private lanai, with its gloriously unobstructed view of the sea and the fiery red sun sinking toward the distant horizon. He had his own beach if he wanted it, at the far end of a winding little path. She could see the white sand gleaming in the last of the daylight, and the waves rocked gently against the shore as if it was doing it for them alone.

And somehow, she managed to wrestle that great ache inside of her into something more compact as she stood there and gazed out at the water, the sunset. Something she could breathe through. Something that wouldn't betray her even further.

Dario was quiet for a long time, but she didn't turn

back to see why. She felt him approach, though she wasn't sure she could actually hear him move, and then he was beside her, buttoning up a shirt made of the same lush linen as his trousers. It was also in black, and she didn't know what was worse. Him bare-chested before her like a thousand desserts she didn't dare touch, or him dressed like some kind of debonair lover, conjured straight up from the darkest part of the dreams she pretended she didn't have.

Both, maybe.

"I'm sorry," Dario said, and that was so shocking she whipped her head around to see if he was pulling her leg. But his moody blue gaze was focused on the sea, not on her. "I didn't mean for this conversation to descend to that level. That's not why I wanted you to come here."

"I imagine you wanted to beat me over the head a little bit with your might and glory," she said, her voice more bitter than she wanted it. More obviously affected. But she couldn't seem to control it the way she should. "This villa has to be at least five thousand dollars a night."

"Are you concerned about how I spend my money? I'm touched, truly."

"Only if it affects Damian." She made herself smile, as if this was an easy little talk. Or as if she was in some way light and airy herself. "That's the beginning and the end of everything, isn't it?"

She saw something move across his beautiful face, ruthless and determined, but then it was gone. She didn't think she'd imagined it, but she couldn't work out what his game was here, so she told herself it didn't matter either way.

"There's no need for us to fight, surely," he said, his voice low. Something like agreeable, which she found instantly alarming. "Six years is a long time. I don't see any reason why we can't have a calm discussion about what's best for Damian. We were rational once. Surely we can be again."

And that was exactly what Anais had told herself she wanted. That was more than she'd dreamed would ever be possible with Dario. So why was it she didn't quite believe him?

"I'd like that," she said. And then, despite that lingering sense that this wasn't real, she tried to be the generous person she thought she *ought* to be. The one she thought her son deserved. "I'd like Damian to get to know you, of course. But you do understand that he's an entire little person all his own, don't you? He came into this world on his own schedule and he's stubbornly stuck to it ever since. If you have some fantasy in your head about an angelic creature who will gaze at you and call you Daddy and serve as some kind of appendage to your whims, that's probably not Damian."

"It didn't occur to me that I would ever be a father until you told me I had a son yesterday," Dario said in a voice that sounded a little too close to grim for Anais's peace of mind. "I have no expectations that require modification."

She realized how close they were standing then, and worse, how obvious it would be if she leaped away from him the way she wanted. How he'd read into that and worse—how he'd be absolutely correct in what he read.

Anais didn't want to be so close to him she could feel the heat he generated, the way she did now, as if that black linen was a radiator even here in the tropics in August. She didn't trust herself.

Around Dario, she couldn't.

The sad truth was that she'd fallen in love with him a

very long time ago. Not quite at first sight, but not long after, and nothing had changed that since. Not the way he'd broken the lonely heart she'd only ever shared with him. Not the way he'd abandoned her so cruelly, as if she'd been unworthy of a backward glance. Not the way she'd tried to hate him in all these years since, and failed, again and again.

How could she hate this man when she saw so much of him in her little boy's face? In that bigger than life laugh that was one hundred percent Dario in her son's body? It wasn't possible. She'd thought she'd come to a place of acceptance with that a long time ago. But of course, that had been when she'd never expected to see Dario again.

She still didn't want to stand this close to him. It made her entirely too aware of her own, eternal weakness where he was concerned.

"Great," she managed to say now, and she eased herself back and put a little more space between them, the better to look him in the eye, as if that would cut him down to size somehow. "Then when he throws a full-scale fit on the floor because he wants to wear a blue shirt instead of a red one the way he did this morning, I'm sure you'll handle it calmly."

Dario's mouth curved, and that wasn't helpful. It only reminded her all over again how susceptible she was to him. How badly some part of her wanted to believe that this—whatever this was—was real. God, how she wanted to believe that.

"If I can handle fractious board members and morally dubious CEOs, one small child shouldn't be a problem."

"I'm glad you're so confident."

The air between them felt taut then. It shimmered like heat. Dario thrust his hands in his pockets in a way that suggested he wanted to do something else entirely with them, and Anais had to fight to conceal her delicious— and traitorous—shiver of reaction.

"I want you to come with me," he told her. "Let's eat a meal like civilized people. Let's talk to each other." That curve in his mouth deepened, and the truth was, Anais wasn't strong enough to resist him. She never had been. And just then, with all his deep blue attention trained on her, she couldn't remember a single reason why that should change. Why she'd want it to change. "Let's do this the right way."

CHAPTER FIVE

MUCH LATER THAT NIGHT, Anais pushed back from the table in the private corner of the resort's outdoor restaurant and tried, yet again, to caution herself. To go slow, to keep her perspective—*something*.

The night had been perfect. Anais was a local, yet she felt like some kind of princess tonight, immersed in old Hawaiian magic on all sides. They'd been whisked to this romantic corner of the hotel restaurant, where there was nothing between them and the sea but a strip of volcanic rock, any other diners lost in the darkness behind them. Torches danced in the thick air all around, and the breeze tugged strands of hair free from her easy chignon to slide over her cheeks like a lover's soft fingers.

But Anais had only ever had one lover, and his fingers were hard, tapered and demanding, no matter how soft his caress.

The meal had been exquisite. The typical Hawaiian fusion of unexpected flavors and marvelous tastes, artfully arranged and beautifully presented, and Anais tried. She tried to sternly keep her attention on her son, not on his father. She tried to withstand the insidious magic of all this grace and ease and quietly luxurious wealth, and the man who had made it happen. She tried her best to keep her walls high, to read nothing into any of this, to stay the glacier she should have been no matter how enticing each bite of food.

No matter the far more worrying beguilement of the man across from her.

Dario had undergone some kind of transformation during the walk from his villa to the restaurant. Gone was that harsh, unforgiving man she'd met at the Fuginawa estate yesterday. In his place was, if not the man she'd married years ago exactly, certainly the closest thing to him she could imagine after these six long years apart.

And what the sound of Dario's laughter after all this time didn't manage to do to her heart, the fine wine he kept pouring did to her head.

She regarded him from across the table now, watching the way the light from the flickering torch flames caressed his beautiful face and made him seem that much more like the many dreams she'd had all these lonely years. That much more the man she'd begun to think she'd made up from the start.

They'd talked about everything and nothing over their meal. She'd talked about Damian—who he was, funny things he did, the sort of stories that highlighted what a delightful little kid she thought he was, most of the time. Dario had talked about the work that clearly consumed his life, in a way that made it clear he was doing exactly what he should. He'd asked her about practicing law and how she enjoyed it all these years into it. She'd asked how he liked becoming so well-known in his own right, having nothing to do with his family. They talked as easily as they ever had, in and around all the submerged rocks and treacherous undercurrents that lurked between them, dancing over the surface of things instead of slamming into the obstacles.

It was all real enough, she supposed. Even…nice. It was lulling her into what she knew damn well was a false sense of security. What she didn't know was what she could do to make her traitorous heart pay attention to warning signs and potential alarms when all it saw— all it wanted to see—was the only man she'd ever loved here with her at last, treating her the way he had when she'd imagined he might love her back.

"Why are you doing this?" she asked softly.

"Eating dinner?" He leaned back in his own chair. "I try to do it at least once an evening. It's an odd personality quirk of mine."

"No." And it terrified her how much—how strongly— she didn't want to do this just then. How terribly she wanted to simply drift off into this fantasy world where there was nothing but faint Hawaiian music on the sweet night air and where Dario, still her husband, looked at her as if he'd never hated her and never could. As if the six years of separation had been the dream, not what had preceded it. "You know what I mean."

He didn't answer. He stood instead, smoothing a hand over the front of his soft black shirt, and Anais's heart sank. She'd ruined it, hadn't she? Would it have really mattered all that much if she'd let this keep on going for another few minutes? An hour? If she'd let herself bask in this no matter how much of a dream it was? Who would it have hurt?

But she already knew the answer to that question. Not Damian—she'd protect him with her last breath. Only her.

Only and ever her.

And yet there was something about the sweet night air that made her imagine she could take it. That a few stolen moments with Dario would be worth whatever pain followed.

Dario stood beside her chair and she braced herself for him to say something hideous and cutting, to slap them both back down to that place they'd been in earlier. His face looked harder than before, no trace of that laughter of his that still split the night open with its rough joy and was clearly where Damian's came from, but she made herself hold his gaze no matter how difficult it was. She owed herself at least that much.

His hard, beautiful mouth moved as if he meant to speak, but he didn't. Instead, he held out his hand.

And Anais knew better. Of course she knew better. She'd been a single mother all this time, while he'd been off building empires and never looking back at all to see what destruction he'd left in his wake. She could have recited the reasons why this—any more time spent with him, especially time spent *touching*—was a terrible idea the same way she could rattle off pertinent case law when necessary at work.

Here, now, none of that seemed to matter.

Nothing seemed to matter except the way he looked at her over his outstretched hand, as if he'd command her to take it if he could but was instead waiting for her to do what he wanted because, deep down, he knew she wanted it, too. She had the strangest feeling he knew exactly what battles she waged inside her head.

And worse, she thought he could see straight through her and deep into her chest, where her poor, battered heart felt swollen and broken at once, all over again—as if this was all something new, these things he conjured up in her.

Anais took a deep, shuddering breath, and then couldn't seem to keep herself from slipping her hand into his.

She didn't gasp out loud at the instant electric surge, at that hot touch as his hard fingers curled around hers, but she thought he felt the jolt of it as it seared through her. He tugged her to her feet and she went to him willingly, and for a moment they stood there with barely a whisper of the sultry summer air between them.

Her shoes were high enough to put her almost at eye level with him, and that made her veins thrum with something that was half music, half delight. His blue eyes looked much too dark, especially when they dropped to her mouth, and she felt that same wild current in him, too, lighting her up from the place their hands were clasped together.

Dario stepped back, though he kept hold of her hand. There was a rueful curve to his mouth and a hard hunger in his gaze, and then he started to walk, pulling her along with him so she fit there at his side.

It took Anais much too long to realize they were weaving their way through the tables of the restaurant she'd forgotten was there. She felt as if she was walking through a dream, or as if the only real thing in the world was the way his fingers held hers tight and their palms touched. As if everything she'd ever felt about this man was boiled down into that tiny little touch, almost innocuous, and yet…not. At all.

The band kicked into a typical Elvis cover, syrupy and deeply Hawaiian, and Dario stopped walking when he reached the line of high palms that rustled there on the outskirts of the restaurant. The singer spoke of wise men and fools, and as Dario tugged her around to face him, Anais knew without a shadow of a doubt that she was very much the latter.

"I can't help it, either," he said in a low voice as he took her in his arms, and it took her a moment to realize he was responding to the famous song, not the words she didn't think she'd said out loud. "I've never been able to help myself when it came to you, Anais."

And it would have taken a far colder and harder woman than she was to pull away from him then. She didn't even try. Anais had never been the glacier she thought she should have been with him, not even all those years ago when she'd known she should have resisted him and hadn't. She wasn't sure she had it in her.

Certainly not when Dario was so close to her in the late-summer dark, his strong arms closing around her as he pulled her flush against him.

It was the middle of the night, she told herself, and she was pretending to be the kind of woman who had dinner with a man like him at all, much less at a stunning resort like this, and who cared if she'd actually married him in a different life? Those quick, painfully bright and deeply hurtful years seemed as if they'd happened to someone else. Surely nothing that happened in the lush dark here, on an island tucked away in the Pacific Ocean so many miles from anywhere, counted.

And she'd been alone so long. So deeply, profoundly alone. Before her marriage and after it. She'd been strong and she'd been brave. Too damned much of both, because she'd had to be to survive her childhood, her lonely early adulthood, the end of her marriage and her new role as Damian's mother and sole source of support. Her whole life had been a series of *had to be*.

Anais wasn't an idiot. This man had abandoned her.

The likelihood was he'd do it again, probably before dawn. But she wasn't the naive creature she'd been back then, so shocked and destroyed when he'd turned on her, and the only good thing about that was that he wasn't likely to surprise her with that kind of betrayal a second time.

She didn't have to trust him to want him.

And she'd always wanted him. He was the only man who had ever touched her, the only man she'd ever let close to her, the only *person* she'd ever let inside. No matter how many dates her aunt and uncle and well-meaning friends had sent her on, no matter how many nice men had said nice things to her, no matter how many times she'd told herself that she wasn't *really* married despite the fact she also wasn't divorced—she'd never been able to bring herself to let another man close. She'd never let them know her at all, much less put their hands on her.

She missed it. She missed *him*.

He's still your husband, a dangerous voice inside of her whispered, as seductive as the whole of this long, perfect evening. *Whatever else happened between you, you loved him once. Maybe he loved you, too. Maybe nothing else matters but that.*

So she swayed closer to him and told herself it didn't matter what happened later. Tomorrow, two weeks from now, whenever. Nothing mattered but this. Here, now, where nobody could see them and no one would know.

She was so tired of being so alone. Maybe that made her weak. She decided she didn't care what it made her. Not when he could make it all go away.

He could. She knew he could. He'd made whole cities disappear with a laugh, the whole world with a kiss. He was far more magical than he deserved to be. She just wanted to taste a little of that oblivion again.

Hell, she'd earned it, hadn't she?

Anais reached up and wound her arms around Dario's neck, angling herself against him. His hands moved up and down the length of her spine in a lazy rhythm, tracing her. Relearning her. Sending a wild heat spiraling all through her until it pooled between her legs, a swollen, delirious ache.

And she was the one who lifted herself up and pressed her mouth to his.

She kissed him with all those dreams she'd kept pent up inside her across so many long years. She poured all the rants she'd aimed at her reflection instead of to him into it, all the tears and the fear and the loss. She kissed him with her broken heart and her new mother's terror. She kissed him and she kissed him, lonely and resolute, as strong as she was afraid, two sides of the same coin.

Finally, all these years later, she kissed Dario goodbye.

And he let her.

He slipped a hand around to the nape of her neck and he met her, as if he knew exactly what she was doing, what this was.

Anais was shaking. That might have been a tear that scraped its way down her cheek. She didn't care. This was a bloodletting. A ritual of loss and leaving, six years overdue.

And when she was finished, she pulled back, not exactly meaning to rest her forehead against his as she gasped for breath. But she didn't pull away when she realized she was doing it.

"Better?" he asked in a rough voice that hardly sounded like his.

It didn't occur to her to tell him anything but the truth, as if the Hawaiian night that brushed against her skin was its own kind of confessional. "No. Not really."

"Good." A small laugh, entirely male, snaked its way down her spine and made her shiver. "My turn."

And then he hauled her mouth back to his, and took control.

Dario should have felt triumph wash over him. He should have been wild with his victory, with a sense of accomplishment. He'd set out to seduce his errant wife and he'd done it.

But all he could concentrate on was the taste of her mouth beneath his, and better, the way she pressed her sweet body against his. Her breasts underneath that soft cream silk were like torture against his chest. Her arms were around his neck as she arched into him and it still wasn't close enough.

He couldn't get close enough no matter how he kissed her, and he couldn't pretend what he was feeling then had anything to do with revenge.

Dario shoved that unnerving truth aside and threw himself straight into the lightning storm instead.

He took her mouth with a ruthlessness that might have concerned him if he'd let himself consider it too closely, but he was lost in the storm. The electric burst of sensation between them. There was nothing but this slick perfection, the tangle of her tongue with his, the sensation of Anais in his arms again at last. It didn't matter why or how or what needed to happen next.

It only mattered that he possess her, totally. Now.

Forever, some traitorous part of him whispered.

Before he lost her all over again.

He didn't know how he managed to pull his mouth from hers when it was the last thing he wanted. He hardly heard the band as they rolled easily into another song. He barely knew where they were and he didn't much care. He only knew he needed her naked and that no matter how accommodating the resort had been so far, they'd likely take a dim view of it if he stripped her here and lost himself in her against the nearest palm tree.

Which meant they needed to go somewhere else.

Immediately.

Dario swept her up and into his arms without a second thought. He begrudged every step he took as he held her high against his chest and strode down the path toward his villa. Every second that he wasn't deep inside her, braced above her, wrapped around her the way he ought to be, was torture. The weight of her against him wasn't enough. The way she looped her arm around his neck was little more than a tease. The way she tipped back her head to watch him with that solemn expression that did nothing to hide the stark, unmistakable need in her gaze made the hunger inside of him threaten to take him to his knees.

It wasn't until he'd shouldered his way back into his villa, striding across the living room and into the sprawling master suite, that he faced the fact that he wasn't acting according to his hastily hammered out plan at all. This was no deliberate seduction, designed to tear her into a thousand pieces and leave her inert and destroyed and unable to lift a finger to stop what happened afterward. This was mutually assured destruction, and he had no idea what the hell he was doing.

He knew he should back off. Stop this right now. He set her down on her sleek red shoes at the foot of his platform bed and forced himself to let go of her. This was the perfect moment to rethink. Regroup. He wasn't in control here and that was unacceptable.

But he couldn't seem to care about that.

Because all these long years after he'd given up imagining any way it could ever happen again, Anais was standing there before him. Her smooth perfection was once again marred by his own hands, and he was so hard it bordered on pain. He reached over and dug his fingers into her thick, black hair, pulling on the bun so the pins scattered everywhere as it all tumbled down to swirl around her shoulders. Her lips were full and lush and faintly swollen from his. Her soft blouse looked crumpled against her breasts.

He still loved it as much as he always had. He was the only one who'd ever seen her like this…

No. A cold voice in his head stopped that line of thought. *Not the only one.*

And the fury that rose in him at that was nothing new, but the way it wound itself around all that need and hunger was. It rolled and twisted all over each other, becoming something new. Something darker and wilder.

He didn't want to think about it. He didn't want to reason it through.

He just wanted her.

God help him, but he'd never stopped wanting her.

As if she could read the turmoil inside of him like a book, a faint shadow moved over her lovely face and a line appeared between her brows.

"Dario?"

He didn't want to talk. He didn't know the difference anymore between his hunger and his fury, his sense of betrayal and his mounting need; he only knew that there was a single cure. He didn't want to think about the implications. He told himself that it didn't matter what he felt while this was happening, as long as in the end it achieved the desired result.

Dario had never believed that the ends justified the means—hadn't he learned that when he'd uncovered all the shifty practices his former silent partner in ICE had signed off on before he'd started there?—but here, now, there was no other way. He refused to allow himself even a moment of regret.

He realized he was staring holes through her when Anais shivered slightly, but the truth of things was the way her nipples poked hard against the soft silk of her top, telling him everything he needed to know about her own need. Her own hunger that had always matched his own. Dario concentrated on that now. He moved closer to her, indulging himself. He traced the stiff little peaks with his fingers, rubbing the silk against her own flesh and smiling slightly when she let out a moan.

Anais let her head fall back, and another beast roared in him then. Pure lust. Sheer desire. He stopped trying to pretend there was anything else inside of him—anything else that mattered. He buried one hand in the fall of her hair and got his lips on the line of her throat, tasting her. Testing the firmness of her skin. Reveling in the scent of her, as delicate and uniquely *her* as he remembered. With his free hand he tugged at her blouse, until he was forced to let go of her hair to tug it the rest of the way over her head.

Her arms were still up in the air when he put his mouth back on her, and he felt as well as heard the way she shuddered into him with a ragged sound. Her small, perfectly formed breasts were as exquisite as he remembered them, and he was delighted to find she still didn't bother with a bra. That meant it was as easy as a memory to hold her where he wanted her with his hands curved over her shoulder blades, and then to get his mouth on one dark-tipped breast.

Then he sucked. Hard.

Anais made a tiny noise that Dario hadn't realized had haunted him for years, that small sound of greed and yearning. And the taste of her was impossibly addicting, sweet musk and a hint of salt against his tongue. He moved his mouth to her other breast to be sure, using his tongue and the hint of his teeth until she was moaning out loud with her head thrown back, her hands gripping his biceps as if she wanted to leave her fingerprints behind on his skin.

He stepped back, then spun her around, so she was braced against the foot of the bed with her bottom in the air. She was still as beautifully formed as he remembered her, and he told himself that wasn't a stab of something like pain he felt. It wasn't loss. He focused on the silken line of her back, the indentation of her spine and the flare of her hips. He couldn't stand the obstacle of her skirt and reached over to unzip it, pulling it from her until it pooled at her feet and she was left in nothing but those wicked, cherry red shoes and a thong in the same bright color.

Dario thought he might explode right there.

Instead, he shrugged out of his shirt and kicked off his trousers, then moved behind her, reveling in the harsh sounds of her uneven breaths in the quiet room.

"What about my shoes?" she whispered when he smoothed his hands over her hips, as if he was trying to memorize them anew, imprint them into his palms.

"Leave them on," he muttered.

And he lost himself in her. He threw the past out of his head and he simply drowned in her the way he wanted to do. The feel of her warm, soft skin beneath his hands. The noises she made, tiny gasps and sweet moans, all leading to that critical point where her breathing became panting instead.

He flipped her over, then tossed her farther up the wide mattress and followed her down. He kissed her again. Deeper, wilder. And this time it didn't matter where they were. This time, he didn't have to stop.

Dario couldn't imagine there would ever be another night with her, not after what he planned to do tomorrow. And this wasn't like the last night he'd spent with her six years ago when he'd had no idea that she was betraying him or that it would be the last time he'd get to touch her. This time he was ready.

This time, he knew exactly what he'd be missing and how much it would hurt, loath as he was to admit it to himself.

So he kissed her like a drowning man, and when he couldn't take any more of it, he moved to lavish attention on her breasts again. And when she was writhing beneath him, her arms thrown over her head in abandon and her back arched high, he moved even lower.

He trailed fire over her belly, then moved over that bright red thong at last. He pulled her long legs over his shoulders, then used his own width to keep her thighs apart. He liked the way she trembled, the way her breath sawed in and out of her and how she came up on her elbows to watch him.

Dario caught her gaze for a moment. If he didn't know better, he'd have believed that sheen of vulnerability in her dark eyes, that faint hint of emotion in her full lower lip. If he was still the fool he'd been, that might have ripped him apart. He could feel something hollow inside of him, as if it had.

But that was nothing more than another ghost, and there was no place here for that.

There was only tonight. There was only this.

Sex, he told himself harshly. *Nothing more.*

And then he pressed his mouth to the V between her legs, covered in that red lace, and made her call out his name.

She shook beneath him, the sharp heels of the high shoes digging at his back, and only when she made that high-pitched sound he liked too much did he tug the bright red thong aside, and lick his way into her heat at last.

He was like a storm.

Anais couldn't catch her breath, couldn't recover. Couldn't do a single thing in all the world but lose herself in the tumult and fire of Dario's wicked, masterful mouth against the part of her that ached so hot and needy she worried it might actually kill her. Or he would, and she doubted she'd mind.

He built up that fire, using his lips and tongue and the scrape of the jaw he still hadn't shaved. It was as if he'd plugged her into an electrical outlet. She hummed. She burned. She burst into flame again and again.

She dug her hands into his hair and held on while he licked her straight over the edge and into oblivion.

She'd almost forgotten the shattering. The sweet splintering. The monstrous ache that only Dario could ease, and the terrible need that only he brought out in her and only he ever assuaged.

And when she came back to herself he was already moving, tugging her thong from her legs and pulling her shoes from her feet, throwing one and then the next aside. She thought she heard them *thunk* against the hardwood floor, but then again, perhaps it was only her poor heart as it beat hard against the cage of her ribs and left her feeling a delicious sort of helpless as she tried to slow her breathing.

She couldn't seem to move. Or think. Or care too much about her inability to do either. One tremor chased another, leaving her boneless in the center of his bed. She heard the crinkle of foil that told her he was sheathing himself and then Dario was crawling over her, hauling her with him into the center of the bed before he propped himself above her on his elbows.

And for a searing moment, all he did was gaze down at her.

His face was drawn and his blue eyes glittered dark with the same passion she could feel sweeping through her, as bright as if she'd never broken apart beneath his talented mouth. As if he'd never thrown her over that cliff once already.

She moved then, lifting the hand that had once worn his ring so proudly and placing it against his beautiful face. She didn't speak. She wasn't sure she could. She didn't know what on earth she'd say even if she could find the words.

Dario reached between them and positioned himself at her entrance, never shifting that intense blue gaze from hers. And then slowly, so slowly, he pushed himself inside her. Inch by glorious, impossible inch.

At last, she thought, *at last...*

Still he continued to slide himself into her as if he had

all the time in the world to let her body accommodate him, for her channel to stretch to fit him. She couldn't help but remember their first time, when she'd been so scared and overwhelmed and in love with him. And he'd taken his time then, too. He'd built that wildfire between them higher and higher, thrown her into bliss twice, before he'd moved to claim her completely.

Just like now, he'd gone slow. So slow. So that his possession had felt inevitable. So that she'd shook beneath him, craving him, desperate to feel him sheathed inside her as far as he could go.

She didn't think she was the only one remembering that faraway night, the two of them wrapped up in each other in his Manhattan bedroom with the whole great city a glittering flame outside his window. Anais had clung to him and welcomed him and found herself in him, and nothing had ever been the same after that.

So, too, would nothing be the same after this. But at least she knew that now. She wasn't that overawed virgin anymore. She knew exactly what she was doing.

If she kept telling herself that, maybe it would eventually be true.

Dario settled himself completely against her, stretching her. Anais could see the tension that corded his neck and made his arms like granite. She could see the mad glitter in his eyes that reminded her of the whole of Manhattan outside that window in his old apartment, and she could feel him, bold and male and uncompromising, so deep inside her it was hard to tell which one of them was which.

As if it was her first time all over again, she felt moisture gather in the corners of her eyes. And the way she had then, she moved her hips experimentally, to see if it made him blow out a breath the way it had before.

When it did, that mouth of his crooked up in the corner.

"This is no time for games, Anais," he told her in that gorgeously dark voice of his that swept through her like a new caress, setting her alight.

And only then did he begin to move.

He set a hard pace, and she met him. He dropped down to take her mouth again, slipping his hands beneath her bottom to lift her and hold her precisely where he wanted her as he thrust into her.

She clung to his shoulders and she wrapped her legs around his hips and she knew this dance. She knew precisely how they fit together, exactly how they moved. As if they'd been made for this. As if no time had passed.

And it took no time at all, or it took a lifetime, before Anais was strung out on that same high cliff all over again. She heard her own voice calling out wordless prayers into the dark, and she heard his low laugh, and then she was shattering all around him all over again.

And this time, he followed her over the edge—and she was sure she heard him shout her name as he fell.

CHAPTER SIX

ANAIS WOKE TO find the sun streaming across her face and the sound of the surf in her ears. She blinked in all the brightness and then sat up too quickly, taking in the vast room, the sleek furnishings, the astonishing softness of the dizzyingly high-thread-count sheets against her skin.

She wasn't particularly surprised to find herself alone. She wasn't necessarily happy about it, of course, but she couldn't claim she was *surprised*. No matter the places they could take each other in bed, out of it she and Dario seemed destined to do nothing but hurt each other.

Over and over again.

Anais moved very slowly, very carefully, to the edge of the bed and was faintly disappointed that nothing sang out in pain as she did. No twinges or tugs to remind her in that raw, physical way of how she'd spent most of the previous night, or with whom. Nothing that would last.

She told herself that was better. Memories were bad enough. They could lurk about for years, as she knew all too well. They snuck into the corners of things and blended into the shadows. They could ruin a woman without her even realizing it, popping up in dreams whenever she closed her eyes and making her unwilling to even consider moving on the way she should. No matter that *he* had, and years before.

But this was neither the place nor the time to worry about the ways Dario would likely haunt her now. Besides, she'd had six years to find a way to handle it before and she'd managed it. This would be no different. She'd be fine.

Eventually, she assured herself, *you'll be perfectly fine.*

Her clothes were draped over the chaise in the corner near the open glass doors, the screen letting in the ocean's song and the summer sunlight but none of Hawaii's less pleasant realities.

Reality is better, no matter how unpleasant, she told herself firmly as she dressed. *This place—Dario—it's all a fantasy that has nothing to do with you or your actual life. It never did. It all might as well be another dream.*

That made her feel better—or at least ready to face him. She raked her fingers through her hair, letting it fall where it would and happy that it conformed to its usual sleek, straight, depressingly unchangeable style without her having to do anything more than that. She'd never before realized how lucky she was to have such hair that allowed her to look a lot more pulled together than a woman wearing last night's outfit should.

She slipped her shoes back on as if they were armor and she then squared her shoulders before she pushed through the door and marched out into the vast living area prepared to do battle—but it was empty.

That confused her. It seemed so unlike him. She stood there for a moment, listening for the usual sounds that indicated Dario was near—the brusque clicking of the keys on his laptop, the sound of his voice issuing orders on the phone. But there was nothing. The villa was hushed. Still.

Empty, she thought. But she couldn't quite believe that.

There was what looked like a stack of papers on the kitchen counter, but she ignored it as she walked to each of the bedrooms and looked inside. Each was as beautifully decorated and as empty as the next. He wasn't in the little den with its massive flat-screen television, or in the separate office space equipped with a massive steel desk. He wasn't on the lanai or out on his secluded beach. He wasn't in the private pool on the far side of the villa, either.

He was gone.

Almost as if he'd never been here on Maui at all.

And Anais could admit it. It surprised her. And, more than that, felt a lot like a slap. The hurt feelings were silly, she recognized, but the other feeling bubbling up inside of her was a complicated sort of disappointment—as if she'd *wanted* what would likely have been another tense, unpleasant scene with Dario.

"Surely not," she murmured to herself, her voice the only sound in the villa.

She shook her head as she crossed the living area again, amazed at herself. At her own capacity for self-delusion and what amounted to self-harm. And she knew—*she knew*—there was a storm waiting there in the distance, bunched up on the horizon, dark and menacing. Thunder rolled deep inside her and the skies were threatening and low, but she was ignoring all of it. She was refusing to play through the images in her head of last night's abandon.

The way he'd touched her, the ways she'd tasted him—*no*.

She was pretending everything was fine—that *she* was fine. She was pretending that she could handle what she'd done last night and the fact he'd disappeared this morning, even though she'd half expected he would. She was desperately pretending she couldn't feel that cold harbinger wind on her skin, making every hair on her body stand on end, letting her know in no uncertain terms that there was no outrunning the storm—the terrible reckoning for all her recklessness—that was headed straight for her.

But maybe she could delay it awhile. Just a little while.

At the kitchen counter, she picked up the bag she'd forgotten she'd even brought with her last night and pulled out her car keys. And she couldn't help but glance over at the stack of papers, which it took her a beat or two longer than it should have to realize was actually a legal document.

With her name on it.

Her stomach flipped over, then plummeted straight down to her feet.

She reached over and pulled the papers toward her, and felt something like frozen solid as she scanned the first page. Once. Twice. It was only the third attempt that she was able to really, truly comprehend that she was looking at divorce papers.

Divorce papers for her and Dario, to be precise.

All drawn up and ready for her signature, demanding the divorce on the grounds of Anais's infidelity and naming his brother Dante as her lover. Just as he'd promised before in what she'd truly believed was simply a hateful, throwaway comment.

It took her another long moment to realize she was

shaking. That the words were blurring there before her on the page.

There was a single sticky note attached to the last page, where the line for her signature sat, blank and cruel, next to the bold dash of Dario's name in an offensively bright blue shade of ink. The shiny yellow note contained nothing but a phone number with a New York City area code.

Dario's, she was certain. Not that she could understand why he'd left her divorce papers and his phone number. It didn't make any sense.

That terrible storm drew closer, the thunder growling ferociously at her as it came. She could feel the leading edge of the rain, battering at her where she stood…

Her phone began to ring in her bag, forcing her to breathe. To look away from the papers and that damned phone number. To shove back that storm as best she could. She tried to gather herself as she rummaged in her bag, and she'd at least taken a few calming breaths by the time she pulled out her smartphone to see her aunt's number on the screen.

"*Bonjour*, Tante," she murmured as she answered it, trying to sound calm. Normal. In one piece.

"Is Damian with you?" her aunt demanded in panicked French, without bothering to greet Anais at all, which could not have been more unlike her.

And Anais forgot about storms and papers and everything else.

"What? Damian? No—"

"The school just called," her aunt told her, her voice a streak of high-pitched upset, hardly intelligible. "I don't know how to tell you this, but he's gone. He went out with the other children for their midmorning recess and he never came back in. They're going to call the police, but I said I'd check with you—"

And that was when she understood. The harsh truth fell through her like a guillotine, swift and gleaming and lethal.

Dario's change in behavior last night. The abrupt switch from antagonist to lover. His absence this morning, the divorce papers, the damned phone number.

He'd planned the whole thing.

Including and especially her sensual surrender to him in bed, not once or even twice, but three times before she'd dropped off into an exhausted, dreamless sleep in the blue light before dawn.

"No, Tante," she managed to say. She would never know how she managed to keep herself from breaking down, right there on the phone. "Tell them not to call the police. Tell them it's fine. I know where he is."

"But, Anais—"

"I'll explain everything when I get home," she managed to grit out, and that wasn't a lie. Not exactly. Though she had no idea where she'd start.

She ended the call with her aunt and yanked the divorce papers toward her, flipping through the pages with numb fingers until she reached the signatures and that scrawled taunt of a phone number. It took her two tries to enter it correctly because her hands shook so badly and her thumbs seemed suddenly twice their previous size.

It rang. Endlessly. Anais thought she aged a thousand years before she heard the line connect and then Dario's smooth, calm voice, as effective as a gut punch. She doubled over, right there at the counter.

"Anais."

"Where is he?" Her voice was rough. Terrible. "What did you do?"

"He's perfectly fine," Dario said coolly. "He's happily watching a movie on his tablet."

"I told you I'd let you see him, you bastard. You didn't have to take him during recess! The school were going to call the police until they realized you were his father!"

"Go ahead," Dario invited her, and he didn't sound particularly cool any longer. "My son and I will be in New York in approximately ten hours. My entire legal team looks forward to handling the issue, however you choose to address it."

She couldn't make her trained legal brain work the way it should. She couldn't *think*.

"Dario, you can't—"

"I can and I did." His voice was the harshest she'd ever heard it. Worse than a stranger's, judgmental and cruel. "You never should have hidden my child from me, Anais. You reap what you sow."

And then, impossibly, he disconnected the call.

The smartphone fell from her hand and clattered against the hard marble, but she was already racing around the counter to pitch herself against the sunken sink and lose the contents of her stomach right there. Once. Again.

For a moment she thought her knees would give out. She could see herself in her head, sliding to the floor in a kind of puddle of despair and staying there until the hotel's housekeeping team swept her out with the trash. Her breath came hard and harsh, loud against the sink's hard walls.

But her knees didn't give out, somehow. Slowly, surely, she straightened. She braced herself against the sides of the sink and then she ran the water cold. She splashed it on her face and rinsed her mouth and slowly, slowly fought back the panic so she could think this through.

Dario wouldn't hurt Damian. That was the most important thing. He might be a terrible bastard to her, but he wasn't a monster. The worst-case scenario was that her baby might be scared, might want her and not be able to find her—she let out a ragged sob at that thought— but Dario had nothing but stacks of money at his disposal. Damian's physical and material needs would be met, no question.

She tried to take a moment to feel thankful for that. To remind herself how many women—many of whom she'd had as clients as part of her pro bono work on the islands—couldn't allow themselves that same confidence in their exes.

But the thought of her little boy afraid, however well Dario might treat him, made her shake again. She fought it back, and that dizzy, swimming thing in her head that was so much worse than a mere sob…she thought it might take her to the ground, after all.

But it didn't. She didn't let it.

She'd been prepared to do what she could to ease Dario's access to Damian. She'd wanted her son to have his father in his life, no matter her complicated feelings about that father. Despite what he'd thought, she'd never wanted to conceal Damian from him in the first place. She shouldn't have slept with him, certainly, but that was a minor misstep, all things considered. She wasn't sure she'd have forgiven herself for succumbing to that old addiction so easily, but she'd have handled it, somehow. She still would have done what she could to make things work well enough that Damian and Dario could build some kind of relationship between them.

He, meanwhile, had deliberately misled her and then kidnapped her child.

Which made what she had to do easy, she decided then and there, braced against an unaffordable sink in this outrageously luxurious resort villa on the edge of the vast, uncaring Pacific.

It felt a little bit like a death, but it wasn't. It was a declaration. He'd made it, but she could answer it—and much, much louder.

Dario wanted a war, apparently.

And this time, she'd damn well give it to him.

It should probably not have come as a surprise to Dario that the child—*his* child, if any of what Anais had said to him in Hawaii could be believed—was an utter terror.

There was no other word for it.

On the fourth day of his surprise fatherhood, Dario stood in the foyer of his sprawling Upper West Side penthouse apartment with its three stories of sweeping views over Central Park, and watched the little demon who supposedly bore his DNA run in screaming circles for no apparent reason, putting priceless artifacts at risk with each lap around the expansive living room.

"I don't understand why you haven't handled this," Dario said coldly to the nanny who'd come with the highest of references from the most prestigious Manhattan agency, which normally boasted a waiting list years long. "Why you haven't done whatever it is I'm paying you to do to stop this kind of insanity at six-thirty in the morning."

"I'm a nanny, Mr. Di Sione," the woman replied

crisply, with the hint of an English accent Dario was ninety percent convinced she faked for effect and her arms crossed over her ample bosom. "Not Albus Dumbledore."

The tiny creature, who was, as far as Dario had been able to tell, made entirely of howls and fists and a boundless, terrifying energy, stopped of his own accord then and shouted something incomprehensible at Dario.

"Can you translate that?" Dario asked the nanny in the same cold tone. "Because if you can't, I might as well fire you and locate a zoologist."

"I'll handle him," the woman said with a sniff.

"See that you do," Dario gritted out, and then he stalked for the door.

None of this was going according to plan.

You do understand that he's an entire little person all his own, don't you? Anais had asked him back in Hawaii. *If you have some fantasy in your head about an angelic creature who will gaze at you and call you Daddy and serve as some kind of appendage to your whims, that's probably not Damian.*

It was definitely not Damian.

"Go to hell," he gritted out as he stabbed at the button of his private elevator, and he hoped Anais heard that, wherever she was. Lying in a heap on some Hawaiian floor, he hoped—and he told himself that pang he felt at the thought was the thrill of his victory over the woman who had wronged him, not something a whole lot more like shame.

He felt slightly more in control when he got to the ground floor of his building and pushed his way out into the sweltering heat of another Manhattan late-summer morning. He waved off his driver and walked instead, thinking the exercise would clear his head. Something had to, or he thought he might implode.

The child—*his son*—was only part of it. The truth was, he'd expected Anais to appear on his doorstep within twelve hours or so of that morning-after phone call, and she hadn't. He didn't know what to make of that. Or, to be precise, one irrepressible part of his body knew exactly what to make of it now it had tasted her again—it counted this as an unacceptable loss and wanted her even more—while the rest of him was as close to confused as he'd been in years.

Not *confused*, exactly, he corrected himself as he strode down Central Park West toward the ICE headquarters farther south. He was only dimly aware that the other pedestrians cleared the way before him, which probably meant he was scowling ferociously. But he refused to call it *confusion*, this heavy, spiked thing in him. It was anger. It was self-righteous indignation, and he'd earned it, by God. It had nothing at all to do with the bright images of their night together that coursed through his head and made him worry he might embarrass himself in the middle of corporate meetings. Nothing to do with that at all.

It came down to one simple point, he told himself as he walked toward his office. If it was all right for Anais to raise their child without him, well, then, that must mean it was all right for him to do the same thing.

Even if the child in question appeared to be the spawn of the devil on an extended sugar high.

His phone kept buzzing in his pocket but he ignored it. It was either a member of his family or of his staff. The earrings Giovanni had demanded he find were the lesser of the two priceless items Dario had brought back from

Hawaii, and he kept forgetting he needed to get them out to the Hamptons and into his grandfather's hands. He made a mental note—because delivering the earrings would stop the calls at least.

And the office could damn well wait until he got in. He'd only fire everyone who crossed his line of sight in his current mood, and more than that, he'd probably enjoy it a lot more than was good for anyone involved. He kept walking. Slowly, surely, the more blocks he covered the more New York worked its usual urban magic on him, the rhythm of the city getting into his blood the way it always did. One block, then another, and he felt the cloud of it all shift, then begin to lift. He was almost feeling back to his normal self when he stopped at a newsstand outside his office building for the paper.

For the first time since he'd turned his back on a stunning tropical view to find his past standing in front of him in a long black dress, Dario felt pretty good.

Until, that was, he saw his own name splashed across the tabloids. Bold and unmistakable.

For a moment he didn't move. He couldn't, no matter how the man behind the counter glared at him and the people behind him muttered. He stared at the obnoxious headlines in sheer disbelief, as if that might make sense of them.

It didn't.

Di Sione in Bitter Custody Battle with Secret Wife— *"He Wanted Nothing to Do with Me or My Baby Until Now!"*

"He Left Me Years Ago to Make His Fortune, but Now He's Stolen My Baby," Cries Abandoned Anais!

Is ICE'S Front Man Cold Enough to Kidnap His Own Child?

And there was Anais's face, treacherous and tearstained, as if she'd camped out in front of the paparazzi giving interviews. It occurred to him that she must have done exactly that. She was front and center on the three largest tabloid papers, her supposedly heartbroken photos side by side with the harshest-looking pictures Dario had ever seen of himself. He couldn't imagine where they'd even found such photographs. He looked like a serial killer.

His stockholders were unlikely to find any of this particularly delightful.

Gritting his teeth, Dario pulled out his still-buzzing phone. Marnie, repeatedly, with a series of 911/SOS texts besides. His lawyers, every fifteen minutes to the second. Numbers he assumed were the usual carrion crows of the so-called press, looking for his response or his reaction, as ever. Some of his usually hands-off siblings, no doubt almost as astonished to discover they had a previously unknown nephew as he'd been to find out he had a son. And his grandfather, who surely deserved better at his advanced age than to see another one of his descendants splashed all over the papers in yet another scandal.

He didn't return any of the calls.

He stalked into the cavernous entry hall of his building and stood stonily in the elevator as everyone else in it pretended not to stare at him, and he wasn't at all surprised to find Marnie waiting for him when he arrived at his floor.

"I'm so sorry," she began the moment he stepped out of the elevator car, which was never good. "I assume you know about the tabloid situation?" He only glared at her. "Of course you do."

"I'll want a copy of each paper that ran this story and the direct number of its managing editor within the hour," he bit out.

"Of course, but—"

Dario didn't wait to hear *but what*. He started moving toward his office in the far corner of the otherwise open, wood-and-steel space, Marnie scurrying along beside him.

"Get Legal on it. I'm not afraid to take every last one of them to court for publishing this crap."

"Yes," Marnie said, "I will, but really—"

He raked a hand through his hair and unclenched his teeth. Or tried, anyway. "Do we know if the stock has taken a hit? Has it gone that far?"

"Mr. Di Sione, I'm sorry, but she's here." Marnie took a deep breath when he scowled at her, but then pushed on, confirming that this unpleasant day really had gone from frying pan to fire, just like that. "Your—Mrs.— *Anais* is here. In the conference room, waiting for you. Right now."

CHAPTER SEVEN

DARIO STOPPED WALKING. Abruptly.

He was aware of too many eyes on him, from people who should have been concentrating on their work instead of on this explosion of his personal life into the public domain. God, but he hated this. He'd hated it when he'd been a kid and his parents' tempestuous lives and tragic deaths had brought the Di Sione family entirely too much unwanted attention. It was worse now.

And even so, he was aware that what leaped in him at the sound of her name was not quite temper or fury or any of the things it should have been. It was that traitor inside his chest, and worse, entirely too much of that same old hunger he'd dared to imagine he'd slaked the other night.

What a laugh. There was no slaking his desire for Anais. There was only indulging it or recovering from that indulgence, and nothing in between.

Dario tried to focus on his secretary. "I was unaware that I'd lifted the standing security alert on her. She should be in a jail cell, not polluting my conference room."

"Yes, well." Marnie shifted her weight from one foot to the other, but held his gaze with such directness it made her sleek, steel-gray bob shake slightly where the razor edge of it scraped her chin. "She told the security officers downstairs that if they didn't let her come up she'd hold a press conference on the front steps. I thought this was better."

Dario made a low noise that was far too close to a growl, but he knew it wasn't Marnie's fault. And there were a thousand things he could have done then. He could have turned and left the building. He could have had Anais wait for him all day while he dealt with the piles of actual work he needed to do. He could have had her thrown out, anyway, and damn her threats.

He didn't do any of those things.

And later, he couldn't remember leaving the elevator bank at all, but there he was, pushing through the glass doors of the conference room, every atom of his being focused on the slender woman who stood at the windows with a studied insouciance that made his blood boil.

And other parts of him stand up and pay far too close attention.

"The tabloids?" he demanded as he strode inside, and he made no attempt to keep the fury from his voice. "Is there nothing you won't do? No depth too low for you to sink?"

Anais shrugged, but she didn't turn from the stretch of windows across the back of the room, with skyscrapers and the distant Manhattan streets spread out before her. As if the great, sprawling city was sunning itself at her feet, the glare of the late-summer sun almost too bright to bear.

"Apparently the tabloids are the only thing that gets your attention. And you have some nerve talking about sinking to new depths, having recently transitioned from corporate shill to kidnapper."

He ignored that, along with the uncomfortable twinge inside of him that suggested a few headlines wasn't quite the same thing as flying off with a child, and no matter that he was supposedly the child's father. "Lying to me in private wasn't enough for you, so you took your lurid fantasies to the gutter press? I'd almost admire the escalation if it weren't so calculated."

"Says the man who seduced me for the sole purpose of abducting my child." She sniffed, still with her gaze fixed on the city outside the windows, her voice irritatingly smooth and cool, like everything else about her. "You could teach the art of calculation to one of your computers, couldn't you?"

"Is this a competition?" His voice was not nearly as smooth as it should have been. Dario found that far more irritating than was at all wise.

"You've been calling me a liar for years when I told you the truth. I thought I'd live down to your expectations." She turned then, and she looked even more perfect and untouchable than she usually did, and God help him, but all he could think about was that wide bed in Hawaii and the way she'd sobbed out her pleasure in his arms. Over and over again. "Where is my son?"

"*My* son. Unless you're ready to confess, at long last, your tryst with my brother? The anxious world you invited into our personal business awaits the truth."

Her gaze cooled even further, but she didn't otherwise react. Not in any way Dario could read, and he hated that. That she could still be a mystery to him and worse—that after all this time and all she'd done he could still want to solve it. What did that say about him?

But he was terribly afraid he knew the answer to that.

"You're a sperm donor to Damian, nothing more," she

said quietly. Too quietly. "Rather than sort things out the proper way, you opted to become a terrifying stranger who plucked an innocent child off a playground as part of some twisted plot to make himself feel better about an imagined slight. I think your actions speak for themselves, but let's not kid ourselves. I think we both already knew you're not a very good man."

Dario would never know how he managed to keep his temper leashed at that. How he kept his cool on the outside while inside he burned in a white-hot fury that he told himself was entirely rage—because it had to be. Because he refused to allow it be any of those darker things he hated that he could still feel for this woman.

He viewed it as a significant victory that his voice remained relatively calm when he replied to her.

"While you are, at best, a faithless cheater who will say and do anything to avoid responsibility for her own actions. Whether that's taking a lover while married or neglecting to inform a man that he has a son in the first place. Which glass house do you think will shatter first, Anais? Yours or mine?"

She smiled. Not nicely.

"I came here as a courtesy," she told him softly. "If you want a war, Dario, I can do that. I don't really care what you do to me. But you should never have touched my child. We can handle this between us like adults or we can handle it in the papers. Your choice. I have nothing to lose either way."

"How amusing that you think so."

"Public opinion tends to back distraught mothers, not the rich, terrible men who abandoned them and their own kids. Maybe you should think about that before you threaten me."

Dario didn't know he'd moved, only that he was standing much too close to her, suddenly. He could see the color in her cheeks, the hectic fury that glittered in her eyes. He was aware of the clothes she wore—a sleek shift in a deep aubergine color with a complicated neckline and another pair of extravagant, deceptively delicate-looking shoes, all her thick black hair secured in a low ponytail at the nape of her neck—but more than that, he was aware of *her*. Every breath she took. Every minute shift of expression on her lovely face. The faint seductive scent she wore, or maybe that was just her skin—

"What the hell are you doing to me?" he growled at her.

"You stole my son, you bastard," she hissed back at him. "I haven't even started yet."

And it hit him then, that she wasn't playing a game with him now. That the brittle expression behind the fury that he hadn't been able to read at first wasn't mysterious at all. It was fear.

Of him. Of what he might do.

He thought he'd never felt so small in all his life. And he couldn't understand it. Wasn't this what he'd thought he wanted? This power over her? The upper hand at last? As much his revenge as her just desserts?

"Damian is perfectly fine," Dario heard himself say grudgingly. From that tiny place inside him that hated what he was doing—hated anything that would put that sort of look on her face, no matter his reasons. "In fact, he's more than fine. He's a holy terror."

Her shoulders relaxed fractionally. Her mouth lost some of its unnatural stiffness. That frozen thing in her dark eyes thawed—if only slightly. And Dario understood that whatever else was true or not about this situation, it was clear Anais truly loved that wild creature of a child. Had he doubted that? Or had he become so used to laying every evil he could at her door that he didn't know how to do anything else where she was concerned?

The trouble was, he didn't know how to stop.

"He's not a holy terror," Anais corrected him. "Or not entirely, anyway. He's five."

"I was under the impression the two are interchangeable."

She almost smiled. Then she reached toward him as if she meant to touch his arm, yet thought better of it at the last moment. Her hand curled into a fist as she dropped it back to her side, and there was no reason on earth he should feel that as some kind of loss. Or why his forearm should throb as if it hurt where she *hadn't* touched him.

"You made your point, Dare," she said quietly. Her gaze was steady, and she raised her chin as she spoke. "You took me on quite a ride. You seduced me and abandoned me and whisked Damian away from beneath my nose. You made me feel exactly as awful as I suspect you've wanted to do for a long, long time."

She paused, and he didn't quite understand why he should feel the trickle of something entirely too much like shame move through his gut at that when it was perfectly true. When he'd done all of those things. Deliberately, if not quite as cold-bloodedly as he'd imagined he would when he'd conceived of this plan the night she hadn't let him step through her front door in Kihei.

"Don't tell me you've come here to claim you're the victim in this," he said softly, because he didn't know what to do with *shame*. It was foreign to him. It certainly had no place here, with her, of all people. Dario had built the last six years of his life on one inescapable truth: he was the victim of terrible betrayals from the only two people in all the world he'd trusted, but their failings didn't define him. He'd risen above them. There was no place in his life for shame or anything like it. "I'll laugh in your face."

"Are we finished now? Can we end this?" She kept her dark gaze on his. "Quite apart from everything else, I can't imagine you have any idea how to raise a child."

"I wasn't aware anyone did. I thought they learned it as they went, like anything else."

He could have told her he'd hired a battalion of highly trained nannies to make sure someone in Damian's vicinity knew a little something about child care, because Anais was absolutely right. He knew nothing about children save that, when he'd been one, it had been largely unpleasant until he and Dante had gone off to boarding school, where they'd had the kind of fun that came hand in hand with daily trips to the headmaster's office. He could have told her he'd never leave something like the care of an innocent child to chance.

He didn't.

"Tell me what you want," she bit out, that cool tone of hers fraying around the edges, and that didn't please him as much as he thought it should have. "To get my attention? To get your revenge? I think you've achieved that."

"I have what I want from you," he said, and he didn't realize until he'd said it that he didn't really mean it. That he'd said it simply to be cruel. Because he could. Because he was supposed to *want* to be as cruel to her as she'd been to him, surely. He should have loved nothing more than to stand there watching her press her lips together, hard, as if she was forcing back a sob, and to see how she had to fight to keep from showing him any of that.

Because there was a part of him, mean and spiked and still raw, that wanted to strike out at her however he could.

And he knew exactly what that black sludge of a feeling was as it moved through him then, rolling over him and sticking to him like a stain. He hated himself. He hated this. He hated hurting her for the sake of hurting her...

When had he become this person? This angry, bitter, horrid man who did these things with such appalling nonchalance?

But he knew. Of course he knew.

And that same old scene unfolded before him the way it always did, with the sickening inevitability of a nightmare. As if he was reliving it instead of simply remembering it. He'd gone out early that Saturday to a meeting with the people at ICE that Dante had refused to attend, in what Dario had thought was his continuing refusal to do his part in their business, and he'd been happy to be headed home after it. Anais had been the only person he could talk to back then, the only person who had understood how torn he'd felt between what he'd believed was the right thing to do for his company and the loyalty he'd felt to his brother. The fact he'd confided in her and had often taken her advice instead of Dante's was, Dario had been aware, something that had driven his brother—no fan of Anais's from the start—absolutely insane.

He could *see* the heedless, carefree way he'd walked into the apartment, throwing his keys on the same table he always did, then heading toward the bedroom to find the lovely wife he'd long since convinced himself was his perfect partner—if nothing more. Never anything more emotionally charged than that.

Because their marriage had been so analytical, so cool and careful, in the light of day. They spoke of their union as if it was a practical business arrangement they'd undertaken for the sake of their common goals with no emotional component whatsoever—and then they tore each other to shuddering pieces in bed every chance they got, again and again and again.

And she was the first person he wanted to find when he had news to share, good or bad. He couldn't even remember how she'd replaced Dante in that role, only that she had. It was as much because he and Dante had stopped thinking and acting as a single unit in those days—the erosion of trust between them, he thought now, that had followed that incident with the girlfriend they hadn't known they'd had in common when they'd been eighteen—as it was because of anything Anais had done herself.

Would he have understood what all of that meant in his own time, if she hadn't played him the way she had? He'd already thought it was astonishing how the two of them, raised in such different yet similarly unpleasant circumstances by hideously selfish parents, had stumbled upon each other the way they had. Would he have eventually comprehended what should have been obvious to him from the start—that their marriage had never been cold in any way at all, and they'd only been pretending otherwise? He'd never know.

Dario could still remember the flush on her cheeks, the wild look in her eyes, when he'd found her standing there in the little hall outside their bedroom with one hand braced against the wall—as if she'd run to stand there, to face him. That was what he'd thought in that last moment before his whole life had imploded.

She'd stared at him, her face pale and her eyes blazing, neither of which had made sense to him. Had he moved closer to her then? He could never remember. Because that was when Dante had stepped out of the bedroom behind her, one of Dario's shirts wide open on his chest and a look Dario couldn't read at all on his face.

And Dario couldn't remember the last time he'd slept. He'd been eating and breathing the company then, juggling meetings all day and preparing for them all night. He'd barely seen his wife at all. He'd certainly not seen enough of Dante while he'd been shoving his whole face to the grindstone night after night. He'd already been feeling shut out of his own life, a stranger in the two most important relationships in his life. It had been a dark time for him already, and he'd even been *worried* about how much the only two people in the world he really cared about seemed to hate each other...

But they didn't hate each other, he'd understood then with sickening clarity. Like a kick to the gut. Clearly, that had never been what was happening between the two of them.

And that was when he'd understood exactly what Anais was to him, what she'd meant to him that whole time. Why he'd moved so quickly with this woman from the start. Why it had seemed something like *destined*, though he'd never have used that word.

Right then and there, in the hallway with his half-dressed twin, he'd understood his own foolish heart much too late.

Here, six years later in a completely different part of the city and the two of them much different people than they'd been back then, he jolted out of his ugly memories to find Anais still standing before him. Still watching him with that same arrested and fearful look on her face.

He still didn't know what it meant, what any of this meant—only that he was clearly hurting her. Whatever she'd done six years ago, whatever karmic reward he believed she deserved, *he* was the one doing the hurting now.

And he couldn't lie to himself any longer and tell himself he didn't care about that. But he also couldn't seem to stop himself.

"The only thing you could possibly do for me requires time travel," he told her, and he didn't know where that came from or why he sounded like that, gritty and nothing like calm or cool. But maybe he'd never been fooling anyone with that, anyway. "And for you to be a completely different person than who you turned out to be."

He realized he was moving as if to touch her again and he jerked himself back. That way led nowhere good, especially in a conference room surrounded by glass walls that his entire company could see through right now.

"Answer me one question," she said, her voice low and strained, though all he could see on her face was the stubborn jut of her jaw and that same glitter in her eyes. "You've made a lot of decisions based on my betrayal. The way you left then. The things you've said. The way you made sure I could never contact you and the way you ended your relationship with your brother. What if you're wrong?"

He laughed at that. "About you?"

"About all of it. About me. About your brother. About what you saw that day. Think about all the things you've done, Dare. Up to and including the kidnap of your own child, transporting him across state lines *and an ocean*, for no other purpose than to get back at me."

Her hands had curled into tight fists by the time she finished speaking, and she was trembling slightly, very slightly, as if the force of her words was tearing her open where she stood.

And Dario hated this. He hated all of this. He was afraid that what he hated most was that there was no way back. There was no pretending she hadn't cheated on him, or ignoring who she'd cheated with, and there was no making believe there wasn't a five-year-old boy in the mix now. There was no road back to what he wanted—what he still wanted, damn her, despite everything—and no way to admit he wanted it.

She was as lost to him as if he'd never met her. More, perhaps.

And what roared in him then was like a hurricane, mighty and vicious.

"That would make me a monster," he told her softly, hardly able to hear his own voice above the din inside him. "Is that what you want to hear? A petty, vicious man, much like the father you claimed to loathe before you treated your own marriage the same way he treated his. But you see, I don't spend any time worrying about such things."

"Because you're so certain you're right?" Her voice cut through the noise inside of him, that endless howl of loss. "There can be no doubt once you've made up your mind? How delightful it must be, to be so perfect and correct at all times. You must find all the rest of us mere mortals a great trial—"

"I told you before it wasn't the first time," Dario bit out, cutting her off. "Did you think you were special,

Anais? Did he tell you that you were? Guess what? He lied. You weren't the first woman he sampled without my knowledge while she was meant to be mine."

He could feel the mirthless smile on his own mouth then. He could feel that hard look in his eyes, because it was ripping him apart, too. He could see the way she flinched at the sight. And he didn't tell her the rest of it—that Dante hadn't known that Lucy was playing them against each other. That they'd both gotten rid of her and supposedly moved on. That he'd had that festering distrust of his brother ever since.

Dario told himself none of that mattered. "But you were the last."

It was a war, Anais told herself, and that meant she used what weapons were available to her.

No matter how much she disliked them.

"Are you sure you want to attack a Di Sione in this way?" her aunt had asked on the drive to the Maui airport, in crisp, rapid French. The sugarcane fields had rustled on the side of the road as if they agreed, right down to their roots in the red Hawaiian dirt. "Particularly the one currently held to be the darling of the tech world, feted in every corner of the world's media? You were adamant that Damian be spared this circus six years ago."

"Six years ago Damian was theoretical," Anais had replied in the same language, the Parisian French of her childhood. The language her father had used to savage her mother, and the language both her parents had used to make certain she knew how she'd ruined both their lives and yet turned out so worthless. She kept her eyes on the fields, the windmills climbing up the rich brown mountain in the distance, and she knew her heart was already flying thirty thousand feet above her in Dario's plane and headed east. "Now he's a little boy who was abducted off a playground. If the circus is what gets him back, I'll hire all the clowns myself."

She'd meant it.

After Dario left her there in his office's conference space—the room still echoing his harsh words and what was, she supposed, the explanation for why it had never crossed his mind to believe her—she'd gotten to work.

She'd set up interviews. She'd answered all of her texts and voice mails from all of the guttersnipe reporters dying to talk to her so they could twist her words into unrecognizable shapes. She settled herself in the center of the long, polished table in Dario's conference room and she told her story again and again, to whoever would listen, while his employees walked by and pretended not to stare.

A few hours later, she'd spread the story of *Secretly Evil Rich Man Drunk with His Own Power* as far and as wide as she possibly could in one day. She smiled sweetly at Dario when he appeared in the doorway again.

If anything, his face looked harder and bleaker than it had before, and her tragedy was that her own heart seemed to hitch a bit at that. It didn't care that he'd done all of this to himself. It only cared that he was in pain.

She couldn't even hate herself for that. He was the first person she'd ever loved like this, heedlessly and recklessly and irrevocably. Until she'd had Damian, he was the only one. Apparently, that hadn't gone anywhere. On some level, she'd always understood it never would.

"Are you finished with whatever performance this was?" he asked in that deceptively quiet voice of his that she recognized now. It meant his temper was right there beneath it, pressing at him to escape and strike. She swore she could see it in the blue glitter of his eyes. "Some of us actually work for a living rather than spin fantasies for the paparazzi. We need access to this room."

"I was done actually." She rose to her feet and tucked her bag beneath her arm. "Did you come here to take me to Damian?"

Dario let out a short laugh. "No."

"How long do you plan to keep this up?"

His gaze was hard then. "I'm thinking at least five years. Just to be fair. I'll contact you when he turns ten."

She wanted to lunge at him for even suggesting something so hideous, but she held herself back. Barely.

"He's a little boy, Dario. He has no idea what game you're playing. He doesn't deserve this."

"He's a Di Sione," Dario countered. "He'll be fine."

She let out a low, insulting sort of laugh. "Like you are, you mean?"

He didn't like that. His eyes flashed.

"If you don't leave this office right now, Anais, I'll have you thrown out on the street," he promised her softly. Very softly. "I don't care what tabloid you hire to plaster it on their front page."

She didn't believe him. But she didn't push it. She only inclined her head and brushed past him on her way out the door.

"Remember that you said that," she advised him. Because this was war, no matter what she felt inside. No matter how much she wished it could be otherwise. He'd made it a war. He'd even taken a hostage—the only person in the world she loved unconditionally. What other choice did she have? "You might come to wish you hadn't."

CHAPTER EIGHT

DARIO WISHED A lot of things over the next few days.

That he'd thought this plan of his through, for one. That he'd paid attention to Anais when she'd warned him about the likely behavior of a small boy so far out of his element and separated from the only parent he knew for the first time in his young life.

That he hadn't imagined in all his hubris that he could simply plop a furious five-year-old into his life without any ripple effects. It wasn't as if the fact they shared genetic material could possibly matter to a small child— hell, it hadn't mattered to his identical twin brother after an entire lifetime spent in each other's pockets. He wished he'd thought a bit more before acting.

Of course, that was nothing new. It was eerily similar to how he'd felt when he'd arrived at ICE—having left his wife and his brother and his former company behind him in a bright blaze of a burned bridge—only to discover that the owner was precisely as shady as Dante had worried he was. That all of the company's business practices were dubious and immoral, exactly as Dante had warned.

He rather doubted that a five-year-old child would appreciate the way he'd handled the ICE situation—with a systemic reworking of the company from the ground up over the course of years, which had included sidelining the owner and making him a silent partner before eventually ousting him altogether.

Dario had only spent a handful of days with Damian, but he knew full well that this child—he found it much too easy to assume the boy really was his son, and that should have worried him more than it did—was never going to be a silent anything.

"Enough," he said one morning, interrupting another tantrum. The nanny wrung her hands in the background but it had been Damian who'd picked up a two hundred and twenty thousand dollar bronze statue from the coffee table and thrown it. At Dario's head.

The fact he'd missed—by a mile—didn't change Damian's intent.

Nor did it change the fact that Dario now had a very heavy bronze stuck like a fork into his hardwood living room floor.

"I want my mom," the little boy said, his face—a perfect replica of every photograph Dario had ever seen of himself and his own memories of his brother, save those eyes that could only be Anais's—very solemn then, with his lower lip on the verge of trembling. "You said she'd come but she hasn't come."

"She'll be here soon."

And Dario wondered when he'd become such a liar. When he'd started tossing them out so easily, so readily. It made him wonder what lies he was telling himself.

"I don't like it here," Damian informed him. But it sounded like more of an observation than a complaint. "I want to go home."

"What if I told you this was your new home?" Dario asked.

Most of the residents of New York City would fling themselves prostrate on the hot asphalt street outside to get the opportunity to so much as glance inside this particular building, so famous was it after the number of colorful, wealthy characters who had graced its Art Deco halls at one point or another. And most of the world would kill for a chance to spend even five minutes in Dario Di Sione's highly coveted penthouse, and only partly because of the view.

This five-year-old who was very probably his own flesh and blood looked around as if he was deeply unimpressed, then screwed up his nose and shrugged.

"It's okay." He considered. "It would be better if my mom was here, though."

Dario met the nanny's gaze from across the room and dismissed her with a jerk of his chin, then returned his attention to Damian.

"I have something to tell you," he said. He felt like an idiot. He felt like a movie villain, ponderous and laughable, except he had no mask to hide behind while he did this. "I'm your father."

He didn't know what he expected. Something out of a movie, perhaps. Something cinematic, dramatic. The child had flung an expensive bit of table art across the room because he'd wanted a different cereal for his breakfast—surely the news that he had a father at all should make him do…something.

Instead, Damian looked as nonchalant as if Dario had shared with him the news that it was sunny outside today, something they could both see quite easily through the sweeping windows that let in the morning light.

"I know," he said after a moment, as if the topic was

boring. Stupid, even. "My mom told me. She lets me keep your picture by my bed."

"You know?" He was so dumbfounded he couldn't quite process the rest of what Damian had told him.

"She said you're very important and busy—that's why you never come to our house." Clearly tired of standing still, Damian started to fidget, working his left arm up over his head for no reason that Dario could discern. He held it there, then began to hop on his right leg. Up, down. Over and over again. "Is she coming soon?"

"Soon," Dario said absently. He couldn't quite get himself to look too closely at what the little boy had said, much less what it could mean. "You've known I was your father this whole time? Even at your school?"

"Of course." Damian stopped hopping and looked at Dario as if he was very dim. "I'm not supposed to go anywhere with strangers."

And then he started using the nearest sofa as a trampoline while shouting out the words to a song he claimed had only dog words, while Dario sat there with an unfamiliar tight feeling in his chest. He didn't know how to process this revelation.

Anais had kept a picture of him by Damian's bed? She hadn't kept the child's paternity a secret at all?

What if you're wrong? she'd asked him.

The truth was, Dario had never considered the possibility. Anais had denied it outright, but she would, wouldn't she? It had been Dante who had made him so utterly certain. Because Dante hadn't denied it. Dante had stared back at him and said nothing, not one word, his silence far more damning than anything he could have said.

And that had been a very dark time for Dario even

before he'd walked into his apartment that day, but what possible reason could his own brother—his identical twin—have for lying about something like sleeping with Dario's wife?

Still, none of that explained why Anais kept his picture next to their son's bed. It was something he knew he wouldn't have done, had their situation been reversed. He would have pretended she'd never existed.

He'd told her it would make him a monster if he was the man she suggested he was. If Dante had lied, if Dario had gotten the wrong idea, if more than half a decade had ticked by like this, rolling on from that single day in his old apartment…

But he knew that was impossible. Dante had been many things back then, but he'd never been a liar—and he'd certainly never looked Dario straight in the eye and lied to him, not once in all their lives. Not even by omission.

Dario knew it was impossible.

Yet somehow, he still felt like a monster.

"What the hell are you doing?" he asked himself, almost under his breath. Because he didn't understand how Anais could be the awkward virgin he'd run after on the Columbia campus and also the woman who'd slept with his twin brother. He'd never understood that progression—and he'd never wanted to hang around and ask for explanations, either. Over time he'd thought he'd figured it out. She'd been so starved for attention, for affection, after the childhood she'd had—no wonder one man hadn't been enough for her. That was what he'd told himself. That was what he'd believed.

But a picture of him next to a child's bed didn't fit in with the character he'd imagined. With who he'd told himself she'd become by having sex with Dante for God only knew how long before he'd discovered them.

He didn't know what to make of it, and he hated that. Anais belonged in the box she'd built with her own deceitful behavior. This past week had been bad enough. Running into her so unexpectedly in that remote house on Maui, then discovering she had a child she claimed was his—it all required a somewhat larger, more unwieldy box than he'd prefer.

Still, this was worse. This struck him as an act of charity and he couldn't understand how such a thing fit with the woman who'd callously pitted one twin against the other. Who might have been doing so all throughout Dario's relationship, for all he knew.

He raked a hand through his hair and picked up his cell phone, aware that calling her was the exact opposite of how he'd normally handle something like this. Why did this woman tie him in knots when she wasn't even in the same room?

But that was when the housekeeper bustled in, placing a stack of new tabloids in front of him and taking Damian by the hand to lead him out. And instead of calling Anais to thank her for a kindness he didn't understand in the first place, he sat where he was and read capital letter denunciations of his character in as overdramatic language as it was possible to find.

The ICE Man Cometh—and He Took My Baby!

And that was when another thought occurred to him, much darker than the previous ones.

He only knew that Anais had placed a photograph next to Damian's bed. Damian hadn't specified what was in that photograph. Which meant Dario had no way of knowing which Di Sione twin was in that photograph, did he?

It was late into the night on that same day when the nanny pushed open the door to Dario's home office suite, startling him where he sat on the leather couch with his laptop and a tumbler of whiskey.

He hit a key to pause the video he was watching—of Anais on some appalling talk show, playing the part of wounded, helpless ingenue swept into all this darkness by a corporate wolf like Dario. He had to admit she was good at it. She'd almost had him convinced he was an evil, heartless bastard and he knew better.

"I was so sheltered," she'd said, her voice choked up. *"No, he never divorced me. He simply reappeared long after I'd given up hope. I thought... I hoped... It sounds so naive to say it out loud, doesn't it? But it was all a trick. A game. He just wanted our son."*

Dario had listened to that part at least fifteen times. If he didn't know better, if he hadn't *lived* the truth of things with Anais, he'd have sworn she hadn't been acting. And even though *he knew* that was impossible, he'd found himself reacting as if she really wasn't putting on a show. As if he really had swooped down upon her like some angel of death, six years ago and now, and ruined her life each time.

She has some kind of magic power, Dante had shouted at him a long time ago, when Dario had first wanted to accept the offer from ICE and Dante had been so adamantly opposed to the very idea. He'd made the mistake of mentioning that Anais thought it made good business sense. *To make you think up is down and black is white. What's next, brother? Will she make me your enemy?*

But no. The two of them had done that together, in Dario's own bedroom.

He had to force himself back into the present, where the nanny was looking at him in concern and he had no idea how long it had taken him to focus on her.

"What is it?" he asked, aware he even sounded off. Wrong. Very much like a man who didn't know if he was crazy or sane any longer, and worse, was almost entirely certain he didn't much care either way.

"It's Damian," the nanny said in a hushed, hurried, almost apologetic voice that wiped all that history straight out of his mind. "I'm afraid he's sick."

"What do you mean?" Dario frowned at the woman. "He was turning cartwheels on the roof deck after dinner."

But he was already up and moving, following the nanny down the guest hall toward the room he'd set up for Damian. He walked inside and found the boy curled up on the bed, shivering and crying and obviously not all right at all.

He was much too hot to the touch, and Dario felt as helpless as he ever had in his life. He sat down on the bed and put his hand on Damian's small back, as if that might give the boy some comfort. He had a dim memory of his grandfather doing the same for him during some long-ago ailment.

"I want my mom," Damian cried.

And Dario had never felt worse than he did then. Had he really been using this *five-year-old* as some kind of pawn? To get his revenge on the child's mother? What was the matter with him? He'd thrown it in Anais's face that she was as bad as the father who'd never wanted to marry her mother and had cheated all throughout their marriage. But meanwhile, he was as bad as his own father, the most selfish creature who'd ever walked the face of the planet. He was worse. At least his father hadn't cared in the slightest about any of his kids—it would never have occurred to him to use them for anything.

He pulled his phone out of his pocket and dialed her number, not sure he'd be able to speak past the constriction of pure self-loathing blocking his throat when she answered at once.

"Dario?"

"You'd better come," he told her with no preamble. He didn't bother to keep his voice even or calm. What could that matter? "Damian is sick."

He didn't know how long it took her. It could have been a handful of minutes. It could have been hours. Time lost meaning to him as he sat there in the dimly lit room with a sick boy in his lap, trying to make soothing noises. He got Damian to stop crying, which made an exultant sort of triumph race through him—far brighter and deeper than anything he'd felt during ICE's last big product launch, which he'd previously imagined was the pinnacle of his life thus far.

Dario didn't know how to process that. He didn't know what it meant, only that somehow this small human who smelled of sweat and something sticky had managed to worm his way into places inside of Dario that he hadn't known were there. And he didn't think Damian even *liked* him. For that matter, he wasn't entirely convinced he wasn't holding his own nephew, not his son.

That didn't appear to have a single thing to do with it.

And then he looked up and Anais was there.

She charged through the door, her eyes snapping to Damian and staying there. She moved so fast her hair flowed behind her like a cloak and she came straight to him, up on her knees on the bed beside Dario to get her hands on the child's hot cheeks.

"Mommy," the little boy whimpered. He didn't seem surprised to see her, and Dario wondered what that was like. To have no doubt that the adults would turn up when they were needed. To expect it. "I'm sick."

"I know, baby," she murmured. Her hands moved all over him as she eased him from Dario's hold. She checked his forehead, his cheeks, and then she clucked her tongue and wrapped her arms around him to rock him. "You have a little fever, that's all. Do you have a headache?"

He moaned something unintelligible with his mouth against her shoulder and she nodded as if he'd made perfect sense. "That's not surprising. Let's cool you down a little bit and see if you can sleep."

She asked the nanny to get her a wet washcloth and while she waited she stripped Damian out of his sweat-soaked pajamas and then got him into a clean pair. Then she laid him down on the bed with the cool cloth on his head, her movements practiced and easy, reminding Dario without a single word what she'd been doing these last five years. She even curled up beside the little boy so he could hold on to her, and then she sang to him.

It was the most hauntingly beautiful thing Dario had ever heard. It broke the heart he'd thought she'd turned to stone and ash years before. Over and over again.

He sat there on the foot of the bed as this mother sang her little boy to sleep, and it took him long, shuddering moments to understand that whatever the truth was, he *wanted* this to be real. To be his in all its uncertainty and noise, silliness and sweetness. He wanted her to have come back to him with this funny little boy who was a perfect blend of both of them. He'd never wanted a family—he barely tolerated his own—but here, now, he wanted *this* family more than he wanted his next breath.

He wanted it almost more than he could bear.

And he could have left when Damian drifted off to sleep, but he didn't. Anais stopped singing eventually, but she didn't move, still curled up next to the boy like some kind of fierce lioness who would shred anyone who ventured near. He had absolutely no doubt that she would. And that he'd help.

"'The ICE Man Cometh'?" Dario asked into the quiet.

"If you ever try to take my child away from me again," she replied in a very soft voice that did nothing to conceal the steel in it, "I'll gut you with something a whole lot sharper than a tabloid newspaper."

He believed it.

They sat like that for a long time, with only Damian's half-snores filling the space between them.

"He already knew I was his father," Dario heard himself say. He hadn't meant to speak. He'd meant to get out of here, in fact—to stand up and leave her here and return to his office, maybe to actually do some work this time. He had no idea why he hadn't done it. "He knew when I found him at his school. He said you kept a picture next to his bed."

Anais didn't say anything for a long time. Dario stopped thinking she would. It was enough, he thought, that they were both here, keeping this strangely peaceful vigil over a sick boy together. Silence was fine. It was more than fine.

It felt a lot like intimacy and, for once, he didn't balk at the notion.

"His best friend is a little girl named Olina," Anais said eventually, her voice sounding scratchy. She was propped up on an elbow next to Damian in the bed, her attention on him as he slept fitfully beside her. "Her father is a fireman on the island, which the kids agreed was very impressive and heroic. Olina told Damian that when she gets scared, her father promised her he'd always be there to fight the monsters or chase away the bad dreams. That she could just call out and he'd come. That was what fathers did, he told her. That was what they were for."

Anais shifted then, her dark gaze finding Dario's in the dim light, and he felt everything inside of him go still.

"Damian asked me how he could call out for *his* father when he didn't know where you were."

Dario was stricken, held fast in some awful grip that he thought might crush him to dust where he sat—but he couldn't bring himself to look away from Anais. Not even to blink.

"I told him that you knew where he was and that all he needed was the reminder of you to fight off the bad dreams and bad things that sometimes turn up in a little boy's closet." She didn't drop her gaze. "I said you were magic. That all fathers were, but especially you."

"Anais."

But she didn't seem to hear him.

"So together we picked out a picture of you from the photo album I have from our wedding day, and then we went to the store and found a frame he liked. He wanted double protection, just to be sure. So it's a Batman frame with you in it looking very magical and fierce and capable. It sits by his bed, and sometimes I catch him talking to it like you're real. To him, you always have been."

Dario couldn't speak. He ran his hands over his face and wasn't entirely surprised to find he was shaking.

And she wasn't finished.

"This thing you did—flying him across the world and whatever you've been doing these past few days? Playing daddy games and indulging yourself? I knew you wouldn't hurt him. I knew he'd be okay. That he'd think it was all a grand adventure with a character he already thinks he knows. You're as real to him as anything he's seen on television, that's all. *This* won't hurt him. He's a resilient kid."

And her gaze seemed to get darker then. Harder. She seemed to reach across the bed and tear him wide open when he knew she hadn't moved an inch. He could see she hadn't moved at all.

"It's when you get bored with this game. When you remember that you're *Dario Di Sione* and you have computer accessories to build and adoring customers to wow. When you throw him back where you found him and forget all the dazzling promises you made him. That's what concerns me, Dare. Because that's when you're going to break his heart."

"I'm not going to break his heart. I'm not going to break anything."

But he didn't believe that even as he said it.

"You swooped in and spirited him away. You're mysterious and fancy and you haven't disappointed him yet," she said.

And she didn't look fierce any longer; that was the part that punched at him, like a fist to the gut. She looked sad. Terribly sad.

"But you will. He'll think it's him, that there's something he could have done to make you stick around. That's what children always think." She shook her head, and looked even sadder, if that was possible. "It would have been kinder to let him keep imagining you as the perfect hero who saves him from bad dreams. Not the real, live man who hates his mother and doesn't have time for him. That's a very common, very boring story. I think he'd prefer to keep you magic. Keep you his."

"Are you talking about him, Anais?" he asked softly. "Or you?"

The way her mouth curved then made him feel scraped raw.

"I gave up on magic a long time ago," she said in the same tone he'd used. "And you were never mine."

He should never have said such a thing. He should never have opened that door, because he didn't like what was behind it. At all.

"I'm not going to do any of those things." He gritted it out, not sure why he felt so defensive. So…exposed, as if he was the one with the dirty history of letting people down instead of her. "None of that is going to happen."

And Anais laughed softly then. Still so sadly, as if it had happened already. As if she knew the bleak future before them, no matter what he said.

"Come on, Dare," she said quietly, piercing him straight through. "You can't help it. It's who you are."

CHAPTER NINE

DAMIAN WOKE UP the next morning fully restored, as if he hadn't had any kind of fever at all.

"He was sick," Dario said flatly over coffee, while Damian chased his own shadow around the expansive roof deck that surrounded the penthouse's lowest level. "I felt his forehead myself."

"Children are mysterious," Anais replied with a shrug.

And so was everything between the two of them, she couldn't help thinking. She expected him to throw her out. She'd been expecting it since she'd woken up this morning, curled up with her squirmy child in a narrow twin bed. But Dario merely sat at the outside table where his housekeeper had served breakfast as if he had nothing on his mind at all. He read the stack of tabloids that had been waiting for him, with ancient pictures of the two of them splashed all over the front pages right there in front of her, but aside from directing a particularly blue look at her now and again, he said nothing about them.

So Anais said nothing in reply, and told herself it wasn't avoidance, exactly. It was strategy. She drank his excellent coffee and she sampled his housekeeper's miraculously fluffy omelets, and she told herself it didn't make her weak or compromised that she didn't try to beat his head in with the serving utensils after what he'd done. Damian was fine, and she was with him again. That was what mattered.

She told herself that was the reason she held her tongue.

When Dario left for work later that morning he asked her where she'd been staying and she braced herself to be tossed out—but he only nodded when she told him the name of the unremarkable hotel in Midtown she'd found at the last minute, then was on his way.

And he wasn't even there an hour later when a courier arrived at his front door with her bags. Or when the housekeeper very efficiently whisked them away and set Anais up not in a room in the guest wing near Damian, but in the room directly opposite the master suite on the top floor.

She should protest all of this, she knew. She should have taken Damian and raced off the moment Dario had left the house this morning. Or at least she should have demanded that they discuss things now that they were all together instead of hurling insults at each other in a conference room or through the papers. She told herself she'd do so the moment he returned from the office. But the nanny took Damian out to the park and left Anais to her work. She made her usual calls and caught up on all the things she'd let slide since Dario had turned up on the island. And when Dario came home in the evening to the meal the housekeeper had prepared for the three of them, it seemed much easier to simply roll with that.

And then keep rolling, one day into the next.

The less they discussed the serious issues that hung between them like so many shimmering veils—the less they talked about what was happening between them, or the dark past they'd never agree on, or what had led them to end up in this penthouse together with the child they'd made—the easier it was to keep right on rolling.

As if this was their real life. As if this was who they were, this...*family unit.*

Every night, weather depending, they would eat dinner together out on that roof deck. The three of them, together.

Like a real family, Anais thought every time, and she knew how dangerous that was. She knew that the dream she'd succumbed to that one night in Hawaii was nothing next to this one, and that single night had put only her heart at risk, not Damian's, too. But she couldn't seem to stop herself from indulging.

She thought Dario felt it, too—the insistent, beguiling tug of the sweet life that wasn't theirs.

But it could be, that seductive voice whispered inside of her, night after night. *It could be exactly like this...*

It was a treacherous landscape to navigate, and every day it got a little bit harder.

Damian loved Dario. Instantly and wholly. That much was clear, and it made Anais feel a little bit bruised inside that he'd had to do without his father all this time. It wasn't that the life she'd given him hadn't been good, it was only that *this* life—this make-believe fairy tale of a shining existence complete with a mother *and* a father all for him—was that much better.

She'd loved Dario six years ago and she despaired of the fact she loved him still, but she thought she hadn't really known what love was at all until she'd rushed through that door to find him cradling their sick son in his lap. Or when she'd watched him read Damian a bedtime story, doing all the voices. Or the many times he let

Damian beat him at the video games the five-year-old adored and the grown man clearly enjoyed just as much.

Anais had always thought love was about tempestuous romances followed by years of emptiness and loss, recrimination and regret. That was what her parents had taught her, in their sad, angry marriage. It was what she'd learned in her own. She'd only started to understand the complexities of different kinds of love these last few years in Hawaii, with Damian and the steady support of her aunt and uncle.

But watching the man she'd loved since very nearly the moment she'd met him take care of the child they'd made together was like watching a new sun dawn on a brand-new world. She certainly couldn't rip Damian away from it. She hardly knew how to contain the joy of this thing she'd barely dared to dream inside herself.

She wasn't sure she managed it at all. She wasn't sure she tried very hard, come to that. And she knew, deep down, it would be one more thing she paid for in the long run.

One night they'd followed their usual pattern. They'd had a carefree family dinner, one marked by their usual easy conversation that never strayed from their preferred path of light, airy, unobjectionable topics, just like every other night since she'd come to stay here. And if there was a growing part of her that hated that—that wanted to dig down into this thing and see what was there beneath the surface, if anything—there was an even larger part of her that would have done absolutely anything to keep from rocking that boat. So she'd smiled and laughed. She'd meant it, the way she did each time, and then they'd put Damian to bed as if they'd been working together like this, like a perfect team, since the day he'd been born.

Anais couldn't control the rueful little laugh she let out at that notion, as Dario pulled the door to Damian's room shut behind him and they started back down the hall. She remembered going into labor all by herself entirely too well. It had been Team Her for a long time, no matter the show they were putting on now.

"Is something funny?" he asked.

She should have shrugged it off. Dario looked deliciously rumpled, the way he always did in the evenings. He'd shrugged out of his jacket the moment he'd stepped into the penthouse's foyer after work, leaving the cuffs of his dress shirt rolled up over those strong, muscled forearms. He'd raked his hands through his dark hair a thousand times or more over the course of their family evening, leaving it in that marvelously disheveled state, and his jaw sported its usual shadow at the end of the day.

Surely she shouldn't find all of that quite as delectable as she did. Surely she shouldn't even notice it any longer, much less after all the things he'd done to her. Anais kept waiting to grow used to Dario. To his undeniable appeal, all that tousled black hair and electric blue eyes. To find him a part of the scenery, nothing more. To stop being so…aware of him the way she always was.

It hadn't happened yet.

Maybe, she thought now, his eyes were simply too blue.

"Nothing's funny," she said. "Not really." Damian's door was closed and all three levels of the penthouse were quiet, hushed and still. And yet her heart was beating loud and hard against her chest as if it knew things she didn't. And she suspected it had more than a little to do with the way he stood there, watching her, an expression she couldn't quite read on his beautiful face. "We make a good team, it turns out. I suppose that surprises me."

She didn't say, *the way we congratulated ourselves for being years ago, before we'd ever been tested.* She didn't ask him if he remembered how sure they'd been that their cool version of marriage, spiced up by those long, hot nights, could handle anything and everything.

It was one more thing to hang in all the shadows between them and pretend she couldn't see.

Anais thought he'd change the subject instantly, pretend he hadn't heard her, steer the conversation back to safe ground. But he only stood there, the light from farther down the hallway playing over his features, making him seem something other than hard as she looked up at him. Something other than the avenging angel he'd been playing for six long years, without ever relenting at all. Something she might have called wistful, had he been a different man.

She told herself she was imagining it.

"I'm no good on a team," Dario said after a while. Almost as if it hurt him to say it out loud. "I'm much better on my own."

"You don't seem better on your own, Dare," she said without thinking. Without paying attention to the precipice it seemed they were standing on suddenly, when she'd thought they were on solid ground. When she'd hoped they were. "You seem alone."

He moved as if he meant to reach out to her, then he slipped his hands in the pockets of his trousers instead, and she thought the sheen in his gaze then was much too close to misery. It echoed that feeling inside her own chest too well.

"I am alone." He shook his head when she started to

speak, and Anais didn't know if he was trying to keep her from arguing with him or if it was himself he feared. "I prefer it that way."

"You're an island all your own?" It was an effort to make her voice dry, to try to sound more amused than shaken. "When you used to be a package deal? That seems a strange evolution."

"It suits me." His voice took on an edge then. "Surely you realized that six years ago."

"Six years ago I was so in love with you I couldn't see straight." Anais regretted it the moment she said it—particularly like that. So casually. Almost as an aside. He shifted, an arrested expression on his face, and she had no choice but to keep going. "I'm not sure I realized anything but that, to be honest."

And this time, the silence between them was anything but comforting. Anais was sure she could see the same old accusations right there between them, dancing in the light and landing hard on the floor. She waited for him to strike out, to knock her down with one of his well-placed barbs, to make her wish she'd never said anything at all. She already wished that.

She'd spent these strange days poking at this odd little peace they'd made, waiting for it to shatter around them, and now she wanted nothing more than for it to carry on forever.

But the look he gave her was shuttered, not cruel.

"It turns out that I have an affinity for solitude," he said in a low voice. "It's what I do best."

And that statement swelled inside of her, like a sob trapped in her chest. Only she didn't know what to cry for. The way their marriage had ended? The years Dario would never get back with his son? Or the way he stood before her now, so obviously lonely and broken and fierce, claiming he *liked it* that way?

Anais didn't know what she felt, what that sob was. What good her tears would do even if she dared let them fall. And she knew, somehow, that if she gave in to that great sobbing thing pressed so hard against her heart, if she let it burst open and drown them both, it would end this strange peace between them as if it had never been.

So instead she closed the distance between them, went up on her toes before she could think better of it and kissed him.

It wasn't a long kiss, or even a particularly carnal one. She pressed her lips to his and felt him jolt at that, felt the usual fire sear through her at that electric, simmering bit of contact. She put one hand to his rough jaw and she let the kiss linger, drinking him in, aware all the while of the way he stood too still, too tense.

When she stepped back, his blue gaze was nearly black with need.

"What the hell was that?" he growled.

"I don't know." She didn't put her hand to her mouth, though she wanted to, to see if she'd tattooed herself somehow. That was how full her lips felt, tingling with almost too much sensation. "You looked as if you needed it."

"I didn't." He bit that out, but she didn't believe him. And more, she didn't think he believed himself. "I don't."

And then he stalked away, leaving her to stand there with that great big sob still trapped in her chest, the brand of that damned kiss on her mouth and no idea what on earth she was doing here.

With him.

Playing games neither one of them could win.

* * *

The call came a few mornings later while Dario was out on his morning run. Only his secretary's personal cell phone was programmed to come through the Do Not Disturb setting he used while he ran his daily lap around Central Park, and she knew better than to use it without a damned good reason.

Before today, she'd used it maybe three other times that he could recall. Dario took his morning run—and his peace and quiet—very seriously.

"It's your grandfather," Marnie said when he answered. "He's taken a turn for the worse. He wants to see you."

After he ended the call and ran the last mile hard to get home faster, Dario realized he had no idea if he'd responded to that or if he'd simply hung up in a daze. Not that he should have been in any kind of a daze at all, he told himself sharply as the elevator rushed him up toward the penthouse again. Giovanni Di Sione was a very old man, even without the leukemia that had beset him this past year, adding insult to the laudable injury of having lived ninety-eight long years. The amazing thing was that the old man was alive at all, he assured himself, not that he'd finally met the thing that might have a chance at killing him.

It was funny how that didn't make him feel any better, the way he'd told himself it had before.

He strode into the penthouse, sweaty and agitated, and stopped when he heard Damian talking. Heedless and excited, the way Damian always seemed to be—because this child had no inkling of the possibility that anyone alive might not find him utterly delightful.

Dario remembered his own childhood. His parents'

sick dependence on each other, the wildness and unpredictability that had haunted every moment of it before they'd died and the sadness that had wreathed it afterward. He'd had nothing to cling to in all the world but the twin brother who would grow up to betray him with his own wife.

His wife.

He found that word didn't infuriate him the way it had for years. Quite the opposite, in fact. He liked it.

He moved quietly through the entry hall and through the great living room, still following Damian's voice. He found the little boy in the kitchen, standing on a pulled-up chair so he could watch his mother make pancakes on the great stove Dario had never personally used.

"We have a housekeeper for that," he said, aware of two things even as he said it.

First, that his voice was all wrong. Ragged and much too dark. It revealed entirely too many things better left hidden.

And second, that he'd said *we*. As if the fact he hadn't divorced her yet, or the fact they'd been living here together as if nothing that had happened between them mattered, made them some kind of unit they'd never been.

Six years ago I was so in love with you I couldn't see straight, she'd said that strange night in the hallway. Then she'd kissed him, sweet and devastating, in a way he could still feel inside of him. He'd spent the time since convincing himself it had been nothing more than Anais up to her usual tricks. He'd almost come around to believing it, too. The only trouble was, he'd seen that raw look in her eyes. He'd heard it in her voice.

And God help him, he'd felt it in her kiss.

He still did.

The truth was, Dario didn't know how to handle any of this. He understood the life he'd lived for the past six years because everything had been in neat, if painfully bleak, boxes and there was none of this blurring of long-drawn lines. In a way, the boxes were easier. There were no surprises, ever.

He didn't understand how his grandfather, who had once told Dario he intended to beat death at its own game by living forever, could possibly be dying this time—no matter how old he was, or how sick. It seemed impossible. Just as he didn't understand how the woman he'd married so quickly, met anew in Hawaii when he'd least expected it, then lived with again these past, peaceful weeks, could be the same woman who had betrayed him so thoroughly.

He wanted this, he thought then. That was the trouble. The real truth beneath all the rest of it. He wanted this woman in his house, making pancakes because she felt like it or because it made a little boy smile. And he wanted that little boy. For the first time since Anais had dropped the news of Damian's existence on him on Maui, Dario didn't care that no genetic test could prove who the real father was. That went both ways. No one could prove Damian *wasn't* his.

And if his grandfather was, in fact, dying, if this really was the end of the only family Dario knew—however inadequate it had been over the years—he knew that what he really wanted was for the old man to meet this small, wild boy with a Di Sione face and his mother's eyes. Even if it was only the once.

"What is it?" There was a frown in Anais's voice, if not on her face, as she slid the last pancake onto Damian's plate and then directed him to the kitchen island to eat. "You look as if there were ghosts out there on your run."

"No ghosts," he said, still not sounding like himself.

Or maybe it was that he'd known exactly who he was for six long years. He'd reveled in that definition and he'd convinced himself it was the truth of not only who he was, but who he could ever become.

And now he had no idea how he'd ever been happy with that.

Because he understood, standing there sweaty and thrown in the room in his home he used the least, watching a domestic scene that should have turned his stomach, that he'd never be happy like that again. That it hadn't been happiness, that in-between state he'd lived in all those years.

Everything had changed that day in Hawaii. Everything was different.

Him most of all. "Not just yet."

CHAPTER TEN

ANAIS HAD ONLY the vaguest memories of the Di Sione estate out in the Hamptons from her scant few visits way back when, but the old man who was the center of the family and the great house's patriarch had remained larger than life in her mind all this time.

Giovanni was exactly as she remembered him, if significantly more frail. He sat in an armchair in one of the drawing rooms of the grand old house, covered in a thick blanket, though the September day outside was warm. And he smiled as they walked in to greet him, that same old glint Anais remembered making his eyes seem much too bright for a man said to be on the brink of death.

"I should have told the world I was dying thirty years ago," Giovanni said, his voice more feeble than Anais remembered it, making the possibility of his death seem much more real, suddenly. "It brings you all running." His canny gaze shifted to Anais, then down to Damian in front of her. "And with such gifts."

"This is Damian," she said, smiling at the old man who she could never remember being anything but kind to her, no matter that her relationship with his grandson had been a mad little whirlwind with an unhappy ending. Then she smiled down at her son, taking her hand from his shoulder as she did. "Damian, this is your great-grandfather."

She thought her heart might burst wide open when her self-possessed little boy walked right up to the oldest man he'd likely ever seen and held out his hand, very much like the man she knew he'd one day become. And this time, there was someone to share that sort of wild maternal pride. This time, she caught Dario's eye and was sure he saw the same thing she did—maybe even felt it himself.

That unexpected moment of communion shook her, deep and hard, making her bones ache.

"It's nice to meet you, young man," Giovanni said with an extra bit of solemnity in his voice, as if speaking to the future man instead of the current boy. But he looked at Dario when he continued, and that glint in his eye seemed more pronounced. "Very nice indeed."

"Behave," Dario told him as Anais took a seat on the couch opposite Giovanni. Her stomach flipped over and she realized it was because there was actual laughter in Dario's voice. It made him sound like a different person. It made him sound *alive*. It made him sound like that young man who'd chased her out of the Columbia University library on a gray winter's afternoon and had talked her into having coffee with him when she'd been convinced he was playing a trick on her. "Or I won't give you the earrings you sent me halfway across the planet to fetch for you."

"Ah," Giovanni said, sounding not in the least bit worried that Dario would do anything but what he'd asked. "My lovely Lost Mistresses are coming back to me at last. Tell me they still sparkle the way I remember them."

"Of course they do, old man," Dario replied, still with

all that rich amusement in his voice. It was mesmerizing. It seemed to wrap around her and pull taut, like a slip-knot she feared she'd never work loose. "They're made almost entirely of diamonds. They make the night sky look dull in comparison."

The old man smiled and then coughed. And coughed. So hard his whole body shook and his hands trembled, and that was when Anais understood that this wasn't some kind of merry joke. Giovanni was truly ill. The force of his personality couldn't change that. Nothing could.

Dario's smile faltered, but he caught himself. Visibly. Anais felt a lump grow in her throat as he reached into his pocket and pulled out the same little box she'd given him in Hawaii. When Giovanni was sitting upright in his chair again and his breathing was less labored, Dario cracked it open and placed it carefully in his grandfather's parchment-pale hands.

"I wish Dante were here," Giovanni said, gazing down at the earrings, a faraway look on his face. "He always has appreciated the shiny things in life just a little bit more than you. You always did think you needed to be the serious one."

Damian chose that moment to stage-whisper his desire to go outside and play, but there was no mistaking the way Dario stiffened at the mention of his twin's name, no matter Anais's momentary distraction. Or the way that long-lost laughter disappeared from his blue gaze and the curve in his mouth flattened out into a line, as if both had been figments of her imagination.

"Why would you bring him up?" Dario asked tautly. "Is he here?"

His grandfather looked old then. Every inch of his ninety-eight years.

"I believe he's out for the day," he said with obvious reluctance.

"I'm not talking about Dante," Dario told his grandfather gruffly. "Ever. And we don't need you meddling, Grandfather. He doesn't need to know I was here."

Giovanni eyed him as if he was inclined to argue, but then merely nodded his head weakly before returning his attention to the open box in his lap. He ran a finger over the bright face of one of the earrings. Then he quietly asked Dario about ICE's much-publicized launch a few weeks back.

While Anais sat frozen on the couch across from them, her heart in a thousand pieces all over the priceless carpet at her feet.

Through the windows she could see her beautiful little boy running in gleeful zigzags on the great lawn, as if the September sun shone for him alone. But here inside this room, an old man was dying after nearly a century on this earth and the man she'd loved for far longer than was wise or healthy was so closed up inside he might as well be dying, too.

Dario was never going to change. He didn't want to talk about his twin to his own grandfather—or at all—even all these years later.

He was never, ever going to believe her.

He was fine with these make-believe spaces, these in-between times, when they pretended nothing was wrong. Meanwhile, the past festered between them. Where would it come out? It was one thing for Dario to periodically vent his spleen on her. Anais could take it, no matter how unjust it was. But what happened when he said the wrong thing one day and Damian heard it?

Because that would happen. It was inevitable.

And she couldn't stand by and allow this man to break her son's heart, simply because he didn't have it in him to trust her.

It was high time she was honest with herself. Dario had never trusted her in the first place. He couldn't have, or he'd never have misinterpreted the scene he'd walked in on that terrible day. He'd never have believed the worst of her, no matter what Dante did or didn't say.

That was the truth she'd been hiding from all this time. Dario had *wanted* to believe the worst of her. He'd seized the opportunity to leave her and he'd made sure there was absolutely no way she could prevail upon him to reconsider. He'd seen an opportunity to get the hell out of their marriage and he'd taken it.

He'd wanted to leave her then; he'd done it with surgical precision, and he'd had no intention of returning to her. Ever. If she'd never had Damian, she imagined that scene on Mr. Fuginawa's lanai would have gone very differently. He'd have insulted her, she'd have returned fire and he'd have swanned back off into the ether.

You've been lying to yourself for a long, long time, she told herself now, watching Dario laugh with his grandfather in a way she hadn't seen him laugh with anyone in years. In a way she'd forgotten he'd ever laughed, even with her. *Those stories you told the tabloids might as well have been the stories you told yourself all this time. That there was some grand misunderstanding. That left to his own devices, away from his brother, none of this would have happened.*

It would have happened. He wanted it to happen. He made *it happen.*

She sat so still, while everything inside of her spun

around too fast and made her worry she might simply fall over with the force of this realization.

And she couldn't push this or any other truth on him. She couldn't *make him* believe her. She couldn't prove Damian was his and she couldn't prove she'd loved him and she couldn't prove there'd never been anyone for her but him, ever. He would have to take that leap of faith on his own; and here, now, in the lovely home where she'd been reminded of the man she'd fallen in love with in the first place, Anais understood that he was never, ever going to do that.

He was never going to trust her, or anyone, no matter what.

And that meant that despite what she felt and had always felt, despite what she still wanted, despite the things her traitorous little heart demanded even as it broke inside her chest, she had to end this.

She had to take Damian and go home.

CHAPTER ELEVEN

IT WAS LATE that night when Dario gave up on trying to sleep in the bed he now found far too empty, when he'd never shared it with another soul. He found himself out on the great balcony that surrounded the master suite and the rest of the top floor of the penthouse. The September night was a warm caress against his bare skin, just the faintest hint of the coming fall in it, and he was glad he hadn't bothered to pull on anything more than a pair of loose black trousers.

Manhattan stretched out in the dark before him, as exultant and bright as it always was, and it echoed deep within him. It played through him like a long, low note of music, altering everything it touched. Knocking apart those careful boxes of his and making him wonder how he'd ever lived in them. How he'd ever managed to survive like that, bound and minimized. For a long while he stood there, simply stood there in the night with the city beneath him, and did nothing at all but breathe.

He sensed her approach in the moment before she appeared there at the rail beside him, her long black hair tumbling over her shoulders as straight and glossy as ever and her lovely arms bare. She wore a tank top and a pair of men's boxers, the very same uniform she'd worn to sleep in for as long as he'd known her. Dario couldn't have said why the sight of it tonight swelled inside him like a song.

He only knew he wanted to sing it so loud he woke the neighborhood. The whole city and all the boroughs. The world.

He settled for turning toward her instead, reaching out to trace a faint pattern down one slim, strong arm and taking note of the goose bumps that shivered alive beneath his touch.

"Life is so short," he said, and he felt her tremble slightly at that beneath his fingers. "Too short, Anais."

She glanced at him, then away, her gaze on the dark heart of Central Park below them. "I know. I can't imagine the world without him."

Dario hadn't been thinking of his grandfather, or not directly.

"He's wily," he said. Because Giovanni always had been. Because he couldn't conceive of anything getting the better of the old man, even leukemia. "He's beaten a thousand enemies in his day, and is never quite as fragile as he looks. I wouldn't count him out yet."

She smiled. And she didn't say what she must have been thinking then—what he knew he ought to be thinking himself. What he'd thought explicitly, in fact, even as he'd arrived in Hawaii and had found himself marooned in all that dangerously seductive tropical heat. That Giovanni was ninety-eight years old. That there was a natural order to things. That living too long must sometimes seem as much a curse as a blessing to a man who had once been so active and was now confined to a few rooms in a house.

She only smiled, this beautiful woman who was still, astonishingly, his wife.

His wife. That was the part that mattered. That was the only part that mattered.

"Anais," he began, his voice serious, because this was long overdue.

But she surprised him. She turned toward him and she shook her head, and when he didn't continue speaking she stepped closer and slid her hands up over the planes of his bare chest. Heat against heat.

And everything inside him burst into flame.

"I don't want to talk," she said, and there was something about her voice. Or maybe it was the way she looked at him, with that gleam of something he couldn't quite read in her eyes. "I want to say a thousand things to you, Dario, but I don't want to talk."

And she was so close, after everything that had happened. And he wasn't playing any games this time, the way he'd tried so hard to pretend when he was on Maui. Her hands were on his bare skin and she gleamed pale and smooth in the light from the city around them, and he was only a man.

"I think we can figure out a better way to communicate," she whispered.

And Dario didn't have it in him to refuse her.

He didn't have it in him to try.

He swept her closer and she was against him then, all those sweet, lean curves pressed tight to him as he bent down and took her mouth the way he'd wanted to for days and days. A lifetime or two, by his reckoning. Every time she laughed, or was still. Every time she frowned at him, or simply breathed the same air.

He wanted this. He wanted her. He wanted *all* of her.

The kiss was a lick of pure fire, of blinding need. And it wasn't nearly enough.

He let the wild thing inside him loose, claiming her and marking her, tasting her deep. And as he kissed her he backed her across the smooth stone deck toward the glass doors that led inside his suite, pulling his mouth from hers only to tug the tank top up and over her head.

Her laugh as she lifted her arms to help him was better than the city's bright gleam, and it moved inside him like the same restless song.

By the time they made it to the side of the wide bed he'd never imagined he'd share with anyone, they were both breathing much too heavily, their clothes strewn behind them in a trail.

"You're perfect," he told her, his voice a guttural rasp against the dark. "You're so damned perfect."

"That sounds like talking," she teased him, nipping at his chin.

And he worshipped her, this woman he'd never recovered from and never gotten past. This woman he'd never divorced, across all these years.

Some part of him must have known it was never over between them. It was never finished, no matter how it seemed. The hunger went on and on and on.

He knelt before her by the side of his bed and he relearned every inch of her gorgeous body, the way he had the night she'd trusted him with her innocence. From her marvelous collarbone to the exquisite arch of her narrow feet, he memorized her. He studied her and he adored her.

With his hands and his mouth and his gaze, he made her his and he made her come. Once. Again.

And the third time he threw her over that edge, this time with two fingers deep in her soft heat and his mouth a small torment against one perfect breast, she cried out so hard and so long he thought she might shatter his windows.

He almost wished she had.

"Enough," she managed to say, spread out across his bed like a feast. "You'll kill me."

"You say that as if you'd mind."

Her mouth curved dangerously and she rolled over, coming up on her knees beside him. "My turn," she murmured.

And she took her time.

She tortured him, with an electric intensity that might have concerned him, had she not been making him feel quite so good. She marked him with her teeth and she indulged herself in him with her mouth, her tongue, the sensual slide of her palms against his skin. She lavished her attention on every part of him, each ridge of his abdomen, the flat disc of each nipple, the line of his neck and all along his jaw, before heading back down the length of his body.

She smiled up at him as she knelt between his legs, something particularly raw in her dark eyes. But before he could question her, she leaned forward and took him deep in her mouth.

He thought he might die. He swore he had. He forgot everything in the world but this. Her. *Anais*.

Her mouth was hot and wet, a benediction and a prayer, and he lost himself in the slide and the suck, the small humming noises she made, the way she rocked herself as she moved over him as if she was as carried away by the sensation as he was.

It was heaven. It was too good. It was so good he thought he might lose his head completely.

He pulled her off him, his jaw clenched tight as he

fought to bring himself back under control. He dealt with the condom swiftly and then he was rolling them both over and bringing her beneath him to thrust himself home at last.

She cried out at his slick possession, and then, at last, he began to move.

And there was no skill in this tonight, no mastery. It was raw and intense, wild and hot. A stripped-down taking. A claiming, elemental and fierce. She wrapped herself around him and dug her nails into his skin, and he pounded into her with all the fury of this thing between them in each and every deep, perfect stroke. He lost himself in the fit of her, so gloriously right beneath him and around him, as if they'd always been meant for this.

And for a while, there was nothing *but* this.

But then Dario could take no more. He reached down between their bodies and pressed against the center of her need, making her throw back her head and cry out his name. Then she bucked against him, writhing out her pleasure, and he hurled her straight over the side of the world.

And he followed right behind her, her name on his lips all the while, as if those long six years had never happened.

Dario knew Anais wasn't in the bed when he woke up the next morning.

He knew it in the same instant he opened his eyes and blinked in the morning sunlight, long before he turned his head to see the wide mattress as empty as it always was. As if her presence here last night, her body tucked against his as they'd finally drifted off to sleep together, had been nothing but a dream.

If it was a dream, he'd have stayed in it awhile longer. He'd have made it last, made it count.

But he knew he hadn't dreamed a single second of it.

He swung out of the bed, pulling on the nearest pair of trousers he could find and leaving them low on his hips. He pushed his way out of the master suite to find the penthouse oddly, strangely, quiet all around him. The door to Anais's bedroom was wide open, showing him it was empty, so he jogged down the wide steel stairs that brought him to the second level. It took him a moment to realize that he couldn't hear Damian. Normally there'd be the usual clamor and howl of a young boy in the house, but not today. That was why it was so quiet.

The nanny must have taken him out, he thought absently, poking his head into one of the small reception rooms on the second level, the one Anais had claimed as her office while she'd been here. It, too, was empty. Not even her laptop open on the small, elegant desk in the corner.

Dario made his way down to the kitchen and poured himself a cup of coffee, then took it into his home office. The penthouse was still oppressively silent all around him, and there was a certain agitated sort of sensation brewing beneath his ribs. He couldn't quite identify it. He rounded his desk and sat down, frowning at the large brown file folder that hadn't been there last night, he was certain.

He picked it up and glanced inside…

And then everything seemed to turn to sheets of ice. Freeze solid, then shatter.

He understood in an instant that what had been bothering him wasn't the absence of Anais's laptop in that second-level room, but of everything else. The stacks of documents, the soft-sided briefcase she'd kept at her feet, the tangle of power cords. Or the suitcase that had sat at the foot of her bed in that bedroom across from his.

He should have realized at a glance that it wasn't her laptop that was gone. She was.

Because he recognized the document in the file folder. It was the stack of divorce papers he'd left for her in his hotel room on Maui.

A dark, terrible thing was unfurling in him, deep and wide and thick, but he made himself flip through the papers to see if she'd signed it. She had. Of course she had. Her signature was just as he recalled it, somehow perfectly French and perfectly her at once, and he thought a bullet to the chest might have been easier. Better, maybe.

He heard a sound at the door and he looked up, somehow unsurprised to see her standing there, dressed head to toe in what he knew, now, were her lawyer clothes. Cool and gorgeous and sleek.

Her armor.

He didn't beat around the bush. "Why?"

Something moved over her face, too quick for him to categorize it.

"You don't trust me," she said simply. "You'll never trust me."

"This can't possibly—"

"Dario."

He stopped, though he thought it might have broken something inside him. He didn't know how there could be anything left to break.

"I can't live like that," Anais told him, that same raw thing he'd seen in her gaze last night there again, and in her voice besides. "I grew up in a house of hatred and contempt. Terrible accusations were thrown about like they were nothing. I won't raise my son that way, surrounded by suspicion and fury at every turn."

Dario was reeling. Unmoored and untethered, and he remembered this feeling all too well from six years ago. The sick thud in his stomach. The noise in his head.

The great black pit of loss that yawned open beneath him and wanted to swallow him whole.

Last time, he'd let it. He'd jumped right in. He'd stayed there for years and called it *realism*. He couldn't bear the thought of sinking into it again. He couldn't imagine there was any way out a second time.

"And last night? What the hell was that?"

"I wanted to say goodbye," she said, and her cool tone slipped a bit. He heard the rawness. The pain. And it didn't make him feel any kind of triumph. It was no victory. It only made him hurt. "I didn't want to walk out on you."

The way he had, without a second thought or a backward glance. She didn't say that. She didn't have to say it.

Dario rose then. He didn't know what he meant to do. If anything.

"Don't do this." He wanted to sound fierce, sure. Instead, he sounded broken. Maybe, this time, he really was. Or maybe that was the point she was making—that he had been all along. "Don't. What do I have to do to keep you here? Name it."

But Anais's expression didn't change. If anything, she looked sadder and more resolute at the same time. And he had the strangest sense of foreboding as she opened her mouth.

"Talk to your brother," she said softly. "That's what you have to do for me to stay."

"No." He gritted the word out, every part of him tense and furious and still reeling closer and closer to that great black pit. "Why would you ask such a thing? Did my grandfather put you up to this?"

And he saw the way her face crumpled, just slightly, before she blinked it away. He saw the way she clenched her hands into fists at her sides. He saw that terrible sadness in her eyes.

"The fact that you don't know is why I'm leaving." She waved a hand, taking in the room, the city, maybe. Him. "This only works if we pretend the past never happened. If you make an effort to act as if it never happened."

He didn't understand this at all. "I'd think that's a good thing, considering."

"Dare." That nickname only she had ever used, but in that hard, hurt voice, and it was worse than a kick to the gut. "I won't live my life as a hostage to a history that you've been getting wrong for six years. How can we ever move forward if you can't look at the past and see the truth?"

"This has nothing to do with that."

"There is no *this* without *that*," she corrected him. "Because *that* never happened. I don't need your forgiveness and I refuse to spend my life trying to convince you to trust me when I never broke your trust in the first place. You know what my parents were like. The screaming fights, the ugly names, the endless horror of it. I won't raise Damian like that. I don't want him to think that kind of war is love."

"It's not like that. We're not like that."

"You can't even imagine calling your brother. Your twin. You can't *imagine* it."

"Dante has nothing to do with us!" he thundered at her.

"I know," she said sadly. "And he never did. But I don't think I'm the one you need to hear that from. And I can't waste my life hoping you see the light and repair what you broke so we can all move forward. I won't."

She was really going to do this. She was really going to leave him, after everything. After they'd made it through what should have been the darkest place. He could see it on her face, in the gleam of moisture in her eyes.

He could feel it in that terrible constriction in his chest.

"Anais…"

"I'm taking Damian back to Maui," she told him, straightening in the doorway, her tone measured. As if she'd been planning out what she would say and was delivering the news to him as calmly as she could. "I'm not taking him away from you and I won't keep him from you. You can see him whenever you like. I'm happy to talk about a formal custody arrangement as we work through the divorce, but informally, I'm perfectly fine with whatever works for you."

"Those are the same papers as before," he said, unable to process this. Unable to understand. "The ones that claim you were unfaithful and name Dante as your lover."

"If that's what you need me to say in open court, then I'll say it," she told him.

And Dario understood that he should have viewed that quiet statement as his most decisive victory yet. But all he could seem to feel was a crushing sense of defeat. Of incalculable loss. Of nothing but grief, rolling on in all directions, forever.

She merely shrugged, and somehow that made it worse. "This needs to end, for all our sakes. I don't care if it takes a lie to do that, as long as it's over."

"Anais. Damn it. This is…"

"Dario." Her voice was hard then. Cold. Very serious. She waited until he met her gaze, and he knew then. He was already in that dark pit. He'd never climbed out. He never would. "You have to let me go."

CHAPTER TWELVE

IT TOOK DARIO less than a day to determine that he was not going to repeat the mistakes of the past. He refused to throw himself into that darkness and hope his work might save him. Not this time.

By the end of the day she left him, taking Damian with her, Dario was fully resolved. He stood on the roof deck without her, staring off into the hectic muddle of the city he hardly saw without her in it, and knew exactly what he wanted.

And Anais had named the single obstacle standing in his way.

Of course, he told himself then, he needed to call his damned brother.

But it took him a little bit longer to actually do it. He'd been so furious at his twin for so long. It was hard for him to let go of that.

Maybe too hard, he thought a few hours later as he waited on the same roof. Maybe some breaches were supposed to be there.

He didn't have to turn around to know that Dante had arrived. That same intuition that had seemed like magic to those around the two of them, dormant for six long years, prickled alive instantly. He knew the very moment Dante stepped out onto the roof.

He didn't simply know it. He *felt* it.

He took his time turning, and his brother was there when he did. It had been six years, and yet it felt…right.

"This is anticlimactic," he said, eyeing the man standing across from him. It was still like looking into a mirror. It was still as if Dante was an extension of himself. *This is right*, he thought again. "I thought you'd at least have the good grace to be horrifically scarred or stunted in some way."

"I could fling myself off the balcony in a show of dramatic atonement," Dante replied in his usual easy manner, though Dario could see the wariness in his eyes. "Of course, that would likely kill me instantly. Much less suffering for me that way, which I'd think would defeat the purpose."

Dario had to catch himself then, because he almost laughed at that—and this was the trouble. This was his *twin*. He knew Dante better than he knew himself, in some ways, or he had. He was genetically predisposed to get along with him. These past six years had been torture—and he couldn't understand how he'd managed to convince himself otherwise. How he'd believed his own lies.

You've been lying to yourself for a long, long time, he thought then.

"You betrayed me," he said starkly, and his brother stiffened. "That was all I knew six years ago. That was all I wanted to know. You hurt me. You, of all people."

Dante only stared back at him, the way he had then, and said nothing.

"Now I want to know the details," Dario continued. He realized he'd tensed every muscle in his body and forced himself to relax. As best he could. "Anais has a child. He looks just like us."

He searched his brother's face. His own face, at a distance, as identical as it had ever been. As children and teenagers they'd played each other for days at a time to see if anyone noticed the switch. No one ever had.

Dario forced himself to ask the question. "Is he yours?"

"No."

The word was like a stone hurled from a great height, and it landed between them with the force of too much gravity. Dario was surprised the roof deck didn't buckle beneath them with the wallop of it. He was surprised he didn't.

Dante looked stricken and fierce at once. "*No.* I never touched Anais, Dario. I never laid a single finger on her. I never would."

And Dario realized that he'd known this, on some level. He must have known this, or he wouldn't have turned and walked away. He wouldn't have cut Dante and Anais off so completely, leaving them no recourse, if he'd thought they'd really cheated on him, because why would he have cared what they said then? And he certainly wouldn't have thrown his revenge aside, ignored the way she'd deliberately aired their private business in the papers, all for the sake of a few family dinners. Not if he'd truly believed she was trying to foist off his brother's child on him.

Because there was only one way Anais could be *so sure* Damian was Dario's. Beyond a shadow of a doubt. Only one explanation.

This was what she'd meant, he understood now. This was what she couldn't live with. It wasn't only that he'd believed the worst of her. It was that he must have been *looking* for something hideous to believe about her as his way out, because look how quickly he'd taken it. Look what damage he'd done.

What he didn't know was why.

"You let me believe otherwise," he said now to the twin who was the lost part of him. How had he pretended all this time that he was whole when that was laughable at best? He didn't care that his voice was too thick. "Deliberately."

Dante moved then, closing the distance between them to stand nearer to Dario at the deck's rail. He frowned down at the traffic on Central Park West, but Dario knew he didn't see it.

He saw the past. Dario had lived in that past for too long. He wanted out.

He wanted to be free.

More than that, he wanted his family.

"I did," Dante admitted. He shook his head. "I hated that you listened to Anais more than to me. I hated that she'd come between us when she was supposed to be nothing more than a business arrangement. You'd married her to give her a green card, not to install her as our third partner."

Lies upon lies, Dario thought, and all of them his own damned fault. "I didn't marry her to give her a green card."

Dante let out a small laugh at that. "That became clear." He shifted to look at Dario. "You were at that damned meeting with ICE. I thought she'd put you up to it, so I took the opportunity to drop by and get in her face." He looked rueful. "She doesn't back down."

"Not usually," Dario agreed. "As you've likely seen in the tabloids."

"She threw a glass of water at me." Dante moved a

hand in the air over his chest. "All over me. And that calmed things down. The irony is that we'd actually started talking to each other when you walked in."

"On you. Coming out of my bedroom, half-dressed."

"It didn't even occur to me that you might read it the wrong way," Dante said in a low voice, "until you did. And I realized you'd obviously never gotten over what happened in college."

"It seemed like a pattern," Dario said then. Though in truth, he thought it was the broken trust he'd never gotten over and never forgotten—and maybe that hadn't been fair. It had been Lucy who had lied, not Dante. But he hadn't wanted to consider that back then. It had all been a mess. ICE, their past, Anais… "But Anais mattered more. Much more."

"I never meant any of this to happen," Dante said fervently. "I never wanted to break up your marriage and I certainly never wanted you to cut *me* off. I assumed things would go back to normal after you'd had time to cool down. I assumed that, at the very least, you'd come after me. Yell at me. Fight with me. Hell, I thought you'd answer the damn phone, Dario."

Dario blew out a breath. "I don't know why I didn't. I don't know why I let a moment of silence ruin two relationships." He looked his brother in the eye, then reached over and clapped his hand to Dante's shoulder. "You might have done nothing to keep me from believing the worst, Dante. But I'm the one who believed it. That isn't your fault. It's mine."

The evening wore on then, but everything was different. Better.

They sat out on the roof and told each other the stories of their lives over the past six years, and while they were no longer finishing each other's sentences the way they had as children, it was remarkably easy to get back in tune. To feel connected again. Whole.

Dario hadn't realized how much he'd missed his brother, or how deeply he'd been fooling himself all this time.

"How did you end up in Hawaii, anyway?" Dante asked. "Didn't you once claim you didn't see the purpose of beaches?"

"Maybe I've had a radical personality transplant and now enjoy nothing more than lying on a bit of sand, waiting for death or boredom to claim me," Dario said.

Dante laughed. "Have you?"

"Certainly not." Dario laughed, too, and it felt good. It felt like a revelation, like another key turned in a lock he hadn't realized was there, to sit beneath the stars and laugh with his twin again. "I was tracking down a pair of earrings for our possibly demented grandfather."

"He sent me off to find a tiara," Dante said. He raked a hand through his hair. "Maybe this has all been an elaborate ruse on the old man's part. Maybe he didn't accidentally sell off a load of trinkets at all. Maybe they were all baubles he handed out."

"What, as gifts? Who hands out priceless jewelry as gifts and calls them 'trinkets'?"

"Remember that Grandfather's from Europe. He's very old school." Dante shrugged, that utterly familiar maverick's grin tugging at his mouth. "Maybe he took a very European view of his wedding vows and kept a string of wealthy mistresses on the side."

It was hard to imagine their grandfather doing any of the things one might logically do with a mistress—especially when the image Dario had of him now was

Giovanni as he'd been at the house the other day, frail and unwell. On the other hand, the old man was famously cagey. And certainly their own father's brief, chaotic life suggested that growing up in Giovanni's house had been something less than perfect.

"The man likes his secrets," he said now.

They looked at each other, and it was back. That instant, wordless communication that the twins had once been so fluent in it had taken them longer to learn actual English than any of their siblings. They hadn't needed it.

They both pulled out their smartphones and started typing various things into the search fields of their browsers.

"'Tiara and earrings,' it turns out," Dante murmured a few moments later, "leads us directly to the Duchess of Cambridge and her pageant of a wedding. Who knew she'd cornered the market on a matched set?"

"I think we can cross Kate Middleton off the list of our grandfather's potential mistresses," Dario replied. "I feel certain the British press would have picked up on it."

But he remembered the snatches of conversation he'd heard over the past few months while he'd been concentrating on the product launch. Little snippets about family matters he hadn't been particularly bothered about at the time.

One of his brothers had found a necklace for Giovanni; one of his sisters had produced a bracelet. He put all of those together, and then threw in a description of the jewels. White diamonds. Bright green emeralds.

"Look at this," he said, leaning closer so Dante could see the screen, as well.

"They were all a commissioned set," Dante said as

Dario scrolled down the page, reading at the same pace. Of course. "I'm surprised they were ever broken apart."

"It says each piece is inscribed with a word."

"Kate Middleton? I knew it."

"BALDO," Dario said, his mouth twitching. He read down further. "No one has ever been able to figure out what that means."

"That's the trouble with secrets," Dante said then, sitting back in his chair. "They must seem like a good idea at the time. Then they're nothing but old words inscribed on the back of lost trinkets, and precious few people to care."

Dante had to head out not long after, but Dario knew that everything had changed between them—and for the better this time. They might not have solved every problem, but they'd started the process.

He had his brother back. He was himself again.

The future was not going to take place in a series of little boxes. Not if he could help it.

And that meant there was only one thing left he needed to do.

It was time to head back to Hawaii and claim his family.

This time, when that same hard knock sounded on her door after dark, Anais told herself it couldn't possibly be Dario. She'd been very clear with him. She and Damian had come home and settled right back into the perfectly decent life they'd been living before Dario had made his reappearance. Everything was exactly as it had been before.

Save that Damian now had a lot more to say to the photograph by his bed, and Anais found herself curled up in her own empty bed with nothing but her broken heart. Broken even harder this time, because she'd been the one to leave.

The knock came again, even louder.

Anais took her time getting to her feet, and longer still crossing to the door. And maybe some part of her had been expecting an impromptu visit one of these days, because she hadn't changed into her usual postwork clothes. Not a single one of the nights since they'd come home from New York.

Had she been hoping he'd show up? Had she imagined that if he did, she'd really feel safer in a pencil skirt and a sleeveless blouse?

She swung open the door and there he was, and her whole body hummed to life, as if she'd locked herself away in a deep freeze here in the tropics. As if Dario was all the heat in the world.

He looked gorgeous and intent, in the kind of sleek, expensive T-shirt that only very rich men thought looked casual and a pair of jeans. He looked rugged and rumpled, his dark hair shoved back from his face at an angle that suggested he'd been raking his hands through it all day. His blue eyes met hers and held.

"This time," he said in that low voice that connected to every part of her that longed for him and lit it all up like fireworks against a dark night, "you need to let me in."

Anais didn't move. She didn't step toward him and she didn't step back. And she was terribly afraid that he could hear how hard her heart was beating in her chest, that he could see how little it would take for her to simply throw herself in his arms and wave away the past...

But she refused to do that. Damian deserved better than that.

And so did she.

"I don't think that's a good idea," Anais said, and it was one of the hardest things she'd ever done in her life. She'd thought that morning in New York had been difficult. She'd had to fight to keep herself from sobbing in front of her five-year-old on that endless flight home. But this was harder.

Because he was here. He'd come after her.

She wanted that to mean a lot more than she suspected it could.

"I meant what I said in New York," she made herself tell him, because she didn't want to say anything of the kind. She wanted to stop gripping the doorjamb. She wanted to launch herself at him. But that was always the trouble, wasn't it? She wanted things she couldn't have, and Dario was at the top of that list. "This can't work."

She expected his eyes to flash dark, for him to argue. She expected threats, harsh words.

Instead, he smiled.

That beautiful smile of his. It was like a perfect sunrise. It was entirely too much like joy, and she didn't understand it at all.

"I'm not going anywhere, Anais," he told her, as if he was reciting a vow. "I'm not walking away again. I'll stay right here on the doorstep for as long as it takes."

"You're not going to stay on the doorstep. Don't be ridiculous."

That smile of his widened. "Maybe not literally."

And she told herself she had no choice. That her heart was a terrible judge of character, or none of this would have happened, would it? She made herself step back.

"Goodbye, Dare," she said.

That smile of his didn't fade. And it hurt her—physically hurt her—to close the front door. Then force herself to walk back into her house and carry on with her life somehow.

She couldn't say she did a good job. She sat there on her sofa and stared across the room at the bookcase where her single photo album of their time together was stored, and she ordered herself not to cry.

Over and over and over. Until she fell asleep slumped sideways on the couch and stayed there until morning.

It was a new day, she told herself when she woke up, cranky and sore. Dario had been seized with something highly uncharacteristic to come all this way and make declarations, but she imagined it was like a tropical sunburn. Painful, but it would peel eventually. Then disappear.

But he came back again that night. And the night after.

And every night that week.

Always after dark, when Damian was already in bed, so there could be no chance of using their son's feelings as any kind of bargaining chip. And he always left with that same smile on his face, as if he really could do this forever.

"I think you have issues," she told him when it continued into a second week. "I never should have gone out to coffee with you in the first place all those years ago. It set a terrible precedent. You think you can wear me down with persistence and a smile."

The scary part was that they both knew he could. She expected him to laugh, but he didn't. He stared at her, the thick dark all around him and his blue gaze serious.

"I don't want to wear you down, Anais," he told her. "You already know that I can walk away when things get tough. Now you know that I can stick around when things don't go my way."

"What if I want you to go away?" Her voice was so hoarse, so soft. She might have thought she hadn't said anything out loud, but she could see that she had in the way he went still.

"Then you have to say that," he said. "You have to tell me there's no hope and that this is never going to change. As long as there's hope, I can do this forever. Tell me that's gone and I'll never bother you again."

And she stood there for a shuddering beat of her heart. Then another. She felt the soft breeze on her face, and curled her bare toes into the cool concrete of her front step. Everything else was the blue of his eyes, the starkness of his expression. The way he held himself, as if braced for the worst.

She should open her mouth right now and tell him there was no hope. It was the kind thing to do—the safe and smart thing to do, for everyone.

"Good night, Dare" was what she said instead, stepping back inside and closing the door.

She could feel him there on the other side. She slumped against the closed door, squeezing her eyes shut, and she could *feel* him there, only that flimsy bit of wood and her own determination separating them.

Anais didn't know how long they stood there. She'd never know how long it was before she heard him turn around and go. Or how much longer she stayed where she was, before she forced her stiff, protesting muscles into a hot shower in the hopes that might stave off insomnia. It didn't help at all.

And two nights later, she let him in.

CHAPTER THIRTEEN

ANAIS DIDN'T KNOW what she expected Dario to do. But it wasn't what he did, which was walk inside as if he'd never had any doubt she'd let him in eventually and then look around, as if searching for something.

"Do you have a fireplace?" he asked.

She scowled at him. It was lowering to realize she'd expected fervent declarations, or at least a discussion of some kind, while he apparently wanted…something else entirely. Whatever that was.

"We have a little fire pit out back," she said. "Damian likes to roast marshmallows every now and again."

He strode past her and she found herself following, then watching in some mix of astonishment and bemusement as he set about building a fire in the hollowed-out center of the table that claimed pride of place on her small patio. It had been an indulgence, that odd little table with the built-in fire pit in its center, but she'd had some of her favorite evenings here with Damian. She had no idea why Dario's being here now made her feel as if she ought to apologize for that.

"Wait here," he said when he got the fire going.

And the crazy thing was, she did as he asked. She waited. She told herself she was simply standing there, waiting to see what would happen next, but it was nothing so passive. She was terrified. She was exhilarated.

Maybe she was paralyzed.

She was too many things at once and she had no idea how she could possibly survive this. Whatever *this* was. She'd lost Dario too many times already. How much of her was left? How could she afford to risk it again?

But she knew, standing there with her eyes on the flames as they leaped against the dark, that this had nothing to do with Damian. People all over the world shared the custody of their children, and the great majority of those children were just fine.

This was about her. This was about the two of them, Anais and Dario. This was about six years ago, and this was about New York, and she didn't know if she had it in her to survive *this*.

Dario came back out on the porch, holding a thick sheaf of papers in his hand. He moved around to the opposite side of the table from where Anais was standing, and he met her gaze over the dancing flames of the fire between them.

"My father was a ruined man," he said.

He tilted the sheaf of papers he held so she could see them, and Anais caught her breath. It was the divorce papers. He'd brought them here.

Dario peeled the first page off, held it aloft, then fed it to the flames. "He was addicted to everything. You know this. He and my mother were as raucous and wild as yours were furious and brooding. I don't know that they ever loved anything. Not each other, not us." He watched her as he added another page to the fire. "After they died, my grandfather took us in, but he was not precisely a warm man. As he grew older, the stories he told were affectionate, interesting and never about us. They were always of other places, lost friends, misplaced trinkets. He was always somewhere else, even when he was in the same room."

"You don't have to tell me this," she whispered, surprised to find she'd shifted to hold herself at some point, her arms wrapped around her middle. "I know your family story."

"All I had was Dante," Dario said, as if he hadn't heard her. "He was my twin, my brother, my best friend. Truly, the first person I ever loved. I would have done anything for him. I did. And there were things that came between us before you, cracks in our relationship, but no one else I loved."

That word. *Loved.* She realized he'd never told her he loved her. She'd accepted that she'd loved him back then, but she'd never have dared to say so. That wasn't their agreement. That broke all the rules. Hearing that word in his mouth now made something inside her flutter. As if, were she not very careful, it might spread out its wings and start to fly away.

"And then you," Dario said quietly, as if he knew. "I looked up, and there you were, and nothing was ever the same after that."

Anais held herself tighter, all of her attention—all of *herself*—focused squarely on Dario, just there on the other side of the small fire, burning page after page of those awful papers as he spoke.

"I spent some time with Dante the other day," he told her.

There was no holding back those wings inside her then. They unfurled. They started to beat. And something inside her soared.

"Then you know." She felt the wetness on her face, but did nothing to stop the tears. She couldn't move. She couldn't look away from him. "You know I never betrayed you. I didn't. He didn't."

"No," Dario agreed, and there was sheer torment in his voice, his eyes. "I betrayed you. I was so ready to believe the worst. I was so lost back then, stressed out and overwhelmed, and maybe I wanted a terrible fight so I could control something, anything that was happening to me. I walked away from the only two people I've ever loved. I told myself cutting you both off was a victory, that it was an act of strength in the face of what you'd done to me. But I understand now it was the worst kind of cowardice."

"Dario…" she whispered.

"Dante and I were twin brothers, the two of us against the world. We had our own language, our own universe. I never learned how to *work* at things. I never had to learn. I was raised by a man who ignored the present all around him, the better to drift off into the past. And my parents dealt with their problems by courting oblivion by any means necessary. Up their noses, down their throats, whatever worked."

He threw another set of pages on the fire and the breeze blew the smoke in her face, sharp and rough at once. Anais didn't turn away.

"My parents were no better," she told him. "They taught me I deserved cruelty. That I was worth nothing."

"I know," Dario gritted out. "And I will never forgive myself for sending you the same message, all because I was too much of a coward to tell you the truth. I didn't marry you because it was good business. I didn't do it out of the goodness of my heart, because you needed

immigration help or because I thought an in-house lawyer would be a great idea. I married you because I fell
in love with you the moment I saw you, and it scared the
hell out of me."

Anais couldn't see then. Tears streamed down her
face, mixing with the fire and the smoke and the thick
Hawaiian night. Somehow forming a kind of paste that
wrapped itself around her broken heart and made it feel
whole again.

Making her imagine. Making her hope.

"I knew Damian was mine the moment I saw that
photograph," Dario continued, his voice rougher than
before, his gestures jerkier as he kept throwing page
after page into the fire. "But more than that, I knew
you. I knew you'd never throw it in my face like that
if there'd ever been the slightest bit of doubt. I didn't
want to know these things. I pretended I didn't know
them. But I did."

He held up the last page, with both of their signatures,
both bold scrawls of blue. He waited while she wiped at
her eyes, her face. He waited until she met his gaze again.

"Anais," he said, "I love you. I've never loved another woman and I never will. I don't want to pretend
anymore."

Then he set their divorce on fire. He held the paper
for another moment, then let it go.

And then there was nothing but flames, and smoke,
and love.

Their twisted, stubborn, fierce love that nothing had
managed to destroy. Not betrayal. Not distance. Not her
own better judgment. Not his vast wealth and ability to
pretend she didn't exist. Nothing.

Here they still were, all these years later. No matter who walked away, the other one always opened the door. Eventually.

"Listen to me," he said urgently.

He moved around the table then to take her shoulders in his hands, as if he thought she planned to reject him yet again. When the truth was, she didn't know what she planned to do.

Don't you? a voice inside of her asked.

"I know this is about trust," he said, his hands so warm against her, sending heat spiraling down into her flesh. "And I know you have no reason to trust me. I can't make you trust me or promise you I won't let you down in the future. I can only tell you that I'm not the same man I was six years ago, or even a month ago. You changed me." His hands moved to her upper arms, drawing her closer to him. "If you give me the chance, I'll spend the rest of my life trying to prove myself to you. I'll do whatever it takes."

She couldn't speak. She could only gaze up at him, almost as if she didn't believe this was happening.

"I love you," he said, and then he said it again, as if to make sure there could be no mistake. "And I love Damian. I want us to have the family we deserve, and I want to give him the family you and I never had. I want the whole package, Anais, if you'll let me. If you'll try."

And life came down to leaps of faith. Running for the edge and jumping out into nothing, hoping something would come to break the fall before landing. Sometimes it did. Other times it didn't, and that was a different lesson altogether. But no matter how many times she'd landed on her face, with Dario in particular, there was something that made Anais want to jump all over again.

Because even if she fell, the falling would be worth it. She had to believe it.

There was a reason she hadn't moved on. There was a reason she'd built a safe little life here, where she could pretend to be getting on with things when all she'd really been doing was waiting. There was a reason she'd never made a very good glacier. She'd made sure Damian loved his father before he'd ever met him. She'd been paving the way back to Dario since she'd left New York. How had she never realized it?

"There are no guarantees," he told her, his hands tightening where he held her. "But I can promise you this. I'll always come back to you. You'll always be my home. I hope I'll never give you reason to doubt that again."

She swayed closer to him. She lifted her hands to cup his face, reveling in the scratch of his unshaven jaw against her palms. She gazed into the eyes of the only man she'd ever loved, just yards away from where the perfect little boy they'd made together slept soundly. Maybe there were more perfect things than this, than him, but not for her.

Anais had only and ever been destined to be right here.

"I love you," she whispered, and she watched that go through him like a wave. "I've always loved you." She went up on her toes and she wrapped her arms around his neck, getting her mouth so close to his she could almost taste him. "And we'll try together, Dario. Again and again and again. Until we get it right."

And then she started off their future with the perfect kiss, right there beneath the dark Hawaiian sky, with nothing left between them but love.

At last.

* * *

Love was the easy part, Dario thought a year later, as he stood outside that same villa at the luxury resort in Wailea and gazed at the beautiful woman who was not only his wife but the true light of his whole world.

Trust took time.

There were no boxes in this life they'd built together, day by day. There was a great deal more laughter. There were perfect nights and stolen moments they found when they could. They'd learned to split their time between New York and Hawaii. They'd learned to talk more and walk away less.

They taught each other how to try, every day. Sometimes they failed. More often, they got there. Wherever they were going, they got there. Together.

Today, Damian stood between them, all three of them with their bare feet in the sand of the private beach. They'd recited a few vows, though their child had declared that "weird."

"It's called renewing our vows," Dario told him.

"Do all married people do that?" Damian asked.

"Only the lucky ones," Anais told him, her dark eyes warm on Dario's.

Damian seemed to accept that, grown-up six-year-old that he was, or perhaps his focus was on other things.

"I thought you said there was going to be a present." He grinned angelically when both his parents frowned at him. "I like presents."

"Holy terror," Dario mouthed to Anais.

Her mouth twitched as she ran her hand over Damian's head.

"What have you always said you wanted more than anything in the world?" she asked him.

"A brother," Damian replied instantly, and when she smiled, he whooped. Then took off to run wild circles up and down the small beach, shouting out his excitement to the surf.

"I hope you're ready for another one," Anais murmured, wrapping her arms around Dario and tilting her head back to gaze up at him.

"I've never been more ready," he promised her gruffly. "Trust me."

And this time, when she gave birth to his son six months later, he was right there beside her. And the very first thing little Didier ever saw.

It got louder and it got messier, and the truth was, Dario loved it. He'd had no idea that he could love so much and so many. His brother was back in his life where he belonged, and better this time, since Dario appreciated what they shared—their twin bond—in a way he never had before. He'd had no idea how much he'd craved the kind of family bonds and deep intimacy he'd thought he'd wanted nothing to do with.

"I have something to tell you," Anais said a couple of years later.

They'd come to Maui for Damian's school vacation, and were sitting out on the lanai of the house where they'd met for the first time six years into their marriage, the house Dario had bought from the Fuginawa estate after the old man had passed on. The rolling hills of the Kaupo countryside gleamed beneath the stars and, far below, he still thought he could hear the sea.

"Because all good conversations start exactly like that," Dario murmured, pushing his laptop aside and closing it. Focusing on Anais. He didn't like the way she stood there, almost mimicking the same positions they'd taken all those years ago, so he hauled her into his lap and got his mouth on her neck.

The same fire roared between them. It always had. It always would.

A wave of goose bumps washed over her, and she shivered in his arms, and only the presence of his children in this house somewhere kept him from pulling up that loose dress she wore and making them both a whole lot happier, right here.

"Remember how I told you I didn't feel well?" she asked, angling her head to one side to give him better access.

"I do." He pushed the silk of her hair aside and trailed heat along the line of her neck. "Remember how I told you my theory and you assured me you couldn't possibly be pregnant?"

She didn't reply and that old fear gripped him—that he'd ruin this again, that he'd ruined *her* irreparably. That she still didn't trust him to be there for her and never would.

"I can't think of anything better than another baby with you," he told her gruffly. He'd never meant anything more. "Another member of this family. Our family. It would be a gift."

And Anais laughed. She tipped back her head to look him in the eye and he knew then. She wasn't afraid of telling him this news, she wasn't worried about their future—she was teasing him. She trusted him.

She trusted him.

He couldn't think of a better gift than that.

"Twins," she said, her dark eyes laughing at him. "And get ready, Dare. They're girls."

He couldn't think of a better gift except that, he

amended as he covered Anais's mouth with his, love and laughter and that same old hunger underneath, making it all sing.

Except that.

* * * * *

DI SIONE'S
VIRGIN MISTRESS

SHARON KENDRICK

For Sarah-Jane Volkers who will know
exactly why this book is dedicated to her when
she reads it! And to the brilliant Rafael Vinoly,
whose words painted such a perfect vignette
of Long Island life...

CHAPTER ONE

DANTE DI SIONE FELT the adrenaline pumping through his body as he walked into the tiny airport terminal. His heart was pounding and his forehead was beaded with sweat. He felt like he'd been running. Or just rolled away from a woman after a bout of particularly energetic sex. Even though it was a long time since he could even remember *having* sex. He frowned. How long?

His mind raced back over the past few weeks spent chasing across continents and flitting in and out of different time zones. He'd visited a dizzying array of countries, been presented with a whole shoal of red herrings and wandered up against several dead ends before arriving here, in the Caribbean. All in pursuit of a priceless piece of jewellery which his grandfather wanted for reasons he'd declined to share. Dante felt the tight clench of his heart. A dying man's wish.

Yet wasn't the truth that he had been tantalised by the task he'd been given and which he had taken on as a favour to someone who had given him so much? That his usually jaded appetite had been sharpened by a taste of the unusual. Truth was, he was dreading going back to his high-octane world of big business and the slightly decadent glamour of his adopted Parisian home. He had enjoyed the unpredictability of the chase and the sense that he was stepping outside his highly privileged comfort zone.

His hand tightened around the handle of his bag which contained the precious tiara. All he needed to do now was to hang on to this and never let it go—at least, not until he had placed it at his grandfather's sickbed so that the old man could do what he wanted with it.

His mouth felt dry. He could use a drink, and... something else. Something to distract him from the fact that the adrenaline was beginning to trickle from his system, leaving him with that flat, empty feeling which he'd spent his whole life trying to avoid.

He looked around. The small terminal was filled with the usual suspects which this kind of upmarket Caribbean destination inevitably attracted. As well as the overtanned and ostentatiously wealthy, there seemed to have been some photo shoot taking place, because the place was full of models. He saw several giraffe-tall young women turn in his direction, their endless legs displayed in tiny denim shorts and their battered straw hats tilted at an angle so all you could see were their cute noses and full lips as they pouted at him. But he wasn't in the mood for anyone as predictable as a model. Maybe he'd just do a little work instead. Get on to René at his office in Paris and discover what had been going on in his busy and thriving company while he'd been away.

And then his gaze was drawn to a woman sitting on her own. The only pale person in a sea of tanned bodies. Her hair was blond and she looked as fragile as spun sugar—with one of those pashmina things wrapped around her narrow shoulders which seemed to swamp her. She looked *clean*. He narrowed his eyes. Like she'd spent most of her life underwater and had just been brought up to the surface. She was sitting at the bar with an untouched glass of pink champagne in front of her, and as their eyes met, she picked up her glass, flustered, and began to stare at it as if it contained the secret to the universe—though he noticed she didn't drink any.

Was it that which made him start walking towards her, bewitched by a sudden demonstration of shyness which was so rare in the world he inhabited? With a few sure strides he reached her and put his bag down on the floor, right next to a remarkably similar brown leather carry-on. But then she lifted her head and all he could think about was the fragile beauty of her features.

'Hi,' he said.

'Hi,' she said in a very English accent as she blinked up at him through thick lashes.

'Have we met before?' he questioned.

She looked startled. Like someone who had been caught in an unexpected spotlight. She dug her teeth into her lower lip and worried them across the smooth rosy surface.

'I don't think so,' she said, then shook her head so that the strands of fair hair shimmered over her narrow shoulders like a silky cascade of water. 'No, we haven't. I would have remembered.'

He leaned on the bar, and smiled. 'But you were staring at me as if you knew me.'

Willow didn't answer—not straight away—her

head was too full of confusion and embarrassment combined with a powerful tug of attraction which she wasn't quite sure how to handle. Yes, *of course* she had been staring at him because—quite honestly— who wouldn't?

Beneath the pashmina, she felt the shiver of goose bumps as she met his mocking gaze, acknowledging that he was probably the most perfect man she'd ever seen—and she worked in an industry which dealt almost exclusively with perfect men. Dressed with the carelessness only the truly wealthy could carry off, he looked as if he'd only just fallen out of bed— though probably not his own. Faded jeans clung to unbelievably muscular thighs, and although his silk shirt was slightly creased, he still managed to convey a sense of power and privilege. His eyes were bright blue, his black hair was tousled and the gleam of his golden olive skin hinted at a Mediterranean lineage. Yet behind the brooding good looks she could detect a definite touch of steel—a dangerous edge which only added to his allure.

And Willow was usually left cold by good-looking men, something she put down to a certain shyness around them. Years of being ill, followed by a spell in an all-girls school, had meant that she'd grown up in an exclusively female environment and the only men she'd ever really met had been doctors. She'd been cocooned in her own little world where she'd felt safe—and safety had been a big deal to her.

So what was it about this man with the intense blue eyes which had made her heart start slamming against her ribcage, as if it was fighting to get out of her chest?

He was still looking at her questioningly and she tried to imagine what her sisters would say in similar circumstances. They certainly wouldn't be struck dumb like this. They'd probably shrug their gym-honed shoulders and make some smart comment, and hold out their half-empty glasses for a refill.

Willow twisted the stem of the champagne glass in between her finger and thumb. *So act like they do. Pretend that gorgeous-looking men talk to you every day of the week.*

'I imagine you must be used to people staring at you,' she said truthfully, taking her first sip of champagne and then another, and feeling it rush straight to her head.

'True.' He gave a flicker of a smile as he slid onto the bar stool beside her. 'What are you drinking?'

'No, honestly.' She shook her head, because surely the champagne must be responsible for the sudden warmth which was making her cheeks grow hot. 'I mustn't have too much. I haven't eaten anything since breakfast.'

He raised his eyebrows. 'I was going to ask if it was any good.'

'Oh. Yes. Of course. Right. Silly of me. It's...' Feeling even more flustered, Willow stared at the fizzing bubbles and drank a little more, even though suddenly it tasted like medicine on her tongue. 'It's the best champagne I've ever had.'

'And you often drink champagne on your own at airports, do you?' he drawled.

She shook her head. 'No. Actually, I'm celebrating the end of a job.'

Dante nodded, knowing this was his cue to ask

her about her job, but the last thing he wanted was to
have to listen to a résumé of her career. Instead, he
asked the bartender for a beer, then leaned against
the bar and began to study her.

He started with her hair—the kind of hair he'd
like to see spread over his groin—because although
he wouldn't kick a brunette or a redhead out of bed
in a hurry, he was drawn to blondes like an ant to the
honeypot. But up close he could see anomalies in her
appearance which made her looks more interesting
than beautiful. He noted the almost-translucent pal-
lor of her skin which was stretched over the highest
cheekbones he'd ever seen. Her eyes were grey—the
soft, misty grey of an English winter sky. Grey like
woodsmoke. And although her lips were plump, that
was the only bit of her which was—because she was
thin. Too thin. Her slim thighs were covered in jeans
onto which tiny peacocks had been embroidered, but
that was as much as he could see because the damned
pashmina was wrapped around her like an oversize
tablecloth.

He wondered what had drawn him towards her
when there were other more beautiful women in the
terminal who would have welcomed his company,
rather than looking as if a tiger had suddenly taken
the seat beside her. Was it the sense that she didn't
really fit in here? That she appeared to be something
of an outsider? And hadn't he always been one of
those himself? *The man on the outside who was always looking in.*

Maybe he just wanted something to distract him
from the thought of returning to the States with the
tiara, and the realisation that there was still so much

which had been left undone or unsaid in his troubled family. Dante felt as if his grandfather's illness had brought him to a sudden crossroads in his life and suddenly he couldn't imagine the world without the man who had always loved him, no matter what.

And in the meantime, this jumpy-looking blonde was making him have all kinds of carnal thoughts, even though she still had that wary look on her face. He smiled, because usually he let women do all the running, which meant that he could walk away with a relatively clear conscience when he ended the affair. Women who chased men had an inbuilt confidence which usually appealed to him and yet suddenly the novelty of someone who was all tongue-tied and flustered was really too delicious to resist.

'So what are you doing here?' he questioned, taking a sip of his beer. 'Apart from the obvious answer of waiting for a flight.'

Willow stared down at her fingernails and wondered how her sisters would have answered *this*. Her three clever, beautiful sisters who had never known a moment of doubt in their charmed lives. Who would each have doubtless murmured something clever or suggestive and had this gorgeous stranger tipping back his dark head and laughing in appreciation at their wit. They certainly wouldn't have been sitting there, tying themselves up in knots, wondering why he had come over here in the first place. Why was it only within the defining boundaries of the work situation that she was able to engage with a member of the opposite sex without wishing that the floor would open up and swallow her?

This close, he was even more spectacular, with

a raw and restless energy which fizzed off him like electricity. But it was his eyes which were truly remarkable. She'd never seen eyes like them. Bluer than the Caribbean sky outside. Bluer even than the wings of those tiny butterflies which used to flutter past on those long-ago summer evenings when she'd been allowed to lie outside. A bright blue, but a hard blue—sharp and clear and focused. They were sweeping over her now, their cerulean glint visible through their forest of dark lashes as he waited for her answer.

She supposed she should tell him about her first solo shoot as a stylist for one of the UK's biggest fashion magazines, and that the job had been a runaway success. But although she was trying very hard to feel happy about that, she couldn't seem to shake off the dread of what was waiting for her back in England. Another wedding. Another celebration of love and romance which she would be attending on her own. Going back to the house which had been both refuge and prison during her growing-up years. Back to her well-meaning sisters and overprotective parents. Back to the stark truth that her real life was nowhere near as glamorous as her working life.

So make it glamorous.

She'd never seen this man before and she was unlikely to see him again. But couldn't she—for once in her life—play the part which had always been denied to her? Couldn't she pretend to be passionate and powerful and *desirable*? She'd worked in the fashion industry for three years now and had watched professional models morph into someone else once the camera was turned on them. She'd seen them become coquettish or slutty or flirtatious with an ease which was breathtaking. Couldn't she pretend that this man was the camera? Couldn't she become the person she'd always secretly dreamed of being, instead of dull Willow Hamilton, who had never been allowed to do *anything* and as a consequence had never really learned how to live like other women her age?

She circled the rim of the champagne glass with her forefinger, the unfamiliar gesture implying—she *hoped*—that she was a sensual and tactile person.

'I've been working on a fashion shoot,' she said.

'Oh.' There was a pause. 'Are you a model?'

Willow wondered if she was imagining the brief sense of *disappointment* which had deepened his transatlantic accent. Didn't he like models? Because if that was the case, he really *was* an unusual man. She curved her lips into a smile and discovered that it was easier than she'd thought.

'Do I look like a model?'

He raised his dark eyebrows. 'I'm not sure you really want me to answer that question.'

Willow stopped stroking the glass. 'Oh?'

His blue eyes glinted. 'Well, if I say no, you'll pout and say, *Why not?* And if I say yes, you'll still pout, and then you'll sigh and say in a weary but very affected voice, *Is it that obvious?*'

Willow laughed—and wasn't it a damning indictment of her social life that she should find herself shocked by the sound? As if she wasn't the kind of person who should be giggling with a handsome stranger at some far-flung spot of the globe. And suddenly she felt a heady rush of freedom. And excitement. She looked into the mocking spark of his eyes and decided that she could play this game after all.

'Thank you for answering me so honestly,' she said gravely. 'Because now I know I don't need to say anything at all.'

His gaze became speculative. 'And why's that?'

She shrugged. 'If women are so unoriginal that you can predict every word they're going say, then you can have this conversation all by yourself, can't you? You certainly don't need me to join in!'

He leaned forward and slanted her a smile in response and Willow felt a sense of giddy triumph.

'And that would be my loss, I think,' he said softly, his hard blue eyes capturing hers. 'What's your name?'

'It's Willow. Willow Hamilton.'

'And is that your real name?'

She gave him an innocent look. 'You mean Hamilton?'

He smiled. 'I mean Willow.'

She nodded. 'It is—though I know it sounds like something which has been made up. But it's a bit of a tradition in our family. My sisters and I are all named after something in nature.'

'You mean like a mountain?'

She laughed—*again*—and shook her head. 'A bit more conventional than that. They're called Flora, Clover and Poppy. And they're all very beautiful,' she added, aware of the sudden defensiveness in her tone.

His gaze grew even more speculative. 'Now you expect me to say, *But you're very beautiful, too.*' His voice dipped. 'And you respond by...'

'And I told you,' interrupted Willow boldly, her heart now pounding so hard against her ribcage that she was having difficulty breathing, 'that if you're so astute, you really ought to be having this conversation with yourself.'

'Indeed I could.' His eyes glittered. 'But we both know there are plenty of things you can do on your own which are far more fun to do with someone else. Wouldn't you agree, Willow?'

Willow might not have been the most experienced person on the block where men were concerned and had never had what you'd call a *real* boyfriend. But although she'd been cosseted and protected, she hadn't spent her life in *total* seclusion. She now worked in an industry where people were almost embarrassingly frank about sex and she knew exactly what he meant. To her horror she felt a blush beginning. It started at the base of her neck and rose to slowly flood her cheeks with hot colour. And all she could think about was that when she was little and blushed like this, her sisters used to call her the Scarlet Pimpernel.

She reached for her glass, but the clamp of his hand over hers stopped her. Actually, it did more than stop her—it made her skin suddenly feel as if it had developed a million new nerve endings she hadn't realised existed. It made her glance down at his olive fingers which contrasted against the paleness of her own hand and to think how perfect their entwined flesh appeared. Dizzily, she lifted her gaze to his.

'Don't,' he said softly. 'A woman blushing is a rare and delightful sight and men like it. So don't hide it and don't be ashamed. And—just for the record—if you drink more alcohol to try to hide your embarrassment, you're only going to make it worse.'

'So you're an expert on blushing as well as being an authority on female conversation?' she said, aware that his hand was still lying on top of hers and that it was making her long for the kind of things she knew she was never going to get. But she made no attempt to move her own from underneath and wondered if he'd noticed.

'I'm an expert on a lot of things.'

'But not modesty, I suspect?'

'No,' he conceded. 'Modesty isn't my strong point.'

The silence which fell between them was broken by the sound of screaming on the other side of the terminal and Willow glanced across to see a child bashing his little fists against his mother's thighs. But the mother was completely ignoring him as she chatted on her cell phone and the little boy's hysteria grew and grew. *Just talk to him*, thought Willow fiercely, wondering why some people even bothered *having* children. Why they treated the gift of birth so lightly.

But then she noticed that Blue Eyes was glancing at his watch and suddenly she realised she was missing her opportunity to prolong this conversation for as long as possible. Because wouldn't it be great to go home with the feeling of having broken out of her perpetual shyness for once? To be able to answer the inevitable question, *So, any men in your life these days, Willow?* with something other than a bright, false smile while she tried to make light of her essentially lonely life, before changing the subject.

So ask him his name. Stop being so tongue-tied and awkward.

'What's your name?' asked Willow, almost as if it was an afterthought—but she forced herself to pull her hand away from his. To break that delicious contact before he did.

'Dante.'

'Just Dante?' she questioned when he didn't elaborate further.

'Di Sione,' he added, and Willow wondered if she'd imagined the faint note of reluctance as he told her.

Dante took a sip of his beer and waited. The world was small, yes—but it was also fractured. There were whole groups of people who lived parallel existences to him and it was possible that this well-spoken young Englishwoman who blushed like a maiden aunt wouldn't have heard of his notorious family. She'd probably never slept with his twin brother or bumped into any of his other screwed-up siblings along the way. His heart grew cold as he thought about his twin, but he pushed the feeling away with a ruthlessness which came easily to him. And still he waited, in case the soft grey eyes of his companion suddenly widened in recognition. But they didn't. She was just looking at him in a way which made him want to lean over and kiss her.

'I'm trying to imagine what you're expecting my response to be,' she said, a smile nudging the edges of her lips. 'So I'm not going to do the obvious thing of asking if your name is Italian when clearly it is. I'm just going to remark on what a lovely name it is. And it is. Di Sione. It makes me think of blue seas and terracotta roofs and those dark cypress trees which don't seem to grow anywhere else in the world except in Italy,' she said, her grey eyes filling with mischief. 'There. Is that a satisfactory response—or was it predictable?'

There was a heartbeat of a pause before Dante

answered. She was so *unexpected*, he thought. Like finding a shaded space in the middle of a sizzling courtyard. Like running cool water over your hot and dirty hands and seeing all the grime trickle away. 'No, not especially predictable,' he said. 'But not satisfactory either.'

He leaned forward and as he did he could smell the tang of salt on her skin and wondered if she'd been swimming earlier that morning. He wondered what her body looked like beneath that all-enveloping shawl. What that blond hair would look like if it fell down over her bare skin. 'The only satisfactory response I can think of right now is that I think you should lean forward and part your lips so that I can kiss you.'

Willow stared at him—shocked—as she felt the whisper of something unfamiliar sliding over her skin. Something which beckoned her with a tantalising finger. And before she had time to consider the wisdom of her action, she did exactly as he suggested. She extended her neck by a fraction and slowly parted her lips so that he could lean in to kiss her. She felt the brush of his mouth against hers as the tip of his tongue edged its way over her lips.

Was it the champagne she'd drunk, or just some bone-deep *yearning* which made her open her mouth a little wider? Or just the feeling of someone who'd been locked away from normal stuff for so long that she wanted to break free. She wanted to toss aside convention and not be treated like some delicate flower, as she had been all her life. She didn't want to be Willow Hamilton right then. She wanted the famous fairy godmother to blast into the Caribbean airport in a cloud of glitter and to wave her wand and transform her, just as Willow had been transforming models for the past week.

She wanted her hair to stream like buttery silk down her back and for her skin to be instantly tanned, shown to advantage by some feminine yet sexy little dress whose apparent simplicity would be confounded by its astronomical price tag. She wanted her feet to be crammed into sky-high stilettos which still wouldn't be enough to allow her to see eye to eye with this spectacular man, if they were both standing. But she didn't want to be standing—and she didn't want to be sitting on a bar stool either. She wanted to be lying on a big bed wearing very sexy underwear and for those olive fingers to be touching her flesh again—only this time in far more intimate spots as he slowly unclothed her.

All those thoughts rushed through her mind in just the time it took for her own tongue to flicker against his and Willow's eyes suddenly snapped open—less in horror at the public spectacle she was making of herself with a man she'd only just met than with the realisation of what was echoing over the loudspeaker. It took a full five seconds before her befuddled brain could take in what the robotic voice was actually saying, and when it did, her heart sank.

'That's me. They're calling my flight,' she said breathlessly, reluctantly drawing her mouth away from his, still hypnotised by the blazing blue of his eyes. With an effort she got off the stool, registering the momentary weakness of her knees as she automatically patted her shoulder bag to check her passport and purse. She screwed up her face, trying to act like what had happened was no big deal. Trying to pretend that her breasts weren't tingling beneath her pashmina and that she kissed total strangers in airports every day of the week. Trying not to hope that he'd spring to his feet and tell her he didn't want her to go. But he didn't.

'Oh, heck,' she croaked. 'It's the last call. I can't believe I didn't hear it.'

'I think we both know very well why you didn't hear it,' he drawled.

But although his eyes glinted, Willow sensed that already he was mentally taking his leave of her and she told herself it was better this way. He was just a gorgeous man she'd flirted with at the airport—and there was no reason why she couldn't do this kind of thing in the future, if she wanted to. It could be the springboard to a new and exciting life if she let it. That is, if she walked away now with her dignity and dreams intact. Better that than the inevitable alternative. The fumbled exchange of business cards and the insincere promises to call. Her waiting anxiously by the phone when she got back to England. Making excuses for why he hadn't rung but unable—for several weeks at least—to acknowledge the reason he hadn't. The reason she'd known all along—that he was way out of her league and had just been playing games with her.

Still flustered, she bent down to grab her carry-on and straightened up to drink in his stunning features and hard blue eyes one last time. She tried her best to keep her voice steady. To not give him any sense of the regret which was already sitting on the horizon, waiting to greet her. 'Goodbye, Dante. It was lovely meeting you. Not a very original thing to say, I know—but it's true. Safe journey—wherever you're going. I'd better dash.'

She nearly extended her hand to shake his before realising how stupid that would look and she turned away before she could make even more of a fool of herself. She ended up running for the plane but told herself that was a good thing, because it distracted her from her teeming thoughts. Her heart was pounding as she strapped herself into her seat, but she was determined not to allow her mind to start meandering down all those pointless *what if* paths. She knew that in life you had to concentrate on what you had, and not what you really wanted.

So every time she thought about those sensual features and amazing eyes, she forced herself to concentrate on the family wedding which was getting closer and the horrible bridesmaid dress she was being made to wear.

She read the in-flight magazines and slept soundly for most of the journey back to England, and it wasn't until she touched down at Heathrow and reached into the overhead locker that she realised the carry-on bag she'd placed in the overhead locker wasn't actually *her* bag at all. Yes, it was brown, and yes, it was made of leather—but there all similarities ended. Her hands began to tremble. Because this was of the softest leather imaginable and there were three glowing gold initials discreetly embossed against the expensive skin. She stared at it with a growing sense of disbelief as she matched the initials in her

head to the only name they could stand for, and her
heart began to pound with a mixture of excitement
and fear.

D.D.S.

Dante Di Sione.

CHAPTER TWO

DANTE'S PLANE WAS halfway over northern Spain when he made the grim discovery which sent his already bad mood shooting into the stratosphere. He'd spent much of the journey with an erection he couldn't get rid of—snapping at the stewardesses who were fussing and flirting around him in such an outrageous way that he wondered whether they'd picked up on the fact that he was sexually excited, and some hormonal instinct was making them hit on him even more than usual.

But he wasn't interested in those women in too-tight uniforms with dollar signs flashing in their eyes when they looked at him. He kept thinking about the understated Englishwoman and wondered why he hadn't insisted she miss her flight, so that he could have taken her on board his plane and made love to her. Most women couldn't resist sex on a private jet, and there was no reason she would be any different.

His mouth dried as he remembered the way she had jumped up from the bar stool like a scalded cat and run off to catch her flight as if she couldn't wait to get away from him. Had that ever happened to him before? He thought not.

She hadn't even asked for his business card!

Pushing her stubbornly persistent image from his mind, he decided to check on his grandfather's precious tiara, reaching for his bag and wondering why the old man wanted the valuable and mysterious piece of jewellery so much. Because time was fast running out for him? Dante felt the sudden painful twist of his heart as he tried to imagine a future without Giovanni, but he couldn't get his head around it. It was almost impossible to envisage a life without the once strong but still powerful figure who had stepped in to look after him and his siblings after fate had dealt them all the cruellest of blows.

Distracted by the turbulent nature of his thoughts, he tugged at the zip of the bag and frowned. He couldn't remember it being so full because he liked to travel light. He tugged again and the zip slid open. But instead of a small leather case surrounded by boxer shorts, an unread novel and some photos of a Spanish castle he really needed to look at for a client before his next meeting—it was stuffed full of what looked suspiciously like…

Dante's brows knitted together in disbelief.

Swimwear?

He looked at the bag more closely and saw that instead of softest brown leather embossed with *his* initials, this carry-on was older and more battered and had clearly seen better days.

Disbelievingly, he began to burrow through the bikinis and swimsuits, throwing them aside with a growing sense of urgency, but instantly he knew he was just going through the motions and that his search was going to be fruitless. His heart gave a leap in his chest as a series of disastrous possibilities occurred to him. How ironic it would be if he'd flown half-way across the globe to purchase a piece of jewellery which had cost a king's ransom, only to find that he'd been hoodwinked by the man who had sold it to him.

But no. He remembered packing the tiara him-self, and although he was no gem expert, Dante had bought enough trinkets as pay-offs for women over the years to know when something was genuine. And the tiara *had* been genuine—of that he'd been cer-tain. A complex and intricate weaving of diamonds and emeralds which had dazzled even him—a man usually far too cynical to be dazzled.

So where the hell was it now?

And suddenly Dante realised what must have hap-pened. Willow—*what the hell had been her sur-name?*—must have picked up his bag by mistake. The blonde he'd been so busy flirting with at the airport, that he'd completely forgotten that he was carrying hundreds of thousands of dollars' worth of precious stones in his hand luggage. He'd been distracted by her misty eyes. He'd read in them a strange kind of longing and he'd fed her fantasy—and his own—by kissing her. It had been one of those instant-chemistry moments, when the combustion of sexual attraction had been impossible to ignore, until the last call for her flight had sounded over the loudspeaker and broken the spell. She'd jumped up and grabbed her bag. Only she hadn't, had she? She'd grabbed *his* bag!

He drummed his fingers on the armrest as he con-sidered his options. Should he ask his pilot to divert the plane to London? He thought about his meeting with the Italian billionaire scheduled for later that evening and knew it would be both insulting and damaging to cancel it.

He scowled as he rang for a stewardess, one of whom almost fell over herself in her eagerness to reach him first.

'What can I get for you, sir?' she questioned, her eyes nearly popping out of her head as she looked at the haphazard collection of swimwear piled in the centre of the table.

Dante quickly shoved all the bikinis back into the bag, but as he did so, his finger hooked on to a particularly tiny pair of bottoms. He felt his body grow hard as he felt the soft silk of the gusset and thought about Willow wearing it. His voice grew husky. 'I want you to get hold of my assistant and ask him to track down a woman for me.'

The stewardess did her best to conceal it, but the look of disappointment on her face was almost comical.

'Certainly, sir,' she said gamely. 'And the woman is?'

'Her name is Willow Hamilton,' Dante ground out. 'I need her number and her address. And I need that information by the time this plane lands.'

There were four missed calls on her phone by the time Willow left the Tube station in central London, blinking as she emerged into the bright July sunshine. She stepped into the shadow of a doorway and looked at the screen. All from the same unknown number and whoever it was hadn't bothered to leave a voicemail. But she knew who the caller must be. *The sexy stranger. The man she'd kissed. The blue-eyed man whose carry-on she had picked up by mistake.*

She felt the race of her heart. She would go home first and then she would ring him. She wasn't going to have a complicated conversation on a busy pavement on a hot day when she was tired and jet-lagged.

She had already made a tentative foray inside, but the bag contained no contact number, just some photos of an amazing Spanish castle, a book which had won a big literary prize last year and—rather distractingly—several pairs of silk boxer shorts which were wrapped around a leather box. She'd found her fingertips sliding over the slippery black material of the shorts and had imagined them clinging to Dante Di Sione's flesh and that's when her cheeks had started doing that Scarlet Pimpernel thing again, and she'd hastily stuffed them back before anyone on the Heathrow Express started wondering why she was ogling a pair of men's underpants.

She let herself into her apartment, which felt blessedly cool and quiet after the heat of the busy London day. She rented the basement from a friend of her father's—a diplomat in some far-flung region whose return visits to the UK were brief and infrequent. Unfortunately one of the conditions of Willow being there was that she wasn't allowed to change the decor, which meant she was stuck with lots of very masculine colour. The walls were painted bottle-green and dark red and there was lots of heavy-looking furniture dotted around the place. But it was affordable, close to work and—more importantly—it got her away from the cloying grip of her family.

She picked up some mail from the mat and went

straight over to the computer where she tapped in
Dante Di Sione's name, reeling a little to discover
that her search had yielded over two hundred thousand entries.

She squinted at the screen, her heart beginning to
pound as she stared into an image which showed his
haunting blue eyes to perfection. It seemed he was
some sort of mega entrepreneur, heading up a company which catered exclusively for the super-rich. She
looked at the company's website.

We don't believe in the word impossible.
Whatever it is you want—we can deliver.

Quite a big promise to make, she thought as she
stared dreamily at photos of a circus tent set up in
somebody's huge garden, and some flower-decked
gondolas which had been provided to celebrate a tenth
wedding anniversary party in Venice.

She scrolled down. There was quite a lot of stuff
about his family. Lots of siblings. *Snap,* she thought.
And there was money. Lots of that. A big estate somewhere in America. Property in Manhattan. Although
according to this, Dante Di Sione lived in Paris—
which might explain why his accent was an intriguing mix of transatlantic and Mediterranean. And yet
some of the detail about his life was vague—though
she couldn't quite put her finger on why. She hadn't
realised precisely what she'd been looking for until
the word *single* flashed up on the screen and a feeling of satisfaction washed over her.

She sat back and stared out at the pavement, where
from this basement-level window she could see the

bottom halves of people's legs as they walked by. A pair of stilettos tapped into view, followed by some bare feet in a pair of flip-flops. Was she really imagining that she was in with a chance with a sexy billionaire like Dante Di Sione, just because he'd briefly kissed her in a foreign airport terminal? Surely she couldn't be *that* naive?

She was startled from her daydream by the sound of her mobile phone and her heart started beating out a primitive tattoo as she saw it was the same number as before. She picked it up with fingers which were shaking so much that she almost declined the call instead of accepting it.

Stay calm, she told herself. *This is the new you. The person who kisses strangers at airports and is about to start embracing life, instead of letting it pass her by.*

'Hello?'

'Is that you, Willow?'

Her heart raced and her skin felt clammy. On the phone, his transatlantic/Mediterranean twang sounded even more sexy, if such a thing was possible. 'Yes,' she said, a little breathlessly. 'It's me.'

'You've got my bag,' he clipped out.

'I know.'

The tone of his voice seemed to change. 'So how the hell did that happen?'

'How do you think it happened?' Stung into defence by the note of irritation in his voice, Willow gripped the phone tightly. 'I picked it up by mistake… *obviously.*'

There was a split-second pause. 'So it wasn't deliberate?'

'Deliberate?' Willow frowned. 'Are you serious? Do you think I'm some sort of thief who hangs around airports targeting rich men?'

There was another pause and this time when he spoke the irritation had completely vanished and his voice sounded almost unnaturally composed. 'Have you opened it?'

A little uncomfortably, Willow rubbed her espadrille toe over the ancient Persian rug beneath the desk. 'Obviously I had to open it, to see if there was any address or phone number inside.'

His voice sounded strained now. 'And you found, what?'

Years of sparring with her sisters made Willow's response automatic. 'Don't you even remember what you were carrying in your own bag?'

'You found, *what*?' he repeated dangerously.

'A book. Some glossy photos of a Spanish castle. And some underpants,' she added on a mumble.

'But nothing else?'

'There's a leather case. But it's locked.'

At the other end of the phone, Dante stared at the imposing iron structure of the Eiffel Tower and breathed out a slow sigh of relief. Of course it was locked—and he doubted she would have had time to get someone to force it open for her even if she'd had the inclination, which he suspected she didn't. There had been something almost *otherworldly* about her... and she seemed the kind of woman who wouldn't be interested in possessions—even if the possession in question happened to be a stunning diadem, worth hundreds of thousands of dollars.

He could feel the strain bunching up the muscles

in his shoulders and he moved them slowly to release some of the tension, realising just how lucky he'd been. Or rather, how lucky *she* had been. Because he'd been travelling on a private jet with all the protection which came with owning your own plane, but Willow had not. He tried to imagine what could have happened if she'd been stopped going through customs, with an undeclared item like that in her possession.

Beads of sweat broke out on his forehead and for a moment he cursed this mission he'd been sent on—but it was too late to question its legitimacy now. He needed to retrieve the tiara as soon as possible and to get it to the old man, so that he could forget all about it.

'I need that bag back,' he said steadily.

'I'm sure you do.'

'And you probably want your swimwear.' He thought about the way his finger had trailed over the gusset of that tiny scarlet bikini bottom and was rewarded with another violent jerk of lust as he thought about her blond hair and grey eyes and the faint taste of champagne on her lips. 'So why don't I send someone round to swap bags?'

There was a pause. 'But you don't know where I live,' she said, and then, before he had a chance to reply, she started talking in the thoughtful tone of someone who had just missed a glaringly obvious fact. 'Come to think of it—how come you're ringing me? I didn't give you my phone number.'

Dante thought quickly. Was she naive enough not to realise that someone like him could find out pretty much anything he wanted? He injected a reassuring note into his voice. 'I had someone who works for me track you down,' he said smoothly. 'I was worried that you'd want your bag back.'

'Actually, you seem to be the one who's worried, Mr Di Sione.'

Her accurate tease stopped him in his tracks and Dante scowled, curling his free hand into a tight fist before slowly releasing his fingers, one by one. This wasn't going as he had intended. 'Am I missing something here?' he questioned coolly. 'Are you playing games with me, Willow, or are you prepared to do a bag-swap so that we can just forget all about it and move on?'

In the muted light of the basement apartment, Willow turned to catch a glimpse of her shadowed features in an antique oval mirror and was suddenly filled with a determination she hadn't felt for a long time. Not since she'd battled illness and defied all the doctors' gloomy expectations. Not since she'd fought to get herself a job, despite her family's reluctance to let her start living an independent life in London. She thought about her sister Clover's wedding, which was due to take place in a few days' time, when she would be kitted out in the hideous pale peach satin which had been chosen for the bridesmaids and which managed to make her look completely washed out and colourless.

But it wasn't just that which was bothering her. Her vanity could easily take a knock because she'd never really had the energy or the inclination to make her looks the main focus of her attention. It was all the questions which would inevitably come her way and which would get worse as the day progressed.

So when are we going to see you walking down the aisle, Willow?

And, of course, the old favourite: *Still no boyfriend, Willow?*

And because she would have been warned to be on her best behaviour, Willow would have to bite back the obvious logic that you couldn't have one without the other, and that since she'd never had a proper boyfriend, it was unlikely that she would be heading down the aisle any time soon.

Unless…

She stared at her computer screen, which was dominated by the rugged features of Dante Di Sione. And although he might have been toying with her—because perhaps kissing random women turned him on—he had managed to make it feel *convincing*. As if he'd really *wanted* to kiss her. And that was all she needed, wasn't it? A creditable performance from a man who would be perfectly capable of delivering one. Dante Di Sione didn't have to be her real boyfriend—he just had to look as if he was.

'Don't I get a reward for keeping your bag safe?' she questioned sweetly.

'I'll buy you a big bunch of flowers.'

'Flowers make me sneeze.'

'Chocolates, then.'

'I'm allergic to cocoa.'

'Stop playing games with me, Willow,' he snapped. 'And tell me what it is you're angling for.'

Willow stared at the piercing blue eyes on the computer screen. His thick black hair looked as if he had been running his fingers through it and she remembered how it had felt to have his lips brushing over hers. It was now or never. It was all about seizing the moment and doing something you wouldn't normally do. Because what was the point of sitting back and moaning about your fate as if it was set in stone, instead of trying to hammer out something new for yourself?

And here was a chance staring her straight in the face.

She drew in a deep breath. 'What I want won't cost you anything but your time. I'm being a bridesmaid at my sister's wedding next weekend and I'm fed up with people asking me why I don't have a boyfriend. All you have to do is pretend to be that man. For one day only, you will be my fictitious but very convincing boyfriend, Mr Di Sione. Do you think you could manage that?'

CHAPTER THREE

HE SHOULD HAVE told her no. Should have told her that he hated weddings. Because marriage stood for everything he despised and distrusted. Lies and deception and manipulation.

Dante straightened the silver-grey tie which complemented his formal charcoal suit and stared at his reflection in the hotel mirror.

So why *hadn't* he said no? Why *had* he agreed to accompany Willow Hamilton to her sister's wedding, where she was being a bridesmaid? It was true that she had his grandfather's tiara in her possession and she had been demonstrating a not-very-subtle form of blackmail to get him to be her plus one. But Dante was not a man who could be manipulated— and certainly not by a woman. If he'd really wanted that tiara back he would have gone straight round to her apartment and *taken* it—either by reason or seduction or quiet threat—because he nearly always got what he wanted.

So why hadn't he?

He gave his tie one final tug and watched as his reflected face gave a grim kind of smile.

Because he wanted her? Because she'd interested

and intrigued him and awoken in him a sexual hunger he'd been neglecting these past weeks?

The reflected smile intensified.

Well, why not?

He picked up his car keys and went outside to the front of the hotel, where the valet was opening the door of the car he'd hired for the weekend. It was an outrageously fast car—a completely over-the-top machine which would inevitably attract the attention of both men and women. And while it wouldn't have been Dante's first choice, if Willow wanted him to play the part of a very rich and super-keen lover, then it followed that he ought to drive something which looked like everyone's idea of a phallic substitute.

He drove through the streets of central London and tooted the horn as he drew up outside Willow's basement apartment. She appeared almost immediately and he watched her walk towards him, narrowing his eyes with instinctive appraisal—because she looked… He swallowed. She looked *incredible*. Gone was the big pashmina which had shielded her from the airport's overzealous air conditioning and hidden most of her body. In its place was a pale dress which skimmed the tiniest waist he'd ever seen, its flouncy skirt swirling provocatively around her narrow knees. Her blond hair was plaited and Dante felt his mouth dry. As she grew closer he could see that the collar of her dress was embroidered with tiny daisies, and it made her look as if she'd been picked fresh from a meadow that morning. She looked ethereal and fragile and he couldn't seem to tear his eyes away from her.

He shook his head slightly as once again he acknowledged her fey beauty and the realisation that she didn't seem quite part of this world. Certainly not *his* world. And then he noticed that she was carrying nothing but a small suitcase.

'Where's my carry-on?' he demanded as he got out of the car to take the case from her.

There was a pause as she met his gaze. 'It will be returned to you after the deal is done.'

'After the deal is done?' he echoed softly.

'When the wedding is over.'

He raised his eyebrows at her mockingly, but made no attempt to conceal the sudden flicker of irritation in his voice. 'And if I insist on taking it now? What then?'

He saw a momentary hesitation cross her fragile features, as if she had suddenly realised just who it was she was dealing with. But bravado won the day and she shot him an almost defiant look which made him want to pin her over the bonnet of the car and kiss her senseless.

'You're not in a position to insist, Dante,' she said, sliding inside with a graceful movement which made him wish she could do it again, in slow motion. 'I have something you want and you have to pay for it.'

He switched on the engine and wondered if she was aware that she had something else *he* wanted, and that by the end of the day he would have taken it… 'So where are we going?' he said.

'My family home. It's in Sussex. I'll direct you.'

'Women are notoriously bad at directions, Willow—we both know that. So why don't you just give me the postcode and I can program it into the satnav?'

She turned to look at him, a frown creasing her

brow. 'Are you for real, or did you just complete a crash course in being patronising? I think I can just about find my way to my family home without needing a robot to guide me.'

'Just don't fall asleep,' he warned.

'I'll do my best. But you're not exactly an aid to relaxation, are you?' Settling back in her seat, she gave him a clear list of instructions, then waited until he had negotiated his way out of London towards the south, before she asked, 'So what's in the bag which makes you want it so much?'

'Boxer shorts.' He shot her a look. 'But you already know that.'

Willow didn't react, even though the mention of his boxer shorts was threatening her with embarrassment, which she suspected was his intention. Because this was the new Willow, wasn't it? The woman who had decided to take control of her own destiny instead of having it decided by other people. The woman who was going to live dangerously. She studied his rugged profile as he stared at the road ahead. 'A few items of underwear wouldn't usually be enough to get a man like you to take a complete stranger to a family wedding and pretend to be her boyfriend.'

'Let's get a couple of things straight, shall we, Willow? Firstly, I have no intention of discussing the contents of that bag with you,' he said as he powered the car into the fast lane. 'And secondly, I intend to play your *lover*—not your damned *boyfriend*—unless your looks are deceiving and you happen to be fifteen.'

'I'm twenty-six,' she said stiffly.

'You look much younger.'

'That's what everyone says.'

There was a pause. 'Is that a roundabout way of telling me I'm unoriginal?'

She shrugged. 'Well, you know what they say… if the cap fits…'

A reluctant smile curved the edges of his lips. 'You need to tell me something about yourself before we get there,' he said. 'If you're hoping to convince people we're an item.'

Willow stared out of the car window as they drove through the sun-dappled lanes, and as more and more trees appeared, she thought about how much she loved the English countryside. The hedgerows were thick with greenery and in the fields she could see yellow and white ox-eye daisies and the purple of snake's head fritillary. And suddenly she found herself wishing that this was all for real and that Dante Di Sione was here because he wanted to be, not because she was holding him to ransom over some mystery package.

She wondered how much to tell him. She didn't want him getting scared. She didn't want him to start treating her as if she was made of glass. She was worried he'd suddenly start being *kind* to her if she learned the truth, and she couldn't stand that. He was rude and arrogant and judgemental, but she rather liked that. He wasn't bending over backwards to please her—or running as fast as he could in the opposite direction, which was the usual effect she had on people once they knew her history.

His words interrupted her silent reverie.

'We could start with you explaining why you need an escort like me in the first place,' he said. 'You're a pretty woman. Surely there must be other men who

could have been your date? Men who know you better than I do and could have carried off a far more
convincing performance.'

She shrugged, staring at the toenails which were
peeping through her open-toed sandals—toenails
which had been painted a hideous shade of peach to
match the equally hideous bridesmaid dresses, because Clover had said that she wanted her sisters to
look like 'a team.'

'Maybe I wanted to take someone who nobody
else knew,' she said.

'True,' he agreed. 'Or you could—and I know this
is controversial—you could always have chosen to
attend the wedding on your own. Don't they say that
weddings are notoriously fertile places for meeting
someone new? You might have got lucky. Or are you
one of those women who believes she isn't a complete
person unless she has a man in tow?'

Willow couldn't believe what he'd just said. Had
she really thought his rudeness was charming? Well,
scrub that. She found herself wishing she'd asked
around at the magazine to see if anyone there could
have been her guest. But most of the men she worked
with were gay—and the place was a hotbed of gossip.
It wouldn't have done her image much good if she'd
had to trawl around for a suitable escort, because the
biggest sin you could commit in the fashion industry
was to admit to being lonely.

She sneaked a glance at Dante. Whatever his short-
comings in the charm department he was certainly a
very suitable escort—in every sense of the word. The
formality of his pristine two-piece looked just as good
against his glowing olive skin as the faded denim

jeans had done. Perhaps even more so. The made-to-measure suit hugged his powerful body and emphasised its muscularity to perfection—making her shockingly aware of his broad shoulders and powerful thighs. The slightly too long black hair appeared more tamed than it had done the other day and suddenly she found herself longing to run her fingers through it and to muss it up.

She felt a rush of something molten tugging at the pit of her belly—something which was making her wriggle her bottom restlessly against the seat. Did she imagine the quick sideways glance he gave her, or the infuriatingly smug smile which followed—as if he was perfectly aware of the sudden aching deep inside her which was making it difficult for her to think straight.

She licked her lips. 'I'm not really like my sisters,' she began. 'You remember I'm one of four?'

'I remember.'

'They've always had millions of boyfriends, and I haven't.'

'Why not?'

He shot the question at her and Willow wondered if now was the time for the big reveal. To tell him how ill she'd been as a child. To tell him that there had been times when nobody had been sure if she would make it. Or to mention that there were residual aspects of that illness which made her a bad long-term choice as a girlfriend.

But suddenly her attention was distracted by the powerful interplay of muscles as he tensed one taut thigh in order to change gear and her mouth dried with longing. No, she was not going to tell him. Why peddle stories of her various woes and make herself look like an inevitable victim in his eyes? Today she was going to be a different Willow. The kind of Willow she'd always wanted to be. She was going to embrace the way he was making her feel, and the way he was making her feel was…*sexy*.

Carelessly, she wriggled her shoulders. 'I've been too wrapped up in my career. The fashion world can be very demanding—and competitive. I've been working at the magazine since I left uni, and they work you very hard. The swimwear shoot I was doing in the Caribbean was my first big break and everyone is very pleased with it. I guess that means I'll have more time to spend on my social life from now on. Take the next turning on the right. We're nearly there. Look. Only seven more miles.' She pointed at a signpost. 'So you'd better tell me a bit about you.'

Dante slowed the car down as he turned into a narrow lane and thought how differently he might have answered this question a few years back. The first thing he would have said was that he was a twin, because being a twin had felt like a fundamental part of his existence—like they were two parts of the same person. But not any more. He and Dario hadn't spoken in years. Six years, to be precise—after an episode when anger and resentment had exploded into misunderstanding and turned into a cold and unforgiving rift. He'd discovered that it was easier to act like his brother no longer existed, rather than acknowledge the fact that they no longer communicated. And that it hurt. It hurt like hell.

'But surely you must have looked me up on the internet,' he murmured.

She quickly turned her head to look at him, and for the first time, she seemed uncertain. 'Well, yes. I did.'

'And didn't that tell you everything you wanted to know?'

'Not really. Bits of it were very vague.'

'I pay people a lot of money to keep my profile vague.'

'Why?'

'To avoid the kind of questions you seem intent on asking.'

'It's just down that long drive. The entrance is just past that big tree on the right.' She leaned forward to point her finger, before settling back against the leather car seat. 'It said you had lots of siblings, and there was something about you having a twin brother and I was wondering what it was like to have a twin. If the two of you are psychic, like people say twins can be. And...'

'And what?' he shot out as her words trailed off.

She shrugged. 'There wasn't much information about your parents,' she said quietly.

Dante's fingers tightened around the steering wheel as he drew up outside a huge old house, whose beauty was slightly diminished by shabby paintwork and a general sense of tiredness. Bad enough that Willow Hamilton should have made breezy assumptions about his estranged twin, but worse that she had touched on the one fact which had ruthlessly been eliminated from his history. Didn't she realise that there was a good reason why there was scant mention of his parents in his personal profile?

He felt a slow anger begin to build inside him, and if it hadn't been for the damned tiara, he would have dropped her off there and then, and driven away so fast that you wouldn't have seen him for smoke. Because personal questions about his family were forbidden; it was one of the ground rules he laid down at the beginning of any date.

But this wasn't a normal date, was it? It was a means to an end. He stared down at her bare knees and felt a whisper of desire. And perhaps it was time he started taking advantage of some of the very obvious compensations available to drive these unwanted irritations from his head.

'I doubt whether knowing about my parentage or siblings is going to be particularly relevant in the circumstances,' he said coolly. 'Of far greater importance is finding out what turns each other on. Because, as lovers, we need to send out the vibe that we've had more than a little...*intimacy*. And in order to convey that to some degree of satisfaction, then I really need to explore you a little more, Willow.'

And before Willow could properly appreciate what was happening, he had undone their seat belts and was pulling her into his arms, as if it was something he had done countless times before. His cold blue eyes swept over her like a searchlight but there was something in their depths which disturbed her. Something which sent foreboding whispering over her spine. Was it the realisation that this man was way too complicated for her to handle and she shouldn't even try? Instinctively, she tried to pull away but he was having none of it, because he gave a silky laugh as he lowered his head to kiss her.

Willow sucked in a disbelieving breath as their lips met, because this wasn't like that lazy kiss at the air-

port. This was a completely different animal—an unashamed display of potent sensuality. This was Dante
Di Sione being outrageously macho and showing her
exactly who was in charge. It was a stamp and an
unmistakable sexual boast and something told Willow that this emotionless kiss meant nothing to him.

But that didn't stop from her reacting, did it?

It didn't stop her from feeling as if she'd just
stepped from the darkest shadows into the bright-
est sunlight.

His seeking lips coaxed her own apart and she felt
the tips of her breasts harden as he deepened the kiss
with his tongue. Did he know she was helpless to resist from the moment he'd first touched her? Was that
why he splayed his fingers over her dress and began
to caress her aching breast? She gave a whimper of
pleasure as she lifted her arms to curl them around
his neck and felt a rush of heat between her legs—
a honeyed throb of need which drove every other
thought and feeling straight from her body. It felt so
good. Unimaginably good. She felt exultant. Hungry
for more. Hungry for him.

Softly, Willow moaned with pleasure and he drew
his head away, his blue eyes smoky with desire and
an unmistakeable trace of mockery glinting in their
lapis lazuli depths.

'Do you want me to stop, Willow?' he taunted
softly, his words a delicious caress which whispered
over her skin, making her want him to talk to her
that way all day long. 'Or do you want me to touch
you a little more?'

His hand was now moving beneath the hem of her
dress and she held her breath. She could feel the tip-

toeing of his fingertips against the bare skin and the heat between her legs was increasing as he started to kiss her again. His words were muffled against her mouth as he repeated that same sensual, taunting question—and all the while he was inching his fingers further and further up her thigh.

'Do you?'

Her heart pounded as she opened her mouth to reply when the sound of footsteps crunching over gravel broke into the kiss like a rock smashing through a thin sheet of ice. Reluctantly Willow opened her eyes and pulled away from him, in time to see her sister's astonished face looking at them through the car window.

CHAPTER FOUR

'FLORA!' SOMEHOW WILLOW managed to stumble her sister's name out through lips which were swollen by the pressure of Dante's kiss. She tried to pull away from him but he wasn't having any of it—keeping his arm anchored tightly around her shoulders. Her voice trembled a little as his fingertips started stroking at the base of her neck, as if he couldn't bear not to be touching her. 'What...what are you doing here?'

But Flora wasn't looking at her. She was staring at Dante as if she couldn't quite believe her eyes. Willow watched as her sister surreptitiously touched her blond hair as if to check that it was pristine—which naturally, it was—and then spread her fingers out over her breastbone, as if to emphasise that at least one of the Hamilton sisters had breasts.

'And just who is *this*, Willow?' she said in a voice which didn't quite manage to hide her disbelief. 'You really must introduce me.'

'He's...' Willow's voice faltered. *He's the man I've bribed to be here. The man who made me feel I was almost going to explode with pleasure, and that was only from a single kiss.*

'My name is Dante Di Sione and I'm Willow's

guest for the wedding,' interjected Dante, and Willow saw Flora almost melt as his sensual lips curved into a lazy smile. 'Didn't she tell you I was coming?'

'No,' said Flora crisply. 'No, she did not. We weren't…well, we weren't expecting her to bring anyone—and as a consequence we've made no special allowances. Which means you'll be in Willow's old bedroom, I'm afraid.'

'And is there a problem with Willow's old bedroom?' he questioned.

'I would say there is, especially for a man of your dimensions.' Flora looked Dante up and down, as if shamelessly assessing his height. 'There's only a single bed.'

Willow wanted to curl up and die, and that was before Dante moved his hand from her neck to place it proprietarily over her thigh. He smiled up at her sister as he pressed his fingers into her flesh. 'Great,' he murmured. 'I do love a good squeeze.'

This clearly wasn't the reaction Flora had expected and the sight of Dante with his hand on her sister's leg must have confused the life out of her. But a lifetime of social training meant that her irritation didn't last long and she made an instant recovery. 'If you'd like to park over by the stables, Dante.' She flashed him a glossy smile. 'Once you've settled in we'll be serving coffee in the drawing room and you'll be able to meet my mother. Oh, and you'll have to try on your bridesmaid dress again, Willow—though I warn you that Clover is going to go ballistic if you've lost any more weight! And don't you think you ought to put a cardigan on? Your arms are covered in goose bumps.'

Dante started up the engine as they watched Flora walk into the main entrance of the grand house. Her blond hair swung down her back in a glossy curtain and she walked with the confident wiggle of a beautiful woman who knew she was being watched.

'So that's one of your sisters,' he said slowly as she disappeared through the open front door.

'Yes.' Willow nodded her head. *So get in first*, she thought. *Say all the stuff he must be thinking and that way you won't come over as vulnerable.* 'I told you my siblings were gorgeous, didn't I? And Flora especially so. Every man she meets falls in love with her. I…I think maybe she's single at the moment, though you can never be…'

'Willow.' He halted her flow of words by placing his finger firmly over her lips. 'Will you please shut up? I may have something of a reputation where women are concerned but even I would draw the line at going to a wedding with one sister, and then making out with another.'

'Not taking into account the fact that she might not be interested in you,' she said indignantly.

'No, of course not,' he murmured as he started up the engine. 'She was looking at me with nothing but cool indifference in her eyes.'

Willow couldn't decide whether to pull him up for his arrogance or simply acknowledge that he was telling the truth, because Flora *had* been looking at him as if she'd like to eat him up for breakfast, lunch and dinner and then maybe go back for a midnight snack. And yet he had been kissing *her*, hadn't he? Kissing her in a way she'd never been kissed before. She could still recall the fizzing excitement in her blood and the way she'd wanted to dissolve beneath his seeking fingers. She'd wanted him to carry on burrowing his fingers beneath her dress and to touch her where she was all hot and aching. Would he laugh or be horrified if he knew she'd never felt like that before? Would he be horrified to discover that she'd never actually had sex before?

They parked the car and she led Dante through the house by one of the back doors, beginning to realise what a big gamble she'd taken by bringing him here. Was he really a good enough actor to pretend to be interested in her when there was going to be so much Grade One crumpet sashaying around the place in their killer heels?

She pushed open the door of her old bedroom, the room where she had spent so much of her childhood—and immediately it felt like stepping back in time. It always did. It made her feel weird and it made her feel small. Little had changed since she'd left home, and whenever she came here, it felt as if her past had been preserved in aspic—and for the first time, she began to question why. Had her parents' refusal to redecorate been based on a longstanding wish not to tempt fate by changing things around?

Willow looked around. There was the portrait done of her when she was six—years before the illness had taken hold—with a blue sparkly clip in her blond hair. How innocent she looked. How totally oblivious to what lay ahead. Next to it was the first embroidery she'd ever done—a sweet, framed cross-stitch saying *Home Sweet Home*. And there were her books—row upon row of them—her beloved connection to the outside world and her only real escape from the sickroom, apart from her sewing. Later on, she'd discovered films—and the more slushy and happy-ever-after, the better. Because fantasy had been a whole lot better than reality.

Sometimes it had felt as if she'd been living in a gilded cage, even though she knew there had been good reasons for that—mainly to keep her away from any rogue infections. But her inevitable isolation and the corresponding protectiveness of her family had left her ill-equipped to deal with certain situations. Like now. She'd missed out on so much. Even at college she'd been watched over and protected by Flora and Clover, who had both been studying at the same university. For a long time she'd only had the energy to deal with maintaining her health and completing her studies and getting a decent degree—she hadn't had the confidence to add men into the mix, even if she'd found anyone attractive enough.

And she had never found anyone as attractive as Dante Di Sione.

She watched him put their bags down and walk over to the window to stare out at the wide green-grey sweep of the Sussex Downs, before turning to face her—his incredible lapis lazuli eyes narrowed. She waited for him to make some comment about the view, or to remark on the massive dimensions of her rather crumbling but beautiful old home, but to her surprise he did neither.

'So,' he said, beginning to walk towards her with stealthy grace. 'How long have we got?'

'Got?' she repeated blankly, not quite sure of his meaning even when he pulled her into his arms and started trailing his fingertips over her body so that she began to shiver beneath the filmy fabric of her delicate dress. 'For...for what?'

Dante smiled, but it was a smile edged with impatience and a danger that even Willow could recognise was sexual.

'That depends on you, and what you want.'

'What I want?' she said faintly.

'Forgive me if I'm mistaken, but I thought that you were as frustrated by your sister's interruption as I was. I was under the distinct impression that our fake relationship was about to get real, and in a very satisfying way. It would certainly be more convincing if we were properly intimate instead of just pretending to be. So are we going to play games with each other or are we going to give in to what we both clearly want?' he murmured as he began to stroke her breasts. 'And have sex?'

Willow quivered as her nipples tightened beneath his expert touch and even though his words were completely unromantic...even though they were the direct opposite of all those mushy rom-coms she used to watch—they were still making her *feel* something, weren't they? They were making her feel like a woman. A *real* woman—not some pale and bloodless creature who'd spent so much time being hooked up to an intravenous drip, while cocktails of drugs were pumped into her system.

Yet this hadn't been what she'd planned when she'd rashly demanded he accompany her here. She'd thought they were engaging in nothing more than an indifferent barter of things they both wanted. Unless she wasn't being honest with herself. *Face the truth, Willow.* And wasn't the truth that from the moment she'd seen him walk into the Caribbean airport terminal, her body had sprung into life with a feeling of lust like she'd never felt before? In which case—why was she hesitating? Wasn't this whole trip supposed to be about changing her life around? To start living like other women her age did.

She tipped up her face so that he could kiss her again. 'Have sex,' she said boldly, meeting the flicker of humour in his smoky blue gaze.

He smiled and then suddenly what was happening *did* feel like a fantasy. Like every one of those mushy films she'd watched. He picked her up and carried her across the room, placing her down on the bed and pausing only to remove the battered old teddy bear that used to accompany her everywhere. She felt a wave of embarrassment as he pushed the bear onto the floor, but then he was bending his lips to hers and suddenly he was kissing her.

It was everything a kiss ought to be. Passionate. Searching. Deep. It made Willow squirm restlessly beneath him, her fingers beginning to scrabble at his shirt as she felt the rush of molten heat between her legs. And maybe he had guessed what was happening—or maybe this was just the way he operated— but he slid his hand beneath her skirt and all the way up her leg, pushing aside the damp panel of her knickers and beginning to tease her there with his finger. Her eyes fluttered to a close and it felt so *perfect* that Willow wanted to cry out her pleasure—but maybe he anticipated that too, because he deepened the kiss. And suddenly it became different. It became hard and hungry and demanding and she was matching it with her own demands—arching her body up towards his, as if she couldn't get close enough.

She could feel the hardness at his groin—the unfamiliar rocky ridge nudging insistently against her—and to her surprise she wasn't daunted, or scared. Maybe it was just her poor starved body demanding what nature had intended it for, because suddenly she was writhing against him—moaning her eagerness and her impatience into his open mouth.

He reached for his belt and Willow heard the rasp of his zip as he began to lower it, when suddenly there was a loud knock on the door.

They both froze and Willow shrank back against the pillows, trying to get her ragged breath back, though it took several seconds before she could speak.

'Who is it?' she demanded in a strangled voice.

'Willow?'

Willow's heart sank. It was Clover's voice. Clover, the bride-to-be. Well-meaning and bossy Clover, the older sister who had protected her as fiercely as a lioness would protect one of her cubs. Just like the rest of her family.

'H-hi, Clover,' she said shakily.

'Can I come in?

Before Willow could answer, Dante shook his head and mouthed, *No*, but she knew what would happen if she didn't comply. There would be an outraged family discussion downstairs. There would be talk of rudeness. They would view Dante with even more suspicion than she suspected he was already going to encounter. The atmosphere would be spoiled before the wedding celebrations had even begun.

She shook her head as she tugged her dress back down, her cheeks flaming bright red as she readjusted her knickers. 'Hang on a minute,' she called, wriggling out of Dante's arms and off the bed, mouthing, *Don't say a word.*

His responding look indicated that he didn't really have much choice but there was no disguising the flicker of fury sparking in his blue eyes.

Willow scuttled over to the door and pulled it open by a crack to see Clover outside, her hair in rollers and an expression on her face which couldn't seem to make up its mind whether to be cross or curious.

'What the hell are you doing?' Clover asked sharply.

For a minute Willow was tempted to tell her to mind her own business, or at least to use her imagination. To snap back that she had just been enjoying a glorious initiation to the mysteries of sex when she had been so rudely interrupted. What was it with her sisters that they kept bursting in on her at the most inopportune moments? But then she reminded herself of everything that Clover had done for her. All those nights she'd sat beside her, holding her hand and helping her keep the nightmares at bay.

Telling herself that her sister was only acting with the best intentions, Willow gave a helpless kind of smile. 'I was just showing Dante the amazing view of the Sussex Downs.'

Clover slanted her a *who-do-you-think-you're-kidding?* look. 'Ah, yes,' she said, loud enough for the entire first floor corridor to hear. 'Dante. The mystery man who drove you here.'

'My guest,' said Willow indignantly.

'Why didn't you tell us you were bringing him?'
said Clover.

'Maybe she wanted it to be a surprise,' came a
drawling voice, and Willow didn't need to turn round
to know that Dante had walked up behind her. She
could tell from her sister's goggle-eyed expression
even before he placed his hand on her shoulder and
started massaging it, the way she'd seen people do
in films when they were trying to help their partner
relax. *So why did the tight tension inside her body
suddenly feel as if it was spiralling out of control?*

'This is…this is Dante,' she said, hearing the hesi-
tance of her words. 'Dante Di Sione.'

'I'm very pleased to meet you, Dante.' Clover's
face took on the judgemental expression for which she
was famous within the family. 'Perhaps Willow could
bear to share you enough to bring you downstairs for
coffee, so that everyone can meet you. My mother is
particularly keen to make your acquaintance.'

'I can hardly wait,' murmured Dante, increasing
the pressure of his impromptu massage by a fraction.

Willow had barely shut the door on her sister before Dante turned her round to face him, his hands
on her upper arms, his lapis lazuli gaze boring into
her.

'Why do you let her speak to you like that?' he demanded. 'Why didn't you just ignore her, or tell her
you were busy? Surely she has enough imagination
to realise we were making out?'

Willow gave a half-hearted shrug. 'She's very persistent. They all are.'

He frowned. 'What usually happens when you
bring a man home with you?'

Willow licked her lips. Now they were on dangerous territory, and if she told him the truth, she suspected he'd run a mile. Instead, she shot him a challenging look. 'Why, are you afraid of my sisters, Dante?'

'I don't give a damn about your sisters.' He pulled her close against him. 'I'd just like to continue what we were doing a few minutes ago. Now…' His hand cupped her aching breast once more. 'Where were we, can you remember?'

For a minute Willow let him caress her nipple and her eyes fluttered to a close as he began to nuzzle at her neck. She could feel the renewed rush of heat to her body and she wondered how long it would take. Whether they would have time to do it properly. But what if it hurt? What if she *bled*? Pulling away from him, she met the frustration in his eyes.

Was she about to lose her mind? *Of course they wouldn't have time.* She'd waited a long time to have sex—years and years, to be precise—so why rush it and then have to go downstairs in an embarrassing walk of shame, to face her judgemental family who would be assembled in the drawing room like a circle of vultures?

'We've got to go downstairs,' she said. 'For…for coffee.'

'I don't want coffee,' he growled. 'I want you.'

There was a pause before she could summon up the courage to say it and when she did it came out in a breathless rush. 'And I want you.'

'So?'

'So I'm going to be a bridesmaid and I have to get my hair and make-up done before the ceremony.'

She swallowed. 'And there'll be plenty of time for that…later.'

Knowing he was fighting a losing battle—something he always went out of his way to avoid—Dante walked over to the window, trying to calm his acutely aroused body before having to go downstairs to face her frightful family.

He wondered what had made her so surprisingly compliant when her sister had come up here snooping around. He wondered what had happened to the woman who had flirted so boldly with him at the airport. The one who had demanded he be her escort as the price for returning his bag. He'd had her down as one of those independent free spirits who would give great sex—and her going-up-in-flames reaction every time he laid a finger on her had only reinforced that theory.

Yet from the moment he'd driven up the long drive to her impressive but rather faded country house, she had become ridiculously docile. He stared out at the breathtaking view. The magnificence of the distant landscape reminded him of his own family home, back in the States. Somewhere he'd left when he'd gone away to boarding school at the age of eight, and to which he had never really returned. Certainly not for any great length of time. His mouth twisted. Because wasn't it something of a travesty to call the Long Island place a *family home*? It was nothing but a grand house built on some very expensive real estate—with a magnificent facade which concealed all kinds of dirty secrets.

He turned back to find Willow watching him, her grey gaze wary and her manner slightly hesitant—

as if she expected him to say that he had changed
his mind and was about to leave. He suddenly found
himself thinking that she reminded him of a delicate gazelle.

'Why are you suddenly so uptight?' he questioned.
'Is something wrong?'

Willow stilled and if she hadn't fancied him so
much she might have told him the whole story. But it
was precisely *because* she fancied him so much that
she couldn't. He'd start treating her differently. He'd
be overcautious when he touched her. He might not
even *want* to touch her. Because that was the thing
with illness—it did more than affect the person it
struck; it affected everyone around you. People who
were mature and sensible might try to deny it, but
didn't they sometimes behave as if the illness she'd
once had was in some way contagious?

And why *shouldn't* she forget about that period in
her life? She'd been given the all-clear ages ago and
now was her chance to get something she'd wanted
for a very long time. Something as powerful and as
uncomplicated as sexual fulfilment, with a man she
suspected would be perfect for the purpose, as long
as she reminded herself not to read too much into it.
For the first time in her life, she had to reach out for
what she wanted. Not the things that other women
wanted—because she wasn't asking for the impossible. She wasn't clamouring for marriage and babies—
just a brief and heady sexual relationship with Dante
Di Sione. But she had to be proactive.

She smiled into his hard blue eyes. 'I think it's
because I'm the youngest, and they've always been
a little protective of me. You know how it is.' She

began to walk across the room towards him, pluck-ing up the courage to put her arms around his neck. This close she could see into his eyes perfectly. And although she was short on experience, she recognised the desire which was making them grow so smoky.

And if she detected a flicker of suspicion lurking in their depths, then surely it was up to her to keep those suspicions at bay.

'I don't want to do it in a rush. I want to savour every single moment,' she whispered, trying to sound as if she made sexual assignations with men every day of the week. 'And don't they say that the best things in life are worth waiting for?'

He framed her face in his hands and there was a split second when she thought he was about to bend his head and kiss her, but he didn't. He just stared at her for a very long time, with the kind of look in his eyes which made a shiver trickle down her spine.

'I hear what you're saying and I am prepared to take it on board. But be very clear that I am not a pa-tient man, Willow—and I have a very low boredom threshold. Better not keep me waiting too long,' he said roughly as he levered her away from him, in the direction of the door.

CHAPTER FIVE

DANTE GLANCED AROUND at the guests who were standing on the newly mown lawn drinking champagne. He risked another glance at his watch and wondered how soon this would be over and he could get Willow into bed—but like all weddings, this one seemed never-ending.

The place had been a hive of activity all afternoon. The faded grandeur of Willow's vast home had been transformed by legions of adoring locals, who had carried armfuls of flowers from the nearby village to decorate the house and gardens. Hedges had been trimmed and Chinese lanterns strung high in the trees. Rough wooden trestle tables had been covered with white cloths before being decked with grapes and roses and tiny flickering tealights.

It quickly dawned on him that the Hamiltons were the kind of aristocratic family with plenty of cachet but very little cash. The ceremony had taken place in *their own church*—he found that quite hard to believe—a small but freezing building situated within the extensive grounds. The bride looked okay—but then, all brides looked the same, in Dante's opinion. She wore a white dress and a veil and the service had been interminable. No change there. But he'd found himself unable to tear his eyes away from Willow as she'd made her way up the aisle. He thought how beautiful she looked, despite a deeply unflattering dress and a smile which suggested that, like him, she'd rather be somewhere else.

Before the ceremony he had endured a meet-and-greet with her family over some unspeakable coffee, drunk in a room hung with dusty old paintings. Flora and Clover he'd already met and the remaining sibling was called Poppy—a startlingly pretty girl with grey eyes like Willow's, who seemed as keen to question him as her sisters had been. Their attitude towards him had been one of unrestrained suspicion. They were curious about where he and Willow had met and how long they'd been an item. They seemed surprised to hear he lived in Paris and they wondered how often he was seeing their sister. And because Dante didn't like being interrogated and because he wasn't sure what Willow had told them, he was deliberately vague.

Her parents had appeared at one point. Her mother was tall and still beautiful, with cheekbones as high as Willow's own. She was wearing what looked like her husband's old smoking jacket over a dress and a pair of wellington boots and smiled rather distractedly when Dante shook her hand.

But her attitude changed the instant she caught sight of Willow, who had been over on the other side of the room, finding him a cup of coffee. 'Are you okay, darling? You're not tiring yourself out?'

Just what *was* it with these people? Dante wondered. Was that a warning look from Sister Number Three being slanted in his direction? He *got* that Willow prob-ably didn't bring a lot of men home and he *got* that as the youngest daughter she would be a little overpro-tected. But they seemed to be fussing around her as if she was some kind of teenager, rather than a woman in her mid-twenties. And she seemed to be letting them.

But now the wedding was over, the photo session was finished and he was standing on a warm sum-mer's evening with a growing sense of sexual antici-pation. He felt his mouth dry as he glanced across the lawn, to where Willow was listening to something her mother was saying, obediently nodding her blond head, which was woven with blooms and making her look even more ethereal than before. Her dress em-phasised the razor-sharp slant of her collarbones and the slenderness of her bare arms.

Maybe her intrinsic delicacy was the reason why everyone seemed to treat her with kid gloves. And why her gaggle of interfering sisters seemed to boss her around so much.

Her mother walked off and Dante put his untouched drink onto a table, walking through the growing dusk until he was standing in front of her. He watched as her expression underwent a series of changes. He saw shy-ness as well as that now-familiar wariness in her eyes, but he saw desire too—and that desire lit something inside him and made him want to touch her again.

'Dance with me,' he said.

With a quick bite of her lip, she shook her head. 'I'd better not. I have masses of things I need to do.'

'It wasn't a question, Willow,' he said, pulling her into his arms. 'It was a command and I won't toler-ate anyone who disobeys my commands.'

'That's an outrageous thing to say.'

'So outrageous it's made you shiver with desire?'

'I'm not.'

'Yes, you are.' Pulling her against his body, he breathed in the scent of flowers which made him long to remove that fussy dress and have her naked in his arms. He'd had enough of behaving like a teenager— only getting so far before another of her damned sisters interrupted them. He slid his hand over her ribcage, his heart thundering as his fingertips stroked the slippery satin. 'So how long does this damned wedding go on for?'

'Oh, ages,' she said, but the sudden breathlessness in her voice coincided with his thumb casually beginning to circle the area beneath her breast. 'We haven't even had the speeches yet.'

'That's what's worrying me,' he said, swinging her round and thinking how slight she was. He remembered how feather-light she'd felt when he'd carried her over to that ridiculously tiny bed and he wished he was on that bed right now with his mouth on her breast and his fingers between her legs. 'I don't know how much longer I can wait,' he said huskily.

'Wait?' She drew her head back and it was as if she had suddenly recognised her power over him, because her grey eyes were dancing with mischief. 'Yes, I suppose you must be hungry. Well, don't worry— supper won't be long. Just as soon as my father and the best man have spoken.'

In answer, he pressed his hardness against her with a sudden calculated stamp of sexual mastery and watched as her pupils dilated in response. 'I want you,' he said, very deliberately. 'And I'm tempted to take you by the hand and get us lost in these enormous grounds. I'd like to find somewhere sheltered, like the shade of a big tree, so that I could explore what you're wearing underneath that monstrosity of a dress. I'd like to make you come very quickly. In fact, I think I could make myself come right now, just by thinking about it.'

'Dante!'

'Yes, Willow?'

She drew away from him, trembling slightly, and once again he was confused, because wasn't she just a mass of contradictions? One minute she was so hot that he almost scorched his fingers when he touched her—and the next she was looking up at him with reproachful grey eyes, like some delicate flower he was in danger of crushing beneath the full force of his desire. And that was how her family treated her, wasn't it? Like she couldn't be trusted to make her own judgements and look after herself.

'You're very…'

'Very what?' He stalled her sentence with the brush of his lips against her cheek and felt her shiver again.

'D-demanding,' she managed.

'Don't you like me being demanding?'

Willow closed her eyes as he tightened his arms around her, distracted by the heat of his body and acutely aware that they were being watched. *Of course they were being watched.* Dante Di Sione was easily the most watchable man here—and hadn't that been one of the reasons she'd demanded his company? To show people that she was capable of attracting such a man? But suddenly it felt like much more than just *pretending* to be his lover; she wanted to *be* his lover. She wanted it to be real. She wanted to be like everyone else, but she couldn't. So she was just going to have to make the best of what she was capable of, wasn't she?

'Yes,' she whispered. 'I like it very much. It's just not very appropriate right now. We're in the middle of a crowd of people and there are things I'm supposed to be doing.'

'Like what?'

'Checking that everyone's got a drink so they can make a toast once the speeches start. And introducing people who don't know each other—that sort of thing.'

'All this hanging around and waiting is very dull,' he observed.

'Then circulate,' she said lightly. 'That's what people do.'

'I've done nothing *but* circulate,' he growled. 'I think I'll go crazy if I have to endure yet another society matron trying to calculate what my net worth is.'

She tilted her head back and studied him. 'So how do you usually cope with weddings?'

'By avoiding them whenever possible.'

'But you were unable to avoid this one?'

'It seems I was.'

She narrowed her eyes at him. 'There must be something very valuable in that bag to make you want it so much.'

'Right now, I want you far more than anything in that damned bag.'

Willow giggled, feeling a sudden heady rush of excitement which had more to do with the way he was making her feel than the glass of punch she'd drunk. 'Which was a very neat way of avoiding my question.'

'I don't remember you actually asking a question and it's the only answer you're going to get. So when can we leave?'

'After the cake has been cut,' she said breathlessly. 'Look, there are the main players getting ready to speak and I'm supposed to be up at the top table. I'll see you in a while.'

She tore herself away from his arms, aware of his gaze burning into her as she walked across the garden, but at that moment she was on such a high that she felt as if she could have floated over the candlelit lawn.

It didn't take Flora long to bring her right back down to earth as she joined her in the throng of Hamiltons at the top table.

'I've looked him up on the internet,' she said as soon as Willow was in earshot.

'Who?'

'Who do you think? The man who drove you here today in his flashy red sports car,' replied her sister. 'Mr Macho.'

Willow reached for a glass of champagne from a passing waitress and took a sip as her gaze drifted over towards Dante's statuesque form, which seemed to stand out from the milling crowd. 'He's gorgeous, isn't he?' she said, without really thinking.

'Nobody's denying that,' said Flora slowly. 'And I'm guessing that if you've brought him here, it must be serious?'

'Well, I suppose so,' said Willow evasively.

Flora lowered her voice. 'So you're aware that he's

an *international playboy* with lovers in every major city in the world who is also known as a complete maverick in the world of business?'

Willow took a mouthful of fizz. 'So what? I'm not planning some kind of corporate takeover with him.'

'He's way out of your league, love,' said Flora gently. 'He's a wolf and you're an innocent little lamb. You haven't exactly had a lot of experience with the opposite sex, have you?'

'Only because my family is too busy mounting an armed guard around me!'

Flora frowned. 'So what exactly is going on between you?'

There was a pause. 'I like him,' said Willow truthfully. 'I like him a lot.'

It was perhaps unfortunate that Great-aunt Maud should have chosen just that moment to drift past in a cloud of magenta chiffon and gardenia perfume, blinking rapidly as she caught the tail end of their conversation. 'So does that mean you're going to be next up the aisle, Willow?' She beamed, without waiting for an answer. 'I must say I'm not surprised. He is quite something, that young man of yours. Quite something.'

Dante listened to the formal speeches which always bored the hell out of him and steadfastly ignored the redhead who was flashing him an eager smile. But for once the sentiments expressed went beyond the usual gags about mothers-in-law and shotguns. The groom thanked all the bridesmaids and told them how beautiful they looked, but he left Willow until last, and suddenly his voice grew serious.

'I'd just like to say how much it meant to Clover, having Willow's support. But much more than that is having her here today, looking so lovely. It means… well, it means everything to us.'

Dante frowned as people began to cheer, wondering why the atmosphere had grown distinctly *poignant* and why Willow's mother was suddenly groping in her bag for a handkerchief.

But then Willow's father began speaking and after he had waxed long and lyrical about the bride, he paused before resuming—his eyes resting affectionately on the slender blonde in the bridesmaid dress who was twisting the peachy satin around her fingers and looking slightly awkward.

'I just want to echo Dominic's words and say how happy we are to see Willow here today looking, if I might add, positively radiant. We just want her to know how proud we are of her, and the way she handled her illness, when all her peers were running around without a care in the world. And how her recovery has made us all feel very, very grateful.'

The applause which followed was deafening and Dante's lips froze as suddenly it all made sense.

Of *course.*

That's why she looked so fragile and that's why her family fussed around her and were so protective of her.

She'd been ill.

How ill? It must have been bad for it to warrant a mention in not one but *two* of the wedding speeches.

He felt momentarily winded. Like that time when a tennis ball hit by his twin had slammed straight into his solar plexus. He had been itching to take Willow away from here as soon as the speeches were over, but suddenly he needed time. And distance. Because how could he now take her to bed in the light of what he had learned?

Did Willow sense where he was in the throng of people? Was that why her grey eyes suddenly turned to meet his? Only this time it was more than desire which pumped through his veins as his gaze connected with hers. It was a cocktail of emotions he was unfamiliar with. He felt sympathy and a flare of something which clenched his heart with a sensation close to pain. The sense that life was unfair. And yet why should that come as a surprise, when he'd learnt the lesson of life's unfairness at the age of eight, when his entire world had changed for ever?

Why the hell hadn't she told him?

He watched as the smile she was directing at him became slightly uncertain and she picked up her glass and took a mouthful of champagne. And part of him wanted to run. To get into his car and drive back to London. To fly on to Paris as soon as possible and put this whole incident behind him. Yet he couldn't do that—and not just because she still had his grandfather's precious tiara. He couldn't just turn his back on her and walk away. If she'd known real suffering, then she deserved his compassion and his respect.

He saw all the women lining up and giggling and wondered what was happening, when he realised that the bride was about to throw her bouquet. And he wondered why it came as no real sense of surprise when Willow caught it, to the accompaniment of more loud cheers.

He couldn't stay here. He could see some of her

relatives smiling at him, almost—*God forbid*—as if they were preparing to welcome him into the fold and he knew that he had to act. Ignoring the redhead with the cleavage who had been edging closer and closer, he walked straight up to Willow and took the empty champagne glass from her hand.

'Let's get out of here.'

He couldn't miss the look of relief on her face.

'I thought you'd never ask,' she said, sounding a little unsteady.

On her high-heeled shoes she was tottering as they walked across the darkening grass as if she'd had a little too much to drink—but for once Dante wasn't about to take the moral high ground.

He waited for her to mention the speeches, but she didn't. She was too busy weaving her fingers into his and squeezing them. He thought again about her father's words and how her experience had affected her. It meant she'd probably learnt in the hardest way possible about the fragility of life and the random way that trouble could strike. He wondered if she'd plumped for recklessness as a result of that. Was that why she would have had sex with him before the wedding had even started, if her damned sister hadn't interrupted them? He wondered if she was this free with everyone—an aristocratic wild child who'd learned to be liberal with her body. And he was unprepared for the sudden dark shaft of anger which slammed into him.

They reached her room without meeting anyone and the sounds of celebration drifted up through the open windows as she shut the bedroom door behind them and switched on a small lamp. He could hear music and laughter and the rising lull of snatched conversation, but there was no joy in Dante's heart right then.

She leaned against the door, her shiny ruffled dress gleaming and her grey eyes looking very bright. 'So,' she said, darting a rather embarrassed glance at the bride's bouquet she was still holding, before quickly putting it down on a nearby table. 'Now what?'

He wished he could wipe what he'd heard from his mind, leaving his conscience free to do what he really wanted—which was to walk over there and remove her dress. To take off her bra and her panties and strip himself bare, before entering that pale and slim body with one slow and exquisite thrust.

He went to stand by the window, with his back to the strings of Chinese lanterns which gleamed in the trees.

'Did you enjoy the wedding, Willow?' he asked carefully.

She walked across the room, pulling the wilting crown of flowers from her head and placing it on the dressing table, and a clip which clattered onto the wooden floor sounded unnaturally loud.

'It was okay,' she said, taking out another clip, and then another, before putting them down. She turned around then, her hair spilling over her shoulders, and there was a faint look of anxiety in her eyes, as if she had just picked up from his tone that something was different. She licked her lips. 'Did you?'

He shook his head. 'No, not really. But then, I'm not really a big fan of weddings.'

Her smile became a little brittle. 'Oh, well, at least

it's over now,' she said. 'So why don't we just take our minds off it?'

She began to walk unsteadily towards him and Dante knew he had to stop this before it went any further. Before he did something he might later regret. But it was hard to resist her when she looked so damned lovely. There was something so compelling about her. Something pure and untouched which contrasted with the hungry look in her eyes and the wanton spill of her half-pinned hair. She looked like a little girl playing the part of vamp.

He shook his head. 'No, Willow.'

But she kept on walking towards him until she was standing in front of him in her long dress. And now she was winding her arms around his neck and clinging on to him like a tender vine and the desire to kiss her was like a fever raging in his blood.

Briefly, he closed his eyes as if that would help him resist temptation, but it didn't—because the feel of her was just as distracting as the sight of her. And maybe she took that as an invitation—because she brushed her mouth over his with a tentative exploration which made him shiver. With an angry little groan he succumbed to the spiralling of desire as he deepened the kiss. He felt the kick of his heart as her hands began to move rather frantically over him, and what could he do but respond?

She was tugging at his tie as he started to caress the slender lines of her body, his fingers sliding helplessly over the slippery material. He felt her sway and picked her up, carrying her over to the bed, like a man acting on autopilot. She lay there, almost swamped by the silky folds of her bridesmaid dress, and as his hand reached out to stroke its way over her satin-covered breast, he felt a savage jerk of lust.

'Oh, Dante,' she breathed—and that heartfelt little note of wonder was almost his undoing.

Would it be so wrong to take her? To have her gasp out her pleasure and him do the same, especially when they both wanted it so badly? Surely it would be a *good* thing to end this rather bizarre day with some uncomplicated and mindless sex.

Except that it wouldn't be uncomplicated. Or mindless. Not in the light of what he'd learned. Because she was vulnerable. Of course she was. And he couldn't treat her as he would treat any other woman. He couldn't just strip her naked and pleasure her and take what he wanted for himself before walking away. She had gone through too much to be treated as something disposable.

With an effort which tore at him like a physical pain, he moved away from the bed and went to stand by the window, where the darkness of the garden was broken by the flickering gleam of candlelight. Tiny pinpricks of light glittered on every surface, like fallen stars. Beneath the open window he could hear a couple talking in low voices which then abruptly stopped and something told him they were kissing. Was that envy he felt? Envy that he couldn't just forget everything he knew and block out his reservations with a kiss?

It took several moments for the hunger to leave him, and when he had composed himself sufficiently, he turned back to find her sitting up on the bed looking at him—confusion alternating with the desire which was skating across her fine-boned features.

He drew in a deep breath. 'Why didn't you tell me you'd been so ill?'

Willow's first reaction was one of rage as his words fired into her skin like sharp little arrows. Rage that her father and Dominic should have seen fit to include the information *in their speeches* and rage that he should suddenly have started talking to her in that new and gentle voice. She didn't want him to be *gentle* with her—she wanted him hot and hungry. She wanted him tugging impatiently at her clothes like he'd been before, as if he couldn't wait to strip her bare.

'What does that have to do with anything?' she demanded. 'I had leukaemia as a child. What's the big deal?'

'It's a pretty big deal, Willow.'

'Only if people choose to make it one,' she gritted out. 'Especially since I've had the all-clear, which makes me as disease-free as you or the rest of the general population. What did you want me to do, Dante? Tell you all about the drugs and the side effects and the way my hair fell out, or how difficult it was to actually keep food down? When it comes to interacting with men, it's not exactly what they want to hear as a chat-up line. It doesn't really make you attractive towards the opposite sex.' She glared. 'Why the hell did Dom and my father have to say anything?'

'I think I might have worked it out for myself,' he said slowly. 'Because I'd had my suspicions ever since we arrived.'

'You had your *suspicions*?' she echoed angrily.

'Sure. I wondered why your sisters were acting as

if I was the big, bad ogre and I wondered why everyone was so protective of you. It took me a while to work out why that might be, but now I think I have.'

'So once I was very sick and now I'm not,' she said flippantly. 'End of subject, surely?'

'But it's a little bit more complicated than that, Willow?' he said slowly. 'Isn't it?'

For a minute she stiffened as she thought he might have learned about her biggest fear and secret, before she told herself he couldn't know. He wasn't *that* perceptive and she'd certainly never discussed it with anyone else. 'What are you talking about?' she questioned.

His eyes narrowed. 'Something tells me you've never brought a man back here before. Have you?'

Willow felt humiliation wash over her and in that moment she hated Dante Di Sione's perception and that concerned way he was looking at her. She didn't want him looking at her with *concern*—she wanted him looking at her with *lust*. *So brazen it out*, she told herself. *You've come this far. You've dismissed your illness, so deal with the rest.* She had him here with her—a captive audience—and judging by his body language, he still wanted her just as much as she wanted him.

'And how did you manage to work that out?' she questioned.

His eyes were boring into her, still with that horrible, unwanted perception.

'Just that every time I was introduced as your partner, people expressed a kind of barely concealed astonishment. I mean, I know I have something of a reputation where women are concerned, but they were acting like I was the devil incarnate.'

For a second Willow thought about lying to him. About telling him that his was just another anonymous face in a sea of men she'd brought here. But why tell him something she'd be unable to carry off? She didn't think she was *that* good a liar. And all she wanted was for that warm feeling to come back. She wanted him to kiss her again. She wasn't asking for commitment—she knew she could never be in a position to ask for that. All she wanted was to be in his arms again.

She thought about the person she'd been when he'd met her at the airport—that bold and flirtatious Willow she'd never dared be before—and Dante had seemed to like that Willow, hadn't he? She was certainly a more attractive proposition than the woman sitting huddled on the bed, meekly listening to him berate her.

'I thought you would be the kind of man who wouldn't particularly want a woman to burden you with every second of her past.'

'That much is true,' he conceded reluctantly.

'So, what's your beef?'

Rather unsteadily, she got off the bed, and before he could stop her she'd reached behind her to slide down the zip of her bridesmaid dress, so that it pooled around her ankles in a shimmering circle.

Willow had never stood in front of a man in her underwear before and she'd always wondered what it would feel like—whether she would feel shy or uninhibited or just plain self-conscious. But she could still feel the effect of the champagne she'd drunk and, more than that, the look on his face was powerful enough to drive every inhibition from her mind. Because Dante looked almost *tortured* as she stepped out from the circle of satin and stood before him wearing nothing but her underwear and a pair of high-heeled shoes.

And although people often told her she looked as if she could do with a decent meal, Willow knew from her time working in the fashion industry that slenderness worked in your favour when you were wearing nothing but a bra and a pair of pants. She could see his gaze lingering on the swell of her breasts in the ivory-coloured lace bra which was embroidered with tiny roses. Reluctantly, it travelled down to her bare stomach before seeming to caress the matching thong, lingering longest on the flimsy triangle and making her ache there.

Feeling as if she was playing out a part she'd seen in a film, she lifted her fingers to her breast and cupped the slight curve. As she ran her finger along a twist of leaves, she thought she saw him move, as if he was about to cross the room and take her in his arms after all, and she held her breath in anticipation.

But he didn't.

Instead a little nerve began working furiously at his temple as he patted his pocket, until he'd found his car keys.

'And I think that's my cue to leave,' he said harshly.

'No!' The word came out in a rush. 'Please, Dante. I don't want you to go.'

'I'm sorry. I'm out of here.'

'Dante…'

'No. Listen to me, Willow.' There was a pause

while he seemed to be composing himself, and when he started speaking, his words sounded very controlled. 'For what it's worth, I think you're lovely. Very lovely. A beautiful butterfly of a woman. But I'm not going to have sex with you.'

She swallowed. 'Because you don't want me?'

His voice grew rough. 'You know damned well I want you.'

She lifted her eyes to his. 'Then why?'

He seemed to hesitate and Willow got the distinct feeling that he was going to say something dismissive, or tell her that he didn't owe her any kind of explanation. But to her surprise, he didn't. His expression took on that almost gentle look again and she found herself wanting to hurl something at him…preferably herself. To tell him not to wrap her up in cotton wool the way everyone else did. To treat her like she was made of flesh and blood instead of something fragile and breakable. To make her feel like that passionate woman he'd brought to life in his arms.

'Because I'm the kind of man who brings women pain, and you've probably had enough of that in your life. Don't make yourself the willing recipient of any more.' He met the question in her eyes. 'I'm incapable of giving women what they want and I'm not talking about sex. I don't do emotion, or love, or commitment, because I don't really know how those things work. When people tell me that I'm cold and unfeeling, I don't get offended—because I know it's true. There's nothing deep about me, Willow—and there never will be.'

Willow drew in a breath. It was now or never. It was a huge risk—but so what? What did she have to lose when the alternative of not having him suddenly seemed unbearable? 'But that's all I want from you,' she whispered. 'Sex.'

His face hardened as he shook his head.

'And I certainly don't have sex with virgins,' he finished flatly.

She stared at him in disbelief. 'But…how on earth could you tell I was a virgin?' she whispered, her voice quivering with disappointment, before realising from his brief, hard smile that she had just walked into some sort of trap.

'Call it an informed guess,' he said drily. 'And it's the reason why I have to leave.'

The hurt and the rejection Willow was feeling was now replaced by a far more real concern as she realised he meant it. He was going to leave her there, aching and alone and having to face everyone in the morning.

Reaching down to the bed, she grabbed at the duvet which was lying on the bed and wrapped it around herself, so that it covered her in an unflattering white cloud. And then she looked into the icy glitter of his eyes, willing him not to walk away. 'If you go now, it will just cause a big scene. It will make people gossip and stir up all kinds of questions. And I don't think I can face them. Or rather, I don't want to face them. Please don't make me. Don't go,' she said urgently. 'At least, not tonight. Let's pretend that you're my lover, even if it's not true. Let me show my sisters and my family that I'm a grown-up woman who doesn't need their protection any more. I want to break free from their well-meaning intervention, and you're the person who can help me. So help me, Dante. Don't make me face them alone in the morning.'

Dante heard the raw appeal in her voice and realised how difficult that must have been for her to say.
She seemed so vulnerable that part of him wanted to
go over there and comfort her. To cradle her in his
arms and tell her everything was going to be all right.
But he couldn't do that with any degree of certainty,
could he? He didn't even trust himself to touch her
without going back on his word and it was vital he
kept to his self-imposed promise.

'This is a crazy situation,' he growled. 'Which
is going to get even crazier if I stay. I'm sorry, Willow—but I can't do it.'

In the distance, the music suddenly came to a halt
and the sound of clapping drifted in through the open
windows.

'But I still have your bag,' she said quietly. 'And I
thought you badly wanted it back.'

There was a pause.

'Are you...*threatening* me?' he questioned.

She shrugged. 'I thought we had a deal.'

He met her grey gaze and an unwilling feeling of
admiration flooded through him as he realised that
she meant it. And even though she wouldn't have
had a leg to stand on if he had decided to offer *real*
resistance, he knew he couldn't do it. Because there
were only so many setbacks a person could take—and
she'd had more than her fair share of them.

'Okay,' he said at last. 'The deal still stands,
though the terms have changed. And this is what
we're going to do. You are going to get ready for
bed in the bathroom and you're going to wear something—anything—I don't care what it is as long as
it covers you up. You are then going to get into bed

and I don't want to hear another word from you until morning, when we will leave for London before anyone else is awake, because I have no intention of facing your family first thing and having to continue with this ridiculous farce.'

'But…where will you sleep?'

With a faint feeling of disbelief that he should be consigning himself to a celibate night, he pointed to a faded velvet chaise longue on the opposite side of the room. 'Over there,' he said.

'Dante…'

'No,' he said, his patience dwindling as he moved away from her, because despite the fact that she was swaddled beneath that fat, white duvet, the image of her slender body wearing nothing but her bra and pants was seared into his memory. He swallowed. 'I want you to do that right now, or the deal is off— and if I have to drive myself back to London and break into your apartment in order to retrieve what is rightfully mine, then I will do it. Do you understand, Willow?'

She met his eyes and nodded with an obedience which somehow made his heart twist.

'Yes, Dante,' she said. 'I understand.'

CHAPTER SIX

THE STRONG SMELL of coffee filtered into her senses, waking Willow from her restless night. Slowly, her eyelids flickered open to see Dante standing by her bed with a steaming mug in his hand. He was already dressed, though looked as if he could do with a shave, because his jaw was dark and shadowed.

So were his eyes.

'Where did you find the coffee?' she asked.

'Where do you think I found it? In the kitchen. And before you ask, the answer is no. Everyone else in the house must be sleeping off their hangover because I didn't bump into anyone else along the way.'

Willow nodded. It was like a bad dream. Actually, it was more like a nightmare. She'd spent the night alone in her childhood bed, covered up in a baggy T-shirt and a pair of pants, while Dante slept on the chaise longue on the other side of the room.

Pushing her hair away from her face, she sat up and stared out of the windows. Neither of them had drawn the drapes last night and the pale blue of the morning sky was edged with puffy little white clouds. The birds were singing fit to burst and the powerful scent of roses drifted in on the still-cool air. It was

an English morning at its loveliest and yet its beauty
seemed to mock her. It reminded her of all the things
she didn't have. All the things she probably never
would have. It made her think about the disaster of
the wedding the day before. She thought about her
sister laughing up at her new husband with love shining from her eyes. About the youngest flower girl,
clutching her posy with dimpled fists. About the tiny
wail of a baby in the church, and the shushing noises
of her mother as she'd carried the crying infant outside, to the understanding smiles of the other women
present, like they were all members of that exclusive
club called *Mothers*.

A twist of pain like a knife in her heart momentarily caught Willow off-guard and it took a moment
before she had composed herself enough to turn to
look into Dante's bright blue eyes.

'What time is it?' she asked.

'Still early.' His iced gaze swept over her. 'How
long will it take you to get ready?'

'Not long.'

'Good,' he said, putting the coffee down on the
bedside table and then walking over to the other side
of the room to stare out of the window. 'Then just do
it, and let's get going as soon as possible, shall we?'

It was couched as a question but there was no disguising the fact that it was another command.

'What about my parents?'

'Leave them a note.'

She wanted to tell him that her mother would hit
the roof if she just slunk away without even having
breakfast, but she guessed what his response would
be. He would shrug and tell her she was welcome to

stay. And she didn't *want* to stay here, without him. She wanted to keep her pathetic fantasy alive for a while longer. She wanted people to see what wasn't really true. Willow with her boyfriend. Willow who'd just spent the night with a devastatingly attractive man. Lucky Willow.

Only she wasn't lucky at all, was she?

Sliding out of bed, she grabbed her clothes and took the quickest shower on record as she tried very hard not to think about the way she'd pleaded with Dante to have sex with her the night before. Or the way he'd turned her down. He'd told her it was because he was cold and sometimes cruel. He'd told her he didn't want to hurt her and maybe that was thoughtfulness on his part—how ironic, then, that he had ended up by hurting her anyway.

Dressing in jeans and a T-shirt and twisting her hair into a single plait, Willow returned to the bedroom, drank her cooled coffee and then walked with Dante through the blessedly quiet corridors towards the back of the house.

She should have realised it was too good to be true, because there, standing by the kitchen door wearing a silky dressing gown and a pair of flip-flops, stood her mother. Willow stared at her in dismay. Had she heard her and Dante creeping through the house, or was this yet another example of the finely tuned antennae her mother always seemed able to call upon whenever she was around?

'M-Mum,' stumbled Willow awkwardly.

A pair of eyebrows were arched in her direction. 'Going somewhere?'

Willow felt her cheeks grow pink and was rack-

ing her brains about what to say, when Dante inter-
cepted.

'You must forgive us for slipping away so early
after such a fabulous day yesterday, Mrs Hamilton—
but I have a pile of work I need to get through before
I go back to Paris and Willow has promised to help
me.' He smiled. 'Haven't you?'

Willow had never seen her mother look quite so
flustered—but how could she possibly object in the
face of all that undeniable charm and charisma Dante
was directing at her? She saw the quick flare of hope
in her mother's eyes. Was she in danger of project-
ing into the future, just as Great-aunt Maud had done
last night?

Kissing her mother goodbye she and Dante went
outside, but during the short time she'd spent getting
ready, the puffy white clouds had accumulated and
spread across the sky like foam on a cup of macchi-
ato. Suddenly, the air had a distinct chill and Willow
shivered as Dante put the car roof up and she slid onto
the passenger seat.

It wasn't like the outward journey, when the wind
had rushed through their hair and the sun had shone
and she had been filled with a distinct sensation of
hope and excitement. Enclosed beneath the soft roof,
the atmosphere felt claustrophobic and tense and the
roar of his powerful car sounded loud as it broke the
early-morning Sunday silence.

They drove for a little way without saying anything, and once out on the narrow, leafy lanes, Willow risked a glance at him. His dark hair curled very
slightly over the collar of his shirt and his olive skin
glowed. Despite his obvious lack of sleep and being in

need of a shave, he looked healthy and glowing—like a man at the very peak of his powers, but his profile was set and unmoving.

She cleared her throat. 'Are you angry with me?'

Dante stared straight ahead as the hedgerows passed in a blur of green. He'd spent an unendurable night. Not just because his six-foot-plus frame had dwarfed the antique piece of furniture on which he'd been attempting to sleep, but because he'd felt bad. And it hadn't got any better. He'd been forced to listen to Willow tossing and turning while she slept. To imagine that pale and slender body moving restlessly against the sheet. He'd remembered how she'd felt. How she'd tasted. How she'd begged him to make love to her. He had been filled with a heady sexual hunger which had made him want to explode. He'd wanted her, and yet rejecting her had been his only honourable choice. Because what he'd said had been true. He *did* hurt women. He'd never found one who was capable of chipping her way through the stony walls he'd erected around his heart, and sometimes he didn't think he ever would. And in the meantime, Willow Hamilton needed protection from a man like him.

'I'm angry with myself,' he said.

'Because?'

'Because I should have chosen a less controversial way of getting my bag back. I shouldn't have agreed to be your plus one.' He gave a short laugh. 'But you were very persuasive.'

She didn't answer immediately. He could see her finger drawing little circles over one of the peacocks which adorned her denim-covered thigh.

'There must be something in that bag you want very badly.'

'There is.'

'But I don't suppose you're going to tell me what it is?'

The car had slowed down to allow a stray sheep to pick its way laboriously across the road, giving them a slightly dazed glance as it did so. Dante's instinct was to tell her that her guess was correct, but suddenly he found himself wanting to tell her. Was that because so far he hadn't discussed it with anyone? Because he and his twin brother were estranged and he wasn't particularly close to any of his other siblings? That all their dark secrets and their heartache seemed to have pushed them all apart, rather than bringing them closer together...

'The bag contains a diamond and emerald tiara,' he said. 'Worth hundreds of thousands of dollars.'

Her finger stopped moving. 'You're kidding?'

'No, I'm not. My grandfather specifically asked me to get it for him and it took me weeks to track the damned thing down. He calls it one of his Lost Mistresses, for reasons he's reluctant to explain. He sold it a long time ago and now he wants it back.'

'Do you know why?'

He shrugged. 'Maybe because he's dying.'

'I'm sorry,' she said softly, and he wondered if she'd heard the slight break in his voice.

'Yeah,' he said gruffly, his tightened lips intended to show her that the topic was now closed.

They drove for a while in silence and had just hit the outskirts of greater London, when her voice broke into his thoughts.

'Your name is Italian,' she commented quietly. 'But your accent isn't. Sometimes you sound American, but at other times your accent could almost be Italian, or French. How come?'

Dante thought how women always wanted to do things the wrong way round. Shouldn't she have made chatty little enquiries about his background *before* he'd had his hand inside her panties yesterday? And yet wasn't he grateful that she'd moved from the subject of his family?

'Because I was born in the States,' he said. 'And spent the first eight years of my life there—until I was sent away to boarding school in Europe.'

She nodded and he half expected the usual squeak of indignation. Because women invariably thought they were showcasing their caring side by professing horror at the thought of a little boy being sent away from home so young. But he remembered that the English were different and her aristocratic class in particular had always sent young boys away to school.

'And did you like it?' she questioned.

Dante nodded, knowing his reaction had been unusual—the supposition being that any child would hate being removed from the heart of their family. Except in his case there hadn't been a heart. That had been torn out one dark and drug-fuelled night—shattered and smashed—leaving behind nothing but emptiness, anger and guilt.

'As it happens, I liked it very much,' he drawled, deliberately pushing the bitter thoughts away. 'It was in the Swiss mountains—pure and white and unbelievably beautiful.' He paused as he remembered how the soft white flakes used to swarm down from the sky, blanketing the world in a pure silence—and how he had eagerly retreated into that cold space where nothing or nobody could touch him. 'We used to ski every day, which wore us out so much that there wasn't really time to think. And there were kids from all over the world, so it was kind of anonymous— and I liked that.'

'You must speak another language.'

'I speak three others,' he said. 'French, Italian and German.'

'And that's why you live in Paris?'

His mouth hardened. 'I don't remember mentioning that I lived in Paris.'

Out of the corner of his eye he saw her shoulders slump a little.

'I must have read that on the internet too. You can't blame me,' she said, her words leaving her mouth in a sudden rush.

'No, I don't blame you,' he said. Just as he couldn't blame her for the sudden sexual tension which seemed to have sprung up between them again, which was making it difficult for him to concentrate. Maybe that was inevitable. They were two people who'd been interrupted while making out, leaving them both aching and frustrated. And even though his head was telling him that was the best thing which could have happened, his body seemed to have other ideas.

Because right now all he could think about was how soft her skin had felt as he had skated his fingertips all the way up beneath that flouncy little dress she'd been wearing. He remembered the slenderness of her hips and breasts as she'd stood before him in her bra and panties—defiant yet innocent as she'd stripped off her bridesmaid dress and let it pool around her feet. He'd resisted her then, even though the scent of her arousal had called out to his hungry body on a primitive level which had made resistance almost unendurable. Was that what was happening now? Why he wanted to stop the car and take her somewhere—anywhere—so that he could be alone with her? Free to pull aside her clothes. To unzip her jeans and tease her until she was writhing in helpless appeal.

He wondered if he'd been out of his mind to say no. He could easily have introduced her to limitless pleasures in his arms—and what better initiation for a virgin than lovemaking with someone like him? But it wasn't his technique which was in question, but his inbuilt emotional distance. He couldn't connect. He didn't know how.

'So why Paris?' she was asking.

Make her get the message, he thought. *Make her realise that she's had a lucky escape from a man like you.*

'It's well placed for central Europe,' he said. 'I like the city and the food and the culture. And, of course, the women,' he added deliberately. 'French women are very easy to like.'

'I can imagine they must be,' she said, her voice sounding unnaturally bright.

The car was soon swallowed up by the heavier London traffic and he noticed she was staring fixedly out of the window.

'We're nearly here,' he said, forcing himself to make some conversational remark. To try to draw a line under this as neatly as possible. 'So…have you got any plans for the rest of the day?'

Willow gazed at the familiar wide streets close to her apartment and realised he was preparing to say goodbye to her. What she would like to do more than anything else was to rail against the unfairness of it all. Not only had he turned her down, but he'd deliberately started talking about other women—*French women*—as if to drive home just how forgettable she really was. And he had done it just as she'd been speculating about his fast, international lifestyle. Thinking that he didn't seem like the sort of man who would ever embrace the role of husband and father…the sort of man who really would have been a perfect lover for a woman like her.

Well, she was just going to have to forget her stupid daydreams. Just tick it off and put it down to experience. She would get over it, as she had got over so much else. No way was she going to leave him with an enduring memory of her behaving like a victim. *Remember how he moaned in your arms when he kissed you*, she reminded herself fiercely as she slanted him a smile. *Remember that* you *have some power here, too.*

'I'll probably go for a walk in Regent's Park,' she said. 'The flowers are gorgeous at this time of the year. And I might meet a friend later and catch a film. How about you?'

'I'll pick up my bag from you and then fly straight back to France.' He stifled a yawn. 'It's been an eventful few days.'

And that, thought Willow, was that.

She was glad of all the times when her mother

had drummed in the importance of posture because it meant that she was able to walk into her apartment with her head held very proud and her shoulders as stiff as a ramrod, as Dante followed her inside.

She pulled out the leather case from the bottom of her wardrobe, her fingers closing around it just before she handed it to him.

'I'd love to see the tiara,' she said.

He shook his head. 'Better not.'

'Even though I inadvertently carried a priceless piece of jewellery through customs without declaring it?'

'You shouldn't have picked up the wrong bag.'

You shouldn't have been distracting me. 'And I could now be languishing in some jail somewhere,' she continued.

He gave a slow smile. 'I would have bailed you out.'

'I only have your word for that,' she said.

'And you don't trust my word?'

She shrugged. 'I don't know you well enough to answer that. Besides, oughtn't you to check that the piece is intact? That I haven't substituted something fake in its place—or stolen one of the stones. That this Lost Mistress is in a decent state to give to your grandfather and…'

But her words died away as he began to unlock the leather case and slowly drew out a jewelled tiara—a glittering coronet of white diamonds and almond-size emeralds as green as new leaves. Against Dante's olive skin they sparked their bright fire and it was impossible for Willow to look anywhere else but at them.

'Oh, but they're beautiful,' she breathed. 'Just beautiful.'

Her eyes were shining as she said it and something about her unselfconscious appreciation touched something inside him. And Dante felt a funny twist of regret as he said goodbye. As if he was walking away from something unfinished. It seemed inappropriate to shake her hand, yet he didn't trust himself to kiss her cheek, for he suspected that even the lightest touch would rekindle his desire. He would send her flowers as a thank-you, he decided. Maybe even a diamond on a fine gold chain—you couldn't go wrong with something like that. She'd be able to show it off to her sisters and pretend that their relationship had been real. And one day she would be grateful to him for his restraint. She would accept the truth of what he'd said and realise that someone like him would bring her nothing but heartache. She would find herself some suitable English aristocrat and move to a big house in the country where she could live a life not unlike that of her parents.

He didn't turn on his phone until he was at the airfield because he despised people who allowed themselves to get distracted on the road. But he wished afterwards that he'd checked his messages while he was closer to Willow's apartment. Close enough to go back for a showdown.

As it was, he drove to the airfield in a state of blissful ignorance, and the first he knew about the disruption was when his assistant, René, rushed up to him brandishing a newspaper—a look of astonishment contorting his Gallic features.

'*C'est impossible!* Why didn't you tell me, boss?'

he accused. 'I have been trying to get hold of you all morning, wondering what you want me to say to the press…'

'Why should I want you to say anything to the press?' demanded Dante impatiently. 'When you know how much I hate them.'

His assistant gave a flamboyant shake of his head. 'I think their sudden interest is understandable, in the circumstances.'

Dante frowned. 'What the hell are you talking about?'

'It is everywhere!' declared René. 'Absolutely everywhere! All of Paris is buzzing with the news that the bad-boy American playboy has fallen in love at last—and that you are engaged to an English aristocrat called Willow Anoushka Hamilton.'

CHAPTER SEVEN

WILLOW FELT RESTLESS after Dante had left, unable to settle to anything. Distractedly, she wandered around her apartment—except that never had it felt more like living in someone else's space than it did right then. It seemed as if the charismatic American had invaded the quiet rooms and left something of himself behind. She couldn't seem to stop thinking about his bright blue eyes and hard body and the plummeting of her heart as he'd said goodbye.

She slipped on a pair of sneakers and let herself outside, but for once the bright colours of the immaculate flower beds in the nearby park were wasted on her. It was funny how your thoughts could keep buzzing and buzzing around your head, just like the pollen-laden bees which were clinging like crazy to stop themselves from toppling off the delicate blooms.

She thought about the chaste night she'd spent with Dante. She thought about the way he'd kissed her and the way she'd been kissed in the past. But up until now she'd always clammed up whenever a man touched her. She'd started to believe that she wasn't capable of real passion. That maybe she was incapable of reacting like a normal woman. But Dante Di Sione had awoken something in her the moment he'd touched her. *And then walked away just because she'd been ill as a kid.*

She bought a pint of milk on her way home from the park and was in the kitchen making coffee when the loud shrill of the doorbell penetrated the uncomfortable swirl of her thoughts. She wasn't really concentrating when she went into the hall to see who it was, startled to see Dante standing on her doorstep with a look on his face she couldn't quite work out.

She blinked at him, aware of the thunder of her heart and the need to keep her reaction hidden. To try to hide the sudden flash of hope inside her. Had he changed his mind? Did he realise that he only had to say the word and she would be sliding between the sheets with him—right now, if he wanted her?

'Did you forget something?' she said, but the dark expression on his face quickly put paid to any lingering hope. And then he was brushing past her, that brief contact only adding to her sense of disorientation. 'What do you think you're doing?'

'Shut the door,' he said tersely.

'You can't just walk in here and start telling me what to do.'

'Shut the door, Willow,' he repeated grimly. 'Unless you want your neighbours to hear what I have to say.'

Part of her wanted to challenge him. To tell him to go right ahead and that she didn't care what her neighbours thought. Because he didn't want her, did he? He'd rejected her—so what right did he have to start throwing his weight around like this?

Yet he looked so golden and gorgeous as he tow-
ered over her, dominating the shaded entrance hall of
the basement apartment, that it was difficult for her
to think straight. And suddenly she couldn't bear to
be this close without wanting to reach out and touch
him. To trace her finger along the dark graze of his
jaw and drift it upwards to his lips. *So start taking
control*, she told herself fiercely. *This is* your *home
and* he's *the trespasser. Don't let him tell you what
you should or shouldn't do.*

'I was just making coffee,' she said with an airi-
ness which belied her pounding heart as she headed
off towards the kitchen, aware that he was very close
behind her. She willed her hand to stay steady as she
poured herself a mug and then flicked him an enquir-
ing gaze. 'Would you like one?'

'I haven't come for coffee.'

'Then why *have* you come here, with a look on
your face which would turn the milk sour?'

His fists clenched by the faded denim of his powerful thighs and his features darkened. 'What did you
hope to achieve by this, Willow?' he hissed. 'Did you
imagine that your petulant display would be enough
to get you what you wanted, and that I'd take you to
bed despite my better judgement?'

She stared at him. 'I don't know what you're talking about.'

'Oh, really?'

'Yes. *Really.*'

'So you have no idea why it's all over the internet
that you and I are engaged to be married?'

Willow could feel all the blood drain from her face.

'No, of course I didn't!' And then her hand flew to her lips. 'Unless...'

'So you do know?' he demanded, firing the words at her like bullets.

Please let me wake up, Willow thought. *Let me close my eyes, and when I open them again he will have disappeared and this will have been nothing but a bad dream.*

But it wasn't and he hadn't. He was still standing there glaring at her, only now his expression had changed from being a potential milk-curdler, to looking as if he would like to put his hands on her shoulders and throttle her.

'I may have...' She took a deep breath. 'I was talking to my sister about you—or rather, she was interrogating me about you. She asked if we were serious and I tried to be vague—and my aunt overheard us, and started getting carried away with talking about weddings and I didn't...well, I didn't bother to correct her.'

His eyes narrowed. 'And why would you do something like that?' he questioned dangerously.

Why?

Willow met his accusing gaze and something inside her flared like a small and painful flame. Couldn't he see? Didn't he realise that the reasons were heartbreakingly simple. Because for once she'd felt like she was part of the real world, instead of someone just watching from the sidelines. Because she'd allowed herself to start believing in her own fantasy.

'I didn't realise it was going to get out of hand like this,' she said. 'And I'm sorry.'

'You're *sorry*?' he repeated incredulously. 'You think a couple of mumbled words of apology and everything's going to go back to normal?' His face darkened again. 'My assistant has been fielding phone calls all morning and my Paris office has been inundated with reporters asking for a comment. I'm in the process of brokering a deal with a man who is fiercely private and yet it seems as if I am about to be surrounded by my own personal press pack. How do you think that's going to look?'

'Can't you just…issue a denial?'

Dante stared into her soft grey eyes and felt close to exploding. 'You think it's that simple?'

'We could say that I was…I don't know…' Helplessly, Willow shrugged. *'Joking?'*

His mouth hardened, and now there was something new in his eyes. Something dark. Something bleak.

'A denial might have worked, were it not for the fact that some enterprising journalist was alerted to the Di Sione name and decided to telephone my grandfather's house on Long Island to ask him for his reaction.' His blue eyes sparked with fury as they captured hers with their shuttered gaze. 'And despite the time difference between here and New York, it just so happened that my grandfather was suffering from insomnia and boredom and pain, and was more than willing to accept the call. Which is why…'

He paused, as if he was only just hanging on to his temper by a shred.

'Why I received a call from the old man, telling me how pleased he is that I'm settling down at last. Telling me how lovely you are—and what a good family you come from. I was trying to find the right moment to tell him that there is nothing going on between us, only the right moment didn't seem to come—or rather, my grandfather didn't give me a chance to say what I wanted to.'

'Dante…'

'Don't you *dare* interrupt me when I haven't finished,' he ground out. 'Because using the kind of shameless emotional blackmail he has always used to ensure he gets his own way, my grandfather then told me how much *better* he'd felt when he heard the news. He said he hadn't felt this good in a long time and that it was high time I took myself a wife.'

'I'm sorry.' She gave him a beseeching look. 'What else can I say?'

Dante felt a feeling of pure rage flood through him and wondered how he could have been stupid enough to take his eye off the ball. Or had he forgotten what women were really like—had he completely wiped Lucy from his memory? Had it conveniently slipped his mind that the so-called *fairer sex* were manipulative and devious and would stop at nothing to get what it was they wanted? How easy it was to forget the past when you had been bewitched by a supposedly shy blonde and a sob story about needing a temporary date which had convinced him to go to the damned wedding in the first place.

He stared at the slight quiver of Willow's lips and at that moment he understood for the first time in his life the meaning of the term *a punishing kiss*, because that was what he wanted to do to her right now. He wanted to punish her for screwing up his plans with her thoughtlessness and her careless tongue. He watched as a slow colour crept up to inject her creamy skin with a faint blush, and felt his body harden. Come to think of it, he'd like to punish her every which way. He'd like to lay her down and flatten her against the floor and…and…

'Are you one of those habitual fantasists?' he demanded hotly. 'One of those women who goes around pretending to be something she isn't, to make herself seem more interesting?'

She put her coffee cup down so suddenly that some of it slopped over the side, but she didn't even seem to notice. Her hands gripped the edge of the table, as if she needed its weathered wooden surface for support.

'That's an unfair thing to say,' she breathed.

'Why? Because you're so delicate and precious that I'm not allowed to tell the truth?' He gave a short laugh. 'I thought you despised being given special treatment just because you'd been ill. Well, you can't have it both ways, Willow. You can't play the shrinking violet whenever it suits you—and a feisty modern woman the next. You need to decide who you really are.'

She met his eyes in the silence which followed. 'You certainly don't pull your punches, do you?'

'I'm treating you the same as I would any other woman.'

'Oh, but that's where you're wrong, because you're not!' she said with a shake of her head. 'If I was any other woman, you would have had sex with me last night. You know you would.'

Dante felt the heavy beat of a pulse at his temple and silently cursed her for bringing that up again. Did she think she would wear him down with her persistence? That what Willow wanted, Willow would get. His mouth hardened, but unfortunately, so did his groin. 'Like I told you. I don't sleep with virgins.'

She turned away, but not before he noticed the dark flare of colour which washed over her cheekbones and he felt his anger morph inconveniently into lust. How easy it would be to vent his feelings by giving her what she wanted. What he wanted. Even now. Despite the accusations he'd hurled at her and the still-unsettled question of how her indiscretion was going to be resolved, it was sexual tension which dominated the air so powerfully that he couldn't hardly breathe without choking on it. He couldn't seem to tear his gaze away from her. She looked as brittle as glass as she held her shoulders stiffly, and although she was staring out of the small basement window, he was willing to lay a bet she didn't see a thing.

But he did. He saw plenty. He could see the slender swell of her bottom beneath the dark denim. He could see the silken cascade of her blond hair as it spilled down her back. Would it make him feel better if he went right over there and slid down her jeans, and laid her down on the kitchen table and straddled her, before feasting on her?

He swallowed as an aching image of her pale, parted thighs flashed vividly into his mind and he felt another powerful tug of desire. On one level, of *course* it would make them both feel better, but on another—what? He would be stirring up yet more consequences, and weren't there more than enough to be going on with?

She turned back again to face him and he saw that the flush had gone, as if her pale skin had absorbed it, like blotting paper. 'Like I said, I'm sorry, but there's nothing I can do about it now.'

He shook his head. 'But that's where you're wrong, little Miss Hamilton. There *is*.'

Did something alert her to the determination which had hardened his voice? Was that why her eyes had grown so wary?

'What? You want me to write to your grandfather and apologise? And then to give some kind of statement to the press, telling them that it was all a misunderstanding? I'll do all that, if that's what it takes.'

'No. That's not what's going to happen,' he said. 'It's a little more complicated than that. My grandfather wants to meet the woman he thinks I'm going to marry. And you, my dear Willow, are going to embrace that role.'

The grey of her eyes was darker now, as if someone had smudged them with charcoal and a faint frown was criss-crossing over her brow. 'I don't understand.'

'Then let me explain it clearly, so there can be no mistake,' he said. 'My grandfather is a sick man and anything which makes him feel better is fine with me. He wants me to bring you to the family home to meet him and that's exactly what's going to happen. You can play the fantasist for a little while longer because you are coming with me to Long Island. As my fiancée.'

CHAPTER EIGHT

A SOFT BREEZE wafted in through the open windows, making the filmy drapes at the window shiver like a bridal veil and the mocking significance of *that* didn't escape Willow. She drew her hand over her clammy brow and looked around the luxurious room. She could hardly believe she was here, on Dante's estate, or that he had persuaded her to come here for a long weekend, despite the many objections she'd raised.

But he'd made her feel guilty—and guilt was a powerful motivator. He'd said that her lies about being his fiancée had given his grandfather hope, and it was in her power to ensure that a dying man's hopes were not dashed.

'You seemed to want to let your family believe that you were going to be my bride,' were his exact, silken words. 'Well, now this is your chance to play the role for real.'

Except that it wasn't real, because a real bride-to-be would be cherished and caressed by her fiancé, wouldn't she? Not kept at a chilly distance as if she was something unwanted but necessary—like a bandage you might be forced to wrap around an injured arm.

They were installed in an unbelievably cute cottage in the extensive grounds, but in a way that was worse than staying in the main house. Because in here there was the illusion of intimacy, while in reality they were two people who couldn't have been further apart. She was closeted alone with a man who clearly despised her. And there was only one bed. Willow swallowed. This time it was a king-size bed, but the principle of where to sleep remained the same. Was he really willing to repeat what had happened at the wedding—sharing a bedroom, while keeping his distance from her?

Dante had telephoned ahead to tell the housekeeper that they wished to be guaranteed privacy. She remembered the look on his face as he'd finished the call. 'They'll think it's because we're crazy about each other and can't keep our hands off each other,' he'd said mockingly.

But Willow knew the real reason. It meant that they wouldn't be forced to continue with the farce for any longer than necessary. There would be no reason for Dante to hide his undeniable hostility towards her. When they were with other people they would be sweetness and light together, while in private...

She bit her lip, trying hard to block out the sound of the powerful shower jets from the en-suite bathroom and not to think about Dante standing naked beneath them, but it wasn't easy. Their enforced proximity had made her achingly aware of him—whether he was in the same room, or not.

They had flown in by helicopter an hour earlier and Willow's first sight of the Di Sione family home had taken her breath away. She'd grown up in a big home, yes—but this was nothing like the crumbling house in which she'd spent her own formative years. This, she'd realised, was what real wealth looked like. It was solid and real, and clearly money was no object. The white marble of the Long Island mansion was gleaming and so pristine that she couldn't imagine anyone actually *living* in it. She had been aware of the endless sweep of emerald lawns, the turquoise flash of a swimming pool and the distant glitter of a huge lake as their helicopter had landed.

A housekeeper named Alma had welcomed them and told Dante that his grandfather was sleeping but looking forward to seeing them both at dinner.

'And your sister is here, of course,' she said.

'Talia?' questioned Dante as the housekeeper nodded.

'That's right. She's out making sketches for a new painting.' Alma had given Willow a friendly smile. 'You'll meet Miss Natalia at dinner.'

And Willow had nodded and tried to look as she thought a newly engaged woman *should* look—and not like someone who had recently been handed a diamond ring by Dante, with all the emotion of someone producing a cheap trinket from the remains of a Christmas cracker.

'What's this?' she'd asked as he had deposited a small velvet box on her lap.

'Your number one prop,' came his mocking response as their helicopter had hovered over the Di Sione landing pad. 'The bling. That thing which women love to flash as a symbol of success—the outward sign that they've *got their man.*'

'What an unbelievably cynical thing to say.'

'You think it's cynical to tell the truth?' he'd demanded. 'Or are you denying that women view the acquisition of diamonds as if it's some new kind of competitive sport?'

The awful thing was that Willow secretly agreed with him. Her sisters were crazy about diamonds—and so were plenty of the women she worked with—yet she'd always found them a cold and emotionless stone. The giant solitaire winked at her now like some malevolent foe, splashing rainbow fire over her pale fingers as Dante emerged from the bathroom.

Quickly, she looked up, her heart beginning to pound. She'd been half expecting him to emerge wearing nothing but a towel slung around his hips, and guessed she should be pleased that he must have dressed in the bathroom. But her overriding sensation was one of disappointment. Had she secretly been hoping to catch a glimpse of that magnificent olive body as he patted himself dry? Was there some masochistic urge lurking inside her which wanted to taunt her with what she hadn't got?

Yet the dark trousers and silk shirt he wore did little to disguise his muscular physique and his fully dressed state did nothing to dim his powerful air of allure. His black hair was still damp and his eyes looked intensely blue, and suddenly Willow felt her heart lurch with a dizzying yet wasted sense of desire. Because since that interrupted seduction at her sister's wedding, he hadn't touched her. Not once. He had avoided all physical contact with the studied exaggeration of someone in the military walking through a field studded with landmines.

His gaze flickered to where she'd been studying

her hand and his eyes gleamed with mockery. As if he'd caught her gloating. 'Do you like your ring?'

'It looks way too big on my hand,' she said truthfully. 'And huge solitaire diamonds aren't really my thing.'

He raised his dark brows mockingly, as if he didn't quite believe her.

'But they have a much better resale value than something bespoke,' he drawled.

'Of course,' she said, and then a rush of nerves washed over her as she thought about the reality of going to dinner that evening and playing the part of his intended bride. 'You know, if we're planning to convince your grandfather that we really are a couple, then I'm going to need to know something about you. And if you could try being a little less hostile towards me that might help.'

He slipped a pair of heavy gold cufflinks in place and clipped them closed before answering. 'What exactly do you want to know?'

She wanted to know why he was so cynical. And why his face had darkened as soon as the helicopter had landed here today.

'You told me about being sent away to boarding school in Switzerland, but you didn't say why.'

'Does there have to be a reason?'

She hesitated. 'I'm thinking that maybe there was. And if there was, then I would probably know about it.'

Dante's instinct was to snap out some terse response—the familiar blocking technique he used whenever questions strayed into the territory of *personal*. Because he didn't trust personal. He didn't trust anyone or anything, and Willow Hamilton was no exception in the trust stakes, with her manipulation and evasion. But suddenly her face had become soft with what looked like genuine concern and he felt a tug of something unfamiliar deep inside him. An inexplicable urge to colour in some of the blank spaces of his past. Was that because he wanted his grandfather to die happy by convincing him that he'd found true love at last? Or because—despite her careless tongue landing them in this ridiculous situation—she possessed a curious sense of vulnerability which somehow managed to burrow beneath his defences.

His lips tightened as he reminded himself how clever Giovanni was. How he would see through a fake engagement in the blinking of an eye if he wasn't careful. So tell her, he thought. She was right. He should tell her the stuff which any fiancée would expect to know.

'I'm one of seven children,' he said, shooting out the facts like bullets. 'And my grandfather stepped in to care for us when my parents died very suddenly.'

'And…how did they die?'

'*Violently,*' he answered succinctly.

Her eyes clouded and Dante saw comprehension written in their soft, grey depths. As if she understood pain. And he didn't want her to *understand*. He wanted her to nod as he presented her with the bare facts—not look at him as if he was some kind of problem she could solve.

Yet there had been times when he'd longed for someone to work their magic on him. He stared out at the distant glitter of the lake. To find a woman he'd be happy to go to bed with, night after night—instead of suffering from chronic boredom as soon as anyone tried to get close to him. To find some kind of *peace* with another human being—the kind of peace which seemed almost unimaginable to him. Was that how his twin had felt about Anais? he wondered.

He thought about Dario and felt the bitter twist of remorse as he remembered what he had done to his brother.

'What exactly happened?' Willow was asking.

Her gentle tone threatened to undermine his resolve. Making him want to show her what his life had been like. To show her that she didn't have the monopoly on difficult childhoods. And suddenly, it was like a dam breaking through and flooding him.

'My father was a screwed-up hedonist,' he said bluntly. 'A kid with too much money who saw salvation in the bottom of a bottle, or in the little pile of white dust he snorted through a hundred dollar bill.' His lips tightened. 'He blamed his addictions on the fact that my grandfather had never been there for him when he was growing up—but plenty of people have absent parents and don't end up having to live their lives on a constant high.'

'And what about your mother?' she questioned as calmly as if he'd just been telling her that his father had been president of the Union.

He shook his head. 'She was cut from the same cloth. Or maybe he taught her to be that way—I don't know. All I do know is that she liked the feeling of being out of her head as well. Or maybe she needed to blot out the reality, because my father wasn't exactly known for his fidelity. Their parties were legendary. I remember I used to creep downstairs to find it looking like some kind of Roman orgy, with people lying around among the empty bottles and glasses and the sounds of women gasping in the pool house. And then one day my mother just stopped. She started seeing a therapist and went into rehab, and although she replaced the drink and the drugs with a shopping addiction, for a while everything was...' He shrugged as he struggled to find a word which would sum up the chaos of his family life.

'Normal?'

He gave a short and bitter laugh. 'No, Willow. It was never normal, but it was better. In fact, for a while it was great. We felt we'd got our mother back. And then...'

'Then?' she prompted again.

He wasn't even angry with her for her persistence because now it felt like some rank poison was throbbing beneath his skin and he needed to cut through the surface to let that poison out.

'One night there was some big row. I don't know what it was about—all I do know is that my father was completely loaded and my mother was shouting at him. I heard him yell back that he was going out and then I heard her going after him. I knew he was in no state to drive and I tried to stop her. I...'

He'd done more than try. He'd begged her not to go. He'd run over and clung to her with all the strength his eight-year-old body could muster, but she hadn't listened. She'd got in the car anyway and the next time he'd seen his mother was when she'd been laid out in her coffin, with white lilies in her hands and that waxy look on her cold, cold cheeks.

'She wouldn't listen to me,' he bit out. 'He crashed

the car and killed them both. And I didn't manage to stop her. Even though deep down I knew what a state my father was in, I let her go.'

He stared out at the grounds of the house he'd moved into soon afterwards when his grandfather had brought them all here. A place where he'd been unable to shake off his sorrow and his guilt. He'd run wild until his grandfather had sent him and Dario away to school. And he'd just kept on running, hadn't he? He wondered now if the failure of his attempt to stop his mother had been the beginning of his fierce need to control. The reason why he always felt compelled to step in and influence what was happening around him. Was that why he'd done what he'd done to his twin brother?

'But maybe you couldn't stop her.'

Willow's voice—suddenly so strong and sure—broke into his thoughts.

'What are you talking about?' he demanded.

'Children can't always make adults behave the way they want them to, Dante,' she said, her words washing over him like balm. 'No matter how hard they try.'

Dante turned round, still unable to believe how much she'd got out of him. She looked like some kind of angel sitting there, with her pale English skin and that waterfall of silky hair. In her simple cotton dress she looked so pure—hell, she *was* pure. But it was more than just about sex. She looked as if she could take all the darkness away from him and wash away the stain of guilt from his heart. And her grey eyes were fixed on him, quite calmly—as if she knew exactly what was going on inside his head and was silently urging him to go right ahead and do it.

He wasn't thinking as he walked across the room to where she sat at an antique writing desk with the oil painting of Sicily which hung on the wall behind it. The hot, scorched brushstrokes and cerulean blue of the sky contrasted vividly with her coolness. Her lips looked soft and inviting. Some warning bell was sounding inside his head, telling him that this was wrong. But some of the poison had left him now. Left him feeling empty and aching and wanting her. Wanting to lose himself in her.

She didn't object when he pulled her out of the chair and onto her feet. In fact, the sudden yearning in her eyes suggested that she'd wanted him to touch her just as badly as he needed to.

His hands were in her hair and his mouth was hovering over hers, their lips not quite touching, as if he'd had a last-minute moment of sanity and this was his chance to pull back from her. Was that why she stood up on tiptoe and anchored her hands to his shoulders? Why she flickered the tip of her tongue inside his mouth?

'Willow,' he whispered as his heart began to pound.

'Yes,' she whispered back. 'I'm right here.'

He groaned as he tasted her—his senses tantalised by the faint drift of her scent. Dropping his hands from her hair, he gripped her waist and he thought how incredibly *light* she felt. As light as those drifts of swansdown you sometimes saw floating across hazy summer lawns. He deepened the kiss, and as she sucked in a breath, it felt like she was sucking him right inside her. For a moment he thought about the very obvious place where he would like to *be* sucked and his hand reached down to cup her breast. He heard the urgent little sigh of delight she made. He felt the restless circle of her narrow hips, and he could feel control leaving him as she kissed him back. He tried to remember where he'd put his condoms and just how long they had before they were expected up at the main house. And all the time he could feel himself going under—as if he was being consumed by a tide of rich, dark honey.

But along with the sweet, sharp kick of desire came the reminder of all the things he'd told himself he wasn't going to do. He'd messed up enough in his life. He'd failed to save his mother. He'd ruptured his relationship with his twin brother. In business he'd achieved outstanding success, but his personal relationships were not the same. Everything he touched turned to dust. He was incapable of experiencing the emotions which other men seemed to feel. And even though Willow Hamilton had allowed her stupid fantasies to manipulate events... Even though she had dragged him into her fantasy and made it impossible for him to walk away from her—that gave him no right to hurt her.

It would be too easy to take her innocence. To be the first man to claim her body for his own. To introduce her to the powerful but ultimately fleeting pleasures of sex. He closed his eyes because imagining her sweet tightness encasing him was almost too much to bear. He thought about easing into her molten heat, with his mouth clamped to one of her tiny nipples. He thought about how good it would feel to be able to come inside her. To pump his seed into her until he was empty and replete. To kiss her and kiss her until she fell asleep in his arms.

But a woman's virginity was a big deal, and someone who had suffered as Willow had suffered deserved more than he could ever give her. Because he was programmed not to trust and never to stay. He would take pleasure and give pleasure and then close the door and leave without a backwards glance.

Dragging his mouth away from hers and dropping his hand from her breast as if it was on fire, he stepped away, trying to quieten down the fierce sexual hunger which was burning inside him. But when he saw the confusion clouding her beautiful eyes, he felt a moment of unfamiliar doubt which he couldn't seem to block out.

His mouth twisted.

'I meant what I said back in England,' he gritted. 'You aren't somebody I intend to get intimate with, Willow. Did you think that because I've just told you something about my *deeply troubled* past…' His voice took on a harsh and mocking tone. 'That I would want you? Did you think any of this was for real? Because if you do, you're making a big mistake. For the sake of my grandfather and his romantic ideals, we will play the part of the happily engaged couple whenever we find ourselves in his company. But when we're alone, the reality will be very different. Just so you know, I'll be sleeping on the couch.' He gave a tight smile. 'And I'll do my best not to disturb you.'

CHAPTER NINE

THE DARK SHAPE was moving almost silently around the room but it was enough to disturb Willow from her troubled sleep. Pushing the hair back from her face, she sat up in bed and snapped on the light to see Dante standing fully dressed, his face shadowed and unfriendly.

'What are you doing?' she whispered.

'Going out for a drive.'

'But it's only…' She picked up her watch and blinked at it. 'Just after five in the morning!'

'I know what the time is,' he growled back as he grabbed a clutch of car keys.

'So…why?' Her voice was full of bewilderment as she looked at him. 'Why in heaven's name are you going out before the sun is even up?'

'Why do you think?' He turned to look at her properly and all his dark and restless energy seemed to wash over her. 'Because I can't sleep.'

Willow swallowed. 'That couch *does* look very uncomfortable,' she agreed carefully. 'It can't be doing your back any good.'

'It's got nothing to do with the damned couch, Willow, and we both know it.'

She leaned back against the pillows, wishing that

he would stop snapping at her, and just end this impasse. Wishing he'd just take off those jeans and that stupid jacket and come and get in bed with her and do what was almost driving her out of her mind with longing. How many nights had they spent here now? And still her virginity was intact. Nothing had changed—at least, not in him—though her desire for him was as strong as ever. She wanted to kiss him. She wanted to hold him. Yet he acted as if she was contaminated.

'It was a mistake to come to this damned cottage,' he bit out. 'And an even bigger mistake to agree to stay on until after Natalia's opening.'

'So why *did* you agree to it?'

'You know damned well why,' he growled. 'Because you managed to make yourself completely irresistible to my grandfather, didn't you? So that I could hardly refuse his suggestion that we hang around for a few more days.' His fingers tightened around his car keys as he glared at her. 'Was this just more of the same kind of behaviour you demonstrated so perfectly at your sister's wedding? Manipulating events so they'd turn out the way you wanted them to?'

'That is an outrageous thing to say,' she retorted, wrapping the duvet more tightly around herself and trying very hard to keep the sight of her tightening nipples away from his accusing eyes. 'Unless you're suggesting that I deliberately went out of my way to be nice to your grandfather, just because I had some sort of hidden agenda to trap you in this cottage?'

He gave an impatient shake of his head. 'That wasn't what I meant.'

'Because, believe me, no one would deliberately angle to have more time alone with you, when you're in *this* kind of mood!'

His eyes narrowed. 'I guess not,' he said.

'And to be honest, I don't know how much longer I can go on like this,' she said. 'Maintaining this crazy fiction of presenting ourselves as the happy couple whenever we're with Giovanni or Natalia—and yet the moment we're alone, we're…we're…'

Dante stilled as he heard the unmistakable break in her voice, which only added to his growing sense of confusion and frustration. Because he hated it when she acted vulnerable—something which was surprisingly rare. When her voice wobbled or she got that puppy-dog look in her eyes, it started making all kinds of unwanted ideas flood into his head. Was it possible that duplicity didn't come as easily to her as he'd originally thought? That the sweet and uncomplicated Willow he'd seen here in his Long Island home—being endlessly patient with his grandfather and lovely towards his sister—was actually the real Willow? His mouth hardened. Or was she trying and managing very successfully to twist him around her little finger?

'We what, Willow?' he questioned silkily.

'We circle each other like two wary animals whenever we're together!'

'Well, let me ease the burden by going out and making sure we're alone for as little time as possible,' he said. 'Like I said, I'm going out for a drive. I'll see you later.'

Walking across the room, he clicked the door shut behind him, and as Willow listened to the sound of his retreating footsteps, she slumped dejectedly back into the pillows.

A heavy sigh escaped from her lips. She was living in a prison. A gilded prison where everything she wanted was right in front of her. The only man she'd ever wanted was constantly within touching distance—only she wasn't allowed to touch. And the fiction of the happy front they presented to the outside world was cancelled out by the spiralling tension whenever they were alone together.

She'd thought she'd been getting close to him. She *had* been getting close to him. On the day they'd arrived, he'd dropped his formidable guard and told her things about his past—things about his childhood and his family which had made her want to reach out to him. She'd seen the bitter sadness distorting his features and had wanted more than anything else to comfort him.

And for a while he had let her. For a few moments he had held her tight and kissed her and something deep and strong had flickered into life as they'd stood, locked in each other's arms. Her experience of men was tiny, but she had *known* that kiss was about more than sexual desire. It had been about understanding and solace. She'd thought it had been about hope.

But then he had pushed her away almost coldly, and since then he hadn't come close. Only when they were being observed by other people did he soften his attitude towards her.

She'd met one of his sisters, Natalia—a talented artist who lived at the house. With her wavy brown hair tied back in a ponytail and tomboyish clothes, she wasn't a bit how Willow had imagined Dante's sister to be. She had recently returned from a trip to Greece, but her clear hazel eyes became shuttered whenever anyone asked about it.

And Willow had at last met the legendary Giovanni, Dante's grandfather. She'd felt a punch of painful recognition after being shown into his room and seeing the pills which the attendant nurse was tipping into a small plastic container. A sense of sadness had curled itself around her heart as she saw the unmistakable signs of sickness. She thought how the Di Sione family had so many of the things which society lusted after. With their lavish wealth and a sprawling mansion in one of the world's most expensive areas of real estate, they were a force to be reckoned with...but nobody could avoid the inevitability of death, no matter how rich they were. And Dante's grandfather's eyes held within them a pain which Willow suspected was caused by more than his illness. Was he trying to get his affairs in order before the end? Was that why he'd asked Dante to trace the costly tiara and bring it to him?

On the first of what became twice daily visits, Willow would perch on a chair beside the bed and chat to the old man. She told him all about her life in England, because she knew better than anyone how being housebound made the dimensions of your world shrink. She was less enthusiastic about her fictitious future with his beloved grandson, even though the old man's eyes softened with obvious emotion when he reached out to examine her sparkling engagement ring. And she hoped she'd done her best to hide her guilt and her pain—and to bite back the urge to confess to him that none of this was real.

After Dante had gone she lay in bed until the light came up, then walked over to the main house for breakfast. The dining room was empty but Alma must have heard her because she came in with a pot of camomile tea, just as Willow was helping herself to a slice of toast.

'Where is everyone?' asked Willow as she reached for a dish of jam.

'Signor Giovanni is resting and Miss Natalia's upstairs, trying on dresses for her exhibition,' replied Alma. 'Would you like Cook to fix you some eggs?'

Willow shook her head. 'I'm good, thanks, Alma. This jam is amazing.'

Alma smiled. 'Thank you. I made it myself.'

Slowly, Willow ate her breakfast and afterwards went for a wander around the house where there was always something new to discover. And it was a relief to be able to distract herself from her endless frustration about Dante by admiring the fabulous views over the Di Sione estate, and the priceless artwork which studded each and every wall of the mansion. She was lost in thought as she studied a beautiful oil painting of Venice when suddenly she heard a small crash on the first floor, followed by the unmistakable sound of Natalia's voice exclaiming something.

Curiosity getting the better of her, she walked up the curving staircase and along a wide corridor, past an open door where she could see Natalia standing in front of a mirror, a heavy silver hairbrush lying by her bare feet. She was wearing a green shift dress—one of the most shapeless garments Willow had ever seen—which did absolutely nothing for her athletic physique.

Instinctively, she winced and the words were out of her mouth before she could stop them. 'You're not wearing that, surely?'

'What?' Natalia looked down at the garment before glancing up again and blinking. 'This is one of my best dresses.'

'Okay,' said Willow doubtfully, going into the room and walking around behind Natalia to see if it looked any better from the back. It didn't.

'So what's wrong with this dress?' Natalia asked.

Willow shrugged as she looked at Dante's sister. 'Honestly? It looks like a green bin bag. Admittedly a very nice shade of green, but still...' She narrowed her eyes in assessment. 'Did Dante tell you that I work in fashion?'

Natalia shook her head. 'Nope. He's been characteristically cagey about you. If you want the truth, I was pretty surprised to meet you. He once told me that he didn't think that marriage was for him, and I believed him.' Her voice softened. 'That's why I'm so happy for him, Willow. Sometimes he seems so... alone...despite all the planes and the parties and the money he's made. I'm so glad he's found you.'

Willow's heart clenched with a guilt even though she felt a perverse kind of pride that their farce of togetherness was working so effectively. She turned her attention to Natalia again.

'You have a knockout figure and gorgeous hair and you don't do much with either.'

'I've never had to.'

'But today is different, isn't it?' persisted Willow. 'I mean, it's meant to be special.'

There was silence for a moment before Natalia answered. 'Yes.'

Willow glanced over at the clock on the mantelpiece. 'Look, we have plenty of time. I can see what you have in your wardrobe or we could raid mine. And I'm a dab hand with a needle and thread. Will you let me give you a bit of a makeover? Only if you want to, of course.'

There was a moment of hesitation before Natalia gave Willow the sweetest smile she'd ever seen. 'Sure,' she said. 'Why not?'

Dante parked the car and walked slowly to the house, his dark glasses shading his eyes against the bright golden glitter of the day. It was a beautiful day and he should have felt invigorated by the air and the drive he'd just had. He should have felt all kinds of things, but he didn't.

Because none of this was turning out the way it was supposed to. He'd thought that maintaining a fake relationship with Willow would be easy. He just hadn't anticipated the reality.

He hadn't thought through what it would be like, being with her day in and day out, because he had no experience of what it *would* be like. Because he didn't do *proximity*. He slept with women, yes. He *loved* sleeping with women and occasionally taking them out to dinner or the theatre—but any time he spent with them was doled out in very manageable slots and always on *his* terms. Yet now he found himself stuck with her in a cottage which seemed way too small and claustrophobic, and with no means of escape. His throat dried. She was there, but not there.

She was tantalisingly close, yet he had forbidden himself to touch her, for reasons which seemed less important as each day passed. And now a terrible sexual hunger raged somewhere deep inside him and it was driving him crazy.

For the first time in a long time, he found himself thinking about his twin. Was it being back here, and seeing the great sweep of lawns where they used to climb trees and throw balls, which had made the pain suddenly feel so raw again? He thought about what he'd done to Dario, and how he'd tried to make amends, and the taste in his mouth grew bitter. Because Dario hadn't wanted amends, had he? There was no forgiveness in his brother's heart.

Deciding to have some coffee before he faced Willow, Dante walked into the house to hear laughter floating down the curving staircase from one of the upstairs bedrooms. His eyes narrowed—the carefree quality of the sound impacting powerfully on his troubled thoughts. Frowning a little, he followed the unfamiliar sound until he reached his sister's bedroom, unprepared for the sight which awaited him.

Talia was standing on a chair, and Willow was kneeling on the floor beside it, with pins in her mouth as she tugged at the hem of a beautiful floaty dress quite unlike anything he'd ever seen his sister wear before. And it wasn't just the dress. He'd never seen Natalia with her hair like that either, or her eyes looking so big. He caught the milky lustre of pearls at her ears—they glowed gently against her skin—and suddenly felt a surge of protectiveness, because this was his baby sister, looking all grown up.

'What's going on?' he said.

Natalia looked up. 'Hi, Dante.' She smiled. 'I'm deciding what to wear to the exhibition of my work.'

He raised an eyebrow. 'But you never go to the exhibition.'

'Not in the past. But tomorrow night I do,' she said softly. 'And Willow has helped me choose what to wear. Isn't she clever?'

Willow.

For the first time, Dante allowed his gaze to linger on the slim blonde scrambling to her feet, her cheeks slightly pink as she removed a pin from her mouth and dropped it into a little pewter box. Her dress was creased and her legs were bare and he was hit by a wave of lust so powerful that he could feel all the blood drain from his head, to go straight to where his body was demanding it.

He'd left their suite early because he'd felt as if he would *explode* if he didn't touch her, and suddenly he began to wonder just what he was doing to himself. Whether pain was such an integral part of his life that he felt duty-bound to inflict it on himself, even when it wasn't necessary. Was he trying to punish himself by denying himself the pleasure which he knew could be his, if only he reached out and took it? Because Willow hungered for him, just as much as he did for her. He could read it in every movement of her body. The way her eyes darkened whenever she looked at him.

Her carelessness had led to that crazy announcement about them being engaged, but hadn't he committed far graver sins than that? Hadn't he once told the biggest lie in the world to his twin brother—a lie by omission. He had stood silent when Dario had accused him of sleeping with his wife, and hadn't their relationship been in tatters ever since?

Pushing away the regret which he'd buried so deep, he thought instead about what his grandfather had said, soon after he'd given him the tiara. That Willow was caring and thoughtful, and that he liked her. And Giovanni wouldn't say something like that unless he meant it. His sister seemed to like her too—and Talia could be notoriously prickly with new people, after all the bad stuff which had happened in *her* life.

He realised that Natalia was waiting for an answer to a question he'd forgotten. Something about Willow, he thought—which was kind of appropriate because it was difficult to concentrate on anything other than a pair of grey eyes and a soft pair of lips he badly needed to kiss.

'Yes, she is,' he said slowly. 'Very clever.'

A funny kind of silence descended as Willow's cheeks grew pink.

'Well, I think that's everything,' she said, brushing her hand down over the creases in her dress. 'You look gorgeous, Natalia.'

'Gorgeous,' Dante agreed steadily. 'And now I'd like to talk to you, Willow. That is, if Natalia has finished with you.'

'Sure.' Natalia gave a quick smile. 'We're all done here.'

In silence Dante followed Willow from Natalia's room, and once he had closed the door, she turned to him, her eyes filled with question.

'What is it?' she asked. 'Has something happened?'

But he shook his head. He didn't want whispered explanations in the corridors of this great house, with Natalia suddenly emerging from the bedroom or Alma or another member of staff stumbling upon them. He badly wanted to kiss her, and once he'd started, he wasn't sure that he'd be able to stop.

'I need to talk to you,' he said. 'In private.'

The journey to their cottage seemed to take for ever, and Willow's heart was pounding as she followed Dante through the grounds because she was aware that something about him was different. When he'd walked into the room and seen her and Natalia giggling together, there had been something in his eyes which had made her want to melt. He'd looked at her in a way which had made goose bumps whisper all over her skin and her heart start thumping with an urgent kind of hope. She'd seen a new tension in his body and hoped she hadn't imagined the hunger she'd seen in his blue eyes, but even if it was true, she wasn't sure she trusted it. Was he going to take her in his arms and run his hands over her body like he'd done before? Was he going to kiss her passionately—to the point where she was gasping with hunger and frustration—only to push her away again and add to that frustration?

In tense silence they walked down an avenue of tall trees, whose leaves were brushed with the first hints of gold, and when finally they reached the cottage, she turned to face him as he closed the door.

'What is it?' she questioned again. 'Why are you acting like this?'

'I'm not acting,' he said unsteadily. 'Up until now, maybe—but not any more. I've wanted you for so long and I've reached a point where I can't go on like this any longer because it's driving me insane. I've tried to resist you, but it seems I can't resist any more. And now I'm through with trying. I want you, Willow. I want you so badly I can hardly breathe.'

Her heart was performing somersaults as she looked at him, scarcely able to believe what she was hearing. 'You make it sound as if you're doing something you don't want to do.'

'Oh, I want to do it, all right,' he said simply. 'I can't remember ever wanting a woman as much as I do right now. Maybe because you've been off-limits for so long that it's stirred my appetite until I can think of little else but you. I don't know. All I know is that I don't want to hurt you.'

'Dante…' she said.

'No. Hear me out, because it's important that you do.' His gaze was very intense—his eyes like blue flames which burned right through her. 'I'm afraid your innocence will make you read too much into this and so I'm flagging it up before that happens. To make sure it doesn't happen. Because the act of sex can be deceptive, Willow. The words spoken during intimacy can often mimic the words of love and it's important you recognise that.'

She dug her teeth into her bottom lip. 'And you're afraid that if I have sex with you, I'll fall hopelessly in love with you?'

His face became shuttered. 'Will you?'

Willow wondered if it was arrogance which had made him ask that—or simply a remarkable honesty. She wondered if she should listen to the voice inside her head which was telling her to heed his warning.

That maybe she was setting herself up for a hurt bigger than any she'd ever known.

But it wasn't as easy as that. She wanted Dante in a way she'd never wanted anyone—a way she suspected she never would again. Even if she met someone else like him—which was doubtful—her fate was always going to be different from other women her age.

Because a normal life and marriage had never been on the cards for her and it never could.

But none of that was relevant now.

She wasn't asking the impossible. She wasn't demanding that he *love* her—all she needed to do was to keep her own emotions in check. *She had to.* Because anything else would frighten him away—instinct told her that. She gave a little shrug.

'I'll try my very hardest not to fall in love with you,' she said lightly.

'Good. Because there isn't going to be some fairy-tale ending to this. This fake engagement of ours isn't suddenly going to become real.'

'I don't care.'

And suddenly neither did he. He didn't care about anything except touching her like he'd wanted to do for so long.

Dante peeled the dress from her body and then couldn't stop staring—as if it was the first time he'd ever undressed a woman. She was all sweetness and delicacy. All blond hair and floral scent and pure white lingerie. He wrapped his arms around her. He wanted to ravish her and protect her. He wanted to spill his seed inside her—and yet surely a virgin of her stature could not take him when he was already this big and this hard.

He brushed a lock of hair away from the smooth-
ness of her cheek. 'I'm afraid I might break you.'

'You won't break me, Dante. I'm a woman, not a
piece of glass.' Her voice trembled a little as she lifted
her chin and he saw the sudden light of determination in her eyes. 'Don't be different towards me just
because I've never done this before, or because once
I was sick. Be the same as you always are.'

'Be careful what you wish for.' With a little growl,
he picked her up and carried her into the bedroom.
Carefully, he laid her down on the bed before moving away and beginning to unbutton his shirt, telling
himself that if she looked in any way daunted as he
stripped off, then he would stop.

But she was watching him like a kid in a candy
store and her widened eyes and parted lips were only
adding to his desire—if such a thing was possible.
He eased the zip down over his straining hardness
and carefully watched her reaction as he stood before her naked—but her face was full of nothing but
wonder, and hunger.

'Oh, Dante,' she said, very softly.

It was the sweetest thing he'd ever heard. He went
over to the bed and bent over her, tracing the pad of
his thumb over her trembling lips and following it
with the slowest, deepest kiss imaginable. It made
his heart kick and his groin throb, and when he drew
back he could see she looked dazed. *You and me both,
sweetheart*, he thought, his fingertip stroking along
the delicate lace of the bra which edged her creamy
skin, and he felt her tremble.

'Scared?' he said.

She gave a little shrug. 'Scared I might not meet your expectations.'

He unclipped the front clasp of her bra, so that her delicious little breasts sprang free and he smiled as he bent his head to trace each budding nipple with his tongue.

'You already have,' he murmured throatily. 'You're perfect.'

Willow didn't react to that because she knew she wasn't. Nobody was and in her time she had felt more imperfect than most. But the look on his face was making her feel pretty close to perfect and she would be grateful to him for ever for that.

And now his thumbs were hooking into the sides of her knickers and he was sliding them all the way down her legs.

'Mmm...' he said, his gaze pausing to linger on her groin. 'A natural blonde.'

And Willow did something she'd never imagined she'd do on her long-anticipated initiation into sex. She burst out laughing.

'You are outrageous,' she said as he dropped the discarded underwear over the edge of the bed.

'But you like me being outrageous, don't you, Willow?'

And that was the thing. She did. Dante Di Sione was both arrogant and outrageous, yes. She could understand why they called him a maverick. But he was a lot of other things too. Most men in his position, she suspected, would have bedded her before now—but Dante had not. He had tried to do the right thing, even though it had gone against all his macho instincts. He had resisted and resisted until he could resist no more. He was strong and masterful, yet he had a conscience which made her feel safe. And safety had always been a big deal for her.

'I think you know the answer to that question,' she murmured as she tipped her head back so that he could kiss her neck.

And Dante did know. He gave a groan of satisfaction as he explored her. He touched her wetness until she was trembling uncontrollably—until she had begun to make distracted little pleas beneath her breath. She was so ready, he thought, his heart giving a thunder of expectation as his hand groped blindly towards the bedside locker.

Thank God for condoms, he thought—though as he rolled the contraceptive on, it was the only time she seemed uncertain. He saw her biting down on her lip and he raised his eyebrows, forcing himself to ask the question, even though he could barely get the words out.

'It won't be easy and I can't promise that it won't half kill me to do it, but if you want to change your mind...'

'No,' she said fiercely, her eager kisses raining over his eyelids, his jaw and his mouth. 'Never! Never, never, never.'

Her eagerness made him smile and when finally he entered her there was only the briefest moment of hesitation as he broke through her hymen, and he was filled with a powerful sense of possession.

'Does it hurt?' he said indistinctly, fighting against every instinct in his body as he forced himself to grow still inside her.

But she shook her head. 'It feels like heaven,' she said simply.

Dante closed his eyes and finally gave himself up to the rhythm which both their bodies seemed to be crying out for, though already he could sense she was very close to the edge.

Gripping her narrow hips he brought himself deeper inside her, bending his head to let his tongue flicker over her peaking nipples while she twisted like some pale and beautiful flower beneath him.

'Dante,' she gasped, but she didn't need to tell him what he already knew.

He had watched with rapt fascination the build-up of tension in her slender frame. The darkening of those wintry eyes. The way her head moved distract-edly from side to side so that her hair fanned the pillow like a silky blond cloud. Her back began to arch and her legs to stiffen, and just as her body began to convulse helplessly around him, he saw the rosy dark-ening of her skin above her tiny breasts.

'Dante,' she gasped again, and mumbled something else, but he didn't know what it was, and frankly, he didn't care. Because he'd been holding off for so long that he couldn't endure it for a second longer, so that when eventually his orgasm came, he felt the rush of blood and pleasure as his senses began to dissolve—and he felt like he was floating.

CHAPTER TEN

To Willow, it felt like living in a dream.

Dante Di Sione was her lover and he couldn't seem to get enough of her. And the feeling was mutual.

But it wasn't a dream. It was real. She needed to remember that. To remind herself that this was temporary. That it meant nothing. It meant nothing but sex. *He'd told her that himself.*

She pulled the rumpled sheet over her and listened to the sound of running water coming from the en-suite bathroom.

The trouble was that when you really wanted something it was easy to start constructing fantasies—the kind of fantasies which had got her into trouble in the first place. She started thinking about Dante's lifestyle. About his dislike of weddings and expressed distaste of settling down and doing the 'normal' stuff. What would he say if she told him she didn't care about all that stuff either? And that they might actually be a lot more compatible than he thought.

But thinking that way could lead to madness. It could make you start hoping for the impossible—and hope was such a random and unfair emotion. Hadn't she watched her young friends die in hospi-

tal and vowed that she would never waste her time
on useless hope?

So just enjoy what you have, she told herself
fiercely. *Store it all up in your mind and your heart—
so that you can pull it out and remember it when
you're back in England and Dante Di Sione is nothing but a fast-fading memory.*

It started to feel like a real holiday as he showed
her around his home territory and introduced her to
places he'd grown up with. He took her to tiny restaurants in New York's Little Italy, where the maître
d' would enquire after his grandfather's health and
where Willow ate the best pasta of her life. They spent
a day at a gorgeous place in Suffolk County called
Water Mill, where a friend of Dante's had the most
beautiful house, surrounded by trees. They visited
Sag Harbor and spent the night having sex in a stunning hotel overlooking the water, and the following
day took a trip out on the Di Sione boat, which was
anchored offshore. But when she told him she wanted
to see the guidebook stuff as well, he took her to
Manhattan and Staten Island, to Greenwich Village
and Gramercy Park—where the beautiful gardens
reminded her of England. And when he teased her
about being such a *tourist*, he couldn't seem to stop
kissing her, even though the wind blowing off the
Hudson River had felt icy cold that day.

'What are you smiling about?' questioned Dante
as he came in from the shower, rubbing his hair dry.

Willow shifted a little on the bed. It was weird how
your life could change so suddenly. One minute she'd
been someone who knew practically nothing about

men—and the next she was someone watching as one headed towards her, completely naked.

Don't get used to it, she thought. *Don't ever get used to it.*

'My thoughts are my own,' she said primly.

'I suspect you were thinking about me,' he drawled. 'Weren't you?'

'That's a very...' His shadow fell over the bed and she looked up into the glint of his blue eyes. 'A very arrogant assumption to make.'

He bent to trace a light fingertip from nipple to belly button, weaving a sensual path which made her shiver. 'But you like my arrogance,' he observed.

Willow shrugged as guilty pleasure washed over her. 'Sometimes,' she murmured. 'I know I shouldn't, but I do.'

I like pretty much everything about you.

He smiled as he sat down on the edge of the bed and slid his hand between her legs.

'What are you doing?' she said.

'I think you know the answer to that question very well, Willow Hamilton.'

She tried telling herself not to succumb as he began to move his fingers against her, because surely it would be good to turn him down once in a while? But she was fighting a losing battle. She couldn't re-sist him when he started to touch her like that. Or when he brushed his lips against her neck. And sud-denly it was not enough. It was never enough. 'Come back to bed,' she whispered.

'I can't. I'm expecting a call from Paris. There isn't time.'

'Then make time.'

'And if I say no?'

'You'll say yes in the end, you know you will.'

Dante laughed softly as he lay down beside her, smoothing his hands over her body as he drew her close. He stroked her breasts and her belly. He brushed his lips over her thrusting nipples and the soft pelt of hair between her thighs. For a while the room was filled with the sounds of breathing and kissing and those disbelieving little gasps she always gave when she came and then in the background the sound of his work phone ringing.

'I'll call them back later,' he murmured.

Afterwards he fought sleep and dressed, though he had to resolutely turn his back on her, for fear she would delay him further. He pulled on a shirt and began to button it, but his thoughts were full of her and he didn't want them to be. He'd told himself time and time again that now Talia's show was over, he needed to finish this. To let Willow go as gently as possible and to move on. It would be better for her. Better for both of them. He frowned. So what was stopping him?

He kept trying to work out what her particular magic was, and suddenly the answer came to him. Why he couldn't seem to get enough of her.

It was because she made him feel special.

And he was not.

He was not the man she thought him to be.

He stared out of the window at the lake and felt the swell of something unfamiliar in his heart. Was this how his twin had felt when he'd met Anais—the sense of being poised on the brink of something significant, something so big that it threatened to take over your whole life?

'Dante, what is it?' Willow was whispering from over on the bed, her brow creased. 'You look as if you've seen a ghost.'

He turned around to face her. Perhaps he had. The ghost of his stupid mistake, which had led to the severing of relations with his twin brother.

He shook his head. 'It's nothing.'

But she was rising from the rumpled sheets like a very slender Venus, her blond hair tumbling all the way down her back as she walked unselfconsciously across the room and looped her arms around his neck.

'It's clearly something,' she said.

And although she was naked and perfectly poised for kissing, in that moment all Dante could see was compassion in her eyes and his instinct was to turn away from her. Because all his life he'd run from compassion…a quality he'd always associated with pity, and he was much too proud to tolerate *pity*—he'd had enough of that to last a lifetime. He'd seen it on the faces of those well-meaning psychologists his grandfather had employed after the fatal crash which had left them all orphaned. He'd seen it etched on the features of those matrons at boarding school, where they'd been sent when Giovanni had finally admitted he couldn't cope any more. They'd all tried to get him to *talk* about stuff and to tell them how he *felt*. But he had clammed up, like those mussels he sometimes ate with frites in France—the ones with the tight shells you weren't supposed to touch.

Yet something about Willow made him want to talk. Made him want to tell her everything.

'You know I have a twin brother?' he said suddenly.

Cautiously, she nodded. 'But you don't talk about him.'

'That's because we are estranged. We haven't spoken in years.'

He untangled her arms from his neck and walked over to the bed, picking up a flimsy silk wrap and throwing it to her, disappointed yet relieved when she slipped it on because he couldn't really think straight when she was naked like that.

He drew in a deep breath as he met the unspoken question in her eyes. 'The two of us were sent away to a fancy boarding school in Europe,' he said slowly. 'And after we left, we started up a business together—catering for the desires of the super-rich. Our motto was *"Nothing's impossible,"* and for a while nothing was. It was successful beyond our wildest dreams...and then my brother met a woman called Anais and married her.'

There was a pause. 'And was that so bad?'

Dante looked into her clear grey eyes and it was as if he'd never really considered the matter dispassionately before. 'I thought it was,' he said slowly. 'I was convinced that she wanted Dario's ring on her finger for all the wrong reasons. Women have always been attracted to the Di Sione name in pursuit of power and privilege. But in Anais's case, I thought it was for the sake of a green card. More than that, I could see that she had her hooks into my brother. I could tell he really cared about her—and I'd never seen him that way before.'

'So what happened?' she said, breaking the brittle silence which followed.

Dante met her eyes. He had done what he had done for a reason and at the time it had seemed like a good reason, only now he was starting to see clearly the havoc he had wrought. He suddenly realised that his dislike of his twin's wife went much deeper than suspecting she just wanted a green card.

'I didn't trust her,' he said. 'But then, I didn't trust any woman.'

'Why not?'

'It's complicated.'

'Life is complicated, Dante.'

His mouth twisted. 'It's not a story I'm particularly proud of, but when we were at college, I was sleeping with a woman called Lucy. She was quite something. Or at least, so I thought—until I discovered she'd been sleeping with my twin brother as well.'

Willow stared at him. 'That's terrible,' she whispered.

He shrugged. 'I laughed it off and made out like it didn't matter. But it did. Maybe it turned her on to have sex with two men who looked identical. Or maybe she was just after the family name and didn't care which brother should be the one to give her that name.' He hesitated. 'All I know is that, afterwards, things were never quite the same between me and Dario. Something had come between us, though neither of us acknowledged it at the time. And after that, I always viewed women with suspicion.'

'I suppose so,' said Willow, and her hand reached up to touch his jaw. 'But after what had happened, it was natural you would be suspicious and examine the motives of the woman he eventually married. You were obviously looking out for him—you shouldn't beat yourself up about it.'

But Dante shook his head, forcing himself to look at the situation squarely for the first time. To see things as they were and not how he'd wanted them to be. And Willow needed to hear this. He didn't want her building up fantasies about him being the kind of caring brother who was just looking out for his twin. She needed to hear the truth.

'It wasn't just that,' he admitted slowly. 'The truth was that I wasn't crazy about Dario's new wife. I didn't like the power she had once she had his ring on her finger. She was so damned...*opinionated* and I hated the way Dario started listening to her, instead of me. Maybe I was just plain jealous.' He gave a ragged sigh. 'When he was out one morning I went round to confront Anais about her real motives in marrying him. I accused her of using him to get herself a green card and we had one hell of a row, which ended up with her throwing a glass of water over me. I guess I deserved it. We both backed down and that might have been the end of it—in fact, we'd both started talking—had Dario not walked in and found me walking out of *his* bedroom, buttoning up one of *his* shirts. He thought we'd been having sex.' He looked into Willow's widened eyes. 'He asked whether we'd been having sex.'

'And what...what did you say?'

'I didn't,' said Dante slowly. 'I didn't say anything. I used my silence to allow him come to his own conclusions, only they were the wrong conclusions. Because even though we'd both slept with Lucy, there was no way I would have ever touched his wife. But that didn't matter. All that mattered was that I felt this fierce kind of anger that he had accused me of such a thing. I thought that their relationship couldn't be so great if he thought his wife would jump straight into bed with his brother at the first opportunity. I thought the only way for things to get back to normal would be for them to break up—and they did. The marriage imploded and Dario cut all ties with me. He held me responsible and I couldn't blame him for that.'

'And did you…did you ever try to make amends?'

He nodded. 'At first I did. I was eaten up with guilt and remorse. But no matter how many times I tried to contact him, his mind was made up and he wouldn't see me, or speak to me. It was like trying to smash my way through a concrete wall with nothing but my bare hands, and in the end I gave up trying.'

He waited for her judgement. For the shock and outrage he would expect from a woman whose innocence he had taken and whose total tally of sexual partners was just one. Wouldn't she be disgusted by what he had done? Wouldn't she want to walk away from him, no matter how good he was between the sheets?

But there was no judgement there. The concern had not left her eyes. And for the first time in his life he was finding compassion tolerable.

'Why don't you go to him?' she asked.

'Because he won't see me.'

'Couldn't you at least…*try*? Because…' She sucked in a deep breath. 'The thing is, Dante…one thing I learnt when I was so ill was just how important family are. They should be the people you can depend on, no matter what. And you never, ever know what's around the corner. If something happened to Dario and you were still estranged, you'd never forgive yourself. Would you? And it's not too late to try again.' Her words became urgent. 'It's *never* too late.'

He shook his head, because hadn't he grown weary with being stonewalled? And all these years down the line, surely rejection would be all the harder to take. But as Dante looked into Willow's face, he realised he needed to be bigger than his pride and his ego. He thought about all the things she'd been through—things she hadn't wanted to tell him but which eventually he'd managed to prise from her. He thought about how she'd minimised her sickness with a few flippant sentences, making it sound no more inconvenient than a temporary power cut. Despite her slight frame and ethereal appearance, she was brave and resilient and he admired her for those strengths.

Walking over to the writing desk, he picked up his phone, but when he saw the name which had flashed onto the screen, he felt a sense of disbelief as he scrolled down to read the message. He looked up, to where Willow hadn't moved, a question darkening her grey eyes.

'What's wrong?'

'It's from Dario,' he said incredulously. 'And he wants to meet me.'

Her expression echoed his own disbelief. 'Just like that? Right out of the blue? Just after we'd been talking about him?'

'He says he heard I was at the house and decided to contact me.'

She gave a slightly nervous laugh. 'So it's just co-incidence.'

'Yeah. Just coincidence.' But Dante found himself thinking about something he hadn't allowed himself to think about for a long time. About the intuition which had always existed between Dario and him—that mythical twin intuition which used to drive everyone crazy with frustration. They'd used it to play tricks on people. They'd loved making their teachers guess which twin they were talking to. But there had been another side too. The internal side which had nothing to do with playacting. His pain had been his brother's pain. Their joy and dreams had been equally shared, until a woman had come between them.

And maybe that was how it was supposed to be. Maybe he had wasted all that energy fighting against the inevitable. For now he could see that not only had he been jealous of Anais, he'd been angry that for once in his life he'd been unable to control the outcome of something he wanted. Because the little boy who'd been unable to save his mother had grown into a man with a need to orchestrate the world and the way it worked. A man who wanted to control people and places and things. And life wasn't like that. It never could be.

He looked at Willow and once again felt that strange kick to his heart. And even though part of him wanted to act like it wasn't happening, something was stubbornly refusing to let him off the hook so easily. Was it so bad to acknowledge the truth? To admit that she made him feel stuff he'd never felt before—stuff he hadn't imagined himself *capable* of feeling. That she had given him a flicker of hope

in a future which before had always seemed so un-
remittingly dark?

'What does your brother say?' she was asking.

'That he wants to meet me.'

'When?'

'As soon as possible. He lives in New York. I could
leave right away.'

'Then shouldn't you get going?'

The words were soft, and the way she said them
curled over his skin, like warm smoke. Smoky like
her eyes. He wanted to take her back to bed. To forget all about the damned text and touch her until he
was drowning in her body and feeling that strange
kind of peace he felt whenever they were together,
but he knew he couldn't. Because this meeting with
Dario was long overdue. The rift was as deep as a
canyon, and he needed to address it. To face it and
accept the outcome, whatever that might be, and then
go forward.

'I shouldn't be more than a few hours,' he said.

'Take as long as you like.'

His eyes narrowed. She was giving him a permission he hadn't asked for and his default setting would
usually have kicked against her interference. Because
he hated the idea of a woman closing in on him…trap-
ping him…trying to get her claws hooked right into
him. Yet he would have welcomed Willow clawing
him—raking those neatly filed fingernails all the way
down his back and making him buck with pleasure.

He wondered when it was that his opinion of her
had changed so radically. When he'd realised she
wasn't some overprivileged aristocrat who wanted
the world to jump whenever she snapped her pretty

fingers—but someone who had quietly overcome her illness? Or when she'd offered him her body and her enduring comfort, despite his arrogance and his hard, black heart?

He walked across to her. The morning sun was gilding her skin and the silky nightgown she wore was that faded pink colour you sometimes found on the inside of a shell. She looked as pink and golden as a sunrise and he put his arms around her and drew her close.

'Have I told you that every time I look at you, I want you?' he said unevenly.

'I believe you said something along those lines last night.'

He tilted up her chin with the tip of his finger. 'Well, I'm telling you again, now—only this time it's not because I'm deep inside your body and about to explode with pleasure.'

Her lips parted. 'Dante…'

He nuzzled his mouth against her neck, before drawing back to stare into her clear eyes, knowing now of all the things he wanted to say to her. But not now. Not yet. Not with so much unfinished business to attend to. 'Now kiss me, Willow,' he said softly. 'Kiss me and give me strength, to help get me through what is going to be a difficult meeting.'

CHAPTER ELEVEN

AFTER DANTE HAD gone Willow tried to keep herself busy—because it was in those quiet moments when he wasn't around that doubts began to crowd into her mind like dark shadows. But she wasn't going to think about the future, or wonder how his Manhattan meeting with his twin brother was going. She was trying to do something she'd been taught a long time ago. To live in the day. To realise that this day was all any of them knew for sure they had.

She set off for a long walk around the grounds, watching the light bouncing off the smooth surface of the lake. The leaves were already on the turn and the whispering canopies above her head hinted at the glorious shades of gold and bronze to come. She watched a squirrel bounding along a path ahead of her and she listened to the sound of birdsong, thinking how incredibly peaceful it was here and how unbelievable it was to think that the buzzing metropolis of the city was only a short distance away.

Later she went to the library and studied row upon row of beautifully bound books, wondering just how many of them had actually been read. She found a copy of *The Adventures of Huckleberry Finn* and settled down to read it, soon finding herself engrossed in the famous story and unable to believe that she'd never read it before.

The hours slid by and she watched the slanting sunlight melt into dusk and shadows fall across the manicured lawns. As evening approached, Alma came to find Willow to tell her that Giovanni was feeling well enough to join her downstairs for dinner.

It was strangely peaceful with just her and Dante's grandfather sitting there in the candlelight, eating the delicious meal which had been brought to them. The old man ate very little, though he told Willow that the tagliatelle with truffle sauce was a meal he had enjoyed in his youth, long before he'd set foot on the shores of America.

They took coffee in one of the smaller reception rooms overlooking the darkened grounds, silhouetted with tall trees and plump bushes. Against the bruised darkness of the sky, the moon was high and it glittered a shining silver path over the surface of the lake. All around her, Willow could feel space and beauty— but she felt there was something unspoken simmering away too. Some deep sadness at Giovanni's core. She wondered what was it with these Di Sione men who, despite all their wealth and very obvious success, had souls which seemed so troubled.

Quietly drinking her espresso, Willow perched on a small stool beside his chair, listening to the sweet strains of the music which he'd requested Alma put on for them. The haunting sound of violins shimmered through the air and Willow felt a glorious sense of happiness. As if there was no place in the world she'd rather be, though it would have been made perfect if Dante had returned home in time to join them.

She thought about the way he'd kissed her good-bye that morning and she could do absolutely nothing about the sudden leap of her heart. Because you could tell yourself over and over that nothing was ever going to come of this strange affair of theirs, but knowing something wasn't always enough to kill off hope.

And once again she found herself wondering if she came clean and told Dante the truth about *her* situation, whether this affair of theirs might last beyond their flight back to Europe.

Giovanni's accented voice filtered into her thoughts.

'You are not saying very much this evening, Willow,' he observed.

Willow looked up into his lined face, into eyes which were dull with age and lined with the struggle of sickness, but which must once have burned as brightly blue as Dante's own.

And I will never know Dante as an old man like this, she thought. *I will never see the passage of time leave its mark on his beautiful face.*

Briefly, she felt the painful clench of her heart and it was a few seconds before she could bring herself to speak.

'I thought you might be enjoying the music,' she said. 'And that you might prefer me not to chatter over something so beautiful.'

'Indeed. Then I must applaud your consideration as well as your taste in music.' He smiled as he put down his delicate coffee cup with a little clatter. 'But time is of the essence, and I suspect that mine is fast running out. I am delighted that my grandson has at last found someone he wishes to marry, but as yet I know little about the woman he has chosen to be his bride.'

Somehow Willow kept her smile intact, hoping her face didn't look clown-like as a result. She'd had been so busy having sex with Dante that she'd almost forgotten about the fake engagement which had brought them here in the first place. And while she didn't want to deceive Giovanni, how could she possibly tell him the truth? She opened her mouth to try to change the subject, but it seemed Giovanni hadn't finished.

'I am something of an expert in the twists and complexities of a relationship between a man and a woman and I know that things are rarely as they seem,' he continued, the slight waver in his voice taking on a stronger note of reflection. 'But I do know one thing…'

Willow felt the punch of fear to her heart as she looked at him. 'What?' she whispered.

He smiled. 'Which is to witness the way you are when you look at Dante or speak of him.' He paused. 'For I can see for myself that your heart is full of love.'

For a moment Willow felt so choked that she couldn't speak. Yes, she'd once told her sister that she liked Dante and that had been true. But love? She thought about his anguish as he'd recounted the story of his childhood and her desire to protect him—weak as she was—from any further pain. She thought about the way he made her laugh. The way he made her feel good about herself, so that she seemed to have a permanently warm glow about her. He made her feel complete—even though, for her, such a feeling could never be more than an illusion.

So could those feelings be defined as love? Could they?

Yes.

The knowledge hit her like a rogue wave which had suddenly raced up out of the sea. Yes, they could.

And even if Dante never loved her back, surely they could still be a couple until he tired of her.

Couldn't they?

'Your grandson is very difficult to resist,' she said with a smile. 'But he is a very complex man.'

Giovanni laughed. 'But of course he is. All Di Sione men are complex—it is written into our DNA. That complexity has been our attraction and our downfall—although pride has played a big part in our actions. Sometimes we make decisions which are the wrong decisions and that is part of life. We must accept the shadows in order to experience light.' His voice suddenly hardened. 'But I know as an old man who has seen much of the world that regret is one of the hardest things to live with. Don't ever risk regret, Willow.'

She nodded as she leaned forward to tuck a corner of the blanket around his knees. 'I'll try not to.'

'And let me tell you something else.' His voice had softened now, shot through with a trace of something which sounded like wistfulness. 'That I long to see the bloodline of my offspring continue before I die, and to know there is another generation of Di Siones on the way.' He smiled. 'I know deep down that Dante would make a wonderful father, even though he might not yet realise that himself. Don't wait too long before giving him a baby, my dear.'

It felt like a knife ripping through her heart as Giovanni's blessing brought all her secret fears bubbling to a head. Willow tried hard not to let her distress show, but she was grateful when the nurse came to help the patriarch to bed. And as she made her way back to the cottage, she couldn't stop Giovanni's unwittingly cruel words from echoing round and round in her head.

Don't wait too long before giving him a baby, my dear.

Stumbling inside, it took a few moments before she could compose herself enough to get ready for bed and to register from the quick glance at her cell phone that there was no missed call or text from Dante. With trembling fingers she put on her silk nightdress, slithering beneath the duvet and staring sightlessly up at the ceiling, as she reminded herself that he hadn't promised to ring.

She had to stop relying on him emotionally. She had to learn to separate from him.

This wasn't going anywhere.

It *couldn't* go anywhere, she reminded herself fiercely. And sooner or later she had to address that fact, instead of existing in la-la land.

She fell asleep—her sleep peppered with heartbreaking dreams of empty cribs—and when she awoke, the pale light of dawn was filtering through the windows, bringing Dante's still and silhouetted form into stark relief.

Brushing the hair from her eyes, Willow sat up.

'How long have you been there?' she questioned sleepily.

He turned round slowly. So slowly that for a minute she was scared of what she might see in his face. Distress, perhaps—if his reconciliation with Dario had come to nothing.

But she couldn't tell what he was thinking because his eyes gave nothing away. They were shadowed, yes, but there was no apparent joy or sorrow in their lapis lazuli depths.

'I got back about an hour ago.'

'You didn't come to bed?'

She could have kicked herself for coming out with something so trite. Obviously he hadn't come to bed, or he wouldn't be standing at the window fully dressed, would he?

But he didn't seem irritated as he walked towards her and sat down on the edge of the mattress.

'No,' he said. 'I thought if I came to bed, then I'd have sex with you, and...'

'And you don't want sex?'

He laughed. 'I always want sex with you, Willow, but it's very distracting and right now I don't want any form of distraction.'

She nodded, staring very hard at the needlepoint bedspread before lifting her eyes to his. 'Do you want to talk about what happened?'

Dante considered her question and thought that of all the women he'd ever known, no one else would have asked it in quite that way. It was curious, yes— but it wasn't intrusive. She was making it plain that she could take it or leave it—it was entirely up to him what he chose to tell her. She didn't want to give him a hard time, he realised. And wasn't her kindness one of the things which kept drawing him back to her, time after time?

He sighed and the sound seemed to come from somewhere very deep in his lungs. It hadn't been an easy meeting with his twin, but it had been necessary. And cathartic. The pain of his remorse had hurt, but not nearly as badly as the realisation of how badly he had hurt his brother. And now that it was over he was aware of feeling lighter as a result.

'Not really. I'm done with talking about it,' he said, taking her hand within the palm of his own and wrapping his fingers around it. 'Would it be enough to tell you that Dario and I are no longer estranged?'

Willow nodded. 'Of course it's enough.' Her fingertips strayed to his shadowed jaw, where she felt the rasp of new growth against her skin.

'Willow, I need to talk to you.'

'I thought you just said you were done with talking.'

'That was about family rifts. This is something else.'

She bit her lip because now he sounded like she'd never heard him sound before. All serious and…*different*. Did he want to end it now? *Already?* 'What is it?' she questioned nervously.

Almost reflectively he began to trace a little circle over her palm before lifting his gaze to hers. And Willow didn't know if it was the fact that the sun was higher in the sky, but suddenly his eyes seemed clearer and bluer than she'd ever seen them before, and that was saying something.

'I'm in love with you,' he said.

Willow froze.

'With me?' she whispered, her voice choking a little.

He reached out his other hand—the one which wasn't holding hers—and touched her hair, as if he was testing how slowly he could slide his fingers over it.

'Yes, with you,' he said. 'The woman who has me twisted up in knots. Who made me do what I told myself I didn't want to do. Who gave herself to me—the sweetest gift I've ever had, as well as the best sex of my life. Who taught me how to forgive myself and to seek forgiveness in others, because that has helped me repair the bitter rift with my brother. You are the strongest and bravest woman I've ever met.'

'Dante…'

'Shh. Who has withstood more than the average person will ever know,' he continued. 'And then just shrugged it off, like the average person would shrug off rain from a shower. But you are not an average person, Willow. You're the most extraordinary person I've ever met—and I want to marry you and have babies with you.'

Her voice was more urgent now. 'Dante…'

'No. Just let me finish, because I need to say this,' he said, his fingers moving from their slow exploration of her hair to alight on her lips, to silence her. And when he next spoke, his words seemed to have taken on a deeper significance and his face had grown thoughtful—as if he'd just discovered something which had taken him by surprise. 'I never thought I wanted marriage or a family because I didn't know what a happy family was, and I wasn't sure I could ever create one of my own. The only thing I did know was that I never wanted to exist in an unhappy family. Not ever again.' His mouth twisted. 'But somehow I believe I can do it with you, because I believe—with you—that anything is possible. And I want you by my side for the rest of my life, Miss Willow Anoushka Hamilton.'

Willow blinked her eyes, trying furiously to hold back the spring of tears as she tried to take in words she'd never expected to hear him say. Beautiful, heartfelt words which made her heart want to melt. Wasn't it funny how you could long for something—even though you tried to tell yourself that it was the wrong thing to long for—and then when it happened, it didn't feel quite real.

It seemed inconceivable that Dante Di Sione should be sitting there holding her hand, with all the restraint and decorum of an old-fashioned suitor and telling her he'd fallen in love with her and wanted her to have his babies. She should have been jumping up and down with excitement, like a child on Christmas morning. She should have been flinging her arms around his neck and whooping with joy, because wasn't this the culmination of all the hopes and dreams which had been building inside her, despite all her efforts to keep them under control?

So why was she sitting there, her heart sinking with dismay as she looked into his beautiful eyes and a feeling of dread making her skin grow cold and clammy?

Because she couldn't do it. She couldn't. She could never be the woman he wanted.

She thought about something else his grandfather

had said to her last night and the wistful expression on his face as he'd said them. *Regret is one of the hardest things to live with. Don't ever risk regret, Willow.*

He was right. She couldn't risk regret—not for her sake, but for Dante's. Because if he married her, he would have a lifetime of regret.

Yet how could she possibly convey that? She didn't want to disclose her own dark secret and have him kiss away her fears and tell her it didn't matter. Because it did. Maybe not now, when they were in the first flush of this powerful feeling which seemed to have crept up on them both—but later, almost certainly it would matter. When the gloss and the lust had worn off and they were faced with the reality of looking at the future. Would Dante still want her then? Wouldn't he long for his heart's desire, knowing she could never give it to him?

She couldn't give him the choice and have him decide to do something out of some misplaced sense of selflessness, or kindness. She had to make the choice for him, because it was easier this way. She drew in a deep breath and knew she had to dig deep into the past, to remember how best to do this. To recall the way she'd managed to convince her weeping parents that no, of course the treatment didn't hurt. She'd worked hard on her acting ability when she'd been sick and realised it was the people around her who needed comfort more than she did. Because in a funny way, what she had been going through had been all-consuming. It was the people who had to stand and watch helplessly from the sidelines who suffered the most.

So use some of that acting talent now. Play the big-

gest part of your life by convincing Dante Di Sione that you don't want to marry him.

'I can't marry you, Dante,' she said, aware that his blue eyes had narrowed. Was that in surprise, or disbelief? Both, probably. He may have just made the most romantic declaration in the world but that hadn't eradicated the natural arrogance which was so much a part of him.

He nodded, but not before she had seen that look of darkness cross over his face, and Willow had to concentrate very hard to tell herself it was better this way. That it might hurt him a bit now—and it would certainly wound his ego—but in the long run it would be better. Much better.

She knew he was waiting for an explanation and she knew she owed him one, but wouldn't all the explanations in the world sound flimsy? She couldn't say that she thought their lifestyles were incompatible, or that she'd never want to live in Paris, or even New York—because she suspected he would be able to talk her out of every single one.

There was only one way to guarantee Dante Di Sione's permanent exit from her life and it was the hardest thing to say. Hard to say it like she really meant it, but she knew she had to try.

So she made her features grow wooden and her voice quiet. Because, for some reason, quiet always worked best. It made people strain towards you to listen. It made them believe what you said.

'I can't marry you because I don't love you, Dante.'

CHAPTER TWELVE

DANTE'S EYES WERE shards of blue so cold that Willow could feel her skin freezing beneath that icy gaze. 'You don't love me?' he repeated slowly.

Willow nodded, hanging on to her composure only by a shred. 'No,' she said. 'I don't.'

She began to babble, as if adding speed to her words would somehow add conviction. 'It was just a part we were both playing for the sake of your grandfather,' she said. 'You know it was. It was the sex which made it start to seem real. Amazing and beautiful sex—although I've got nothing to compare it to, of course. But I'm guessing from your reaction that it was pretty special, and I guess that's what made us get carried away.'

He gave a short laugh. 'Made *me* get carried away, you mean?'

Keep going, she told herself. *Not much longer now. Make him think you're a cold hard bitch, if that helps.* 'Yes,' she said with a shrug of her shoulders. 'I guess.'

A strange note had entered his voice and now his eyes had grown more thoughtful. 'So it's only ever really been about sex, is that what you're saying, Willow? You decided early on that I was to be the man who took your virginity, and you were prepared to do pretty much anything to get that to happen, were you?'

All she had to do was agree with him and very soon it would be finished. Except that something in the way he was looking at her was making her throat grow dry. Because the softness had left his face and her breasts were beginning to prickle under that new, hard look in his eyes. Willow licked her lips. 'That's right.'

Dante stared at her, wondering how he could have got it so wrong. Had he been so bewitched by her proximity that he had started believing the fantasy which they'd both created? Had his reconciliation with his brother made him overly sentimental—making him want to grab at something which up until recently hadn't even been on his agenda? Perhaps his grandfather's illness had stirred up a primitive need inside him and he had made a bad judgement call. She didn't want him, or his babies. She didn't love him. She didn't care.

A smile twisted his lips. Ironic, really. He could think of a hundred women who would fight to wear his ring for real. Just not Willow Hamilton. And just because she'd never had sex with anyone before him didn't make her a saint, did it? He'd turned her on in a big way and it seemed he had liberated her enough to want to go out there and find her pleasure with other men. He felt a savage spear of something else which was new to him. Something he automatically despised because deep down he knew it would weaken him. Something he instinctively recognised as jealousy.

And suddenly he knew that in order to let her go,

he had to have her one last time. To remind himself
of how good she felt. To lick every inch of her soft,
pale skin and touch every sinew of her slender body.
To rid himself of this hateful need which was making his groin throb, even though he told himself he
should be fighting it. But he couldn't. For the first
time in his life, he couldn't. His sexual self-control
was legendary and he had walked away from women
when they'd been begging him to take them. Willow
was not begging—not any more. His bitter smile returned. But pretty soon she would be.

'Well, if it's only ever been about sex, then maybe
we ought to go out with a bang.' He smiled as her
head jerked back, her shock palpable. 'If you'll pardon the pun.'

Willow's heart pounded as she looked into his eyes
and saw the smoulder of intent there. She told herself
that this was dangerous. Very dangerous. That she
needed to get out of here before anything happened.

'Dante,' she whispered. But the words she'd been
about to say had died on her lips because he was
walking towards her with an expression on his face
which was making her blood alternatively grow hot
and cold. She could *see* the tension hardening his
powerful body as he reached her. She could *smell*
the raw scent of his arousal in the air. As he stroked
a finger down over her arm, she began to shiver uncontrollably. This was wrong. It was wrong and dangerous and would lead to nowhere but pain and she
knew she had to stop it. She *had* to. 'Dante,' she whispered again.

'One for the road,' he said in a cruel voice.

And then he kissed her in a way which shocked her

almost as much as it turned her on. It was hard and it was masterful—an unashamed assertion of sexual power. It was all about technique and dominance—but there was no affection there.

So why did she kiss him back with a hunger which was escalating by the second? Why didn't she just press her hands against that broad chest and push him away, instead of clinging on to him like some sort of limpet? He was strong enough and proud enough to accept her refusal. To just turn and walk away. They could end this strange relationship without stoking up any more emotional turmoil and then try to put the whole affair behind them.

But she couldn't. She wanted him too much. She always had and she always would. She wanted—how had he put it?—*one for the road*.

Did he see the sudden softening of her body, or did her face betray her change of feelings? Was that why he reached down to her delicate silk nightdress and ripped it open so that it flapped about her in tatters? His eyes were fixed on hers and she wanted to turn her head away, but she was like a starving dog sitting outside a butcher's shop as he swiftly bared his magnificent body and carelessly dropped his clothes to the floor.

Naked now, he was pressing her down against the mattress as he moved over her, his fingertips whispering expertly over her skin, making her writhe with hungry impatience. His big body was fiercely aroused, and even though his face looked dark and forbidding, Willow didn't care. Because how could she care about anything when he was making her feel like *this*?

She shuddered as he palmed her breasts and then bent his head to lick them in turn, his breath warm against her skin as she arched against his tongue. She could feel the rough rasp of his unshaved jaw rubbing against her skin and knew that it would be reddened by the time he had finished. And when he drew his head back she almost gasped when she saw the intense look of hunger on his face, his cheekbones flushed and his blue eyes smoky.

'Ride me,' he said deliberately.

She wanted to say no. She wanted him to kiss her deeply and passionately, the way he usually did—but she recognised that she had forfeited that luxury by telling him she didn't love him. All she had left was sex—and this was the very last time she would have even that. So make it raunchy, she told herself fiercely. Make him believe that this was what the whole thing had been about.

She slid out from underneath him to position herself on top, taking his moist and swollen tip and groping on the nearby bedside table for the condoms he always kept there. He had taught her to do this as he had taught her so much else, and she had worked on her condom application skills as diligently as a novice pianist practising her scales. So now she teased him with her fingertips as she slid the rubber over his erect shaft, enjoying his moan of satisfaction—even though it was breaking her heart to realise she would never hear it again. And when she took him deep inside her and began to move slowly up and down, he felt so big that she was certain he would split her in two. But he didn't. Her body quickly adapted to him, slickly tightening around him until she saw his fingers claw desperately at the rucked sheet on which they lay.

For a while she played the part expected of her and for a while it came so easily. Her fingers were tangled in her hair and her head was thrown back in mindless ecstasy as she rode him, glad she didn't have to stare into his beautiful face, scared that she might falter and give away her true feelings. Blurt out something stupid, and very loving. But suddenly he caught hold of her hips and levered her off him. Ignoring her murmur of protest, he laid her down flat against the mattress and moved over her again.

'No,' he said, his voice very intent as he made that first renewed thrust deep inside her. 'I want to dominate you, Willow. I want to remind myself that everything you know you have learned from me. I want to watch your face as you come, and I want you to realise that never again will you feel me doing this… and this…and *this*…'

She cried out then, because the pleasure was so intense it was close to pain. And if the first time they'd ever made love she had begged him not to be gentle with her—not to treat her as if she was made of glass—he certainly wasn't gentle now. It was as if he was determined to show her everything he was capable of, as he drove into her with a power which had her nails digging helplessly into his shoulders.

She almost didn't *want* to come—as if her orgasm would be a sign of weakness and by holding it back she could retain some control over what was happening— but already it was too late. Her back was beginning to arch, her body spasming around him as she opened her mouth to cry out her satisfaction.

But for once he didn't kiss the sound away and blot it into silence with his lips. Instead he just watched her as she screamed, as cold-bloodedly as a scientist might observe an experiment which was taking place in the laboratory. Only then did he give in to his own orgasm and she thought it seemed brief and almost perfunctory. He didn't collapse against her, whispering the soft words in French or Italian which turned her on so much. He simply pumped his seed efficiently into the condom before withdrawing from her and rolling away to the other side of the bed.

Several agonisingly long minutes passed before he turned to look at her and something about the coldness of his blue gaze made her want to shiver again.

'Time to get on that road,' he said softly.

And he walked straight towards the bathroom without a backward glance.

Willow's hands were trembling as she gathered up the tattered fragments of her torn nightdress and stuffed them into her suitcase, terrified that one of the staff would find them. She had composed herself a little by the time Dante emerged, freshly showered and shaved and wearing a dark and immaculate suit which made him seem even more distant than the look in his eyes suggested he was.

'Are you…are you going somewhere?' she said.

'I am.' He gave a cold smile. 'I'm leaving. And obviously, you'll be coming with me. We will drive to the airport—only we'll be going our separate ways from now on. You'll be heading for London, while my destination is Paris. But first, I need to speak to my grandfather.'

'Dante…'

'Save your breath, Willow,' he said coolly. 'I think we've said everything which needs to be said. I guess I should thank you for playing such a convincing fiancée. But I'm going to sit down with Giovanni and tell him that our relationship is over, and to remind him that he knows better than anyone that marriages simply don't work if there is no love involved.' His eyes glittered. 'If you're willing to sign a confidentiality clause, you can keep the ring. You should be able to get a decent amount of money for it.'

'I don't need to sign a confidentiality clause. And I won't talk about this to anyone. Why would I? It's not exactly something I'm very proud of.' Her voice was trembling as she stared at the huge diamond and thought about how much it must be worth. Shouldn't she keep it and sell it, and use the money to do some real good—for people who badly needed it? And wouldn't it help if he thought of her as greedy and grasping? If she could give him yet another reason to hate her? She curved her mouth into a speculative smile. 'But yes, I will keep the ring.'

The look of contempt on his lips was unmistakable as he turned away. 'Be my guest. And now pack your case and get dressed,' he said harshly. 'And let's get out of here.'

CHAPTER THIRTEEN

BEHIND THE FLASHING blue and gold illuminations of
the Eiffel Tower, the Parisian sky was dark and star-
less and the streets were quiet. Far below the windows
of his offices, the river Seine looked cold and unin-
viting and Dante was lost in thought when he heard
the door open behind him and someone walk in. He
swivelled round in his chair to see his assistant standing there, a pointed expression on his face.

'Yes, what is it, René?' he questioned impatiently.

'You are due at a drinks party at the Ritz…' René
looked down at his watch. 'Ten minutes ago actually.'

Dante scowled. 'Ring them. Tell them that I've
been held up and unlikely to make it in time.'

'I could do that, of course,' said René carefully.
'But it is the birthday party of the countess—and you
know how much she wants you there.'

Dante leaned back. Yes, he knew. The whole world
always wanted him, women especially. Except for one
woman. His mouth hardened as he stared into space.

*One woman. One infernal, infuriating woman who
had made it clear that wanting him was the last thing
on her particular wish list.*

'Is there…is there something wrong, boss?'

Dante glanced across the room, tempted to confide in his loyal assistant—not something he ever did usually. But then, he didn't *usually* feel as if a heavy weight was pressing down hard on his heart, did he? Or his life seem as if there was something fundamental missing which made him feel only half complete. He shut his eyes. Had he imagined that the heartless way that the beautiful blonde had rejected him would have been enough to make him see sense? And that it would somehow be easy to forget her? Because if that was the case then it seemed that yet again he had been wrong, and he didn't like being wrong.

He thought about the contradiction she'd been. The tender and passionate woman in his arms who had rapturously embraced the joys of sex. He remembered her childlike delight when he'd taken her to Shelter Island for breakfast. The way she'd charmed his grandfather and made his tomboy sister look like a million dollars. He thought about the crazy hope she'd awoken in his heart, along with the realisation that, suddenly, all the things he'd never dared dream of felt as if they could be possible with her. He remembered the trembling expression on her face when he'd asked her to marry him. The way she'd tried to blink back the sudden tears of joy as she looked at him.

And then?

Then…nothing. In a voice which was deathly quiet and a face devoid of emotion, she had told him she couldn't marry him. She'd told him she didn't love him when those words belied her every action. It didn't make sense. He shook his head. None of it made sense. If she hadn't been so innocent, he might have suspected the presence of another man. Though maybe that wasn't such a crazy idea? She'd grabbed at the diamond ring quickly enough, hadn't she? So maybe she wasn't quite as naive as she seemed.

He watched as the lights on the tower turned to red, and then to gold. Perhaps he had been nothing but her *stud*—an alpha male chosen as the ideal candidate for her sexual initiation. Maybe the fact that he was a foreigner had allowed her to shed all her inhibitions—he knew some women were like that—when all along she'd intended to marry an English aristocrat of the same class as herself.

Once again, an unwanted streak of jealousy flooded through his veins like dark poison and he opened his eyes to find René looking at him with that same expression of concern. He thought about his assistant's question and he realised that yes, something was *very* wrong and it was more to do with his own behaviour. Because since when had he taken to asking himself questions, without bothering to seek out the answers?

'I need some information about a woman.'

'Same woman as before?' asked René innocently. 'It wouldn't happen to be a Miss Willow Hamilton, would it?'

'As quickly as possible,' said Dante impatiently.

'Bien sûr.' René's lips twitched. 'This is getting to be a bit of a habit if you don't mind my saying so, boss.'

'Well, I do mind.' Dante glowered as he stood up and pulled off his tie. 'I don't pay you to give your opinion when it isn't wanted. Have the car brought round and I will call at the countess's party for a while. And will you please wipe that smug expression from your face, because it is starting to infuriate me.'

Dante was driven to the first *arrondissement*, to the glittering cocktail party being held in one of the famous hotel's penthouse suites, but his heart wasn't in it—nor in any of the stellar guests who were present. The countess was delectable, but she left him cold—as did the other women who smiled at him with open invitation in their eyes. He endured it for a while, then slipped away—and when he arrived at work early the following morning, it was to find René already in the office, with a look of triumph on his face.

'I have the information you require,' he said.

'Go on.'

'She is living in London…'

'I already know that,' interrupted Dante impatiently.

'And she will be attending a fundraiser for the Leukaemia Society being held at the Granchester Hotel in London this Saturday.' René paused, his dark eyes hooded. 'You might also be interested to know that she has put her diamond engagement ring up for the charity auction.'

And for the first time in his life, Dante was speechless.

Willow looked up from behind the podium and for a moment there was complete silence in the large ballroom, before she spoke again. 'And that is why I consider it such an honour to be your new patron.'

An expectant hush fell over the assembled throng and she drew in a deep breath, knowing that she had to get this right. 'I wanted to give fellow sufferers hope, as well as supporting the fantastic new research which is taking place all over the world. I'm prepared to step out of the shadows and talk openly about what happened to me, instead of hiding it away. Because I'm better. And because, every day, there are more and more people like me, getting better. And I...'

Her words tailed off because, for a moment there, a trick of the light made her think she saw Dante standing at the back of the ballroom. She blinked, slightly impatient with herself. Was she now beginning to conjure him up from nowhere, so that he was about to become a constant presence in her daytime as well as her night-time thoughts?

'I...' She couldn't remember what she had been saying and someone held a glass of water towards her, but she shook her head. She stared to where the man stood, her eyes drinking him in—registering every pore of his sensual face. It *was* him. Very definitely him. Because nobody in the world looked quite like Dante Di Sione. Tall and broad and strong and magnificent and somehow managing to dominate the entire room.

And she couldn't allow herself to go to pieces at this point. Too many people were relying on her.

She fumbled around for the words which had been on the tip of her tongue and somehow managed to produce them. 'I just want to say that I think you are all wonderful, and I'm delighted to be able to tell you that the silent auction has raised almost half a million pounds.' She swallowed, and then smiled— a big smile which just grew and grew. 'So thank you again from the bottom of my heart—for allowing me to give something back.'

The sound of clapping began and swelled, echoing loudly throughout the vast room as Willow stepped carefully down from the stage, her narrow silver dress not the easiest of garments to move around in. Now what did she do? She risked a glance to where Dante had stood, but he was no longer there and she felt her heart plummet. Of course he wasn't there! She had dreamt him up. It had been a fantasy—nothing more. Why would he be here when he'd flown straight back to Paris and they hadn't spoken since he had boarded his jet in New York, all those weeks ago?

'Willow.'

The sound of his voice was unmistakable and her knees buckled, but even though his hand was instantly on her elbow and his strength seemed to flow straight into her, she shook herself free. Because she had to learn to live without him. She had to.

'Dante,' she said, but her voice sounded faint. 'What are you doing here?'

His eyes were curious, but his tone was dry. 'No ideas?'

She licked her lips. 'You were in London?'

'And happened to be passing? Yeah, you could say that.' He gave a mirthless smile. 'Is there anywhere quieter we can go to talk?'

She knew she should tell him that no, there wasn't. She knew she ought to fetch her wrap and go outside to find a cab. Go home and forget she'd ever seen him. Her gaze travelled over his face and stayed fixed on the features she'd missed so much. His blue eyes. His sensual lips. The faint darkness which always lingered around his jaw. 'There's the hotel's Garden Room,' she croaked.

In silence they walked to the plant-filled bar, with its white baby grand piano tucked away in the corner. Dante immediately managed to commandeer a quiet table at the back of the room but Willow knew instantly that she'd made a mistake in her choice of venue. A big mistake. Because the air was filled with the scent of jasmine and gardenia—heady scent which seemed unbearably romantic, as did the soft music which the pianist was playing. And the flickering candlelight didn't help. Maybe she could concentrate on her drink. Order some complicated cocktail with a cherry and an umbrella and give it her full attention.

But Dante waved the hovering waiter away and she guessed it was an indication of his charisma that he should be allowed to occupy the best table in the place without even ordering a drink.

She waited to hear what he would say and she tried to second-guess him, desperately trying to work out the right answers to whatever he was going to say. Trouble was, he asked the last question she wanted to hear. The one question she didn't want to answer. She'd lied about this once before, but she had been stronger then. She'd been so certain it had been the right thing to do and she hadn't been starved of his presence for almost five weeks, so that she could barely stop herself from reaching out to touch him.

'Do you love me, Willow?'

She looked into his eyes—which were the colour of midnight in this candlelit room—and she opened her mouth to tell him no. But a rush of stupid tears filled

her own eyes and prevented her from saying anything, and mutely, she found herself shaking her head.

'Do you?' he said again. 'Just tell me, Willow. Say
it out loud. That's all I'm asking. Tell me you don't
love me and I'll walk out of here and you'll never
see me again.'

She tried. For almost a minute she tried. Tried to
force the words out of her mouth in the same way
that you sometimes had to prise a stubborn Brazil
nut from its shell. But the words wouldn't come. They
just wouldn't come. At least, not the words she knew
she should say. The other ones—the eager, greedy
ones—they suddenly came pouring from her lips as
if she had no control over them.

'Yes,' she burst out. 'Yes, I love you. Of course
I do. I didn't want to. I still don't want to. And I'm
sorry. I don't want to mess you around and I certainly
don't want to send out mixed messages. So it's probably better if you forget everything I've just said.
Because…because it can't lead anywhere, Dante—
it just *can't*.'

His eyes narrowed, like someone who had just
been presented with a locked room and was working
out how best to open it without a key. 'Do you want
to tell me why?'

'Because I can't give you what you want,' she
whispered. 'You told me you wanted marriage. And
babies. Your grandfather told me that he longed for
nothing more than to see the next generation of Di
Siones.'

'And?'

'And I can't promise you that. I had…' She swallowed and licked her lips. 'I had treatment for my

illness before I started my periods and they said it's possible—even likely—that I may not be able to have children.'

'But you didn't ever find out for sure?'

She shook her head. 'No. I know it's stupid, but I preferred to live in a state of not knowing. I guess I was too scared to confront it and I didn't want yet another negative thing to define me. It seemed much easier to just bury my head in the sand.' She shrugged and bit her lip. 'But I suppose that's difficult for you to understand.'

She didn't know what she had expected but it hadn't been for Dante to pick up her hand—her left hand—and to turn it over and study her palm as if he was able to read her future, before lifting his solemn gaze to hers.

'No,' he said. 'It's not difficult at all, because all of us are sometimes guilty of not facing a truth which is too hard to take. I did it with my own brother—refused to accept that my reluctance to share him was what lay at the root of our rift. But listen to me very carefully, Willow—because you're not thinking logically.'

Her blurry gaze fixed on his stern features. 'What do you mean?'

'There is *always* the chance that you or I can't have a baby. That applies to every couple in the world until they try themselves. Unless you're advocating putting all prospective brides and grooms through some kind of fertility test before they're allowed to marry?' He raised his eyebrows. 'I don't think even royal families adopt that strategy any more.'

'Dante…'

'No,' he said. 'You've had your say and now I'm having mine. Understand?'

Pressing her lips in on themselves, she nodded.

'I love you,' he said simply. 'And the past few weeks have made me realise how much. Time spent away from you has only increased the certainty that I want to spend the rest of my life with you, and only you.' He placed a warning finger over her lips as they began to open. 'With or without children of our own. Because children aren't a deal-breaker. You not loving me would be the only deal-breaker. That's the only thing which would stop me from wanting to marry you, and I'm afraid you've just signed your own fate by telling me that you *do* love me.'

Dazed, she stared at him. 'Am I allowed to say anything yet?'

'Only if you're prepared to see sense and accept my proposal—unless you want me to go down on one knee in this very public place and ask you all over again, despite the fact that you've already auctioned off the first ring I gave you?'

'No! No, please don't do that. Don't you *dare* do that.'

'So you will marry me?'

'It seems I have no choice!'

She was laughing but somehow she seemed to be crying at the same time and Dante was standing up and pulling her into his arms and wiping her tears away with his fingers, before kissing her in a way that made the last of her reservations melt away.

And when the picture of that ecstatic kiss made its way into the gossip columns of next day's news-papers—with the headline *Society Girl to Wed No-*

torious Playboy—Willow didn't care. Because now she realised what mattered—the only thing which mattered. She was going to focus on what was truly important, and that was yet another thing Dante had taught her.

He'd taught her that love made you strong enough to overcome anything.

So she threw the newspaper down onto the carpet and turned to look at him, running her fingers over his olive skin and thinking how magnificent he looked in *her* bed.

Sleepily, he opened his eyes and gave a huge yawn as he glanced down at the bare hand which was currently inching its way up his thigh. 'I guess we'd better go out and buy you another ring. Would you like that?'

'I'd like that very much.'

'But not a diamond.' He smiled. 'A rare grey pearl, I think.'

'Mmm… That sounds perfect.' She moved over him, skin against skin, mouth against mouth—and ripples of desire shivered over her as she felt his hardness pressing against her. 'Just not now,' she whispered indistinctly. 'The ring can wait. But this can't.'

EPILOGUE

'COME AND SIT in the shade,' Dante said lazily. 'I don't want you getting burned.'

Willow pushed her straw hat back and smiled up into her husband's face. 'I'm unlikely to burn when you insist on applying factor fifty to my skin at every opportunity, am I?'

'True. In fact, I think you need another application right now,' he murmured, rising to his feet and standing over her. 'Come here.'

'That sounds like another excuse for you to start rubbing cream into my body.'

'You really think I need an excuse, Mrs Di Sione?' he growled, lifting her off the sun lounger and leading her inside to the air-conditioned cool of their beach-side house.

Willow bit her lip with sheer pleasure as she felt his lips whisper over her throat, thinking she couldn't remember ever feeling so happy. Or lucky. So very lucky. For the past month they'd been honeymooning in a Caribbean beach house, while nearby the crystal waters lapped contentedly against sugar-fine sands. They swam in the mornings, napped in the after-noons and took lazy days out on the Di Sione boat,

which had been sailed from New York and was now
anchored off the island.

They had married quietly in the small church built
in the grounds of her parents' house and the building had been transformed for the occasion, discreetly
bankrolled by her future husband. The badly repaired
hole in the ceiling had been miraculously fixed and
the air was scented with gardenias and jasmine similar to those which had perfumed the Garden Room
at the Granchester on the night Dante had asked her
to marry him.

'Did you like our wedding?' she questioned softly.

'I loved it. Every second.'

'You didn't think it was too quiet?'

'No. It was perfect. Just like you.' Dante unclipped
her bikini top and began to skate his fingertips over
her nipples. He had wanted a quiet wedding. There
had still been so much *stuff* going on about Giovanni's Lost Mistresses—with his brothers and his sisters all over the place trying to find random pieces
of jewellery and other stuff which had once belonged
to his grandfather, and nothing completely resolved.
The uncertainty about who would be able to attend
and who wouldn't had made Dante decide to have
the smallest of weddings, with only his brother Dario
in attendance as his best man. He told Willow he
planned for them to visit the Long Island estate during the forthcoming holidays, where they would have
a big post-wedding party.

But he'd known all along that he didn't need pomp,
or ceremony. If it could have been just him and Willow, he wouldn't have complained. In the end, he was
the one who badly wanted to place a gold ring on

her finger and make her his. He'd wanted to marry her more than he could ever remember wanting anything. Because she gave him everything he needed—and more.

And if she'd questioned him over and over about his need for children, he had reassured her with a certainty which went bone-deep. He'd told her that there were lots of possibilities open to them if they couldn't conceive. Like he'd said, it wasn't a deal-breaker. Until one day she'd started believing him and never mentioned it again. And if either of them had been able to see into the future, they would have seen Willow Di Sione holding two baby girls—beautiful, blue-eyed twins, just like their daddy.

Dante gave a contented sigh as he remembered back to their wedding day. Without a doubt she had made the most exquisite bride in the history of the world—with a veil which had been worn by her grandmother, held in place with the glittering tiara of white diamonds and emeralds as green as new leaves. Dario had offered her use of the matching earrings, but although Willow had been very grateful, she had declined the offer. 'A woman can wear *too* much jewellery, you know,' she'd whispered to her prospective husband—and Dante had laughed with a feeling of pure pleasure.

Her slender figure had been showcased by a pale, gauzy dress, beneath which she'd sported a garter embroidered with dramatic flames of yellow and red. And when slowly he'd been removing it on their wedding night, his hand had lingered on the raised surface of vibrant hues, which she'd so lovingly stitched.

'Flames?' he questioned with a frown.

'As a kind of homage to an earlier Dante and his famous inferno.' She smiled. 'But mainly because my life would be hell without you.'

He smiled back. 'Interesting. But I thought brides were traditionally supposed to have something blue?'

And that was when her fingertips reached up to trace over his cheeks with the most gentle touch he had ever known. A touch which had made him shiver with pleasure and count his blessings.

'Your eyes are the bluest thing I've ever seen, Dante Di Sione.' Her voice had been low and trembling. 'I'll settle for those.'

* * * * *

A DI SIONE FOR
THE GREEK'S
PLEASURE

KATE HEWITT

CHAPTER ONE

'I WANT YOU to do something for me.'

Natalia Di Sione smiled at her grandfather as she adjusted the blanket over his legs and sat down across from him. Even though it was the hottest part of a June day, Giovanni Di Sione still shivered slightly in the wind coming off the Long Island Sound.

'Anything, Nonno,' Natalia said, using the name she'd called him since she was a little girl.

Giovanni gave her a whimsical smile as he shook his head. 'You are so quick to agree, Talia, yet you do not know what I am going to ask.'

'You know I'd do anything for you.' Giovanni had raised Talia and her siblings after her parents had died in a car accident when she, as the youngest of seven, had been little more than a baby. He was father, mother and grandfather rolled into one, and since she'd been living on the Di Sione estate with him for the last seven years, he was also the closest thing she had to a confidant and best friend.

She knew some of her older siblings had retained a little distance from their hardworking and sometimes remote grandfather, but in the last seven years Talia had embraced him wholly. He'd offered her refuge when she'd crawled back here, wounded in both body and mind. He'd been her salvation.

'Anything, Talia?' Giovanni asked, arching one eyebrow in wry challenge. 'Even, perhaps, leave the estate?'

She laughed lightly. 'Surely you wouldn't ask me to do something as terrible as that.' She pretended to shudder, although the truth was just the prospect of stepping foot outside the lavish gated estate made her insides clench in fear. She liked her ivory tower, the security of knowing she was protected, behind gates, *safe*. Because she knew what it was like not to feel safe, to feel as if your very life hung by a single, slender thread, and she refused ever to feel that way again…even if it meant living like a prisoner.

She left the villa at most only a few times a year, usually to visit one of her siblings or attend a private viewing at the occasional art exhibition nearby. She avoided cities and even Long Island's Gold Coast's small, well-heeled towns, and restricted travel to short jaunts in a chauffeured car.

When Giovanni suggested Talia get out more, she insisted she preferred a quiet life on the estate, with its sprawling villa, rolling manicured lawns and the winking blue of the Long Island Sound in the distance. Why, she teased her grandfather, did she need to go anywhere else?

Giovanni was kind enough not to push. Yet Talia knew he was concerned about her isolation, even if he never said it. She saw how worry often shadowed his eyes or drew his bushy eyebrows together as he watched her pottering about the villa.

'You know I do not have long left, Talia,' Giovanni said now, and she merely nodded, not trusting her voice. A few months ago Giovanni had been given a year to live. Considering he was ninety-eight years old and had already beaten cancer once, nearly twenty years ago, a year was a long time. But it wasn't long enough for Talia.

She couldn't imagine the villa without Giovanni, his gentle smiles and wise words, his often silent yet steady presence. The huge, elegant rooms would seem emptier than ever, the estate yawning in all directions, inhabited only by her and its skeleton staff. She hated the thought, and so her mind skittered away from it.

'So what would you like me to do?' Talia asked. 'Paint your portrait?' For the last few years she had built up a small but thriving career painting portraits. For her twenty-first birthday Giovanni had given her a studio on the grounds of the estate, a small, shingled building with a glorious view of the Sound. Clients came to her studio to sit for their portraits, and she enjoyed the social interaction as well as the creative work, all in the secure environment she craved.

'A portrait?' Giovanni chuckled. 'Who would like to see an old man such as me? No, *cara*, I'd like something else. I'd like you to find something for me.' He sat back in his chair, his gnarled hands folded in his lap, and watched her, waiting.

'Find something?' Talia leaned forward, surprised and curious, as well as more than a little apprehensive. She recognised that knowing gleam in her grandfather's eyes, the way he went silent, content to let her be the one to ask. 'Have you lost something, Nonno?'

'I have lost many things over the years,' Giovanni answered. Talia heard a touch of sad whimsy in his voice, saw how his face took on a faraway look. A faint smile curved his mouth, as if he was remembering something sweet or perhaps poignant. Then he turned back to Talia. 'I want you to find one of them. One of my Lost Mistresses.'

Talia knew about Giovanni's Lost Mistresses; it was a tale cloaked in mystery that she'd grown up on: a collection of precious objects that Giovanni had carried with him into the new world, when he'd emigrated from Italy as a young man. He'd been forced to sell them off one by one to survive, although he'd loved them all dearly. He'd always refused to say any more than that, claiming an old man must have some secrets. Talia suspected Giovanni had many secrets, and now, with a flicker of curiosity, she wondered if he would tell her at least one of them.

'One of your Lost Mistresses?' she repeated. 'But you've never actually said what they are. Which one is it?'

'A book, a very special book, and one that will be very difficult to find.'

She raised her eyebrows. 'And you think *I* can find it?'

'Yes, I do. I trust your intelligence and ingenuity, Talia. Your creativity. It shines from your soul.'

She laughed and shook her head, embarrassed and touched. Her grandfather did not often speak so sentimentally, but she knew that the years weighed on him now and she suspected he felt the need to say things he'd kept hidden for so long.

'What kind of book?' she asked.

'A book of love poems, written by an anonymous poet from the Mediterranean. It is called *Il Libro d'Amore.*'

'The Book of Love,' Talia translated. 'Are there many copies of it available?'

'A handful perhaps, but the one I possessed was unlike any other, a first edition with a cover of hand-tooled leather. It is truly unique.'

'And yet you think I can find it?' Talia said, doubt creeping into her voice. She'd been envisioning doing a quick Internet search, maybe tracking the book down through a used book dealer. But of course Giovanni could do that himself. He'd bought a tablet years ago, and innovative entrepreneur that he'd always been, he regularly surfed the Internet.

But of course he wanted her to do something far more

difficult. Something far more important. And she knew she didn't want to let him down.

Her grandfather hadn't asked much of her over the years; he'd graciously given her her own private living quarters on his estate when she'd been just nineteen years old and barely able to cope. He'd never pushed her too hard to get out or to try new things, and he'd made her career as an artist possible without ever having to leave the villa. She owed a lot to her *nonno*.

'Yes, I want you to find that particular book,' he said, smiling sadly. 'There is an inscription on the inside cover: "Dearest Lucia, For ever in my heart, always. B.A."' His voice choked a little and he looked down, blinking rapidly, before he gazed back up at Talia with his usual whimsical smile. 'That is how you will know it is the right one.'

'Who is Lucia?' Talia felt oddly moved by the inscription, as well as her grandfather's obvious and unusual emotion. 'And who is B.A.? Were they friends of yours?'

'You could say that, yes. They were very dear to me, and they loved each other very much.' Giovanni sat back, adjusting the blanket over his legs, his face pale. Talia had been noticing how easily he tired lately; clearly their conversation had worn him out. 'But that,' Giovanni said, a note of finality in his voice, 'is a story for another time.'

'But what happened to the book?' Talia asked. 'Did you sell it when you reached America?'

'No, I never took it to America. I left it behind, and that is why it will be difficult to find. But I think you are capable, Talia. Even if finding it may take you on a journey in more ways than one.'

'A journey…' Talia pressed her lips together. She was pretty sure that finding this book was her grandfather's way of getting her off the estate, out into life. She knew he'd been wanting her to spread her wings for some time now, and she'd always resisted, insisted she was happy here on the estate. How could she not be? She had everything she wanted right here. She didn't need more, didn't want adventure or excitement. Not as she once had.

Because look where that had got her.

'Nonno…' she began, and Giovanni shook a finger at her in gentle admonition.

'You are not going to refuse an old man a dying wish?'

'Don't say that—'

'*Cara*, it's true. And I wish to have this book very much. To turn its fragile pages and read of how love surpasses any glory, any tragedy…' His voice choked once more and Talia bit her lip as guilt flooded through her.

How on earth could she even consider refusing her grandfather's request, all out of her own selfish fear? How could she say no to Giovanni, her *nonno* who had taken care of her since she was a baby? Who had been as both mother and father, and lived with her these last seven years, accepting her limitations, loving her anyway?

'I'll try, Nonno,' she said finally, and Giovanni leaned forward to rest his bony hand on top of hers.

'I know you will, *cara*,' he said, his voice hoarse as he smiled at her. 'I know you will try your hardest. And you will succeed.'

'There is one more woman to see you, Kyrie Mena.'

Angelos Mena looked up from his desk and the stack of CVs he'd scanned and then discarded. None of the young women he'd interviewed that afternoon had been remotely appropriate for the position. In fact, he suspected they'd been more interested in cosying up to him than getting to know his daughter, Sofia, just as the last three nannies had been.

His mouth thinning in disgust, he ran his hand through

his hair and then shook his head. 'One more? But that should be all.' He tapped the discarded pile of papers on his desk. 'I have no more CVs.'

His assistant, Eleni, spread her hands in helpless ignorance. 'She has been waiting here for several hours, saying she needs to see you.'

'She has tenacity, then, at least.' He pushed away from the desk. 'You might as well send her in.'

With a click of heels Eleni left his office and Angelos rose to stand by the floor-to-ceiling window that overlooked Athens. Tension knotted the muscles of his shoulders and made his temples throb. He really hadn't needed the complication of his new nanny delaying her start by six weeks. Finding an acceptable temporary replacement was a challenge he did not relish, especially considering that not one of the dozen women he'd interviewed today had been suitable.

Some had had experience, yes, but when he'd called Sofia in to see if his daughter approved, she'd resisted the women's cloying attempts at friendship. Even Angelos had been able to see how patently false they were. He'd noticed how several of the women hadn't wanted to look at Sofia; several others had stared. Both reactions had made his daughter shrink back in shame, and the injustice of it made Angelos seethe with fury. His daughter had nothing to be ashamed about.

Not like he did.

'Mr Menos?'

Angelos turned around to see a slender young woman standing in the doorway. She looked pale but resolute, her sandy brown hair tousled, the simple pink cotton sundress she wore hopelessly wrinkled. Angelos frowned at the sight of her dishevelment. Clearly she did not dress to impress.

'And you are?' he asked, his tone deliberately curt.

'I'm sorry…um…*signomi*…but I don't speak…*den*… uh…*milau*…' She stammered, a flush washing over her face, making her hazel eyes seem luminous in her freckled, heart-shaped face.

'You don't speak Greek?' Angelos finished for her in flawless, clipped English. 'And yet my daughter's only language is Greek. How…interesting, Miss…?' He arched an eyebrow, smiling coldly. He did not have time for another completely unsuitable candidate to witter her way through an interview. Better to have her scurry away now.

'Miss Natalia Di Sione,' the woman said. She straightened her spine, fire flashing in those golden-green eyes, surprising Angelos. The woman had spirit. 'And actually, your daughter does speak a bit of English, if you are referring to the young girl who has been sitting outside the office all afternoon.'

Angelos's eyebrows snapped together. 'You have been talking to her?'

'Yes.' She eyed him uncertainly, the tip of her tongue coming out to moisten her lips. Angelos acknowledged the tiny gesture with an uncomfortable tightening in his insides that he resolutely ignored. 'Was I not supposed to?'

'That is neither here nor there.' He tapped the pile of CVs on his desk. 'You have not provided me with a CV, Miss Di Sione.'

'A CV?' She looked blank and irritation rose within him. She was clearly unsuitable and hopelessly unprepared. A change from the hard polish of the last few candidates, but irritating nonetheless.

'I am afraid I do not have time to indulge you, Miss Di Sione,' he said. 'You are clearly completely unsuitable for the position.'

'The position…' For a moment she looked utterly flummoxed, her forehead crinkling, her mouth pursing. Angelos moved from around his desk and towards the door. As he passed her he caught a whiff of her scent, something clean and simple. Almonds, perhaps. He reached for the door handle. 'Thank you for your time, Miss Di Sione, but I prefer you don't waste mine.'

'But I haven't even talked to you yet,' she protested, turning around to face him. She tucked her unruly hair behind her ears, drawing his attention to the long, golden-brown strands, her small, perfectly formed ears.

Good grief. He was staring at her *ears.* What was wrong with him?

His gaze dropped from her ears to the shoulders that she'd thrown back, and now he noticed her slender yet gently curving body. He yanked his gaze back upwards to her face and determinedly kept it there.

'I've learned enough from our brief conversation. You have no CV, you wear a crumpled dress to a job interview—'

'I just got off a plane,' she shot back, and her gaze widened. 'A *job* interview...'

'You are here,' Angelos bit out, sarcasm edging every word, 'to interview for the temporary position as nanny?'

'Nanny? To your daughter?'

'Who else?' Angelos exploded, and she nodded quickly.

'Of course, of course. I... I apologise for not having my CV with me.' The tip of her tongue touched her lips again and Angelos looked away. 'I only heard about this... position recently. Could you...could you tell me exactly what it entails?'

He frowned, wanting to dismiss her, needing to, because he knew she was completely unsuitable. And yet... something about her clear gaze, the stiffness of her spine, made him hesitate. 'You would care for my eight-year-old daughter, Sofia. The nanny I hired has had to look after her ill mother, and she cannot start until the end of August. Therefore I require a replacement for the six weeks until then. This was all in the advertisement?'

She nodded slowly, her hazel eyes wide, sweeping him with that unsettlingly clear gaze. 'Yes, of course. I remember now.'

His breath released in an impatient hiss. 'Do you have any child-care experience, Miss Di Sione?'

'Please, call me Talia. And the answer to that is no.'

He stared at her in disbelief. 'None?' She shook her head, her wavy hair falling about her face once more. She tucked it behind her ears, smiling at him almost impishly, and Angelos's simmering temper came to a boil. She had an unfortunate amount of gall to demand an interview with absolutely no experience to recommend her. He shook his head. 'You are, as I suspected from the moment you entered this office, wasting my time.'

Talia Di Sione blinked, recoiling a little bit at his tone. Angelos felt no sympathy. Why had the woman come here? She had no CV, no experience, no chance whatsoever. Surely she should have realised that.

'Perhaps you should ask your daughter if I wasted her time,' she said quietly, and then Angelos stilled.

Talia watched Angelos Mena's pupils flare, his mouth tighten. Animosity and impatience rolled off the man in waves, along with something else. Something disturbing… a power like a magnetic force, making her realise how dangerous this man could be. And yet she didn't feel remotely threatened, despite all the challenges she'd faced today, leaving her emotionally raw and physically exhausted.

Angelos folded his arms, the fabric of his suit stretching across impressive biceps. If he didn't look so utterly forbidding, Talia would have considered Angelos Mena a handsome man. Actually, she would have considered him a stunning, sexy and potently virile man. His tall, powerful body was encased in that very expensive-looking suit, and the silver and gold links of a designer wristwatch glinted from one powerful wrist. Crisp dark hair cut very short framed a chiselled face with straight slashes of eyebrows and deep brown eyes that had been glowering at her like banked coals for the entirety of this unfortunate interview.

Not that she'd been expecting to be *interviewed*. She'd been waiting outside Angelos Mena's office for four hours, hoping for a chance to meet him and ask him about *Il Libro d'Amore*. It had taken her several weeks of painstaking research to track down the precious book to the man standing in front of her, and she still wasn't positive he had it in his possession. The Internet had taken her only so far, and when she'd called Mena Consultancy several times she'd been unable to reach the man himself. She'd left a few vague messages with his PA, wanting to explain what she was looking for in an actual conversation, but judging by Angelos Mena's attitude now, she didn't think he'd received any of them. Her name clearly hadn't rung any bells, and it had only taken ten seconds in the man's presence to realise that a simple conversation probably wouldn't get her very far.

But was she really going to try to be hired as Angelos Mena's daughter's *nanny*?

'I'll go get her,' he said in a clipped voice, and as he strode out of the room Talia sank into one of the chairs in front of the desk. Her knees were shaking and her head throbbed. Getting this far had taken all of her physical and mental resources. Nine hours in a plane, sweating and shaking the whole time, and then wandering through the crowded streets of Athens, flinching every time someone so much as jostled her shoulder, fighting back the memories she never let herself think about, the ones that could bring bile to her throat and send her heart rate crashing in panic.

It had been utterly exhausting. And yet... Talia rose from the chair and went to the huge window that overlooked the city. In the distance she could see the crumbling ruins of the ancient Acropolis underneath a hard blue sky, and the sight was powerful enough to make her feel a flicker of awe, a lick of excitement. For a second she could remember how it had felt to be eighteen years old and full of hope and vigour, the whole world stretched out in front of her, shimmering with promise, everything an enticing adventure...

'Miss Di Sione?'

Talia whirled around, flushing guiltily at the look of disapproval on Angelos Mena's face. Should she not have looked out the window? Goodness but the man was tightly wired.

'This is Sofia.'

'Yes, of course.' Talia stepped towards the slight girl who blinked owlishly from behind her glasses. Her dark, curly hair framed a lovely, heart-shaped face; most of her right cheek was covered in the puckered red flesh of a scar. While waiting outside Talia had noticed how the girl would let her hair fall in front of her face to hide it, and her heart had twisted with sympathy. She knew what it was like to have scars. It just happened that hers were invisible.

'Hello, Sofia,' she said now, smiling, and just as before the girl bent her head forward so her hair slid in front of her face. Angelos frowned.

No, actually, he glowered. Talia quelled at the scowl on his face, and she could only wonder what his daughter felt. She'd watched Sofia covertly as she'd waited to see Angelos; she'd seen how the girl's gaze followed each woman into the office, and then how her shoulders had slumped when each woman had come out again, usually looking annoyed or embarrassed or both. A couple of times Sofia had been ushered in, and Talia had watched how her slight body had trembled and she'd gripped her hands together, her knuckles showing bony and white, as she'd stepped into that inner sanctum.

After about an hour of waiting, Talia had tried to befriend her. She'd shown her the pad of paper and pack of coloured pencils she always kept in her bag, and for fun she'd done a quick sketch of one of the women who had been waiting, exaggerating her face so she was a caricature, but still recognisable. When Sofia had recognised the woman with her beaky nose and protuberant eyes, hands like claws planted on bony hips, she'd let out a little giggle, and then clapped her hand over her mouth, her eyes wide and panicked.

Talia had grinned at her, reassuring and conspiratorial, and slowly Sofia had relaxed, dropping her hand and then pushing the pad of paper towards Talia, silently inviting her to draw another sketch. And so she had.

They'd whiled away a pleasant hour with Talia doing sketches of as many of the women as she could remember before she'd handed the pencils to Sofia and encouraged her to draw something.

Sofia had sketched a sunset, a stretch of golden sand and a wash of blue water.

'Lovely,' Talia had murmured.

'*Spiti*,' she'd said, and when Talia had looked blank, she'd translated hesitantly, 'Home.'

'Sofia?' Angelos said now, his tone sharpening. He rested a hand on his daughter's shoulder, gentle yet heavy, and spoke in Greek to her.

Sofia looked up, smiling shyly. *'Yassou.'*

Angelos spoke again in Greek and then glanced pointedly at Talia. 'I am telling my daughter that you do not know Greek.'

'Don't worry,' Talia replied lightly. 'She already knows. We've been miming for most of the afternoon, but we've managed to get along. And Sofia knows more English than you think, Mr Mena.'

'Kyrie Mena,' he corrected, and she nodded, only just keeping from rolling her eyes.

'Kyrie,' she agreed, and she didn't need Angelos Mena's wince to know she'd butchered the pronunciation.

Angelos spoke again in Greek to Sofia, and his daughter said something back in reply. Although Talia didn't know what either of them was saying, she could feel both Angelos's disapproval and Sofia's anxiety. She stood there, trying to smile even as exhaustion crashed over her again.

What was she doing here, really? She'd come all this way to find her grandfather's precious book, not interview for a nanny position. If she had any sense she'd stop this farce before it went any further, and explain to Angelos Mena the real reason why she'd come.

And then, no doubt, have him boot her out the door, and any chance to recover Giovanni's book would be gone for ever.

Angelos was talking to Sofia again in Greek and Talia could feel her vision blur as the headache that had been skirting the fringes of her mind threatened to take over. The room felt hot, the air stale, and her legs were starting to tremble again.

'Do you mind...' she murmured, and sank into the chair, dropping her head into her hands as she took several deep breaths.

Angelos broke off his conversation with his daughter to enquire sharply, 'Miss Di Sione? Are you all right?'

Talia took another deep breath as her vision started to swim.

'Miss Di Sione?'

'Talia,' she corrected him. 'And no, actually, I think I'm going to faint.'

CHAPTER TWO

ANGELOS SWORE UNDER his breath as the woman in front of him went limp, her head drooping down between her knees.

He shouted for Eleni and then went over to Talia, crouching down by her chair as he put an arm around her shoulders and attempted to prop her up.

'Sorry,' she managed as her head lolled against his arm. She felt like a rag doll in his arms, boneless and light. Her hair brushed his cheek.

'Papa, is she going to be all right?' Sofia asked anxiously, and Angelos nearly swore again. The last thing his daughter needed was to worry about some stranger.

'Yes, of course,' he said, more tersely than he intended. 'She's just come over faint for a moment.'

His assistant came hurrying into the room, and Angelos barked out an order for a glass of water. 'Make it juice,' he snapped as Eleni headed out to the reception area. 'Her blood sugar might be low.'

He glanced back at Talia, whose eyes were closed, her once rosy face now pale and bloodless. Her golden lashes fanned her cheeks and her lips parted slightly on a shaky breath. Then her eyes fluttered open and her gaze clashed with Angelos's. For a second he felt jarred, as if he'd missed the last step on a staircase. He was suddenly conscious of his arm around her shoulders, her breasts pressed against his chest. Then she struggled to sit upright and he let his arm fall away.

'I'm so sorry,' she murmured. 'I don't normally do that.'

'Don't you?' he bit out, and she glanced at him uncertainly.

'No…'

'The thing is,' Angelos said, his voice still hard, 'I don't know the first thing about you, Miss Di Sione. And yet you want me to entrust my daughter into your care.'

She gazed at him for a moment, the hazel of her eyes so clear he felt a sudden flicker of shame at his curt tone and implied accusation. Then she looked away from him, to Sofia.

'I'm all right, Sofia,' she said softly, and Angelos saw his daughter's expression brighten as she gave Talia a trembling smile.

She was the first woman today, Angelos acknowledged, who had actually cared what his daughter was feeling. Had concerned herself with Sofia at all. And he realised that from the moment Sofia had entered his office, Talia had not made anything of his daughter's scarred face. She hadn't overcompensated either way; she'd simply acted as if it hadn't mattered at all. The realisation made him feel both glad and completely wrong-footed, because it was still obvious to him that Talia Di Sione was utterly unsuitable to be a nanny. No qualifications, no references… he didn't even know how she'd heard of the job or why she'd shown up for it.

And yet he felt on a gut level that she was the right choice, the only choice. Because she cared about his daughter.

Eleni came in with a crystal glass of apple juice on a tray and Talia took it with a murmured thanks. 'I'm sorry to be a bother,' she said, glancing at Angelos from under her lashes as she took a sip of juice. 'I'm fine now, really.'

'It's no bother.' Angelos paused. Talia was clearly the best choice for the position, and yet still he resisted. He liked things to be clear-cut, to make sense. He appreciated quantitative qualifications, experience over instinct. God knows his instincts had been wrong in the past. He trusted facts now, hard and solid and certain. Emotion, instinctual or otherwise, had no place in his life.

And yet… He watched as Talia smiled at Sofia and said something that made his daughter smile shyly back. Sofia caught his frowning gaze and gave him a hesitant smile and a discreet thumbs-up. This was the first woman she'd approved of. Should he trust his daughter's instinct as well as his own?

His resolve hardened along with the set of his jaw. He had no choice. He needed to hire a nanny today, so he could return to work and Sofia could be cared for. He turned to Talia. 'Can you be ready to leave in an hour?'

Talia blinked, her vision starting to swim again as she took in Angelos's request. *'Leave…?'* she repeated, and he gave an impatient nod.

'I'd like to return to Kallos within the hour.'

Knowing she was sounding stupid, Talia couldn't keep herself from repeating him yet again. 'Kallos…?'

'My home,' Angelos clarified. 'Did you not read the advertisement I placed, Miss Di Sione?'

'Spiti,' Talia said, remembering Sofia's drawing, and surprise flickered in Angelos's mahogany eyes.

'Yes, home.' He paused, his gaze sweeping over her in a way that made goose bumps rise on Talia's arms. 'So you do know a little Greek.'

'Very little.' Talia dragged a deep breath into her lungs

and tried to force her mind to clear. She felt a hot tide of embarrassment wash over her to think how weak and helpless she must have looked to Angelos Mena, practically collapsing in his office. It was just that she hadn't eaten anything for hours, and the emotional and physical exhaustion of dealing with so many strange things had finally overwhelmed her. But she was better now. She'd make herself be.

She straightened, putting the glass of juice on the desk with a clink. 'Mr—Kyrie Mena, I'm afraid this has all got a little out of hand…' She felt another blush rising as Angelos's eyebrows snapped together in irritated confusion. If she told him the real reason for her being here now, he'd be utterly furious. She might have only met the man a few minutes ago, but she knew him well enough to understand that Angelos Mena would be enraged to learn she actually had no intention or interest in being his daughter's nanny.

Except…could she really say that? Talia's gaze slid to Sofia, who was watching her anxiously, her dark hair swinging in front of her face to hide her scarred cheek. Sofia met her gaze and gave a fragile smile.

'Parakalo,' she whispered, which Talia knew meant *please*. 'Come,' she added, her voice tentative, the English word sounding hesitant on her lips.

Talia's heart twisted hard in sympathy, just as it had when she'd first laid eyes on this girl. Sofia wanted her to come, and it was only for six weeks. And surely in six weeks she'd find an opportunity to ask Angelos about the book, even to get him to give her the book. More importantly, she might be able to help Sofia. At least she could offer her friendship.

Why shouldn't she accept this job?

Because it was strange and unexpected, and she'd have to deal with all sorts of things she'd avoided for the last seven years. Because she was in no position to help anyone, when she hadn't been able to help herself. When she was already out of her depth, suffering panic attacks, afraid of the future.

And never mind her own deficiencies, by accepting this job she'd be deceiving this family, even if it was out of good intentions. She was pretty sure Angelos Mena would see her actions as questionable, perhaps even reprehensible. She was no nanny.

'I…' she began, helplessly, because she had no idea what to do. Sofia was gazing at her with puppy dog eyes and Angelos Mena was clearly seething with impatience. How could she refuse? How could she not?

'You did come here to apply for the position, didn't you, Miss Di Sione?' Angelos demanded. 'I am now *offering* you the position. Are you prepared to take it or not?'

Still Talia hesitated, caught by Sofia's silently imploring look. She turned back to Angelos, whose gaze was narrowed, everything about his powerful form exuding impatience and irritation. 'Yes,' she said, the word catching in her throat. She cleared her throat, and then lifted her chin. 'I am.'

The words seemed to set everything in motion, and the next hour was a blur as Angelos barked out orders to his assistant and Talia was shunted back to the reception area with Sofia. She got out her pad and pencils while people bustled around them, and she and Sofia took turns drawing funny pictures, laughing softly together, until Angelos stood before them, hands on trim hips, his dark and commanding gaze fastened on Talia in a way that made every thought evaporate from her brain.

'Where are your things, Miss Di Sione?'

'Um, back at the hotel where I checked in.'

'And that is?'

'Near the Acropolis…'

Angelos let out a sigh, no more than a hiss of breath. 'The name of the hotel, please?'

'The Adriana,' Talia recalled, wishing she could act a bit more with it in front of Angelos Mena. She'd dealt with plenty of rich and powerful people through her work as a portrait artist, but no one had reduced her to insensible babbling the way Angelos Mena did with his narrowed gaze and overwhelming presence, not to mention his obvious annoyance. He clearly did not suffer fools gladly, and from the moment she'd entered his impressive office she'd felt like a fool.

'I'll arrange for someone to collect your bags,' Angelos said. 'In the meantime you can wait here with Sofia.' He strode away without waiting for her reply, and Talia watched him leave. He had not even looked at his daughter, much less spared her a kind word or a smile.

She glanced at Sofia, wondering how they were going to overcome the language barrier for the next six weeks. 'Perhaps you should teach me some Greek,' she suggested, and Sofia's forehead furrowed. *'Elinika,'* she tried, fishing for the few phrases of Greek she'd learned on the plane trip over here. She touched her mouth to indicate speaking, and Sofia brightened.

'Ne, ne.' She pointed to her chest. 'Speak *Anglika.'*

Talia nodded, smiling in understanding. 'We can teach each other.'

They spent the next hour teaching each other words and phrases in both English and Greek, amidst much laughter when one of them, usually Talia, got it wrong.

'Gi-neck-a,' Talia repeated after Sofia. 'Now what is that?' Laughing, Sofia pointed to her. 'Nanny?' Talia guessed. 'American? Foreigner?'

'Woman,' Angelos said quietly, and everything in Talia

jolted as she turned to look at him. He was standing in front of them, gazing at her with an inscrutable expression, which was better than his usual scowl, although it still made Talia feel uncertain. *'Gyneka,'* he added, making Talia realise she'd butchered the pronunciation once again. 'Woman.' For a second, no more, his gaze remained on Talia; she felt as if he'd pinned her there, so she was unable to look away, or even to breathe.

Then he flicked his gaze away, towards his daughter. Talia couldn't understand the Greek but the quick jerk of his head towards the elevator conveyed his meaning well enough. It was time to go.

She slipped the pad and pencils back into her bag and stood with Sofia. Angelos turned back to her.

'The helicopter is ready, and your things have been fetched from the hotel.'

'Helicopter…' She stared at him in alarm. 'You didn't say anything about a helicopter.'

Angelos frowned. 'How else would we get to Kallos?'

'By car?' she guessed hopefully, and Angelos's nostrils flared.

'Kallos is an island, Miss Di Sione. We will travel there by helicopter. It should only take an hour.'

An island. She thought of Sofia's drawing, the blue water, the beach. Of course it was an island.

She realised she must have been gaping at him because Angelos's lips compressed as he looked at her. 'Is that a problem?' he asked, his tone deceptively mild.

'No, of course not.' But she was lying, because she could already feel the panic starting its insistent staccato pulse inside her. What on earth was she doing, going goodness knew where with this stranger? In a *helicopter*?

Her breath hitched and Angelos glanced at her. 'You aren't going to faint again?'

'No,' Talia said with far more certainty than she felt. In the past twenty-four hours she'd gone about five thousand miles outside her comfort zone. She wasn't sure she could manage another step.

Then she felt a small, cold hand slide into hers and she looked down to see Sofia smiling at her. 'Okay?' she asked, and Talia was touched and humbled by the girl's obvious concern.

'Okay,' she confirmed shakily, and hand in hand they walked towards the lift.

Even with Sofia's support Talia couldn't keep the fear from kicking up her heart rate as they took the lift up to the top of the building where a helicopter was waiting on a helipad.

She glanced at Angelos, who was striding towards the machine, the wind from the whirring propellers moulding his shirt and suit jacket close to his body so Talia could see the impressive outline of his well-defined pecs. The helicopter looked small and menacing, its curved windshield looking like the giant eyes of a bug. Talia clutched Sofia's hand harder.

She really didn't think she could do this.

Angelos climbed into the helicopter, and then reached down first for Sofia's hand. Talia watched as the little girl clambered easily inside and then sat down. Angelos turned back to her, the wind whipping about him, his hand outstretched. Talia simply stared.

'Miss Di Sione,' he shouted over the noise of the propeller blades. 'Take my hand.'

Talia's heart was pounding painfully, and her palms were icy and damp with sweat. She couldn't do this. She couldn't deal with confined spaces, ones where it was impossible to get out. A closed door, a dark room, a locked car...she avoided them all. And the passenger jet she'd been on a few hours ago had been hard enough, but a *helicopter*…

And then suddenly she thought of Giovanni smiling at her as he'd given her his instructions. *'I know you will try your hardest. And you will succeed.'*

Taking a deep breath, she reached for Angelos's hand and then she let him pull her up into the helicopter. She practically collapsed into her seat, her legs rubbery and her heart thudding sickly. She had just managed to jam her seat belt together when the helicopter lifted off the building and began its ascent into a cloudless blue sky, heading for the Aegean Sea.

CHAPTER THREE

ANGELOS STUDIED HIS new nanny, noting dispassionately how pale she'd gone, her eyes closed as she leaned back against the seat and took several deep, even breaths. What on earth was the woman's problem?

'Do you suffer from travel sickness?' he asked abruptly, raising his voice to be heard above the noise of the helicopter, and her eyes flew open.

'No.'

'Then why do you look so terrible?'

'You're quite the flatterer, aren't you,' she muttered, and Angelos stared at her, nonplussed.

'You look as if you are about to be sick.'

'You'd better hope I'm not,' Talia answered, and he grimaced in distaste.

'Indeed, I do. It would make for a most unpleasant journey.'

'That it would.' Talia let out a shuddering breath as she shifted in her seat. 'And it's already pretty awful.'

'You do not like helicopters.'

'No.' She'd closed her eyes again, her face scrunched up, and Angelos inspected her for another moment. Her hair was going curly in the heat and he could see a sprinkling of golden freckles across her nose. He wondered how old she was, and realised afresh how little he knew about her besides her name. What on earth had possessed him to hire her?

Talia opened her eyes and turned to Sofia. 'You don't mind helicopters,' she remarked, and with a bit of play-acting, miming the propeller blades and making a face, she communicated her meaning.

Sofia grinned. 'Home,' she said in English. 'I like home.'

'I like home too,' Talia said with a sigh. 'But I'm sure I'll like yours as well.' Sofia wrinkled her nose, not understanding, and Talia leaned over and patted her hand before she sank back against the seat and closed her eyes.

Angelos continued to study her for a moment, wondering how she'd ended up in his office. How had she even heard of the advertisement, and why had she come without a CV? Questions, he decided, he would not ask her in the noisy confines of the helicopter, with Sofia trying to catch every word. He would have time to discover just who his new nanny was later, and make sure she was an appropriate companion for his daughter.

His gaze moved to Sofia; she was leaning towards the window, watching the sea slide by. She never liked leaving the safety of Kallos, and she seemed to shrink even more into herself whenever he took her to Athens. He knew people stared at her scarred face, and the attention made Sofia embarrassed and exceedingly shy. He was grateful that Talia Di Sione, for all her idiosyncrasies, had not once made Sofia feel ashamed of her scar.

'Look, Papa,' Sofia called in Greek, and he leaned forward to see a sleek white sailboat cutting through the blue-green waters.

'Beautiful,' he murmured, and then glanced back at Talia. She still had her eyes closed. Impulsively he reached over and touched her shoulder. Her eyes flew

KATE HEWITT 33

open and she jerked upright as if he'd branded her with a hot poker.

'Relax,' he said. 'I just thought you might appreciate the view.'

'I'd rather just get onto land,' Talia muttered, but she obligingly looked out the window of the helicopter, and Angelos watched as her face softened into a smile as she took in the stunning vista of sea and sky.

'I always wanted to see the Greek islands,' she said.

'You have not been here before?'

'No, this was my first time in Athens.'

'How long had you been in the city?'

She shot him a wry look. 'About six hours.'

'Six hours?' Angelos frowned. 'Do you mean you arrived in Athens *today*?' She nodded. 'But what on earth made you apply for the job, having just arrived?'

She looked away, seeming uneasy. Suspicion hardened inside him. What was going on with this woman? 'It seemed like a good idea,' she said at last.

Angelos didn't answer. He could see Sofia looking at them both and he had no intention of pursuing an uncomfortable line of enquiry with Talia Di Sione when his daughter was present. But he *would* get to the bottom of why she was here.

Fifteen minutes later the helicopter began to make its descent to Kallos. As soon as they'd landed Angelos clambered out of the helicopter, and then reached back a hand for Sofia and then Talia.

He was conscious of how small and slender her hand felt in his as she stepped down onto the rocky earth, shading her eyes with her other hand as she gazed round the island.

'Is this a private island?' she asked.

'Yes, it is my home. But you will have everything you need. The villa is well supplied by nearby Naxos.'

She nodded slowly, letting out a breath she must have been holding for a while. 'Okay,' she said, and she sounded as if she were talking to herself. 'Okay.'

Angelos led the way from the helipad to the villa. The salt-tinged sea breeze buffeted him and the sun was hot above and for a moment he breathed in the air and let himself relax. Let himself believe that he had things under control, that Sofia was safe.

That he'd done the best he could, even when he hadn't before.

Talia took several deep breaths of fresh sea air as she followed Angelos and Sofia down the winding path to the sprawling whitewashed villa by the beach. The tension that had been throbbing in her temples since she'd stepped into the helicopter was finally starting to ease.

From the vantage point of the helipad she'd been able to see how small the island was: a large villa with extensive gardens, a staff cottage and a stony, hilly rise to a beach on the other side. *Small.* But small could be good, she told herself. She didn't have to feel claustrophobic here. She wasn't in a closed space, with the open air and sea all around her, and at least she wouldn't have to deal with a lot of strange people.

Still she felt tense. She felt like sprinting back to the safety of her grandfather's estate, the quiet studio with its views of sea and sky, where she could paint in blissful solitude. Where she didn't have to come up hard against all her old fears and insecurities.

She took a deep breath and tilted her face to the sun. She could do this. She *was* doing this. She'd survived a plane trip, a taxi ride through a heaving city, a helicopter ride and near constant interactions with strangers. It was more than she'd had to deal with in seven years, and it had exhausted her, but she'd survived.

'Are you all right?' Angelos called, and Talia realised she'd stopped walking, and had dropped behind Angelos and Sofia.

'I'm fine,' she said, and hurried down the path to join her employer and his daughter.

As they came into the villa, the rooms airy and spacious and light, a housekeeper bustled up to them, exclaiming in Greek as she kissed Sofia on both cheeks. Then she stopped in front of Talia and, planting her hands on ample hips, gave her a thorough once-over with narrowed eyes. She spoke to Angelos, who answered in Greek. Talia had no idea what they were saying, but she suspected she'd come up wanting in the housekeeper's well-trained eye.

'Do I pass?' she asked Angelos when there was a break in the conversation. She'd meant to sound teasing but it came out anxious instead. Tension knotted her stomach muscles again as she realised afresh how *strange* this all was. And she really didn't like strange.

Angelos looked startled, and then his mouth compressed in a way she was already finding familiar. 'My housekeeper's opinion is of no concern. I have already hired you.'

'It's that bad, huh?' Talia only half joked. At least this time she sounded light, even if she didn't feel it. 'I know my dress is wrinkled, but I *have* been on a plane.'

He inclined his head towards the stairs. 'Maria will show you your room. You will have time to refresh yourself and dress appropriately before dinner.'

The man had no sense of humour, Talia decided as she followed Maria up the stairs. No sense of compassion or friendliness or sensitivity. He was a machine. A robot. A drone…

She was so busy thinking she almost slammed into Maria's substantial form as the housekeeper stopped in the doorway of a bedroom.

'Your room,' she said in heavily accented English, and Talia peeked around her to see a gorgeous room decorated in sea-green and cream, the louvered shutters of the windows open to the beach.

'It's lovely,' she said. *'Efharisto.'* Maria grunted her grudging approval at Talia's passable Greek, and then with her fingers mimed seven o'clock. 'Dinner at seven?' Talia guessed, and as the housekeeper nodded and left she wondered if she could take a crash course in Greek.

She moved to the windows, taking in the spectacular sight. Gardens bursting with bougainvillea and heliotrope ran down a sloping hill to the beach, a stretch of white sand that met up with the blue-green water, just like in Sofia's picture.

The housekeeper had directed Sofia to the kitchen as soon as they arrived, and judging from the tantalising baking smells coming from that direction, Talia had suspected there was a snack in store. Her own stomach growled at the thought and she checked her watch. Two hours until dinner. Time, hopefully, to make herself presentable, although she had a feeling Angelos Mena would judge her wanting no matter what she wore or how much effort she took with her appearance. But at least he'd hired her.

Still Talia relished a soak in the huge marble tub, washing away the grime of nearly twenty-four hours of travel and reviving her tired spirits. She unpacked her single suitcase, realising belatedly that she had not brought nearly enough for six weeks. In fact, she'd packed nothing but serviceable T-shirts and shorts, a single fleece and a pair of jeans, and the crumpled sundress she'd worn on the plane.

Biting her lip, Talia acknowledged she had nothing remotely *appropriate* to wear for dinner that night. In her normal life she never needed to dress to impress, and her career as an artist meant work wear was usually paint-splattered jeans and old T-shirts. She hadn't even considered bringing something businesslike to wear for her meeting with Angelos Mena; in truth, she hadn't thought much beyond surviving the journey. She hadn't had the heart or head space for more.

Sighing, she wondered if she had time to wash her sun-dress and let it dry in the sea breeze.

She discovered that she *almost* had time, when she headed out of her bedroom at five to seven, the dress clean and far less wrinkled, but slightly damp across the shoulders. Hopefully Angelos wouldn't notice.

The villa was quiet as Talia came down the stairs, the rooms darkened and empty. She peeked into an enormous living room scattered with linen sofas in natural shades, and then a masculine-looking study with a huge mahogany desk and book-lined walls. Finally she found the dining room towards the back of the house; Angelos was already standing in the room, gazing up at a large portrait of a woman hanging on the far wall.

He turned as Talia tiptoed in, his face snapping into its usual frown. 'You're late.'

'I'm sorry. I was looking for the dining room.'

His frown deepened as he took in her outfit. 'You have not changed.'

'Actually, I have. I washed my dress and put it back on.' For some reason that made her blush, and to cover it she did a ridiculous little twirl. 'Can't you tell?' She stopped, her dress swishing around her legs, and saw that Angelos's frown had morphed into a positive scowl, grooves visible from nose to mouth, eyes dangerously narrowed.

Even scowling, the man was devastatingly attractive.

He'd changed his grey business suit for a crisp white shirt, open at the throat, and dark trousers. The clothes were basic and should have been boring, but on his powerful frame the white cotton drew Talia's attention to his broad shoulders, the dark trousers to his trim hips and powerful thighs.

Appalled by her perusal, she yanked her gaze away from his muscular form. She'd been looking at his *thighs*, for heaven's sake. Hopefully he hadn't noticed her moment of shameless goggling.

Now she saw the plush velvet chairs and huge polished table set for two. 'Is Sofia not joining us?'

'You *washed* your dress?' Angelos sounded incredulous and Talia lifted her chin.

'I'm sorry, I didn't realise I'd be required to wear an evening gown.' She walked to the place setting at one end of the table, resting her hand on the back of the chair. 'Where's Sofia?'

'She's eating with Maria.'

'Is that what usually happens?' Talia watched as Angelos walked around the table to pull out her chair.

'In future, you may dine with her if you wish, but tonight I wanted to speak to you alone.'

'Oh.' Since he was holding out her chair Talia sat down. She breathed in the woodsy scent of his aftershave as he pushed her chair in; his face was close to hers, close enough to make goose bumps rise on her arms, and she suppressed the urge to shiver. She wondered what his jaw would feel like, if his clean-shaven face would be smooth, or possess a hint of roughness. Like the man himself, urbanity not quite cloaking a cold, ruthless interior.

Angelos walked smoothly around the table and sat down at the opposite end, placing his napkin in his lap with a brisk flourish. Talia did the same. Although she lived in a house that more than rivalled Angelos Mena's in terms of space and sheer luxury, she still felt awed by his home and his presence. Back on Giovanni's estate, she took most meals in the kitchen or in her studio while she was working. When she ate with Giovanni, they had a quiet meal listening to the radio or watching TV. She hadn't been to a dinner party since…well, she couldn't even remember since when. A Christmas or Thanksgiving meal with her brothers and sisters hadn't felt as ornate or intimidating as a meal alone with this man.

Maria came in with the first course, a salad of plump tomatoes and slices of cucumber sprinkled with feta cheese. 'This is very civilised,' Talia said when the housekeeper had left. 'Thank you.'

'May I never be accused of being uncivilised,' Angelos responded dryly.

Talia watched him covertly as she ate her salad, wondering at this man who, if her research was correct, possessed a priceless volume of poetry and had bid on a second by the same anonymous poet. That was how she'd tracked him down; she'd found an obscure website with a message board where people could post the rare books they were looking for. She'd stumbled across a message posted by an agent acting on Angelos's behalf, or at least on the behalf of Mena Consultancy. She just hoped it meant that Angelos actually had the book.

What if after everything she'd endured and agreed to, this was nothing more than a wild goose chase?

'So do you and Sofia live on Kallos all year long?' she asked.

'Sofia does. I travel for work. In fact, I have to leave tomorrow.'

So he wouldn't be here for the six weeks of her stay? Talia felt a wave of relief at the thought, as well as a twinge

of disappointment for Sofia. No matter how stern or auto-
cratic Angelos seemed, it couldn't be good for him to be
away from his daughter so much.

'Isn't it rather lonely here for a girl her age?' she asked.

'Sofia prefers it. She has a tutor who comes in by boat
for her lessons, and Maria and the other staff for company.
And, of course, now you.'

'Has she had other nannies?'

'Yes, but I'm afraid none of them have lasted very long.'
Angelos's voice was clipped, his gaze shuttered. 'I hope
this next one will be a better fit.'

'Why haven't they lasted very long?' Talia asked, curious. Sofia didn't seem like a difficult child, and the setting was practically paradise. Surely it was a dream job
for anyone looking for a position in child care.

Angelos shrugged. 'They did not find the situation to
their liking. But you are asking all the questions, Miss
Di Sione, and I invited you to dinner so *I* could ask the
questions.'

'And here I thought we were just having a conversation,'
Talia answered lightly, but Angelos did not give so much
as a flicker of a smile. She speared a cucumber. 'Ask away,
then,' she said with an insouciance she didn't remotely
feel. She didn't want Angelos Mena asking her probing
questions, at least not yet. She had no idea how to answer
anything. She hated the thought of lying, but total honesty felt impossible at this point. 'But first,' she added, 'I
must ask one last thing, and that is that you call me Talia.'

She popped the cucumber in her mouth only to have
it stick in her throat as Angelos answered, an edge to his
smooth voice, 'Very well, *Talia*. I want to ask you just
why you came to Athens, and more to the point, to my *office*, since it obviously wasn't to seek a position as nanny.'

CHAPTER FOUR

WITH THE CUCUMBER stuck in her throat, Talia erupted into an inelegant fit of coughing. Angelos poured her a glass of water and pushed it across the table, watching unsympathetically all the while.

Talia took a few sips, thankful that she'd managed at least to stop coughing. 'Sorry about that,' she said on a gasp.

'You haven't answered my question.' Angelos's gaze was narrowed, his lips compressed, his arms folded. He wasn't exuding warm fuzzies—that was for sure.

Talia took another forkful of salad in order to give her time to think of a reply. How much to admit? She felt instinctively that if she were to talk about her true reason for coming to Greece now, Angelos would have her back on that helicopter so quick her head would be spinning as fast as the propeller blades.

And the truth was, she didn't want to leave. Not just because she needed to find her grandfather's book, but for Sofia's sake as well. Already she was forming a picture of what the little girl's life here on Kallos had to be like, lonely and isolated, with only a few elderly staff for company.

Kind of like yours, then.

The realisation gave her an uncomfortable jolt. She didn't think of herself as either lonely or isolated, not with her work for stimulation and her grandfather for company. Perhaps Sofia was happy here, just as she was happy on her grandfather's estate. Maybe she wasn't as needed as she'd felt she was…which still left her with no idea how to answer Angelos's question.

'Talia? I am waiting.'

Talia jerked her unfocused gaze back to Angelos. He'd laid down his fork and put his hands flat on the table, his dark gaze fastened on hers, hard and unyielding. The man looked seriously annoyed, but even with the irritation flashing in his whisky-brown eyes Talia couldn't keep from noticing the lean planes of his cheek and jaw, the warm olive tone of his skin. If he'd just smile a bit more, she might start seriously crushing on him.

But considering their situation, it was probably better that he didn't smile.

'You're right that I wasn't looking to be a nanny,' Talia said finally, choosing her words with care. 'I came to Athens for a…a different reason. But when you assumed I was there for the nanny position, it seemed…fortuitous that I apply. And accept.' That much was true at least.

'Fortuitous,' Angelos repeated flatly. 'How so?'

'I like Sofia, Mr—Kyrie Mena. She seems a very kind girl. I want to help her, or at least be her friend.'

'And yet with, by your own admission, absolutely no child-care experience, you think you have the ability, even the expertise, to help her?'

Talia blinked at his scathing tone. 'I may not have child-care experience, but I know what it is like to be a child—'

'As does every person on this planet.'

'I know what it's like to be lonely,' she burst out, and then wished she hadn't. She wasn't lonely. She'd always told Giovanni she wasn't, and she'd believed herself. She *had*.

'My daughter is not lonely,' Angelos informed her shortly. 'She has everything she needs here on Kallos.'

'Everything?' Exasperated, Talia shook her head. 'Then why did you hire me?'

'I'm asking myself that question as well,' he retorted. He sat back, taking a measured breath. Talia could feel the crackle of tension in the air. 'The truth is,' he continued, 'I was running out of both time and options. And,' he conceded grudgingly, 'Sofia seems to have formed some kind of attachment to you. But I must confess, in our short acquaintance, you have not recommended yourself to me, Miss Di Sione.'

'Talia.'

'*Talia*. You have in fact seemed extraordinarily short-sighted and, dare I say it, flighty—'

'I think you just dared,' Talia snapped before she could think better of it. She felt annoyed and bizarrely hurt by his quick and brutal judgement. What did Angelos Mena know about her, really? Only that she hadn't packed very much and she didn't do well in helicopters. And for that he felt capable of dismissing her as a person?

'You disagree with me?' he enquired, and she let out a huff of disbelieving laughter. No doubt Angelos Mena expected her to bow and scrape and apologise—and for what? Coming over a little dizzy?

'Of course I do. You don't know me, Kyrie Mena. You didn't know I existed until a couple of hours ago. How can you say I'm anything when you've barely met me?'

'I am basing my opinions on what I've seen so far. I'm a consultant, Miss—'

'Talia.'

'Talia.' He expelled her name on a hiss of breath. 'It's my job to come into a situation and assess it swiftly.'

'Too swiftly, maybe. What are you basing your judgement on? That I didn't pack more than one dress or that I was a little nervous in your helicopter?' She raised her eyebrows in challenge, half amazed at her own daring. She didn't normally pick a fight, but then she didn't normally need to. She'd cocooned herself in safety and isolation instead. It felt kind of good to come out swinging. Strangely empowering. She'd much rather stand tall than shrink back. 'Well?' she challenged when he didn't answer. 'Which is it?'

Angelos leaned back in his chair. 'I take your point,' he said after a pause. His face was expressionless, his gaze implacable. Of course it would be too much to expect to see a glimmer of apology in those darkly glowing eyes. 'But surely you can understand my concern,' he continued. 'I am entrusting my daughter, my only child, to your care.'

'Of course I can understand your concern.' Talia sighed, the fight going out of her. 'If I had a daughter, I'd feel the same.' Angelos had hired her without knowing anything about her. He had the right to ask some questions, to be a bit sceptical. And she was hiding something, just as he suspected. Perhaps if she admitted her interest in the book…but no. She needed him to get to know her first. 'If you'd like to know more about me,' she said, trying to smile, 'then all you have to do is ask.'

He studied her for a moment, his gaze assessing and speculative. Talia suppressed the urge to squirm or fidget under his unnervingly direct and unblinking stare. 'You're American,' he said at last, and she gave a shaky breath of relief at the innocuousness of that statement.

'Yes.'

'Where do you come from?'

'Outside New York City.'

He nodded slowly. 'You must be in your mid-twenties. You had a job before this?'

'Yes, and I still have it. I'm an artist.'

'An artist,' he repeated, sounding decidedly unimpressed. He spoke as if she dabbled in finger paints in her free time.

'A portrait artist,' Talia clarified. 'I work on commissions.'

'I see.'

What he saw, Talia suspected, was that she was an unemployed airhead who traipsed around the world, being short-sighted and flighty. It was foolish of her to be so rankled, so hurt, by his assessment, and yet she was. No one had ever sized her up and dismissed her so thoroughly before. She'd worked hard for her reputation as a reclusive but talented artist. She hated the thought that Angelos was judging her, and so harshly at that.

'You said you wished to help my daughter,' Angelos said after a pause. Again with that direct stare, and Talia forced herself not to look away, to find some way to hide from Angelos Mena's searching gaze and questions. Being the focus of his full attention felt like standing on a beach, watching as a tidal wave gained in towering power, readying to crash down on you. 'How do you think you could help her?' he pressed.

'By being her friend,' Talia answered.

His gaze blazed into hers. 'I am not paying you to be her friend.'

'Very well,' Talia answered, trying not to quake under that unyielding stare, 'perhaps you should tell me what you're paying me for exactly. You haven't actually told me what my duties are.' Angelos had the grace to look slightly discomfited, his gaze thankfully flicking away from hers for a second, giving Talia the courage to add, 'Not to mention an actual job contract or reference check or any of the usual protocols. I mean,' she continued as she shrugged expansively, 'if you want to talk about being short-sighted or, I don't know, *flighty.*'

Angelos turned back to her, his lips tightening, his nostrils flared with annoyance, and Talia wondered if she'd gone too far. She didn't actually want to be fired. She certainly didn't want to get in that helicopter again anytime soon. But she hadn't been able to resist pushing back just a little. If Angelos Mena was a different kind of man, he might have even smiled at her pointed joke.

For one tantalising second she imagined that granite gaze softening, those sensual lips curving into an answering smile, that hard body relaxing towards her, and she felt a weird leaping sensation in her middle. She pressed one hand to her stomach to soothe those sudden butterflies. Better for him not to tease. He was so much easier to resist that way.

'Very well,' he said stiffly. 'I am happy to give you the details now. You are to be a companion to my daughter and provide her with stimulating conversation and activities when she is not at her lessons.'

'And when is she at her lessons?'

'Her tutor comes to the island every weekday morning, for a few hours until lunchtime.'

'Could she not go to a school near here?' Talia asked. 'On Naxos, maybe? To be with other children?'

'She prefers to be on the island.' Angelos's tone was final, and despite the iron warning she heard in his voice not to ask any more questions, Talia continued.

'Is that because of her scarring?' she asked quietly, and Angelos stilled.

'What about her scarring?'

'I noticed she seemed self-conscious about it,' she explained carefully. 'And it's hard for any child to feel different.'

Angelos hesitated, and in the ensuing silence Maria came in to clear the plates. Talia thanked her in clumsy Greek and the woman brusquely nodded her acceptance before turning away. Talia wondered if the housekeeper would ever thaw towards her. She'd seemed suspicious and unimpressed from the moment Talia had stepped into the villa. Someone else who'd judged her and found her wanting.

'Sofia suffered burns in a fire when she was a baby,' Angelos said abruptly. Talia opened her mouth to reply, but he cut her off before she could frame a syllable. 'It is a very painful memory for her. We do not discuss it. Ever.' He held her gaze for one long, taut moment, and Talia's mouth dried at the implacable look in his eyes. *Message received.*

Then Maria came in with the main course and Talia knew the chance, if there ever had been one, to say anything about the fire had passed. Angelos would clearly brook no more discussion of it, and she wasn't brave enough to press.

Still her mind whirled with this new information as Maria set plates of lamb souvlaki in front of them. Was it a house fire? Had Angelos been there? And what of his wife? She hadn't even given the woman a thought, and she realised she hadn't because it had been so glaringly obvious that no woman was around. She knew what a motherless home looked like, felt like. That had been another point of sympathy with Sofia, one that had been so innate Talia hadn't even realised it until now.

'Do you have any other questions?' Angelos asked. 'I will have my assistant in Athens draw up a contract and fax it to my office here. If you have any concerns while I am away, you can reach me by email, which Maria has.'

'While you're away?' Talia repeated, remembering that

he'd said he was leaving tomorrow. 'How long will you be gone?'

Angelos's mouth thinned. 'A few weeks. I can hardly work from an island in the middle of the Aegean.'

'It seems like everyone is telecommuting these days,' Talia answered. 'Can't you?'

'I'm afraid not.' He took a sip of water, effectively closing down the conversation.

Talia stared at him, wondering how close he was to Sofia. She'd sensed a yearning in the girl, a desire to please her father even as she tensed when she was around him. But what did Angelos feel for Sofia? Didn't he realise how important he was to her, especially with her mother gone? 'Won't you miss your daughter?' she asked.

He set his glass down with a firm clink. 'That is hardly your concern.'

'No, but it may be Sofia's,' Talia answered. 'Surely she'd like to spend more time with her father. Especially considering—'

'Your job,' Angelos cut across her in a hard voice, 'is to be her companion, not form an opinion on any aspect of her or my life.'

Talia nodded and swallowed down her protests. She knew she'd been terribly outspoken. She was this man's employee and she barely knew him. But she *knew* what it felt like to be without a mother or father, and she was incredibly thankful for Giovanni's care and devotion during her childhood. But Sofia didn't have a doting grandfather in her life, at least as far as Talia could tell.

'So you have no other questions,' Angelos said, a statement, and Talia merely shook her head.

They ate in tense silence for a few moments; the souvlaki was delicious but Talia barely registered a mouthful. Finally she couldn't stand the silence any longer and so she nodded towards the large portrait of a woman that hung in pride of place on the far wall.

'That is a beautiful portrait. Is it of a relative?' The portrait was of a young woman with dark hair pulled back in a loose bun, her heavy-lidded gaze full of secret amusement, her lips curved in a small, knowing smile. 'She reminds me of the *Mona Lisa.*'

Angelos didn't look at the portrait as he answered. 'It is of my late wife,' he said, and after that Talia didn't dare ask any more questions.

An hour later Angelos strode through his bedroom, shrugging out of his suit jacket and loosening his tie. Outside a silver sickle moon hung in an endless starlit sky, the sea like a smooth, dark plate underneath. Angelos braced a forearm against the window frame as he let the serene beauty of the scene wash over him.

His dinner with Talia Di Sione had left him feeling unsettled, even angry; she'd been like a stick prodding the hornet's nest of emotions he'd kept buried deep inside for the last seven years. He'd seen the judgement in her clear hazel eyes when he'd said he was leaving Sofia. He'd felt her censure at learning he would be away for several weeks.

But Talia Di Sione had no idea how it felt to gaze at his daughter every day and know it was his fault, *entirely* his fault, that she felt more comfortable hidden away on an island than living the kind of life any young girl would want, with friends and school and a mother who loved her with all of her heart.

The emotion Talia had stirred up rose within him, and resolutely, relentlessly, Angelos clamped it down. Now was not the time to indulge in self-pity, especially considering he was the last person who was deserving of any such sentiment.

He let out a long, low breath and then turned from the window. He would work; work always made him focus, helped him to forget, at least for a little while.

He moved through the villa to his study downstairs, turning on a lamp and powering up his laptop. Yet even as he reread the notes he'd made on the latest company he was helping to turn around, his mind wandered back upstairs to the woman occupying a bedroom only a few doors down from his own.

Talia Di Sione was an impossible, aggravating mystery. He had never had someone speak to him with such flippant irreverence as she had, and he found himself, to his own irritation, to feel both appalled and reluctantly admiring of her spirit. And yet she'd seemed positively terrified when they'd boarded the helicopter, and she'd practically fainted in his office. The woman was an utter contradiction, and he still knew very little about her.

He knew Maria would tell him if Talia was unsuitable in any way; she'd kept an eye on the previous nannies, most of them unfortunate young women who had taken the post in the hopes of becoming the next Kyria Mena. A few of those women Angelos had had no choice but to fire; others had left in a huff when their cringingly obvious seduction attempts had failed.

Talia, at least, didn't seem interested in him that way, if her snappy comebacks were anything to go by. Yet before he could keep himself from it, he imagined what a seduction attempt by Talia Di Sione would look like. Her hair loose and wavy about her face, her hazel eyes sparkling, her lips parted invitingly as she walked towards him, hips subtly swaying, that sundress sliding over her slight curves…

Horrified by the nature of his thoughts and his body's insistent and alarming response, Angelos quashed the provocative image immediately. He slammed the lid of his laptop down and rose from his desk, pacing the confines of his study in an attempt to keep his body under tight control. It had been a long time since he'd been with a woman, but he wasn't so desperate or deprived that he needed to fantasise about his nanny.

Shaking his head in self-disgust, he left his study and headed back upstairs. The hall was quiet, no light shining from under any of the doors. His body now firmly under control, Angelos walked past Talia's bedroom to his daughter's, quietly opening the door and slipping inside the darkened room.

Sofia was asleep in bed, her knees tucked up to her chest, one hand resting palm upwards on the pillow next to her face. Lying as she was, her scarred cheek against the pillow, she almost looked whole. Healthy in both mind and body. Angelos could almost believe she hadn't been burned, that he hadn't damaged his daughter for ever.

Gently he smoothed a tendril of curly dark hair, hair just like Xanthe's, away from her forehead. She stirred slightly, her lips pursing in a frown before her expression smoothed out and she settled back into sleep.

'*S'agapo, manaria mou,*' he whispered. His little lamb. With a sad smile Angelos touched his daughter's cheek and then quietly left the room.

CHAPTER FIVE

TALIA WOKE TO sunlight streaming through the latticed shutters of her bedroom and the sound of the surf outside. Buoyed by both the light and sound, she threw off the covers and went to the window, opening the shutters wide.

The sight that greeted her was enough to make her sigh in pure pleasure. Sunlight gilded a perfect paradise: blue-green waters and soft white sand, the riot of pink and red flowers tumbling all the way to the beach. Leaning her elbows on the sill she inhaled the scents of flowers and sand and sea, the prospect and possibilities of the next six weeks filling her with something close to joy.

When had she last had an adventure or felt excitement at what the day might bring? Smiling at the thought, she reached for her smartphone to send a quick email to her grandfather.

Arrived in Greece safely. Having a surprising and wonderful time.
Love, T.

Tossing her phone on the bed, she acknowledged that she wasn't actually having a wonderful time. *Yet.* The memory of her dinner last night with Angelos and his scathing assessment of her still stung. But Angelos was leaving today, and she'd be spending most of her time with Sofia. Wonderful might be just around the corner.

She was just getting dressed in a pair of shorts and a T-shirt when the loud, insistent sound of a helicopter starting up sent her to the window again. She watched as the helicopter she'd flown in last night lifted off the helipad and like some large, ugly insect rose in the sky and began to move away.

Angelos was leaving already? It wasn't even eight in the morning. Clearly he couldn't wait to get away from Kallos, a thought that made her frown. She wondered how much time Angelos spent with his daughter, if any. And then she reminded herself, as Angelos had told her last night, that it wasn't her concern.

Dressed, her hair caught back in a practical ponytail, Talia headed downstairs. She found Maria in the kitchen, chopping vegetables for lunch. She barely glanced at Talia before nodding to the table, where two places had been set. Talia could see from one of the settings that Sofia had already eaten, and so she sat at the other and spooned yogurt and honey into a bowl.

'Sofia?' she asked the housekeeper, searching for some of the Greek phrases she'd tried to memorise. *'Apu pu iste?'* she tried, and Maria looked at her, clearly amused.

'Where am I from?'

'Oh.' Talia stared at her, nonplussed. 'You speak English.'

'A bit,' Maria answered. 'I am from Naxos.'

'Sorry, I meant where Sofia is. Currently.' Talia shook her head. 'I admit, my Greek is severely limited. But last night you seemed like you didn't speak English at all.'

'Well.' Maria let out a huff of breath. 'I wasn't sure of you.'

Talia laughed at that. 'And now you are?'

'No,' Maria answered bluntly, 'but you didn't make eyes at Kyrie Mena last night, so I am reassured that you are not trying to seduce him.'

'*Seduce...*' Talia nearly choked on her mouthful of yogurt. 'I most certainly am not. He is doing his best to terrify me though.'

Maria nodded sagely. 'That is what Kyrie Mena does. And rather well.'

'You speak more than a bit of English,' Talia exclaimed, and Maria smiled slyly.

'I'm a quick learner.'

Talia laughed again and shook her head. Somehow she seemed to have made an ally of the housekeeper, and for that she was glad. She had a feeling she would need allies. 'So...are you telling me that some of the other nannies have tried to...to seduce Kyrie Mena?'

Maria pursed her lips and then turned back to her vegetables, beheading a bunch of carrots with one swift chop. 'You could say that. If a woman crawls naked into a man's bed, it is a seduction, *ne*?'

This time Talia did choke on her yogurt. She grabbed a napkin and pressed it to her mouth, gazing at Maria in stunned disbelief. 'Not really...' she finally managed.

Maria nodded grimly. 'It is true. The woman was shown the door that night. Kyrie Mena did not even wait until morning to have her back on the mainland.' She gave Talia a quick, sideways glance. 'But I do not gossip.'

'No, of course not.' Talia took another spoonful of yogurt, her mind now full of rather salacious images of some eager nanny spread out like a centrefold, lying in wait for Angelos. And Angelos coming into his darkened bedroom, loosening his tie, unbuttoning his shirt...

Before she could stop herself she was imagining his brisk strip tease, the way he'd shrug out of a shirt, and how solid and muscular his chest would be, the moonlight casting silver shadows over his olive skin…

Good grief. A blush rose to Talia's face as she realised just how far she'd strayed into fantasy territory. And about Angelos Mena of all people, whom she didn't even like. He certainly had no regard for her. What on earth was she thinking?

'Sofia is upstairs,' Maria said, and Talia was grateful for the distraction. 'She is waiting for Ava, who comes for her lessons.'

Talia nodded and quickly finished her breakfast, taking her dishes to the sink before going in search of Sofia.

She still felt weirdly affected by that stupid little fantasy, as if someone might be able to guess the nature of her thoughts just from looking at her. All right, Angelos Mena was a handsome man. A very handsome man. A stunningly virile and sexy man, *fine*. And maybe she had extremely limited experience with the opposite sex. A boyfriend at seventeen, a couple of kisses. So what?

It didn't mean she had to fantasise about the first good-looking man who came into her orbit. And anyway, it wasn't as if Angelos Mena was the first good-looking man she'd ever seen. William Talbot III, whose portrait she had painted just a few months ago, was very attractive. Admittedly, he thought so too, and he'd insisted on being painted with his golf clubs and two yappy terriers, but *still*. He was, objectively speaking, a good-looking man.

But he was, Talia acknowledged wryly, no Angelos Mena.

She walked down the hallway, checking several spare rooms, before she finally found Sofia in a large, airy room at the end of the hall, its gabled windows overlooking the sea. Sofia was curled up in the wide window seat, looking out at the glittering waters.

'Kalimera,' Talia tried as she came into the room. Sofia turned to look at her, smiling shyly although Talia could still see sorrow in her big, dark eyes.

'Hello.'

'We're both learning,' Talia approved. She came to sit on the window seat next to Sofia. 'You have lessons this morning?' With a bit of miming of reading and writing, Talia was able to communicate what she meant, and Sofia nodded.

They sat in silence for a moment before Talia ventured, 'Papa? *Yia sou?'* She mimed waving goodbye, and Sofia shook her head.

'Papa…not…say,' she said in halting English.

'He didn't say goodbye?' Talia struggled to keep the dismay from her voice. Sofia shook her head again.

*'Ohi…*no. But…' She pointed to a sheet of paper in her lap, the single page filled with strong, slanting handwriting.

'He wrote you a letter,' Talia surmised, and Sofia nodded.

The letter was in Greek, of course, and Talia would never read someone else's correspondence, yet she found she was intensely curious to know what Angelos had written to his daughter…and why he hadn't said goodbye.

The sound of a motorboat cut through the still air, and Sofia leaned out the window to wave to the woman approaching the dock. 'Ava,' she said, turning back to Talia, and then said something in Greek Talia didn't understand but could guess the nature of.

'Your teacher,' she said, and Sofia repeated the new word.

'Teacher. *Ne.* Yes.'

A few minutes later Ava, a friendly woman in her forties, came upstairs. Fortunately she spoke English, and when Talia had explained who she was she offered to help her learn Greek after her lessons with Sofia.

'I'll have to ask Kyrie Mena,' Talia said, suspecting that Angelos would want to hear about any changes in plan. 'But I'm sure he'd like me to know more Greek.'

Ava laughed knowingly at that and Talia headed downstairs while Sofia had her lessons. Maria had disappeared from the kitchen, and so after standing uncertainly in the spacious hallway for a moment, Talia decided to go outside.

The air was hot and dry even though it was only a little past nine in the morning, and the sun shone brightly above, glinting off the sea.

Talia made her way through the garden, enjoying the colour and scent of the jumble of flowers. The gardens at the estate back in New York were lovely, but in a careful, manicured way. She liked the wildness here, felt its surprising answer in herself.

Funny, really, to think that Angelos Mena, of all people, would have a wild garden. But perhaps he wasn't here enough to keep it in order.

The thought made her frown as she stepped onto the beach, slipping off her sandals so she could feel the warm sand between her toes.

She made her way to the water's edge, letting the warm sea lap at her toes. She imagined Angelos back in Athens, sitting down at some important business meeting, making his so-called swift decisions. Athens was only an hour away, and yet he'd said he wouldn't be back for weeks. Why couldn't he make the trip more often, for Sofia's sake?

Talia knew it wasn't her concern; Angelos had certainly said as much. Besides, she was only here for six weeks, and she could hardly entangle herself in the lives of the Menas.

And yet…thoughts and questions whirled through her mind. The portrait of the secretly smiling woman; the fire Angelos refused to speak about. The sorrow she saw in Sofia's eyes, and the letter that had lain on her lap.

And of course the book. The real reason she was here, she reminded herself, was to find Giovanni's book. Sighing, Talia turned from the beach and headed back up to the villa.

Sofia was still in her lessons so Talia stayed in the kitchen with Maria, watching her as she kneaded bread. She'd offered to help, but Maria had vociferously refused, instead sitting her back down at the table, this time with a cup of what she called mountain tea. Talia took a cautious sip—Maria had made it by boiling what looked like a bunch of stems and leaves in a little brass pot—and found it surprisingly pleasant, a cross between chamomile and peppermint.

'It cures everything,' Maria assured her, 'except heartbreak. But you are not heartbroken, are you?'

'No, definitely not,' Talia assured her.

'You did not come all this way to Greece because of a failed romance?' Maria asked, sounding almost hopeful. Talia smothered a smile at the housekeeper's not so subtle attempt at digging into her past.

'No failed romances,' Talia answered. 'No romances at all, unless you count the boy I dated when I was seventeen.'

'You're waiting for someone special,' Maria said sagely. 'That is good.'

'I think I might be waiting a long time.' Talia shrugged the woman's sympathy aside. 'I've been happy on my own. I still am.'

'Every woman needs a man.'

Talia decided not to argue this point. 'But you don't

want me crawling into Angelos's bed, do you?' she joked, only to flush as Maria eyed her appraisingly.

'It was Kyrie Mena this morning.'

'It still is,' she promised. 'That was a slip. Trust me, I'm not going to be crawling into anyone's bed but my own.' She closed her eyes briefly, wondering if this conversation could actually get any more awkward.

'You do not want to set your sights on Kyrie Mena,' Maria said firmly. She gave the bread dough a few firm kneads. 'He is not a whole man.'

Intrigued, Talia leaned forward. 'Not a whole man?' He certainly looked like a whole man, devastatingly attractive in every part. 'What do you mean by that?'

Maria shook her head. 'I should not have said it. It is only there has been much tragedy in his life. He is not able to give a woman all she would need here.' Maria pressed a hand to her heart.

So Angelos was emotionally repressed? Not exactly a surprise. 'When you say tragedy,' Talia asked, 'do you mean the fire?'

Maria pressed her lips together. 'I should not have said.'

Talia could tell she wasn't going to get anything else out of the housekeeper about that, and so she asked if there was a library instead.

'A library? You want a book?'

'I thought I might see if there was anything to read,' Talia demurred, squashing a feeling of guilt at her duplicity. She did want a book, one specific book. But she had no idea if it was on Kallos, or in Angelos's possession at all.

'There is a room at the top of the house,' Maria said. 'Above the bedrooms. You will find some books there.'

Since Sofia was still busy with her teacher, Talia followed Maria's directions, up a winding staircase to a single, airy room on the top floor, with windows in every direction and bookshelves lining all the walls.

She stood in the centre of the room for a moment, enjoying the view of the sea all around her, before she began to study the books lining the shelves. Angelos had an eclectic collection of books: history, politics, art and music, even a little light fiction. None of the books looked like the one Giovanni had described, handcrafted with a cover of tooled leather.

Sighing, Talia berated herself for hoping it could be so simple. Did she actually think she'd just find the rare book lying on a shelf for anyone to pick up? She didn't know if it was on this island, or even in Angelos's possession. If he did own it, he might well keep it in Athens, in a safe. And maybe he didn't own it. The only way she would know, Talia acknowledged, was by asking the man himself.

She was just about to head back downstairs when Sofia popped her head up over the banister. 'I look for you!' she exclaimed in English, and Talia laughed.

'And you found me. How was your lesson?'

'Good,' Sofia said, and ducked her head in shy pride at how much English she'd spoken. Then she pointed to Talia. 'You now.'

'My Greek lesson?' Talia surmised. 'Bring it on.' She followed Sofia downstairs, where Ava was waiting.

Ten days passed by faster than Talia felt she could blink. It was easy to lose herself in the sunny haze of days; she spent the mornings reading or sketching or simply lazing on the beach, and then had a Greek lesson with Ava. The afternoons were with Sofia, either inside doing crafts or playing games, or outside walking, swimming and exploring some of the island.

She and Sofia managed to communicate through miming and bits of broken English and Greek, improvement showing on both sides with every passing day.

And with each day Talia saw Sofia becoming more confident and comfortable, although whenever Angelos came into the conversation a cloud passed over her face, and shadows came into her eyes. Talia started trying to keep her employer out of the conversation, even as her heart ached for Sofia and the lack of a loving parent in her life.

Several times she tried to find out more information about her grandfather's book, but when she asked Maria if Angelos liked poetry, she received an utterly blank look.

'Poetry? No.'

'He seems an educated man,' Talia tried. 'He has so many books upstairs... I thought he might enjoy a bit of poetry.'

'Are we talking about the same Kyrie Mena?' Maria asked with raised eyebrows. 'The man I know does not like poetry. He certainly doesn't read it.' Her gaze narrowed as she glanced at Talia. 'Why do you ask?'

'No reason,' Talia answered with a weak smile, guilt flashing through her. In the ten days since she'd arrived on Kallos she'd grown close to both Maria and Sofia, and Ava as well. She hated the thought that she was deceiving anyone, but she didn't know how to admit the truth without hurting everyone involved, and potentially enraging her boss.

Although she tried not to talk to Sofia about Angelos, Talia spent an inordinate amount of time wondering about him. How long had he been a widower? Had he loved his wife very much? Sometimes she would pause in the dining room and gaze up at the portrait of Xanthe Mena, with her heavy-lidded look and small, secretive smile, and wonder what she'd been like, and how she'd captured the heart of her husband.

Not that she was concerned about Angelos Mena's heart, Talia told herself. She was just curious. It was only natural.

Ten days into her time on Kallos her grandfather wrote her an email, asking about the book. Talia read the few lines with a growing sense of guilt, because she knew that she'd only made a few half-hearted attempts to find out any information.

When Angelos returned, she decided, she'd ask him about the book flat out. She'd try, at least.

Quickly she typed an email back to Giovanni.

Dear Nonno,
I am doing my best. I hope to have news soon. But please don't worry about me. I am having a good time and I hope you are keeping well.
Love, Talia.

For a second she pictured him in the conservatory where they'd shared so many meals, and a wave of homesickness washed over her. He'd become so frail in the last few months, his once robust and commanding figure diminished by age and illness. She hated the thought that she was missing time with him, precious days and weeks she'd never have again.

Which made her more determined than ever to find his book.

She was just pressing Send when she heard a distant whirring. She left her laptop open on her bed and hurried to the window, where she saw a helicopter touch down on the helipad. Her heart seemed to leap in her throat as the hatch opened and a familiar figure stepped out before striding down the path to the house.

Angelos Mena was home.

CHAPTER SIX

HE HADN'T MEANT to come back. Angelos Mena headed down the garden path, half inclined to turn around and climb back into the helicopter. He hadn't been intending to return to Kallos for another two weeks at least.

But he'd found himself thinking about returning almost since the moment he'd left. He wanted to make sure Talia Di Sione was indeed a suitable nanny, and even though Maria had assured him in several emails that she was, Angelos needed to see for himself. His daughter's welfare was paramount.

At least that was why he told himself he was back so soon. He just didn't completely believe it.

Now he stepped into the quiet of the villa, breathed in the scents of bougainvillea and heliotrope from outside. Maria hurried towards him.

'Kyrie Mena! I was not expecting you. You didn't send word you were coming.'

'It was a last-minute decision,' Angelos said as he shed his suit jacket. 'I'm sorry if I've inconvenienced you.'

'Not at all,' Maria clucked, bustling around him as she always did. 'I will make up your bedroom. And as for dinner…?'

Angelos hesitated. He normally didn't stay on Kallos for many meals, and those he took were by his desk, working. 'Have you eaten?' he asked. Maria shook her head.

'No, not yet. We were just going to have something simple in the kitchen...'

'Then I will join you for dinner.' Maria looked flummoxed; Angelos never joined them in the kitchen.

'Very good, sir,' she murmured, and he turned away, towards the solitude of his study.

He worked until he heard Sofia and Talia come downstairs; he listened to their chatter, a pidgin mixture of English and Greek, punctuated by much laughter. He couldn't remember the last time he'd heard his daughter sound so excited, so happy.

The realisation felt like a fist clenching his heart.

Finally when he could hear Maria putting the meal on the table he rose from his desk and went into the kitchen. The moment he stepped into the doorway the room fell silent, and three heads swivelled expectantly towards him.

'Kalispera,' Angelos greeted them, his voice terser than he would have liked. 'You are all well?'

'Very well,' Maria answered when no one else seemed inclined to say anything. Angelos sat down at the table and after a brief pause Talia and Sofia joined him there.

'Hello, Papa,' Sofia whispered, and Angelos smiled at her. She ducked her head, letting her hair fall forward to hide her scarred cheek. Everything inside him tightened in regret and dismay, and he looked away to compose himself. His interactions with Sofia were always like this.

As he put his napkin in his lap he could feel Talia watching him, and when he looked up he saw how she was gazing at him in what almost seemed like disapproval, her lips pursed, her eyes narrowed.

He raised his eyebrows in silent enquiry, and flushing, she looked away.

She looked good, he noticed. The last week had left her

tanned, the freckles across her nose coming out in bold relief. Her hair had golden streaks, and she seemed more relaxed than she had a week ago, even if she seemed determined to give him a death stare all dinner long.

The meal was awful. The food was as delicious as always, but the conversation was stilted and awkward, punctuated by long, taut silences. Whenever Angelos asked Sofia a question she stammered or mumbled an answer, and then hung her head.

Talia didn't speak at all, but Angelos could feel the censure and even the animosity rolling off her in waves and when the plates were cleared Angelos decided he had had enough of it. He excused himself before dessert was served, claiming he needed to work.

Back in his study he paced the room before he reached for the bottle of ouzo he kept in a drinks cabinet and poured himself a small measure. Then he cursed and slammed the glass back onto the desk. Alcohol was not the answer.

He went to his laptop, but he'd finished writing his notes on the last consultancy and he'd done nearly all the prep work on his next client. He had an unprecedented five days to spend at his leisure, and the truth was he didn't know what to do with it. At least when he worked he didn't have time to think. To remember.

He was staring blindly into the empty hearth when a quiet knock sounded at the door.

Angelos stiffened. No one disturbed him in his study. Maria knew it was off-limits, and Sofia would never dare. Which left one person who could be knocking at his door, one person who dared to disturb his privacy.

'Enter,' he barked, and the door swung open to reveal Talia standing there, her hands on her hips, her eyes blazing.

* * *

Talia was furious. She'd been furious ever since Angelos's helicopter had landed three hours ago, and he hadn't even come upstairs to say hello to his daughter.

When he'd appeared for dinner, she'd managed to calm down a little. Maybe he really was busy with work. He'd come back earlier than he'd intended, and he was making the effort to have a meal with them. She was willing to be appeased, even impressed. But then his behaviour during that meal—the bitten-off questions, the stony looks—had made her fury return in full force. And no matter what happened, even if the man fired her, she knew she couldn't stay silent any longer. For Sofia's sake she had to speak.

'Did you need something?' Angelos asked, his tone as curt as ever. He looked devastatingly sexy standing there, with the top two buttons of his crisp white shirt unbuttoned, revealing the tanned column of his throat, and the sleeves rolled up to show his powerful forearms. His hair was slightly mussed, and a five-o'clock shadow glinted on his strong jaw. Just the sight of him was enough to make every thought empty out of Talia's head, and she had a hard time remembering why she was so angry.

'I thought,' Angelos continued as he turned to his desk, effectively dismissing her, 'that Maria would have told you my study is off-limits.'

'You mean you're off-limits,' Talia returned. She was fast recalling her fury, especially when Angelos didn't even look up as he answered her. No matter how sexy the man was, he could still act like an ass.

'When I am working, yes.'

She gestured to his closed laptop. 'Have you been working, Kyrie Mena?'

Angelos glanced up then, clearly annoyed by her challenge. 'What is it you want, Miss Di Sione?'

'I thought you were going to call me Talia,' she reminded him with acid sweetness. 'Not that you've ever asked me to call you by your first name.'

'I am your employer.'

Talia rolled her eyes. 'You are also the most stiff and formal man I've ever met. In this day and age, I think it would be perfectly appropriate for us to call each other by our first names.'

He looked utterly nonplussed by this apparently outrageous suggestion. 'Is this why you came into my study? To discuss how we address each other?'

'No.' Talia let out her breath in a huff. She was picking the wrong fight, but there was so much about Angelos and his distant, disdainful attitude that got up her nose. Made her want to come out swinging for Sofia's sake. 'But I thought I'd mention it, as an aside.'

'Fine. You've mentioned it.' He turned away again and Talia clenched her hands into fists.

'You know, I *think* you love your daughter,' she said, her voice shaking with the force of her feeling, 'but I wouldn't be able to tell from your behaviour. At all.'

Angelos turned around slowly. His face was blank, his eyes like two dark pools, his huge body radiating menace. Talia felt a tremor of trepidation go through her; she'd already learned that Angelos was at his most terrifying when she couldn't tell anything from his expression.

'I have no interest in what you think,' he said, enunciating each harsh word with cold precision. 'And no desire for you to come and invade my privacy with your ridiculous presumption.'

She blinked, half amazed at the blatant insults he delivered with such deliberate cruelty, even as part of her recognised it as a tactic. A defence, and one she was determined to break through. 'You really are incredibly rude,' she told him, glad her voice came out evenly. 'As well as—dare I say it?—*short-sighted*. I spend more time with your daughter than anyone else does. Maybe you should care what I think.'

Two spots of colour appeared high on Angelos's sharp cheekbones, but his expression remained glacial, his eyes like chips of dark ice. 'You overstep yourself, Miss Di Sione,' he said, his voice a quiet, warning hiss. Talia felt a tremble of fear, and yet courage or perhaps just a deep conviction of what Sofia needed propelled her onwards.

'So what are you going to do, fire me?' she demanded as she took a step towards him, felt the heat from his body and inhaled the clean male scent of him. 'I'm overstepping myself because I care about your daughter. And your behaviour hurts her terribly, even though she tries to hide it. Why can't you be more—' She broke off, searching for a word, and Angelos raised his eyebrows, his whole body tensed with suppressed fury.

'Be more what?' he asked, biting off each word and spitting it out.

'*Loving,*' she burst out. 'She's a little girl. She has so few people in her life. She wants to be loved by her papa.'

Her words seemed to echo in the taut stillness of the room, and for one brief second Angelos's features twisted in what looked like a grimace of anguish, and Talia felt as if her heart was suspended in her chest as realisation slammed into her. *He was hurting...just as Sofia was hurting.*

Just as she was hurting.

Then his expression ironed out and he turned away, busying himself with some papers on his desk, his back to her.

'This conversation is over.'

'Angelos...' It was the first time she'd dared to call him

by his first name, and it felt weirdly intimate, as if she had just used an endearment. She took a step towards him, reaching a hand out, wanting to touch him, to offer him that little comfort, and her too. She imagined the feel of his shoulder under her palm, hot and hard and strong. She craved that connection, however brief and illusory it was, and she imagined, foolishly perhaps, he craved it too. Yet even so she didn't dare. 'Surely someone else,' she said quietly, 'Maria or one of the nannies, has spoken to you about this? Has been as concerned as I have?'

'The other nannies were not nearly as interested in Sofia as you seem to be,' Angelos answered tonelessly. 'Now I wonder if that was no bad thing.' He glanced up at her, his expression as cold and implacable as it ever had been, and Talia knew any moment of connection she had been hoping for was well and truly severed. 'I am not asking for your opinion on these matters. You are here for a short time only, Talia. You are not part of our lives. In a month you will be gone from here, as good as forgotten.'

The deliberate brutality of his words felt like a slap to the face, a fist to the gut. She blinked rapidly, startled by how hurt she felt by Angelos's cold statement. She may have only been on Kallos for ten days, but she felt as if she'd become part of Sofia's life, as if she *mattered*. And, Talia realised with a stab of remorse, she mattered to so few people in her life. Her grandfather, her brothers and sisters…her circle of loved ones was incredibly small. She hadn't thought she minded, but now…

'That may be true,' she managed when she trusted her voice not to tremble with the force of her hurt. 'But I'm part of Sofia's life now. I matter to her *now*, and she matters to me.' Angelos simply stared, blatantly unimpressed. Talia fought the urge to cry, or maybe scream. She felt as if she were banging her head against a wall. A very hard wall. Maybe Angelos was right, and she should just stop. It wasn't as if she'd ever see these people again after the next month. Why was she pushing so much? Why did she care so much?

Because you know how Sofia feels.

She took a deep breath and forced all the feelings back. 'How long are you staying for this time?' she asked, and she saw surprise flicker across Angelos's face at the abrupt change in topic.

'I have not yet decided. I came to make sure you were doing an adequate job—'

'And am I?'

'That remains to be seen,' Angelos answered coolly. 'Now, as I said before, this conversation is—'

'Perhaps you should assess my performance,' Talia suggested before she lost her courage. She felt reckless now, almost wild; he'd already hurt her so what did she really have to lose? 'Surely you need to see if I really am doing the thing properly. *Appropriately.*' Angelos narrowed his eyes, clearly trying to figure out her game. Talia gave him her sunniest smile, even though she felt fragile inside, ready to break. 'Tomorrow Sofia and I are going on a picnic,' she stated, although she hadn't planned any such thing. 'I've been wanting to walk to the far side of the island. Why don't you come with us?'

He stared at her for a long moment, a muscle flickering in his jaw, his eyes utterly opaque. Talia waited for his answer, her breath held, trying not to hope too hard.

'Well played, Miss Di Sione,' he finally said, and there was a faint note of reluctant admiration in his voice that made Talia release her breath in a relieved rush. 'You are a positive terrier.'

'I'll take that as a compliment.'

'It wasn't necessarily meant as one.' Angelos turned

back to his desk, bracing his hands flat on the burnished surface, almost as if he were steeling himself—but for what? 'As tempting as a picnic sounds,' he said, 'I'm afraid I will have to forego such pleasures. I have a lot of work to do.'

'Why did you come back at all, then?' Talia demanded, hurt audible in her voice, making her cringe. She'd thought he'd been going to accept, and the intense disappointment she felt at his refusal felt like an overreaction, yet one she couldn't keep herself from.

'I told you—'

'To assess my capabilities? But you haven't spent any time with me or Sofia. How can you possibly know how capable I am?'

He swung around, anger igniting in his eyes again, making them burn. 'Why are you so damnably persistent?'

'Because I know what it's like to be without a father,' Talia confessed. She felt the blood rush to her face at this unwarranted admission. 'Or a mother. I lost both my parents when I was a year old.'

Angelos stared at her for a long moment, his jaw bunched, his arms still folded, and yet Talia sensed a softening in him. 'I'm sorry,' he finally said, his voice gruff. 'I would not wish that on anyone.'

'Sofia's already lost her mother,' Talia pressed while she had an advantage. 'She needs you—'

'And she has me.' He cut her off swiftly, his tone and expression hardening once more. 'I provide for her every need, and I visit here as often as I can. And frankly, Miss Di Sione, Sofia is better off without me around.' He swung away again, driving a hand through his hair, his back, taut and quivering with tension, to her. 'Now, go please,' he said in a low voice. 'Before either of us says something we will later regret.'

Talia stared at him for a long moment, everything in her wanting to go comfort this man. She sensed a grief and even a darkness in him that she hadn't expected, and it called to a similar emotion in her that she'd long suppressed.

'Angelos…' she tried, hesitantly, because they did not remotely have the kind of relationship that would allow her to offer comfort, and she wasn't sure she wanted to give it anyway. Reaching out to this man, actually connecting with him, would be dangerous for both of them.

And yet she stayed, even lifted her hand as she had before, fingers trembling, straining… Her fingertips brushed his shoulder, and she felt his muscles quiver and jerk in response, or perhaps she was the one who moved, a jolt running through her body that surprised her with its impossible force. She'd barely touched him.

'Go,' Angelos said, his voice low and insistent, his head bowed, and dropping her hand, her whole body reacting to that tiny touch, Talia went.

Angelos stayed in his study working until the small hours of the morning. Better to work and try to blot out all the damning accusations Talia had hurled at him. The pleas to spend time with his daughter, when that was the one thing he couldn't do.

For a second, staring blankly at the page of notes he'd been making on his new client, Angelos remembered what it had been like to be close to Sofia. To hold the warm baby weight of her in his arms, tuck her head against his shoulder and rest his chin on top of her silky hair. He remembered how she'd always tugged on his ears, giving a great big baby's belly laugh. How Xanthe had watched them, smiling that secret smile, love shining in her eyes…

With a curse he shoved the pad of paper away, driving

his hands through his hair, his nails raking his scalp, as if he could push the memories right out of his head. As if he could change the past, the night that had claimed Xanthe's life and scarred Sofia for ever. The night that had been his fault.

He glanced at the ouzo in the drinks cabinet, and then turned away.

The house was quiet as he headed upstairs, the night breeze cool. He paused outside Talia's room, wondering how she'd taken his rebuttals. He'd been harsh, he knew, but she'd been so damnably determined. She'd been trying to make him see, and the trouble was, he saw all too clearly. He saw that when he was near his daughter he made her uncomfortable, reminded her of all they'd lost. Sofia might need a father, but she needed a better one than him.

And yet Talia didn't know that, didn't realise how unworthy he was. She'd tried to comfort him, and for a second, his eyes clenched shut, Angelos remembered the feel of her fingers on his shoulder, barely the brush of a hand, and yet it had made him feel as if his skin had been scraped raw, every nerve exposed to stinging air. Not a pleasant feeling, and yet it had made him feel so *alive*. For a second he'd craved even more; the kind of connection to another human being that he hadn't had in seven years. It would have felt like the ripping of a bandage from a wound, the sudden exposure to light and air and life, painful and necessary and good.

And not for him.

Banishing all thoughts of Talia, he moved past her room to Sofia's, slipping inside silently as he did every night he was on Kallos, while his daughter slept.

Sofia lay on her side, her knees tucked up as they always were. As Angelos came closer, his throat constricted as he saw the dried traces of tears on his daughter's cheek.

She'd been crying…because of him? Because of what he had or hadn't done? He glanced down and saw the last letter he'd written her on the floor, having slipped from her fingers as she'd fallen asleep.

Guilt lashed him, a scourge whose sting he accepted as his due. Sofia's sadness was his fault. He knew that. He'd always known that. He just didn't know how he could make it better.

'S'agapo manaria mou,' he said softly, and then, as he always did, he slipped silently from the room before she could wake.

Talia woke the next morning determined to give Sofia the day she should have had with her father, if he'd only been willing. She asked Maria to pack a picnic, and, a few games to play on the beach and plenty of sun cream.

As soon as Sofia had finished her lessons, she announced her intentions.

'A picnic?' Sofia's face lit up as she smiled shyly. Talia had noticed how quiet and downhearted she'd seemed since Angelos's arrival yesterday afternoon, and she was glad to see the girl brightening now. 'Just…just the two of us?' She glanced inadvertently towards her father's study, the door firmly closed.

'Yes,' Talia said, injecting as much cheer as she could into her voice. 'Won't it be fun? I've been wanting to explore the other side of the island. We can swim on the other beach.' Sofia frowned in confusion, and with exaggerated movements Talia mimed what she meant. She deserved an Academy Award for her acting talents, she thought wryly as Sofia nodded in understanding.

Talia slathered them both in sun cream, and cramming the wide straw hat she'd borrowed from Maria on her head, she headed outside with Sofia.

The sky was cloudless blue, the sun already high and hot above, and the other side of the island beckoned enticingly. Kallos wasn't very big, a few square miles at most, but Talia hadn't ventured much beyond the landscaped gardens and beach right in front of the villa.

Now, despite the disappointment caused by Angelos's absence, she found she was looking forward to seeing a little more of the island. The sense of adventure that had been dormant for so long rose up once more, so she walked with a spring in her step as they left the bright tangle of the villa's gardens for the stony hill above the house.

They'd just crested the hill and Talia was gazing in interest at the rock-strewn valley below when Sofia suddenly exclaimed in Greek.

Afraid she'd seen a snake or something dangerous, Talia whirled around. Sofia was pointing back towards the villa.

'Papa,' she exclaimed.

Talia held up her hand to shade her eyes from the sun, and her heart felt as if it had leapt into her throat when she saw Angelos coming up the hill they'd just climbed with long, purposeful strides.

'Papa,' she agreed cautiously, and she glanced down at Sofia to see a look of apprehension coming over her face as Angelos drew nearer. He was dressed as casually as she'd ever seen him, in shorts that emphasised his powerful thighs and calves and a T-shirt that clung to the well-defined muscles of his chest. He was also, Talia saw as her heart sunk from her throat to her toes, scowling ferociously.

CHAPTER SEVEN

TALIA AND SOFIA watched Angelos climb up the hill, his stride easy and powerful, the scowl on his face deepening with every step. Sofia slid her hand into Talia's and hid slightly behind her.

Talia lifted her chin, determined to brazen out whatever Angelos had in mind. What on earth could he be angry about? Taking his daughter on a picnic?

'Well.' He stood in front of them, his hands on his hips, the scowl still on his face. 'I'm here.'

'So you are,' Talia agreed warily. 'Why?'

His gaze snapped to hers, his eyes widening in disbelief. 'Did you not ask me to come on a picnic, even though it is a wretchedly hot day? And so I came.'

Talia simply stared at him for a long moment before she finally realised what he was saying. 'You mean…you're coming with us? And you're…you're not angry?'

'Angry?' Angelos stared at her, nonplussed. 'Why do you think I am angry?'

A grin split her face as relief zinged through her. 'Maybe you should look in a mirror on occasion,' she dared to tease. 'You've been scowling the whole time you were climbing the hill, and scaring the dickens out of your daughter and me.'

For a second Angelos looked almost embarrassed.

'Well.' He rubbed his chin, looking away. 'Like I said, it is very hot out here.'

And then the full realisation of what he'd done bloomed inside her, and she felt caught between laughter and tears. Angelos was coming on their picnic. He was *trying*, and maybe that was what had brought the scowl to his face, because this was unfamiliar territory, and it was hard. Harder, perhaps, than Talia even knew.

He was coming out of his comfort zone, and she admired him for it. She knew how incredibly hard that could be.

'We're glad you're here,' she said, and stepped aside so Sofia couldn't hide behind her any longer. 'Aren't we, Sofia?'

'Ne,' Sofia answered after a moment, ducking her head so her hair hid her face. Talia suppressed the urge to tuck it behind Sofia's ears; she knew it was a defence mechanism, and one she employed whenever she was in her father's presence.

'Good.' Angelos's expression clouded as he saw the way Sofia hid, but then he gave one brisk nod and surveyed the valley before them. 'So where are you intending to have this picnic?'

'I thought we could walk to the far side of the island. There are some rocks there that look interesting.' Talia pointed to some large boulders that bordered the shoreline, perfect for scrambling.

'Very well.' Angelos nodded again, and Talia had to smother a laugh as she realised how out of his element he was. He had the most commanding, confident presence of anyone she'd encountered, and yet he was clearly out of his depth here, no doubt trying to manage a picnic like a business meeting. 'Shall we?'

'Yes, we shall,' she agreed, and she must not have been

able to keep a teasing note from her voice because Angelos gave her a swift, suspicious look before he started
down towards the valley.

They walked down the hill towards the opposite shore;
the hillside was dotted with the ancient, gnarled trunks
of olive trees, the ground strewn with stones. Talia stumbled on one, and before she'd even had a chance to right
herself, Angelos steadied her with one strong hand on her
elbow, the touch of his skin against hers a shock to her
system just as it had been last night, like being doused in
ice water, or jolted with electricity.

Except, Talia reflected as Angelos dropped his hand and
they walked on, both of those sensations were unpleasant and Angelos's touch hadn't been unpleasant at all. Far
from it. The few times his skin had brushed hers she'd felt
a warmth blooming inside her, spreading outward, taking
over. It was the kind of feeling that made her want more,
made her wonder how to get it.

She was still feeling the aftershocks of his hand on her
elbow as they approached the shore, little zinging sensations arrowing low down in her belly. Amazing how a
hand on her elbow of all places could make her feel so...
tingly. Dangerous too, because she knew she couldn't en-
tertain some kind of crush or attraction for her boss. For
a whole lot of reasons.

Not least of all the complication of Giovanni's book.
But she didn't want to think about the book today, or how
she was going to bring up the subject with Angelos. She
just wanted to enjoy their time together, as Sofia was.

She looked down at Sofia walking between them, her
shy glance darting from Talia to Angelos, as if she couldn't
believe they were both here. And in truth, Talia couldn't
believe it. She'd spent hours last night, lying on her bed,

staring into the darkness and wondering what Angelos had meant, saying Sofia was better off without him around.

How could he, how could any father, think such a thing? Talia knew what it was like to grow up motherless, fatherless, longing for so much as a memory of the parents she'd had and having only an empty space in her heart and head instead.

She knew her parents hadn't been perfect, far from it. Her oldest brother, Alessandro, had hard memories of her mother and father, memories he wouldn't speak of to anyone, or at least not to Talia. She knew her father had had an affair, which had resulted in a half-brother she barely knew, Nate.

But surely any parents were better than none? Sometimes she and her sister Bianca, who had only a few shadowy memories of their mother—the smell of perfume, the jingle of bracelets—talked about how they missed their parents, missed having ever known them. Missed having a memory of a conversation or cuddle. Giovanni was wonderful, but he'd been only one old and sometimes ill man to care for seven very different and sometimes difficult children.

So why did Angelos shy away from his daughter? Last night, when she'd been in his study and heard the anguish in his voice, seen it in his face for a moment, Talia had been sure there was some private torment that kept Angelos from his daughter, and she'd longed to know what it was, so she could try to relieve him of such an awful burden.

But who was she, she'd asked herself in the darkness of her bedroom last night, to relieve anyone of anything? She'd chosen a life of isolation rather than brave the world around her. She wasn't in any position to offer advice.

But you're different. You're protecting yourself physi-

cally. Angelos is cutting himself off from the person he loves.

'Shall we stop here?' Angelos asked, and Talia blinked the world into focus. She'd been so lost in her thoughts she'd barely been aware of the island around her, the sea shimmering with sunlight, the boulders they'd reached pointing proudly to a hard, blue sky.

'Yes, this looks good.' Talia took the blanket from her bag and spread it over a patch of even sand. Sofia sat down, kicking off her sandals and then digging her toes into the sand with a sigh of pleasure.

Angelos sat nearby, his long, muscular legs stretched out in front him, his arms braced behind him, as he gazed out at the sea.

'Now this isn't so bad, is it?' Talia teased, and he shot her a dark look.

'It's hot. But the breeze is pleasant.'

'You know I'm not talking about the weather.'

'No.' His forehead furrowed, he glanced at Sofia, who was now kneeling in the sand, scooping it up in handfuls.

'How about we make a sandcastle?' Talia suggested, waving a bucket, and clearly taking her meaning, Sofia clapped her hands. Angelos looked nonplussed.

'A what?'

'A sandcastle? You have made one, haven't you, when you were a child at least?'

'No, not as a child.' He drew his legs up and rested his forearms on his knees, his expression becoming distant and veiled. 'I… I used to make them with Sofia.' He glanced at his daughter, who was watching him warily, not understanding the English. 'But she'd always eat the sand.'

'I'm assuming she was a baby at the time?' Talia said. She was oddly moved by the arrested look on Angelos's face, the sense that this was a precious memory, and one he didn't access often. Again she felt that sense of grief and even torment, so private it felt as if she were glimpsing something she wasn't meant to see, an emotional peeping Tom.

'Yes, she was a baby,' Angelos said, and he looked away. 'Not quite a year old.'

No one spoke, and Talia tried to think of something to say, some way to bridge the moment between darkness and light, between painful memory and carefree present.

Then Angelos turned back to them and gave his daughter a rusty smile, his gaze deliberately averted from Talia. 'Do we have a spade?'

Talia handed him a plastic shovel, her heart precariously full as she watched Angelos begin to dig. They were merely making a sandcastle, and yet it felt like they were building something more, the beginning of something important, its foundation the memories that had gone before.

After a few minutes of them all working together Talia scooted back, content to let father and daughter create their palace. She started to unpack the food Maria had made them, casting a glance every so often to Angelos and Sofia. Neither of them was speaking, so she couldn't say it was a huge bonding success, but at least they were doing something together. It still felt like a lot.

Carefully Angelos turned the bucket over and lifted it so a perfect dome of damp sand emerged. Sofia peeped up at him, a shy smile lighting her features, making the old guilt and grief inside him twist painfully. He could tell his daughter was pleased to have him here, and it made him wonder if he'd been remiss, even wrong, in staying away for so long.

But he'd felt he'd had no choice. He'd honestly believed he was doing the best thing for Sofia. And maybe he had been. A single, sunny afternoon was simply that. A moment in time. The reality of his presence in Sofia's life was that he was inept, inexperienced, and it brought back painful reminders of everything his daughter didn't have.

He glanced at Talia, who had unpacked several containers of food and was now sitting on the edge of the blanket, her hands clasped around her knees as she stared out at the sea. Her hair blew in tangles around her face, making Angelos itch to tuck it behind her ears, let his fingers skim the silky softness of her cheek.

His insides clenched at the thought as he grimly acknowledged that he was attracted to his temporary nanny. Ironic, really, that he'd had his choice of svelte beauties before and he'd always refused them. He hadn't felt so much as a flicker of desire for the other nannies, not to mention the women at work and in Athens who had offered themselves to him. It had been so long he'd wondered if his libido had simply gone for good. He hadn't even minded; life was simpler that way, and pleasure was something he hadn't so much as considered in a long, long time.

But since Talia Di Sione had catapulted into his life, his libido had become positively wakeful. Desire had roared through him last night when she'd touched his shoulder. His *shoulder*. For heaven's sake, it wasn't as if she'd rubbed up against him, or tried to kiss him, those petal-soft lips opening and yielding under his...

At these thoughts his body stirred to life and Angelos shifted where he sat. What was he doing, thinking like this?

Talia caught his glance and smiled at him. Sofia was busy completing her castle, and so they had a moment of private conversation.

'So you didn't make sandcastles as a child? How come?'

Jolted by the question, as well as the nature of his own

recent thoughts, Angelos answered without thinking. 'I had no opportunity. I grew up in Piraeus.'

'Piraeus?' Talia wrinkled her nose. 'But isn't that near the beach?'

Angelos shook his head, wishing he hadn't said so much. He never talked about his childhood, not even to Xanthe. She hadn't wanted to know, had preferred to think they were starting something new and better together. 'The docks,' he explained succinctly. And then, for no reason he could fathom except that Talia was looking at him with such honest, interested curiosity, he clarified, 'I was a street rat.'

'A street rat?' Her eyebrows rose in disbelief even as her expression clouded with sympathy. 'What do you mean exactly?'

Angelos shrugged. 'I was—am—an orphan. My father was never around and my mother gave me up when I was a baby. I grew up in a home for children, but when I was fourteen I left to work on the docks.' He looked away, not wanting to see the revulsion and pity he knew would be in her eyes. Xanthe had been horrified by his past. She'd accepted it, accepted him, but she'd wanted to pretend the ugly parts of his story didn't exist. And so Angelos had acted as if they hadn't.

'That's terrible,' Talia said quietly. 'And it must have been so hard for you. I'm so, so sorry.'

Her obvious sincerity left him feeling nonplussed, even disoriented. 'I survived.'

'But how did you go from working the docks to owning your own management consultancy?' she asked. She sounded quietly awed, which made no sense. Angelos turned back, still expecting to see pity, and instead he saw admiration shining in her eyes.

It felt like a kick to the gut, to the heart. Suddenly he

was breathless. 'I had a lot of luck,' he said gruffly. 'I went to night school and received my high school accreditation, and then a scholarship to university. I started my own firm fifteen years ago, a single room in a shabby building in the wrong part of Athens.'

'That doesn't sound like luck,' Talia said. 'That sounds like a lot of hard work and determination.'

Angelos just shrugged again. He didn't know how to handle her admiration; he was so unused to it. Xanthe had met him when he was already successful, and the people from his past had disappeared a long time ago. In any case, he didn't deserve it, not really. So he'd worked hard. He'd made money. What did it matter? He hadn't been able to protect his family at the most crucial time. He hadn't been able to save his wife.

'Angelos, I'm proud of you,' Talia said, laying a hand on his arm. He tensed beneath her touch, every nerve twanging to life from the simple brush of her fingers. He had a mad, nearly irresistible urge to pull her into his arms and plunder the soft mouth he hadn't been able to stop looking at. No one had ever said they were proud of him, not even Xanthe.

Talia's fingers tightened on his arm and Angelos felt his insides coil in expectation. It would be so easy to turn to her, to take her face in his hands and draw her lovely mouth towards his. Everything in him pulsed with the desire to do so.

And he sensed that she wanted him to, that she wouldn't resist. The attraction was mutual, which both excited and alarmed him. It would be so, so easy...

Then Sofia turned from her finished sandcastle, chattering to Talia, and she let her hand slip from his arm. Angelos let out a long, low, silent breath of relief—and disappointment. The moment, whatever it had been, had passed.

Talia started putting food on plastic plates, and handing them around, and after a few seconds when his libido lay down again, Angelos rejoined the conversation.

He picked at the delicious offerings of cheese and bread and olives, a restlessness inside him that he'd quieted for a long time, and this not to do with the overwhelming physical attraction he had for his nanny. This was caused by something deeper, something more emotional. At first he hadn't liked Talia's prying questions, but then part of him had. Part of him had been glad to share something of who he was, to be honest and open with another person.

Disturbed by this thought, he put the plate aside and started walking towards the sea. He kicked off his sandals and let the cool water lap over his feet, cool his blood. What was *wrong* with him today?

From behind him he could hear Talia clearing the dishes, talking to Sofia. Then he heard them both coming across the sand, and he saw that Sofia had stripped to her one-piece and Talia...

Every thought flew out of his head as he gazed at Talia in a forest-green bikini. It was, for a bikini, quite modest: boy shorts and a halter top. He was able to acknowledge that even as his pulse skyrocketed and his mouth dried, his gaze moving inexorably towards the gentle swell of her breasts under the thin fabric, the enticing dip of her waist and flare of her hips. His palms ached to smooth across her golden skin, to anchor her hips in his hands....

Horrified by how quickly he'd envisioned that fantasy, how instantly his blood had heated and his body had responded, Angelos stripped off his shirt and dived cleanly into the sea, letting the shock of the cold water cool his response.

'How is it, Papa?' Sofia asked, and Angelos stood, making sure he was waist-deep to hide any lingering effects of seeing Talia.

'Cold but fine,' he called. 'Why don't you come in?'

He told himself not to so much as glance at Talia, but clearly his body was not receiving his brain's signals because his gaze slid that way, and he inhaled sharply as he saw the desire in her eyes. Watched her gaze drop to his bare chest before flicking away.

So he'd been right. She wanted him. She wanted him just as he wanted her.

The realisation shocked him, not because he was so surprised that Talia would desire him physically, but because it had been so long since he'd felt the same. And for a second, no more, he considered acting on the attraction they both felt.

It could be simple, if they let it be. She was here only for six weeks; they could have a fling, get each other out of their systems. The sex would be good, fantastic even, and it had been so *long*…

And what about Sofia? In the last twenty-four hours he'd seen how Sofia was happier, more confident and comfortable, with Talia around. He could not risk his daughter's well-being simply to scratch an itch he'd only just developed.

He turned away from Talia, effectively ignoring her as she dove into the water, and watched Sofia instead.

Angelos Mena in nothing but shorts was an unbearably gorgeous sight. Talia knew she was probably making a fool of herself, letting her gaze linger on his broad, bronzed chest, watching the muscles in his shoulders and arms ripple enticingly as he held his hands out to Sofia. His stomach was perfectly flat, every contour of his six-pack abs defined.

She imagined brushing her fingers against those ridged muscles, exploring their shape, letting her hand slide lower…

A blush scorched her cheeks as she realised what she was imagining. She, who had absolutely no bedroom experience, hadn't done anything but buss lips with a boy a lifetime ago, was picturing *that*? She didn't even know what *that* would look like. Feel like.

Quickly Talia ducked her head under the water, kicking hard away from Angelos and Sofia. She had to shut down this line of thinking now. She couldn't bear the thought of Angelos seeing the overwhelming desire she felt in her face. What if he sent her away, suspecting she was trying to seduce him?

The thought that she could seduce anyone, much less a man as powerful and commanding as Angelos, was utterly absurd. He would never be attracted to someone like her, someone with absolutely zero worldly experience.

She thought of that portrait in the dining room, the elegant sophistication of the woman who had been his wife, with her dark eyes and knowing smile. Whereas she didn't know anything.

Suddenly, to her shock, she felt strong hands close around her shoulders like iron bands and she was jerked out of the sea, coughing and sputtering as she inhaled a mouthful of salt water.

'Why did you swim underwater for so long?' Angelos demanded. His face was thrust close to hers, his eyes glittering with fury, droplets of water beading on his bare chest.

'I don't know… I was just swimming.' Her body pressed

close to his, Talia could barely form a coherent thought. She could feel his thighs against hers, hard and powerful, his hands still clasping her shoulders, her breasts brushing his chest, making them tighten and ache.

'I thought you'd hit your head or something when you dove in,' Angelos gritted out. 'I couldn't see you...'

Despite the desire swirling through her like a delicious fog, Talia could tell Angelos had been genuinely worried.

'I'm sorry,' she said. 'I've always liked swimming. I grew up by the water. You don't need to worry about me in the water.'

He released her so suddenly she nearly fell backwards. She found her footing as Angelos stepped back, his expression shuttering. 'Next time come up for air a little sooner,' he bit out, and then turned away, back to Sofia, who was paddling in the shallows.

Talia watched them together, wondering at Angelos's extreme reaction. All right, she may have been underwater for a little while, but she'd always liked swimming, the way the water cocooned her, made her feel safe. And she'd been trying to get over her physical reaction to her boss.

Unfortunately Angelos's manhandling of her had only made it worse. Her arms burned where he'd touched her, and every part of her tingled. The peaks of her breasts ached where they'd brushed against his bare chest.

Best not to think of that again, Talia told herself, and dove back under the water, making sure to resurface before Angelos came looking for her again.

They stayed on the beach for most of the afternoon, swimming and lazing around, but Angelos didn't attempt to make conversation again beyond a few basic pleasantries.

Talia knew it was better that way, and yet the little

he'd said about his childhood had provided an intriguing glimpse into the emotional interior of a man who had, on appearance, always seemed hard and cold and, frankly, unfriendly.

It made her want to get to know him more, but Angelos was providing no opportunity. Clearly he didn't feel the same way.

After a few hours, their skin encrusted with salt and a sunburn starting on her nose, Talia suggested they pack up. Sofia's face dropped but Talia could see her charge was flagging; they'd spent a lot of time out in the wind and sun.

Wordlessly Angelos helped to pack up and then took the picnic basket from her as they started back towards the villa. Talia had the pleasantly tired sensation of having had a full day out, although after suffering one of Angelos's frowning glances she realised she must look a complete mess.

Her hair was tangled and salty, hanging in damp ropes down her back, and her nose was probably Rudolph-red by now. She'd put her T-shirt and shorts back on over her swimsuit, which had made damp patches on the fabric. Yes, she was really rocking a sexy, seductive look right now. Not that she wanted Angelos to see her as sexy or seductive, of course. Not that he ever would, even if she wore a black lace bustier and fire-engine-red stilettos.

Now where had that image come from? Talia let out an incredulous little laugh as she pictured herself in such a ridiculous getup. She hated heels and the only thing she wore to bed was a very old, very large and very comfy T-shirt. This made her smother another laugh, and Angelos glanced at her, eyes narrowed.

'What's so funny?'

For a second she imagined telling him, and that made

her laughter cut off like a tap being turned off. Would he be appalled or incredulous or both? She knew Angelos Mena was way, way out of her league. 'Nothing,' she assured him. 'Nothing at all.'

CHAPTER EIGHT

BY THE TIME they reached home, dark clouds were billowing up on the horizon and the wind that had been teasing and warm while they'd been on the beach had turned hard, buffeting them as they crested the hill above Angelos's villa.

'There will be a storm tonight,' Angelos remarked as he led the way down the hill towards the house. 'Make sure you close the shutters in your bedroom.'

'A storm?' Alarm prickled along Talia's skin at the thought.

Angelos must have heard the anxiety in her voice for he glanced at her, eyebrows raised. 'We will be perfectly safe in the villa. It is built to withstand such things.'

'I'm sure,' Talia murmured. She hated storms. Hated, hated, *hated* them. So much so that she had, in the past, swallowed a couple of sleeping pills while she waited one out. She'd rather be dead to the world than trembling in terror as it raged around her.

But she didn't want to knock herself out here, with Sofia needing her. Maybe the storm wouldn't be that bad. A little rain and wind was fine. It was the thunder and lightning that she couldn't stand, the booming that reverberated through her chest, the lightning that streaked through the sky and, for one blazing second, illuminated everything.

Just the thought of it made her head start to feel light, and a buzzing began in her ears. Talia took a deep breath, willing the panic away. She'd been so good, these last eleven days, in controlling her fear. Being on Kallos had felt, in a way, like being on the estate. Isolated. Safe.

But a storm...

'Talia?' Angelos asked, his voice harsh and insistent. 'Are you all right?'

'What?' She blinked up at him, swaying slightly where she stood. They'd walked down the hillside without her even realising it and they now stood on the terrace outside the kitchen. Sofia must have gone inside. 'I'm fine,' she said, even though she knew she wasn't. She dragged another deep breath into her lungs. 'Totally fine. Where's Sofia?'

'She went inside to change.' Angelos was still frowning at her, his gaze moving over her like a doctor checking for broken bones. 'Do you not like storms?'

'Not particularly.' The smile she gave him felt like a horrible rictus. The wind was picking up so much now her hair blew about her face, and then she heard a distant rumble and her heart free-fell towards her toes. 'I'll be fine,' she said as firmly as she could. She didn't want Angelos to see her anxiety, even though she knew she must be showing it, at least a little. She hated for anyone to know her weaknesses; it was bad enough for her grandfather and siblings to feel sorry for her, to know how damaged she was. She couldn't bear for others to see it, and especially someone like Angelos, who was so strong and capable. He probably wasn't afraid of anything.

'If you're sure,' he said, sounding doubtful, and Talia forced a nod.

'I'm sure.'

She walked up to her bedroom and ran a shower, glad

that the rush of water drowned out the noise of the thunder rumbling in the distance, like a discontented giant. She rested her head against the tile as she let the water stream over her and tried to calm the racing of her heart.

It's just a storm. It can't hurt you. No one can hurt you now. You're safe. You're safe.

Words she'd repeated to herself countless times over the last seven years, but she never really believed them, not deep down. She'd never trusted that she would be safe, not unless she was hidden behind high walls, locked gates, like some frightened Rapunzel up in her tower.

You're on an island. No one can hurt you here. No one can get to you.

Really, she was so much safer on Kallos than anywhere else. She had to believe that, because if she didn't, she'd start thinking about how small the island was, how confined and cut off. And then her claustrophobia would kick in, and she'd *really* be in trouble.

Resolutely Talia turned off the shower and dressed in her one pair of jeans and a thick fleece. With the approaching storm the weather had cooled down and she stood by the window for a moment, gazing out at a wide sky the colour of a livid bruise before she closed and latched the shutters, releasing a shaky breath. She still had dinner to get through.

Downstairs the house was dark, the shutters all closed against the storm. Somewhere in the distance a loose shutter banged, and the sound made unease prickle along Talia's scalp. She hated that lonely, mournful sound. She shivered, and then jumped when she heard Angelos's low voice coming from right behind her.

'Are you cold?'

'No...' She turned, blinking in the gloom to see him emerge from his study. His hair was damp from a shower and he'd changed into faded jeans that moulded to his thighs and a grey crew-neck sweater that clung to his chest. Even in the midst of her panic Talia couldn't keep from feeling a kick of desire at the sight of him. He was glorious, utterly and wonderfully male.

'You shivered,' Angelos explained, coming closer so she breathed in the scent of his skin, warm male and soap. Her mind spun crazily. 'So I thought you were cold.'

'I'm fine.' She took a needed step backwards. If he came any closer she'd start purring. 'Shall we go into the kitchen?' She turned away without waiting for a reply, her heart bumping in her chest both from Angelos's closeness and the storm outside. Did Angelos realise the effect he had on her? She had a feeling she might as well have her attraction to him spelled out in blazing letters on a neon sign, but even so she hoped he didn't notice.

In any case, he was probably used to women lighting up like a firework when he was around. Maria had mentioned the other nannies trying to get into his bed, after all. Angelos probably found her obvious desire amusing and a little pitiful, which of course it was.

She had to get a handle on it, as well as on her panic. *Control.* That was what was needed here. Deep, even breathing to steady her heart rate, and a logical reminder that she really was safe.

Taking a deep breath, Talia joined Maria and Sofia at the table. The kitchen was warm and brightly lit, the spicy smell of roasted lamb filling the air, and all of it helped to push back her anxiety about the storm.

Then Angelos came into the room and her stomach flip-flopped at the nearness of him. She was a *mess.*

Talia ate her dinner as quickly as she could without being rude, and then chivvied Sofia upstairs to get ready for bed without waiting for coffee. Angelos looked bemused, but since he'd been the first to leave the table last night Talia didn't think he could complain.

She stood by the window while Sofia readied for bed, listening to the rain sleet against the shutters. It sounded like a herd of elephants had taken residence on the roof, but the noise didn't bother her. She could handle rain.

Then a distant rumbling sounded, followed by the ear-splitting crack of thunder. Talia let out a little shriek, clutching at the wall to balance herself, and Sofia came out of the bathroom, toothbrush in hand, a frown on her face.

'Okay?' she asked, and Talia nodded quickly.

'Yes, I'm okay.' Maybe if she kept saying it, it would actually become true.

She read Sofia a chapter from the English book they both enjoyed, although Talia didn't know how much the girl understood. Then she kissed her goodnight and hurried to her own bedroom, where she prayed she could shut out this awful storm.

Two hours later Talia was contemplating taking the sleeping pills. She lay on her bed, a pillow clutched to her stomach, her body drenched in icy sweat as the storm swirled and raged around the house. The lightning was coming every thirty seconds or so, a savage crack and then a blinding light that lit up the room like a disco and made Talia whimper as memories streaked through her.

Cowering in the corner, her arms wrapped around herself, wondering if this would be her last night on earth. The rain thundering on the tin roof over her, the thunder shaking the shed's flimsy sides, the sound of raised voices right outside the door, and then the door *opening*…

She whimpered again and closed her eyes, her whole body trembling with a terror as elemental as the storm outside.

She could take a shower again, and let the noise drown

out the sounds of the storm, but at this point Talia wasn't sure she could get off her bed. She felt paralyzed by her own fear, her mind a terrible blank, and it took all her strength simply to lie there and survive. Surely it would be over soon. Surely this nightmare would end...

Just as it had ended before. She tried to cling to that, to the memory of her salvation, but the thunder boomed again and lightning streaked through the cracks in the shutters and all she could think about, all she could feel, was the icy, overwhelming terror at being locked in a tiny room while the storm raged ahead and her life hung by a single, precarious thread.

Angelos closed his laptop, unable to concentrate on work with the storm raging outside. Although if he were honest, it wasn't the rain and wind outside that was distracting him; it was the storm inside himself.

He'd been feeling restless and uneasy all day, ever since he'd gone on the picnic with Talia and Sofia. Ever since he'd told Talia a little bit about his childhood, cracked open the firmly closed door to his soul. And, he admitted reluctantly, ever since he'd felt her soft, pliant body against his, had seen her breasts rise and fall with agitated breaths, had absorbed the impact of the desire lighting those golden-green eyes...

Groaning, Angelos rose from his desk. No more work tonight. He'd settle for a cold shower and a sleepless night, and perhaps tomorrow he would return to Athens.

Except he didn't want to go to Athens. Despite the restlessness surging through him, he'd enjoyed his time with Sofia today.

And Talia. You enjoyed your time with her too.

For Sofia's sake he would stay. It was her birthday in a few days and he tried to be present for that at least. Tried to be the kind of father he knew he never really could be, not when it had mattered.

Angelos headed upstairs, the house dark all around him, the beams and shutters creaking from the force of the wind. He'd just crossed the landing when he heard a sound he first mistook for the wind, a low moaning. He stilled, frowning, and then he heard it again. An animal sound, one of pain or fear.

Frowning, Angelos went down the hallway, his heart rate kicking up at the thought that Sofia might be distressed by the storm. Then he recognised the sound was not coming from his daughter's room at the end of the hall, but from behind the closed door right in front of him. Talia's room.

Again he heard the moan. 'Talia?' he called softly, knocking on the door. No answer. Angelos cocked his head, his brow furrowed as he strained to hear. All was silent, but unease prickled along his spine. What if Talia was ill? She'd been terribly quiet at dinner, but Angelos had put it down to all the sun and sea, plus the fact that she didn't like storms. She'd still been attentive and loving to Sofia, and he hadn't been able to fault her. He'd just been sorry when she'd gone, as if a light had left the room, energy draining from it.

He heard the moaning again and, rapping sharply first, Angelos opened the door.

He stopped on the threshold, appalled at the sight before him. Talia was curled in a foetal position on the bed, a pillow clutched to her chest. Her hair was damp with sweat, her face sickly white with a greenish tinge.

Angelos swore under his breath before he strode towards her. 'Talia, what has happened, are you ill…?'

She barely seemed aware of him as he crouched next to her and peered anxiously into her face. He touched his hand to her forehead, sucking in a hard breath as his palm came in contact with the iciness of her skin. He'd been expecting her to be hot with fever, but she was terribly, terrifyingly cold.

'Talia…' he murmured, and brushed her damp hair away from her forehead. She barely looked at him, her eyes glassy, her gaze unfocused. Her whole body was rigid.

Realisation slammed into Angelos with breathless force. She wasn't ill; she was *scared*. Utterly and completely terrified. He'd seen how she'd been nervous about the storm, but he'd had no idea she had a full-fledged phobia.

'Talia, it's all right,' he murmured as he continued to stroke her damp hair away from her face. She didn't look at him, hardly seemed aware of him. 'It's all right,' he said again, uselessly, because he could see that it wasn't all right at all.

A shudder ran through her body, wracking her slender frame, and her eyes closed in what seemed like surrender to the fear that gripped her.

'Come on,' Angelos said, and he put one arm around her shoulders, sliding the other under her body. 'Let's get you cleaned up at least.' She was incredibly light and fragile in his arms, even as a dead weight, although after a few seconds she curled into him, resting her cheek against his chest, her legs tucked up, her arms around his neck.

Angelos's heart stumbled and for a moment he just stood there, conscious of the closeness of her, the way she trusted him completely.

Then he moved into the en-suite bathroom, reaching out with one hand to turn on the shower before he gently put her back down on her feet, supporting her with one arm.

'Can you undress?' he asked, and she just looked at him, her eyes still wide and glassily blank.

He hesitated only for a second before he stripped the roomy T-shirt and men's boxers she'd been wearing as pyjamas from her body. He kept his movements efficient yet gentle, but even so he couldn't keep his insides from tightening at the sight of her body, golden, lithe and perfect. Small, high breasts sprinkled with freckles. A tiny waist and endless legs. He jerked his gaze back up to her face, ashamed that he'd been staring, but she wasn't even looking at him. Her whole body had started to tremble, her teeth chattering.

'Come on,' Angelos said, and helped her into the shower. She stood under the warm spray, her eyes closed, and then she leaned against the shower wall and slowly sank to the floor, her legs crumpling underneath her.

Muttering a curse Angelos went to her, mindless of the water that streamed over his clothed body, and pulled her into his arms.

She clung to him, her naked body curling into his, and after a while—Angelos didn't know how long—she stopped trembling.

Eventually she came to, like someone coming out of a trance. She moved away from him, water streaming down her naked body and slicking back her hair, appalled realisation swamping her eyes.

She opened her mouth but no words come out and Angelos knew she was beyond embarrassed. And yet he was not, even though he'd been sitting in the shower fully dressed, cradling a naked woman, for the better part of an hour.

Calmly he reached up and turned off the taps. The bathroom was plunged suddenly into steamy silence; Angelos rose, conscious of the way his shirt stuck to his body and his hair was plastered to his head.

'Let me get you a towel,' he said. Talia didn't answer.

He reached for one of the big fluffy towels piled on a shelf and she rose from the shower on unsteady legs, one arm braced against the wall as she stepped out of the shower.

'I...' she began, her voice wobbling all over the place.

'Don't,' Angelos said. Gently he wrapped her in the towel, covering her nakedness. 'Don't be embarrassed, I mean,' he clarified. Her face was fiery, and not just, he knew, from the heat and steam of the shower. She'd ducked her head low so she didn't have to look at him.

'How can I not be?' she returned in a suffocated whisper. She closed her eyes and a single tear squeezed out, trickling down her cheek.

'Talia...' Angelos's heart constricted with unfamiliar emotion as he wiped it away with his thumb. 'I'm sorry I didn't realise how storms affected you.'

'How could you know?' Her eyes were still closed, and another tear snaked down her cheek.

'Oh, Talia.' Without thinking Angelos gathered her up in his arms and carried her into the bedroom. He laid her down gently on the bed and she stared up at him, clutching the towel to her.

'You're soaked.'

He glanced down at his drenched clothes. 'And dripping onto your floor.'

'I don't mind.'

'I should go change.' He saw, to his gratification, a flicker of disappointment pass across her face like a shadow. 'I'll come back,' he promised. 'To check on you.'

She nodded and reluctantly he left the room. Back in his bedroom Angelos peeled off his damp clothes, wondering at his audacity at stripping his nanny naked, cradling her in the shower—what had he been *thinking*? But he hadn't been. He'd simply been reacting to her pain and need, and also to his own.

It had felt amazingly good to hold a woman after so long. To comfort a woman, to be the person she needed in a crisis. He'd needed to be needed. He'd craved being the comforter and protector, being *enough*.

Was it wrong of him, to have taken advantage of her pain to soothe his own?

But no, he'd helped her, or at least he hoped he had. And she'd helped him.

He pulled on a pair of loose pyjama trousers and a T-shirt, clothes he didn't normally wear since he preferred to sleep in a pair of boxer shorts or nothing at all. Then, combing his fingers through his damp hair, he went back to check on Talia.

In his absence she'd taken the opportunity to change into another billowy T-shirt and shorts, and she'd brushed her hair so it curled about her face in damp tendrils. She was sitting on her bed, her knees brought up to her chest, her eyes huge in her face. In the distance thunder rumbled.

Angelos sat on the edge of the bed. 'The storm's moving off now, I think,' he said quietly.

'Yes.' She nodded jerkily, her chin bumping the tops of her knees.

'Do you want to talk about it?' he asked, and she let out a shaky laugh.

'Not particularly.' The thunder rumbled again, and lightning flashed briefly, barely lighting the room, but it was enough to have Talia tensing again.

'You don't have to talk, if you don't want to,' Angelos said. God knew he had a few secrets himself. He glanced at the shuttered window. 'Are you going to be okay?'

She nodded again. 'I'm fine.'

'You don't sound fine,' Angelos said.

'It's okay…'

But it wasn't okay. Even though the storm was moving

away from Kallos, Talia still looked frightened. And Angelos didn't want to leave her alone. He *wouldn't* leave her alone, refused to leave anyone who needed him.

Except Sofia. You left Sofia.

But his daughter was better without him. At least, he'd thought she was, until Talia had started showing him otherwise.

'Move over,' he said, and her eyes widened, her spine straightening as she looked at him.

'What…?'

He nudged her leg with his own, and then gently took her by the shoulders and moved her to the side of the bed. He stretched out alongside her, smiling a bit at her obvious surprise. 'I'll stay,' he said. 'Until the storm ends completely.' And then, because it felt so natural and he couldn't keep himself from it even if he had wanted to, he took her into his arms.

Talia remained rigid in his embrace for a few seconds, and then, just as she had before, she relaxed into him, her body softening against his as she let out a breathy little sigh of contentment.

Angelos rested his chin on top of her head, enjoying the feel of her in his arms, the simple closeness of another person. She smelled like almonds and she was so warm and soft and slender. His libido stirred insistently; it was impossible not to imagine sliding his hands under her voluminous T-shirt, feeling her warm, satiny skin under his palms as he cupped the small, perfect breasts he'd seen earlier, kissed each freckle…

As surreptitiously as he could Angelos shifted slightly away from Talia. The last thing she needed right now was to feel the hard evidence of his arousal. It was, he acknowledged wryly, going to be a long night.

CHAPTER NINE

TALIA WOKE TO sunlight and an empty bed. She blinked the world into focus, her heart giving a funny little dip at the sight of the smooth expanse of sheet next to her. At some point in the night, and she had no idea when, Angelos had left her.

Talia flipped onto her back and stared up at the ceiling as memories of last night unspooled through her mind like scenes from a movie. Angelos coming in and seeing her drenched with sweat and shaking with terror. Angelos gently removing her clothes, stepping into the shower with her, holding her in his arms.

And she'd let him. Of course she'd let him. She'd never felt so treasured, so *protected*, and it had been the most amazing and incredible feeling in the world. It had felt deeper and more important than any physical desire that she'd felt for him, although there had been that last night too.

Resting her cheek against his chest, hearing the steady thud of his heart as he cradled her…she'd been so tempted to tilt her head upwards and let him kiss her.

But of course he probably *wouldn't* have kissed her. He'd been wonderfully kind last night, comforting her when she'd been in the grip of a major panic attack, but that's all it had been. Comfort.

And for what he'd done, Talia knew, he deserved an explanation. One she didn't relish giving, because she hated for anyone to pity her, to know her weakness. But Angelos had already seen her weakness, so perhaps she had nothing left to lose.

Sighing she rose from the bed and went to get dressed. Sofia was just finishing her breakfast as Talia came into the kitchen, instinctively glancing around for Angelos. She didn't know whether to feel relieved or disappointed when she saw he wasn't there, but she caught Maria noticing her wandering gaze and a blush rose to her cheeks. Maria's lips pursed. The housekeeper didn't miss *anything*.

'Hey, Sofia,' Talia said brightly, and avoiding Maria's speculative gaze, she sat down at the table and helped herself to fresh fruit.

After breakfast Sofia went off with Ava for her lessons, and resolutely Talia went in search of Angelos. She found him, predictably, in his study, and his terse, 'Enter,' when she knocked on the door made her wonder if last night had happened at all.

Then she opened the door and saw him sitting at his desk, dressed in his usual button-down shirt and pressed trousers, seeming brisk and remote and yet so utterly wonderful, and colour flared into her face.

To her surprise an answering colour touched Angelos's sharp cheekbones as he looked up at her. He cleared his throat and then closed his laptop. 'How are you feeling this morning?'

'I'm fine. Good actually.' She closed the door behind her and took a deep breath. 'I'm sorry for being so...' Her mind spun as she tried to think of a word for what she'd been.

'Don't be sorry, Talia,' Angelos filled in quietly. 'I'm

the one who should be sorry, for not realising how the storm affected you. I would have checked on you, if I'd known.'

'There was nothing you could have done. That is...' She swallowed convulsively, resisting the urge to press her hands to her hot face. 'Besides what you did. Which was wonderful and way beyond the call of...'

'Duty?' he supplied, quirking an eyebrow, amusement lighting his eyes, turning them almost golden, and making her insides fizz in response. Scowling the man was almost unbearably attractive. Smiling he was impossible to resist.

'Yes,' she managed, dragging her gaze away from his. 'I suppose.'

'I said last night and I will say it again, there is no need to feel embarrassed.'

'You don't think?' Talia blurted. 'You saw me *naked*. Not to mention sweaty and shaking and...' She closed her eyes briefly. 'I'd really rather not remember.'

His mouth twitched in what she thought was amusement. 'I've seen women naked before, Talia.'

'Like most of your nannies?' Angelos's eyebrows snapped together and, horrified, Talia slapped a hand over her mouth. 'I mean,' she said through her fingers, 'Maria mentioned that they've tried to seduce you. And failed.'

'Maria talks too much,' he replied, but he didn't sound angry.

Slowly Talia dropped her hand, knotted her fingers together. 'It's just I don't want you to think...' What? That her sweating and shaking was supposed to have been a turn-on? She was absolutely no good at this, Talia thought as a fresh wave of mortification swept over her. She had absolutely no experience with sex, or even talking about sex, and especially not with a man as gorgeous as Angelos Mena.

'I don't think that, Talia,' Angelos said. 'Last night you were in no shape for a seduction.'

'Right. Sorry.' She gave a little shake of her head. 'I'm handling this really badly. I actually came in here to thank you, and also to explain why I reacted the way I did last night. Because, contrary to what you may think now, I'm not actually scared of storms.'

Angelos's look was one of almost comical disbelief. 'You could have fooled me last night.'

'I know.' She gave a shaky laugh. 'Would you believe I actually liked storms when I was little? I loved watching them from the window of my bedroom, especially in summer. They were so...wild.'

Briefly, so briefly she almost missed it, something flared in Angelos's eyes. She felt a kick in her stomach and she forced herself to continue, to ignore the helpless desire this man so easily ignited in her, simply by saying a word. *Wild.* What would it be like, if Angelos let go of his tightly held control? Images flared in her mind, vague swirling pictures of limbs tangling, mouths pressing, hands reaching. She shoved them away and met Angelos's gaze. 'It's not the storm I'm scared of,' she explained. 'It's what it makes me remember.'

Angelos stilled, his hands resting flat on his desk. 'You don't have to tell me—'

'I know. But after what you did, how you helped me, you deserve to know.' And actually, she realised, she *wanted* to tell him—even though she'd tried to keep the whole awful episode hidden from everyone, just as her grandfather had kept it out of the press, both of them pretending it had never happened, because that was easier. She wanted someone to know, someone who, amazingly, might understand a little. She drew a deep breath, let the air fill her lungs and buoy her courage. 'When I was eighteen,' she stated, 'I was kidnapped.'

Angelos opened his mouth, but no words came out. 'Kidnapped...' he finally said, and his voice sounded hoarse, his tone horrified.

'I was travelling in Europe, after my high school graduation. It was meant to be my big exciting summer, exploring the world, having endless adventures. I was with a couple of friends...we took precautions and we didn't do anything stupid...' Even now she felt the need to justify herself, to explain how it wasn't her fault, because for years she'd tormented herself with the what-ifs. What if she'd been more careful? What if she'd travelled with more people? What if she could have done something to keep the disaster from unfolding the way it had?

Angelos had recovered himself and was now looking at her with his familiar hard stare, his eyes dangerously dark. 'What happened exactly?'

'We were in Paris. The City of Love.' She let out a short, sharp laugh and shook her head. 'Right in front of the Eiffel Tower. It felt like it should have been the safest place in the world. My friend Anna had gone to see about tickets to go up the tower and I was just taking a photo.' She felt her chest start to go tight, her throat constrict, as memories assailed her, memories she'd kept locked tightly away. 'I'd raised the camera up to my face, and was looking through the lens when...' She stopped, closing her eyes. That moment when her world had shifted, shattered. One second was all it had taken to go from carefree insouciance to utter, incredulous terror.

'Talia,' Angelos said in a low voice. 'You don't have to—'

'No, I want to,' she insisted. 'I do. I never talk about this, but I want to now...after what you did...'

'It wasn't that much—'

'It was, Angelos,' she responded, and she heard how her voice throbbed with sincerity. She saw something flash across Angelos's face and she realised he'd never given permission to call him by his first name. 'Sorry, should I not have…'

'Not have what?'

'Called you Angelos,' she muttered. Angelos let out a wryly disbelieving laugh.

'After everything, Talia, I think you can call me Angelos. In fact, I think it would be strange if you didn't.'

After everything. Two little words that made her remember how he'd held her so tenderly, how hard and solid his chest had felt beneath her cheek. How she'd wanted to stay there for ever, wrapped in his arms, protected and safe.

Angelos rose from behind his desk, and taking her by the hand, he drew her to the two club chairs in front of the fireplace. She sank onto one, her legs shaky, and he sat in the other. 'So they took you from the Eiffel Tower,' he prompted, his voice low and steady.

'They grabbed me so quickly. I didn't even see…' She swallowed hard, remembering how brutally and ruthlessly efficient the man had been, pulling her tightly to him, leaning down as if he were whispering in her ear, looking all for the world as if they were two lovers sharing an intimate moment. In reality he'd been pressing a chloroform-soaked cloth to her mouth and nose. She'd been unconscious in seconds.

She forced herself to meet Angelos's gaze and continue. 'They drugged me. When I woke up, I was in some kind of shed. It was locked, of course, and there was nothing in there. A dirt floor, a tin ceiling…barely room to stand up. And it was so dark.' A shudder ran through her. 'I had no idea where I was, or what they were going to do to me.'

Angelos's face was pale, his eyes like burning dark coals. 'That must have been utterly terrifying.'

'It was.' She pressed her lips together, memory rising inside her, choking her. 'A man brought me food and water, although he never spoke to me. After a while I actually started to feel bored, which sounds ridiculous, but I just wanted something to *happen*.' She shook her head. 'I was so naïve.' She lapsed into silence, remembering the endless days and weeks of sitting in that cramped cabin, filthy, exhausted, emotionally spent. Almost wanting it to be over...for good. She knew what despair felt like. She understood hopelessness.

'What happened then, Talia?'

She jerked her gaze up, refocusing on Angelos. 'There was a storm one night. A terrible storm, worse than the one we had here. I think the lightning must have struck something nearby, because there was a terrific crash, and I heard something fall nearby, a tree, I suppose. I was afraid they would leave me to die in there and save themselves. Or maybe they'd died, and no one would ever find me.' Her fists had become bloody and bruised from banging on the door, a useless but instinctive bid for freedom.

'But they didn't?' he prompted quietly when she'd fallen into silence once more.

'No, they didn't. In the middle of the storm the door opened and there were several men, some I hadn't seen before. I couldn't see their faces...they dragged me out of the room. I had no idea what was going to happen. One of them had a knife.' She stopped, expelling a trembling breath, and heard Angelos mutter a curse. 'They didn't actually hurt me,' she said. 'They held a knife to my throat, but it was only for a picture. A ransom note. I didn't realise that at the time though. I couldn't think about anything. I could barely stand up.' She tried to smile ruefully but her facial muscles felt like they weren't working properly. 'They took the photo, and then they pushed me around a bit, and then they shoved me back in the shed.'

'I cannot imagine, Talia,' Angelos said. He was gripping the armrests of his chair, his knuckles white, his face bloodless.

'They weren't as smart as they thought they were though,' Talia continued, trying to inject a cheerful note into her voice and failing. 'They sent the photo of me to my grandfather, and he used his resources to locate me from what they'd seen in the photo and then to prosecute the kidnappers. Just twenty-four hours after they sent the photograph a helicopter came with a SWAT team to rescue me.'

'A helicopter,' Angelos repeated after a pause. 'Is that why you are scared of helicopters?'

'Sort of. The sound reminds me of that whole time, and the rescue effort was…intense.' She remembered the shouts, the staccato gunfire, the stranger who yanked her arm so hard he nearly dislocated her shoulder as he pulled her towards the waiting helicopter. At that point she hadn't even known if the man was friend or foe, or if she was facing freedom or death. She'd collapsed inside the helicopter, watching in disbelief as a man was shot and killed right in front of her. And then the soul-freezing terror had morphed into an incredulous and numb relief, both emotions overwhelming.

'But really,' she told Angelos, 'any confined space is difficult. From…from being in that shed. I've tried some different therapies for it, but none of them have worked.' She gave him a lopsided smile. 'But I supposed claustrophobia and a fear of thunderstorms is a small price to pay for my freedom.'

Angelos shook his head, his hands still clenched on the armrests. 'I don't know how you survived such a thing.'

'How does anyone survive?' she answered. 'And *survive* is the right word, because sometimes it's felt as if that's all I'm doing.'

'What do you mean?'

'Coming to Athens was the first time I'd got on an airplane in seven years. The first time I used public transportation, or ventured out of my comfort zone at all. After the kidnapping I dropped out of college and retreated to my grandfather's estate. I couldn't face people, and just being in a small space, even in a classroom, sent me into a blind panic. My grandfather was understanding, and he let me hide myself away. I think he thought I'd come out again, but I never did.'

Confusion clouded Angelos's eyes and he shook his head. 'But you must have. You said you were an artist—'

'I have a private studio there. Clients come to me. I hardly ever leave. I can't stand crowds, or cities, or small spaces. Which leaves me feeling pretty limited sometimes, but I've been happy. At least, I thought I was happy.' But now, with a taste of what it felt like to truly live again, to feel excitement and happiness and desire, Talia knew she hadn't been. She'd been content, maybe, but that was all. She'd been living a half-life without realising it, telling herself it was enough.

'But you did come to Athens,' Angelos said. 'You *tried*. That's important, Talia.'

'Yes…' But he didn't know why she'd tried. Talia could tell that Angelos assumed she'd come to Greece simply to break out of her cocoon. Now would be the perfect time to tell him about the book, the real reason she was here.

And yet she stayed silent. She might have been brave in coming here, but in many ways she was still a coward. Because she didn't want to risk Angelos's anger at learning her true motives, feeling deceived. She didn't want to leave Kallos or Sofia. She didn't want to leave *him*.

The realisation of how much she was starting to care about this man drove her upright. 'I should go. Sofia's lessons will be finished, and we were going to sketch today, outside.'

Angelos rose also and reached for her hand. The slide of his fingers along hers was infinitely, achingly sweet, and it lit a flame of need in her belly. 'Thank you,' he said quietly. 'For telling me all of that.'

'Thank you,' Talia answered, 'for comforting me last night.'

And then, because she didn't trust herself not to throw herself into Angelos's arms just as she had last night, she yanked her hand away and hurried from the room.

CHAPTER TEN

CONSIDERING EVERYTHING SHE'D confessed, everything that had *happened*, Talia expected to feel embarrassed and exposed. Yet sitting on the beach with Sofia, sketchpads on their laps, she found she wasn't squirming internally with humiliation at how much she'd revealed. She felt…free. At peace in a way she hadn't expected.

For the last seven years she hadn't talked about the kidnapping to anyone. She knew Giovanni blamed himself for the whole affair, because the men had kidnapped her for money, knowing her to be an heiress. But Giovanni had rescued her; it was he who had accessed satellite photos to identify where she was being held from the picture the kidnappers had sent. She'd never blamed Giovanni. He'd been her saviour. And she'd respected his desire to forget the whole episode…or at least act as if she had. Her siblings had followed suit.

But secretly, or not so secretly considering her phobias and isolation, the kidnapping had tormented her with its terrible memories. For years she'd suffered nightmares that left her shaking, and the tiniest things could set her off: the sound of a lock turning, the creak of a door. She'd tried therapy, but talking to a stranger had only made her feel more exposed and raw. She'd learned to avoid triggers and read up on PTSD and kept everything buried deep inside.

Until Angelos.

Amazing, how *validating* it had felt when he'd told her it must have been terrifying. To have him sympathise and understand without pity or judgement.

She wished she could do something in return, help him in some way, for she knew that Angelos must have his own dark memories, his closely guarded secrets. But despite the comfort he'd offered her last night, she knew they still didn't have the kind of relationship that would allow that conversation.

'Hello, you two.'

Talia stiffened in surprise, pleasure flooding through her as she saw Angelos strolling down the beach. Sofia's face lit up as Angelos came to stand in front of them, the wind off the sea ruffling his hair.

'How's the sketching?' he asked, and Talia nudged Sofia to show her father her work. Shyly she offered up the paper and Angelos took it and studied it carefully.

Talia couldn't understand the Greek he spoke to her, but even she basked in his smile. She loved that he was trying more with Sofia, and that it was working.

They spoke in Greek for a few moments and then he turned to Talia. 'It is Sofia's birthday in a few days—'

'Is it?' Talia interjected in surprise. She wagged a finger at Sofia, smiling. 'You should have told me.'

'Perhaps we can do something to celebrate,' Angelos said, and Talia felt as if her heart was a balloon expanding in her chest, full of hope. He almost sounded as if they were a family.

'Of course we must celebrate,' she said. She turned back to Sofia. 'What would you like to do?'

Timidly Sofia spoke in Greek to her father. Angelos listened, a frown furrowing his forehead, and the balloon inside Talia started to deflate. Why did he have to look so angry?

He spoke sharply back and Talia watched in dismay as Sofia nodded in acceptance, the light dimming from her eyes. She ducked her head so her hair slid in front of her face, hiding her scarred cheek, an action Talia had come to associate with Sofia's lack of confidence, and one she thankfully hadn't done for a while.

'What is it?' she burst out. 'Surely whatever Sofia wants to do, we can manage…' Sofia hardly seemed the type of girl to ask for something unreasonable.

'She wants to go sailing,' Angelos said tightly. 'To Naxos. I told her it was not possible.'

'Why?'

'Because she wants to go with you,' Angelos explained. 'I don't think you want to be on a small boat in the middle of the sea.'

'*Oh.*' For a moment all Talia could do was gape. He was thinking of her, and her fear of being confined. She was so surprised and touched that it took her a few seconds to gather her composure. She turned to Sofia with a smile. 'I think sailing sounds like a lot of fun.'

'Talia,' Angelos protested. 'You don't have to—'

'But I do,' she said quietly. 'It's Sofia's birthday. If this is how she wants to celebrate, then I want it too.' And she just wouldn't think about how long she'd be on a small boat. 'Besides,' she told Angelos with more conviction than she actually felt, 'it's not as bad as a helicopter. The sides are open, and we'll be out on the sea. It'll be fine.'

Angelos was still frowning. 'I don't like it,' he said, and Talia saw Sofia's hopeful smile slide off her face once more.

'It'll be fine,' she said again. She'd make sure it was.

She was still telling herself that three days later, as she

and Sofia stood on the beach while Angelos readied the sailboat. It was a very small boat, barely big enough for all three of them to sit in. Nerves coiled tightly in her belly and she tried to keep her fists from clenching. She could do this. It wasn't as if she had four walls bearing down on her. There was no reason to feel trapped.

Except once she was out on the water, she *would* be trapped. And Angelos had told her it would take an hour to sail to Naxos, which felt like an incredibly long time.

'Ready, Papa?' Sofia called. She was jumping up and down in her excitement and the sight of the little girl looking so happy was enough to calm Talia's fears for a moment. They'd started the day with a special birthday breakfast and Sofia had opened presents from everyone.

Talia hadn't known what to get for Sofia's birthday; she hadn't left Kallos since she'd arrived two weeks ago and she hadn't brought anything remotely suitable to give her as a present. In the end she'd painted Sofia a picture of the villa and the beach, remembering how Sofia had sketched it when they were back in Athens. The little girl had been incredibly pleased with the picture, and Talia had promised to look for a frame for it when they went to Naxos.

'All right, I think we're just about there,' Angelos called. He looked amazing and remarkably at ease, wearing board shorts and a T-shirt that the wind pressed to his well-muscled chest. Over the last few days he'd spent a fair amount of time with Sofia and Talia, coming in as soon as Sofia's lessons were finished. At first he'd merely watched and smiled as Talia and Sofia played a game or did some sketching, but in the last day or two he'd started, at Talia's gentle urging, to join in. It made her heart ache with bittersweet joy to see how clumsily yet sincerely Angelos tried with his daughter, how hard these simple interactions were for him, and yet he *tried*. And that, just as he'd told her, was important.

Now he extended a hand towards Sofia, and helped her to clamber into the boat. Once Sofia was seated he turned to Talia, who was still rooted on the shore, unable to keep from eyeing the boat nervously.

His eyebrows snapped together as he held out his hand. 'Are you all right?'

'Yes…' Her voice wavered and she tried to smile. 'It's just…it is a pretty small boat. I thought you'd have a yacht or something.'

'I do have a yacht,' Angelos answered. 'It's docked in Piraeus. Sofia prefers the sailboat.'

'Oh. Right.' Of course he had a yacht. No matter how humble his beginnings, Angelos was a millionaire now. He exuded power from every pore. Masculine power. Over the last few days Talia had tried to hide her attraction to Angelos, but at times she felt overwhelmed with the desire, the need, to touch him. To feel his heart beating against her cheek once more, to taste his lips…

At night she lay in bed, restless and aching, amazed at how many new desires this man had awoken in her. She'd never felt this way about anyone before, hadn't even known such strong feelings existed.

And Angelos, as far as she could tell, seemed utterly unmoved.

'Talia?' he prompted, and taking a deep breath, she reached for his hand. The feel of his fingers closing over hers was enough to send her heart rate skittering and she tried to hide how uneven her breathing was, but the flush to her face was unavoidable. Maybe Angelos would chalk it up to the sun, or maybe he knew she found him irresistible and was being polite by ignoring it.

He guided Talia to her seat by the tiller, one arm around

her shoulders, which only made it worse, and yet also wonderfully, achingly better. She loved it when he touched her. She just wished he'd touch her more.

'Everyone ready?' Angelos asked as Talia buckled her life vest. She managed a sunny smile and a nod.

'Totally.'

Angelos pushed out, and as the boat bobbed into the deeper waters, the wind caught and filled the sails.

It felt like flying. Talia had been out on a sailboat as a child, although not since the kidnapping, for the obvious reason. Now she knelt by the tiller, her face tilted to the wind and sun, enjoying the way the boat skimmed across the glinting water. She could hardly credit, but she was actually enjoying this, and it reminded her of how much she'd used to enjoy, how adventurous she'd been. Seven years ago she'd lost a big part of herself and it had taken coming to Greece to begin to find it again. It had taken her grandfather to push her gently. Without Giovanni, she never would have left the safety of the estate.

Thinking of her grandfather made Talia flinch inwardly with guilt. She'd emailed him several times over the course of the last few weeks, reassuring him she was looking for the book…which was a lie. Beyond looking in the villa's library, she hadn't done anything. She hadn't wanted to risk this fragile peace and happiness she'd found here, with Angelos.

Who you are kidding? You don't have anything with him.

Angelos was a powerful, attractive, worldly man. Who knew how many women he had in Athens, or indeed around the world? He'd never be interested in someone like her, who cringed at her own shadow, who had no experience in anything.

And in any case, in a month's time she'd never see him

again. She had no reason whatsoever not to ask about her grandfather's book.

Angelos had come to sit beside her, one hand on the tiller, the other shading his eyes from the sun. Sofia was on the other side of the small craft, gazing down at the shimmering water speeding by, the wake from the boat as white as whipped cream.

'Do you like poetry?' Talia blurted, and then winced inwardly at the abrupt absurdity of the question.

Angelos stared at her for a moment, bemused. 'Now where did that question come from?'

'I was just curious.' She bit her lip, misery and indecision swamping her. She knew of no good way to come clean to Angelos and admit why she'd come here in the first place. But maybe he wouldn't be angry. Maybe he'd understand. And even if he didn't, she knew she had to say something. She had to find a way to mention her grandfather's book.

'I can't say I'm particularly well-versed,' Angelos answered, 'if that isn't too terrible a pun.'

'I only wondered, because my grandfather mentioned a Mediterranean poet that he liked,' Talia said, and Angelos's forehead furrowed. Clearly he didn't see the connection, and that's because there wasn't one.

'Tell me about your grandfather. You speak about him quite a lot.'

'Do I? I suppose that's because he raised me.' Relief trickled through her at the realisation that Angelos was providing her with an out. 'He took over the raising of me and my brothers and sisters after my parents died.'

'How many brothers and sisters do you have?'

'Seven,' Talia answered, 'including my half-brother, Nate. Five brothers and two sisters.'

'That's a lot,' Angelos remarked. 'Are you close to all of them?'

'Mostly, in different ways, although I don't see Nate very much.' She frowned, thinking of the elusive half-brother who had always skirted the fringes of her family. 'My father had an affair, before I was born, and Nate was the result.' She grimaced. 'Which puts my parents in a bad light, I know. They were…weak people, I think. But I still missed them, the idea of them.'

'I suppose bad parents are better than none.'

'Do you think that? You didn't grow up with any parents…'

'No.' Angelos stared out at the sea, his mouth pressed into a firm line. 'I don't know. I suppose I would have preferred almost anyone to the care home, or scratching a living on the docks.'

Talia shook her head in genuine admiration. 'It's amazing, how far you've come.'

'Just luck,' Angelos dismissed with a shrug of his shoulders, as he had before.

'More than luck,' Talia insisted. 'Not many people could do what you have done, Angelos.'

A brief look of something close to anguish contorted Angelos's features and then he looked out to sea again. 'Maybe,' he allowed, 'but I've failed in other ways.'

Talia felt as if her heart was bumping its way up her throat. 'What do you mean?'

Angelos shook his head, and then nodded towards Sofia. 'This is her day. Let's not ruin it by talk of the past.'

Which made her even more intrigued, but Talia knew better than to press it. She turned to Sofia with a smile, and they spent the next few minutes chatting in a mixture of broken English and Greek, both of them managing to get their meaning across. Mostly.

Several times she sneaked a glance at Angelos; he was still staring out at the sea, his eyes narrowed against the sun, the set of his mouth seeming bleak, and Talia wondered if she'd ever get an opportunity to ask Angelos what he'd meant when he'd said he'd failed.

He didn't talk about the past. He certainly didn't mention his failures. But he had to Talia; he'd almost told her about the fire. The realisation made Angelos's shoulders tense and his chest go tight. He didn't want to relive that awful day, the worst day of his whole life. He'd put those memories in a box and slammed the lid shut, but for some reason getting to know Talia was prying it open again. And that was not a good thing.

What was it about this woman with her clear, hazel gaze and her impish smile and incredible bravery that got to him? That made him want to tell her things, just as she'd told him? She'd been so honest with him, and he admired that deeply. But he wasn't capable of it himself.

In any case, she was leaving in a month. He'd enjoyed these last few days, and he was grateful to Talia for helping him to reconnect, at least a little, with his daughter. But it wasn't as if he and Talia had any kind of *relationship*. In a matter of weeks he'd never see her again.

He glanced at Talia; she'd stopped chatting to Sofia and was sitting back, her hands in her lap, the wind blowing her hair into golden tangles about her face. Her incredibly pale face, and belatedly Angelos noticed how her fists were clenched, how she was starting to tremble.

He knew they shouldn't have gone in the boat.

'Talia.' He slid off his seat and reached for her hands; they were ice cold. She didn't even look at him. 'Talia,' he said again, his voice hard and insistent, and she blinked him back into focus.

'Sorry…' she whispered, and Angelos muttered a curse.

'You have nothing to be sorry about.'

'It's just…we can't see land any more…' Her teeth chattered and Angelos slid next to her, putting an arm around her shoulders. She leaned into him, closing her eyes.

'It's okay,' he murmured. 'It's going to be okay. We'll get to land, we'll be safe. I'll keep you safe.' The words echoed through him, a promise he meant utterly and yet feared was hollow. After all, he'd broken it before.

Sofia turned to look at them, her face going nearly as pale as Talia's as she took in her nanny's sickly expression.

'Talia…'

Talia gave her a weak, apologetic smile and silently Sofia slid her hand into hers. Angelos went back to the tiller, guiding them as quickly as he could towards the shore.

The boat sped swiftly over the water; he kept glancing at Talia, making sure she was okay. Her face was pale but she lifted her chin bravely and squeezed Sofia's hand.

'I'm okay, Sofia,' she told the girl. 'Don't worry, please.'

The realisation that even in the midst of her suffering and fear, Talia was able to comfort his daughter, *cared* enough to comfort her, made something expand painfully in Angelos's chest.

He turned away quickly, not trusting the expression on his face, and steered them on to Naxos.

CHAPTER ELEVEN

As soon as the sailboat reached the jetty, Angelos leapt out and tethered it before turning to Talia, his arms outstretched. She fell into his embrace clumsily, because her legs were so shaky, and heat scorched her once pale face as her panic started to recede, replaced by an almost as awful embarrassment.

'You must think…' she muttered as she stepped away from him.

'I think you're very brave, to go on this boat for my daughter's sake,' Angelos murmured. His hands still rested on her shoulders, his palms warm through the thin fabric of her sundress. 'Thank you,' he added, and then he released her to help Sofia out of the boat.

His words whirled through her mind as they set up camp on the stretch of beach by the harbour, the sand soft and warm beneath her bare feet.

I think you're very brave. Did Angelos really mean that? She didn't feel brave. She felt like the worst wimp, unable to hack so much as an hour in a sailboat. What kind of sad sack wasn't able to manage that?

Talia had accepted her limitations for so long they had stopped bothering her. At least, she'd thought they had. But now that she was experiencing more of life, both with Sofia and Angelos, she was coming to realise how little she'd had these last seven years…and how much she still wanted.

They spent the morning on the beach and then walked into the town of Chora for lunch. As they approached the whitewashed buildings, colourful cafés with striped awnings and tables outside, Talia watched as Sofia seemed to shrink into herself. Her hair slid in front of her face, her shoulders hunched, her whole demeanour making Talia think the girl wanted to hide herself.

In the nearly two weeks since she'd been on Kallos, Talia had grown so used to Sofia's face, to her bright smile and beautiful eyes as well as the puckered, reddened flesh that covered her entire cheek. She'd stopped noticing it at all, and Sofia had been much less self-conscious. But now she saw the shyness and insecurity come back, and she could tell Angelos noticed it too. As his daughter hid behind a curtain of curly dark hair, Angelos's scowl deepened, a deep furrow carved between his straight eyebrows.

'Where shall we go?' Talia asked brightly. She was determined to rescue this day and keep it special and happy for Sofia's sake. It wasn't every day a girl turned nine, after all. In hesitant, clumsy Greek, she asked Sofia where she would like to eat.

'There,' Sofia said, pointing to a café at the end of the street, and they headed towards it.

'You have learned some Greek,' Angelos remarked as they took their seats at one of the tables outside.

'Ava has been teaching me. I did ask Maria to ask you—'

'Yes, I remember. I said yes. And I am pleased you have made the effort.' He smiled, his eyes crinkling up at the corners, and Talia just about melted into a pool of slushy sentimentality.

She'd known she'd be a sucker for Angelos's smile.

In fact, as they ordered their meals and enjoyed the sunshine, chatting in a mixture of English and Greek, she started daydreaming that they were actually a family. That Angelos actually loved her.

The realisation of what she was fantasising about had her jolting upright, nearly spilling her drink.

Angelos's smile disappeared as he took in her pale face and slack jaw. 'Are you all right?' he asked in a low voice. 'This isn't too much for you?'

'It's fine,' Talia assured him with a shaky smile. And actually it *was* fine. She, who avoided crowds and cities, was actually enjoying sitting in a restaurant like a normal person.

It was Sofia she had been concerned about, until her fantasies about Angelos had derailed her whole thought process. Did she really want him to *love* her?

Did she love him?

'Talia?' Angelos's voice was tight with tension as he frowned at her, clearly concerned.

'It's okay.' She rested her hand on his, and then snatched it back when just the slide of skin across skin sent sensation skittering through her nerve endings. 'I'm fine. Really.'

Yet thoughts continued to zing through her mind as they ate lunch and then wandered through the town's street market. Love was such a huge concept, and one she didn't have a lot of experience with. Not romantic love anyway.

And you can't be in love with Angelos. You barely know him. A week together, a single night of comfort...

Mindlessly she studied some fabric piled on a market stall, green silk shot through with gold thread. Angelos joined her, standing so close she could feel the heat of his body, inhaled the scent of his aftershave, and had to close her eyes against the wave of desire that crashed over her.

'You would look lovely in that,' he said, gesturing to the silk.

Talia's heart lurched alarmingly. 'Oh, I don't know...' she demurred. She had a crazy and near irresistible urge to lean against him, to have him wrap one strong arm around her.

What was happening to her?

'Why don't I buy some for a dress?' He spoke to the shopkeeper in Greek, who was more than happy to accommodate him.

'I don't need a dress...'

'You are wearing the only one you brought,' Angelos reminded her. 'And perhaps you will go somewhere special. Perhaps we all will.' He pointed to another fabric, this one bright pink. 'And that for Sofia,' he said, and addressed the shopkeeper again in Greek.

Impulsively Talia put a hand on his arm. 'Thank you,' she said softly, and Angelos turned to her, his mouth turning down in self-deprecation.

'It is only a bit of silk.'

'I don't mean that. I mean the way you are with Sofia.' She nodded towards the girl, who was inspecting some cloth dolls hanging from pegs on the other side of the stall. 'She is so pleased to have this time with you. I know it means a lot to her.'

Angelos shrugged, his gaze sliding away. 'It is very little.'

'Even so...'

'It is you I should thank, for making me realise she wants to spend time with me.'

'Why would you think she wouldn't?'

Angelos turned back to her, his gaze dark, his frown deepening. 'Because I disappointed her terribly. I have not been the father she wants or needs.'

'But you are, Angelos, because you *are* her father. No mattered what happened before—'

He shook his head, the movement abrupt, as he handed some euros to the shopkeeper and took the cut fabric, now wrapped in paper. 'We will not talk about this.'

Talia watched as he strode towards Sofia, and then showed her the fabric he bought. Her shy, answering smile lit up her whole face and made Talia ache. Why did Angelos think he wasn't a good father? Why had he virtually ignored his daughter for so long? She wanted to know the answers, but she doubted she'd get them from him.

By early evening they were all feeling pleasantly drowsy. As they walked back towards the boat, Angelos tapped his finger against Talia's nose.

'You're a bit burned.'

'Which means more freckles,' she answered with a playful grimace.

'I like your freckles,' Angelos replied, and while Talia gaped at him he turned back to say something to Sofia.

He liked her freckles? Was she crazy, thinking that Angelos might like *her*? She had no experience with flirting or romance or love. She had no idea how to gauge Angelos's feelings, or even her own. And yet his simple statement had sent bubbles of excitement racing through her, as if she'd just imbibed a bottle of champagne.

'Will you be all right on the journey back?' he asked in a low voice as he helped Sofia scramble into the sailboat.

'I think so.' She smiled at him, trying not to let her gaze rove helplessly over his rugged features as those bubbles fizzed and popped. He'd had a bit of sun too, and his skin was even more bronzed and beautiful, the sharp planes of his cheekbones and the golden brown of his eyes making her breathless. 'Actually, I'm amazed at how easy this whole day has been,' she confessed. 'I haven't wandered around a town like this, in the crowds, for years.'

'Since…?' Angelos asked, his eyes darkening, and she nodded.

'I couldn't stand crowds. But I didn't mind them today.' *Because I was with you. Because you made me feel safe and protected.* She swallowed down the words and smiled instead. 'Thank you.'

'I didn't have anything to do with it—'

'You did,' she asserted, and then, throwing caution to the winds, she explained, 'When you held me that night… it was the first time I'd felt truly safe, really protected, in seven years. It gave me a confidence, Angelos, that I never thought I'd have again. So you see, you did have something to do with it. And I thank you for that.'

She didn't dare look at him, afraid she'd revealed too much, and so she scrambled into the boat by herself and sat next to Sofia, her face hot.

The moon rose over the Aegean as the boat skimmed the placid, dark waters and the breeze cooled their sunburned skin. Talia put her arm around Sofia while the girl dozed against her and Angelos sat down, one hand resting on the tiller. He nodded towards Sofia.

'It's been a big day for her.'

'A big day for all of us.'

'Yes.' He paused, and in the gathering twilight she couldn't see his face. 'I'm proud of you, Talia. For facing your fears. Not everyone has the courage to do so.'

'I said before, you're the one who helped me.' She was glad for the darkness that hid her blush. 'The truth is I didn't plan on facing them. It's being here and seeing how Sofia…' She paused, afraid this might be too sensitive a subject for Angelos.

'What about Sofia?' he asked.

'She reminds me of me,' Talia said softly. 'How I've been inside for so long. Hiding myself. Ashamed of who I am.'

She felt Angelos stiffen even though he was several feet away from her. Pain emanated from him, seeming to tauten the very air. 'You think Sofia is ashamed of herself?' he asked, his voice low and aching. 'Of…of her scar?'

'She's certainly self-conscious about it,' Talia said carefully. She didn't have the courage to add, *Especially when you're around.* 'Have you noticed the way she hides her cheek with her hair?'

'Of course I've noticed it.' Angelos pressed his lips together and looked away. 'But she has no reason to be ashamed. None at all. She is a beautiful girl, inside and out.'

'Maybe you should tell her so,' Talia suggested. 'I think she'd like to hear it.'

'I do tell her,' Angelos answered, and she wondered if he wrote as much in her letters. 'Let us not talk of this any more,' he added, his tone final, and Talia knew she would have to let it go.

Neither of them spoke as Kallos appeared on the horizon, the villa washed in moonlight. Angelos moored the boat and then carefully scooped Sofia up into his arms; in sleep she snuggled against her father, her scarred cheek resting against his chest.

Seeing him acting so tenderly with Sofia made a lump form in Talia's throat. This man had so much love to give, and yet he seemed determined to lock it all away.

Or was she simply being foolishly hopeful, to think such a thing? To think he could fall in love with her?

Because she knew she was falling in love with him, whether it made sense or not. She might be inexperienced, but even she could recognise the ache in her heart, the hope in her soul and the need that flooded her body, all of it overwhelming, undeniable. Silently she followed Angelos across the beach and up to the villa.

The house was quiet and dark as they entered, Maria having already gone to bed. Angelos went upstairs to put Sofia to bed and Talia followed slowly, reluctant to end what had been, on the whole, a wonderful day. She wondered if she'd pushed Angelos too hard. Would he retreat back into his brusque, businesslike shell tomorrow, and once again ignore her and Sofia? She hated the thought.

Sighing she turned to her bedroom, only to still when she heard Angelos's voice, soft and disembodied in the darkness, coming from down the upstairs hallway.

'Thank you, Talia.'

'For what?' She turned around, her heart bumping hard as she saw him standing in the darkened corridor. Moonlight streamed through the high windows, touching his hair with silver. She couldn't see the expression on his face, but she felt his sincerity.

'For making this day possible,' he said. 'For making me realise it was necessary. I do take your point, you know. Sofia needs me, even if I'm not...'

'Not what?' Talia prompted softly when he'd trailed off with a little shake of his head.

'Not the father I want to be. The father I should be.' He'd stepped closer to her, close enough that she could touch him if she simply reached out one hand. Her fingertips tingled with the need to do so, to feel his solid strength beneath her palm, to comfort him as well as herself.

'You've said that before, Angelos, and I don't understand it. I'm not sure I believe it. I know you love Sofia. Why can't you be the father you want to be? The father Sofia needs?'

'Too much has happened,' he murmured. 'Things that can't be forgiven.'

'Anything can be forgiven.'

'Do you really believe that?' His voice had sharpened. 'Could you forgive the men who kidnapped you?'

Talia blinked, startled. 'How can you compare yourself to those brutes?'

'You don't know me, Talia. You don't know what I've—'

'I do know you,' she interjected, her voice turning ragged with the force of her conviction. 'I've seen you these last few days, Angelos, and I *do* know you. I know you love Sofia. I know you can be the father she needs, the man I—' She stopped suddenly, horrified by what she'd been about to blurt. *The man I love.*

'The man you what?' Angelos asked. He took a step closer to her, heat and intent evident in his hard stare.

'The man I've—I've come to know,' Talia answered, stammering in her embarrassment and anxiety. 'I have come to know you these last few days, Angelos. And I... I like the man I know.' *And so much more than that.* But she'd admitted more than enough already.

'Talia...' Angelos's voice broke on her name, and then, before she could even process what was happening, he pulled her towards him, his hands hard on her shoulders as his mouth crashed down on hers.

It had been ten years since she'd been kissed, and then only a schoolboy's buss. She'd never been kissed like this, never felt every sense blaze to life, every nerve ending tingle with awareness, nearly painful in its intensity, as Angelos's mouth moved on hers and he pulled her tightly to him.

His hard contours collided against her softness, each point of contact creating an unbearably exquisite ache of longing as she tangled her hands in his hair and fit her mouth against his.

She was a clumsy, inexpert kisser, not sure what to do with her lips or tongue, only knowing that she wanted more of this. Of him.

She felt his hand slide down to cup her breast, his palm hot and hard through the thin material of her dress, and a gasp of surprise and delight escaped her.

That small sound of pleasure was enough to jolt Angelos out of his passion-fogged daze, for he dropped his hand and in one awful, abrupt movement tore his mouth from hers and stepped back.

'I'm sorry,' he said, his voice coming out in a ragged gasp.

'No...' Talia pressed one shaky hand to her buzzing lips as she tried to blink the world back into focus. 'Don't be sorry,' she whispered. 'It was wonderful.'

'I shouldn't have—'

'Why not?' she challenged. She felt frantic with the desperate need to feel and taste him again, and more importantly, not to have him withdraw from her, not just physically, but emotionally. Angelos didn't answer and she forced herself to ask the question again. 'Why not, Angelos?'

'Because you are my employee, and I was taking advantage of you,' he gritted out. 'It was not appropriate...'

'I don't care about appropriate,' she cried. She knew she sounded desperate and even pathetic but she didn't care. She wanted him. She *needed* him. 'I care about you,' she confessed, her voice dropping to a choked whisper, and surprise and something worse flashed across Angelos's face. He shook his head, the movement almost violent and terribly final.

'No, Talia,' he told her flatly. 'You don't.'

And without giving her a chance to reply, he turned and strode towards his bedroom.

Talia remained in the darkened hallway, her body still throbbing with the need Angelos had lit inside her. She heard his door close, a soft, final-sounding click, and then with a shuddering sigh she turned towards her own bedroom.

She peeled off her clothes in the dark, gasping as the simple movements made the ache of need flare up inside her. She wanted Angelos to be the one to undress her, to touch her in ways she'd never been touched but now felt as if she couldn't live without. His mouth on hers, his hands on her skin...

But he obviously didn't feel the same way, and she'd humiliated herself in practically begging him to keep kissing her. In telling him she cared.

Cringing at the memory, Talia curled up on her bed, her knees tucked to her chest, and tried to will herself to sleep. It seemed to take an age before she finally fell into an uneasy, restless doze, only to wake to sunlight streaming through the shutters and the staccato sound of a helicopter whirring in the distance.

CHAPTER TWELVE

ANGELOS LEANED BACK against the seat in the helicopter and closed his eyes, forcing back the memories of last night, of Talia pressing herself against him, her mouth opening under his like the sweetest of flowers. It was better this way. It had to be.

'Sir?' The pilot's voice broke into his thoughts and he opened his eyes, blinking in the bright sunshine of a summer morning.

'Yes, Theo?'

Theo waved towards the tarmac surrounding the helipad, raising his voice over the loud whirring of the helicopter's propeller. 'There is a woman…'

Angelos leaned forward, stiffening in surprise at the sight of Talia, wearing nothing but one of her huge T-shirts and a pair of skimpy boy shorts, striding towards the helicopter, a look of fury on her face.

'Cut the engine,' Angelos said tersely. The last thing he wanted was for Talia to be hurt. The wind generated from the propeller's blades was whipping her hair about her face in golden tangles, and her T-shirt to her body so Angelos could see every perfect, slender contour—and so could his pilot.

A jealousy so primal and fierce it would have shocked him had he possessed the sangfroid to consider it rose up inside him, making him leap out of the helicopter and swallow the space between him and Talia in two giant steps.

'What the hell do you think you're doing?'

'What the hell do you think *you're* doing?' she challenged. Her eyes glittered with golden-green fury and she jutted her chin at a proud, stubborn angle. 'Running away?'

'I am returning to Athens,' Angelos bit out. 'For business.'

'Liar. Liar *and* coward.'

'How dare you insult me in such a way,' he snapped. 'I am your employer—'

'As you reminded me last night. You bring that one out whenever it suits you—'

'This is not the place for such a conversation. Anyone can see you are barely dressed.'

She arched an eyebrow, magnificent even in a pair of pyjamas. 'Anyone? I don't see a crowd of bystanders.'

'My pilot, Theo.' Angelos gestured to the helicopter. 'I don't particularly want him to see what—' He stopped, swallowing the words he'd been going to say. *What is mine.*

Talia wasn't his. Not remotely. And she never could be.

'Fine, I'll go back to the house. But only if you'll come with me.' She folded her arms, chin still tilted proudly. 'Will you?'

'Fine,' Angelos answered. And when they were back in the house he would make it abundantly clear that they had no relationship, and that her place in his household was only as his daughter's nanny. Clearly last night had given Talia the presumption to take liberties with her position.

Suppressing the urge to drape his jacket over her, he strode back to the villa as Talia followed.

'Go change,' he instructed as they came into the house. 'And then you will meet me in my study.'

He didn't so much as look at her as he slammed into his study. It was time to put things back the way they were. Last night had been a moment of weakness and need that he intended never to show again.

Five minutes later a knock sounded on the door, and before Angelos could bid enter, Talia came in. She was wearing a pair of shorts that showcased her long gold legs and a T-shirt that was positively skimpy. Angelos could see the high, small breasts that he'd touched last night and, irritated, he yanked his gaze away.

'Don't you have any suitable clothes?'

'I've been wearing these clothes since I arrived,' Talia answered. Her voice was even but he sensed the tension and anger underneath, cracks in her calm surface. 'Why are you harping on about my clothes anyway? They hardly matter—'

'What matters,' Angelos cut across her, 'is the appalling liberties you've taken in your position as nanny.'

'*What?*' The word was expelled in an incredulous rush of air, Talia's jaw slackening and her eyes going wide as she stared at him in angry shock.

Angelos stood behind his desk, one hand resting on the back of his chair. 'I made it clear when I hired you what your position was to be. To supervise my daughter—'

'Are you implying I have been *negligent* in my duties?' Talia asked, her eyes now narrowing to golden-green slits.

'I'm implying that you have allowed your relationship with my daughter to give you the presumption to take liberties with me—'

'*I* take liberties with you?' Talia gasped in outrage. 'Correct me if my memory is faulty, but you're the one who kissed me last night.'

Angelos felt heat rush into his face and he stiffened his stance. 'I am not talking about that. In that instance I was at fault and I can assure you it will never happen again. I'm talking about your position in my family, Miss Di Sione, and the way you think you can—'

'We're back to Miss Di Sione?' she interjected with a sharp laugh. 'You really do feel backed into a corner, don't you?'

'Don't be ridiculous.'

'I don't think I am.' She took a step towards him. 'What is this really about, Angelos? Why were you leaving this morning?'

'I have business in Athens.'

'Did you even say goodbye to Sofia?'

'That is none of your concern—'

'Yes, it is, because I'm the one taking care of her. Did you?' Her question rang through the room and Angelos met her accusing stare unflinchingly.

'I wrote her a letter, which suffices.'

'You really believe that?'

'It is not for you to question my actions.'

She shook her head slowly, disbelievingly. 'You're scared,' she stated, and he stared at her coldly.

'Scared? Of what?'

Too late he realised he shouldn't have asked the question. He should have shut down this conversation before it had begun. Talia had no right—

'Scared of getting close to people. To Sofia, to me—'

'A single kiss does not mean we're close,' he informed her, knowing he was hurting her—and that he was a liar.

'I'm not talking about the kiss,' Talia answered quietly. Her face was flushed and humiliation sparkled in her eyes but she still stood straight and tall, holding his gaze, and it made Angelos feel a reluctant admiration for her. She was proud and beautiful and, considering all she'd endured, so very strong.

He wasn't worthy of her, not remotely.

'I'm talking about the conversations we had yesterday,' she continued, her voice trembling slightly. 'The things you admitted to me about your childhood, and how you feel you aren't a good father to Sofia. You feel threatened because I know all that, and you're wishing you hadn't said those things.'

She was utterly right, and his sense of honour forced him to admit as much. 'I am wishing it,' he told her. 'I never should have allowed us to have such…a connection.'

'Why not?'

'Because nothing can happen between us.'

She took a deep breath as she held his stare. 'Why not?'

He stared at her, flummoxed by her tenacity. 'Why not? Because…because it is simply not possible.'

'Do I have to say it again?'

'Why not?' he filled in for her, irritation creeping into his voice. 'Are you a glutton for punishment, Talia? Do you want me to spell it out for you?'

'I don't consider myself a glutton for punishment,' she answered, her voice wobbling a little, 'but yes, I do. Tell me why—why there couldn't be anything between us. I think we like each other…' Her face was fiery and she looked away for a few seconds, blinking rapidly, before she swung her gaze resolutely back to his.

'Because I am not interested in a romantic relationship with you,' Angelos informed her shortly. 'I have my daughter to consider—'

'I don't think Sofia would mind—'

'And my business,' he cut across her. 'In any case, you are American, and will be leaving here in a few short weeks. This whole conversation is the height of absurdity.'

He swung away from her, discomfited by how tempted he was to take her up on her blatant offer. He desired her, God knew; in the last seven years his libido had been like a dormant volcano that was now bubbling hotly to life. He wanted her very badly indeed.

And even more alarmingly, he *liked* her. He liked her sense of humour and her gentleness with Sofia, her understanding and her courage and her kindness.

He liked her so much that he couldn't stand the thought of her knowing how he'd disappointed the people he loved in the worst way possible. He couldn't stand the thought of her walking away from him.

'You are here,' he told her in a cold voice, his back still to her, 'as Sofia's nanny. That is all. Any…illusion of intimacy that occurred between us is simply that. An illusion. And you would do best to forget it ever happened.'

The silence after this pronouncement was awful, endless. Angelos could hear Talia's soft breathing; the gentle, hitched breaths reminding him of a hurt animal, of someone in pain.

'Very well,' she said at last. 'I will accept what you've said. I can hardly do otherwise. But I would ask, for Sofia's sake, that you not leave Kallos just yet. It was her birthday only yesterday, and she treasures this time with you. For her sake, will you stay? I will keep myself out of the way when the two of you are together. But just…' Her voice broke and Angelos closed his eyes, a shudder of pain ripping through him. 'Don't leave yet. Please.'

A long moment passed as Angelos mastered his composure. 'Fine,' he said, his voice toneless. 'But I do need to return to Athens. But I'll stay for a few more days. For Sofia's sake.'

'Thank you,' Talia said softly, and then he heard the door open and click softly shut as she left the room.

* * *

She was so stupid. Slowly Talia walked upstairs, barricading herself in her bedroom as the realisation of how utterly she'd revealed and humiliated herself reverberated through her. She was so painfully, horribly stupid, to think Angelos cared about her. To demand he give a fledgling relationship between them a chance, when he obviously had no interest or intention of doing so. *I think we like each other.* What was she, in seventh grade?

She leaned against the door and slid slowly to the floor, cradling her head in her hands. *Stupid, stupid Talia. The first time you get a taste of life and love and you go crazy.* At least she was wiser now. Next time, if there was a next time, she'd know not to go begging. She'd wait for a man to show her he cared for more than just a kiss, amazing as it had been.

She heard Sofia go downstairs for breakfast, and then Angelos's low, murmured greeting as he came out of the study. At least he'd said he would stay. If she left Kallos in a few weeks having helped to strengthen the relationship between Angelos and his daughter, she would be happy.

Almost.

The day dragged, with Talia both hopeful and afraid of seeing Angelos around the house. He closeted himself in his study, and after lunch she took Sofia swimming. They splashed around in the water for a while, enjoying the sun, joking in their strange yet workable mixture of English and Greek.

'Sofia,' Talia asked when they were lying on the beach, the salt drying on their skin, 'did you like being on Naxos?'

Sofia turned to look at her in surprise. *'Ne...'*

'Would you like to go to school there? I saw there was a school in Chora. It's not so far in a boat, and you could have friends, then, besides us boring old grown-ups.'

Sofia frowned, trying to make out Talia's meaning, and so she explained it more clearly. 'School,' she said. '*Scholeio*? In Chora?'

Understanding brightened Sofia's face before it fell and she shook her head. 'Papa *ohi*,' she said. 'No.'

'Papa said no?'

'He not…want.' She shrugged, and Talia nodded in understanding.

'You think your father doesn't want you to go to school in Chora,' she surmised, and after a brief pause Sofia touched her scarred cheek, her fingers brushing the ridged flesh as she gazed at Talia with wide, sorrow-filled eyes. 'Because of that?' Talia exclaimed in surprise and dismay. 'Sofia, no. *Ohi*. Your papa doesn't care about that.'

But Sofia just shook her head and looked away.

The conversation lingered with her for the rest of the day, and after a sleepless night Talia decided she would have to confront Angelos about this latest revelation. She knew he would not take kindly to her interference, and worse, she was afraid the idea that Sofia thought he wanted her to hide away because of her scar would hurt him. But he had to realise how his behaviour was affecting his daughter.

It took three more days before she was finally able to find a moment alone with Angelos. He'd gone off the island for an overnight; Maria had said he was having a quick trip to Athens before returning, an explanation that satisfied Talia as she suspected previously he would have gone for weeks.

When he came back he spent his time with Sofia and she tried to make herself scarce. She watched from her bedroom window as they built a sandcastle together, a ridiculously elaborate construction that made her smile even as her heart gave a little pulsing ache of sorrow. She wanted to be down there on the beach with them. She wanted Angelos to want it, but she knew he didn't.

Finally, the next morning while Sofia was at her lessons, Talia confronted Angelos in his study.

His gaze sharpened and his mouth thinned as she stepped into his inner sanctum, trying not to let her fear show at his unwelcoming look.

'What is it?' he asked. 'I trust nothing is wrong with Sofia?'

'Actually,' Talia said as she closed the door, 'something is.'

Angelos straightened in his chair. 'What do you mean?'

'I spoke with her a few days ago, Angelos, and she said something that I think you need to know about.'

'Which is?'

'I asked her about going to school on Naxos…'

'You what?' His voice came out like a boom of thunder, and made her tremble nearly as much. 'You had no right—'

'I wanted to know if she'd ever considered going to school,' Talia replied stubbornly, locking her knees and lifting her chin. 'She had fun when we were on Naxos, and it seemed like a reasonable question to me…'

'You know why she doesn't want to go,' Angelos said in a low voice that thrummed with anger.

'I do now,' Talia returned. 'But do you?'

He glared at her, fury simmering in his eyes and a muscle flickering in his temple. Even angry he was gorgeous, and she still longed for him. 'What do you mean by that question?'

'Sofia told me *you* don't want her to go to school on Naxos.'

'I want her to be comfortable,' Angelos snapped. 'And protected. I've seen how she is when we're out in public. She hides her face—'

'From you.' Talia took a deep breath, knowing her next words would hurt, and perhaps even get her fired. 'I think she believes you are ashamed of her, Angelos. Of her scar.'

'What!' Angelos's voice came out in a crack like a gunshot, and he jerked back as if she'd been the one to fire the bullet. 'How can you even…? I have never been ashamed of it. *Never.* Why would she think such a thing?' He shook his head, his eyes snapping with fury and hurt. 'Why would you think it? Is that—is that the kind of man you believe I am?'

'No,' she said, her voice rising, ringing with sincerity, as tears pricked her eyes. 'No, Angelos, I don't. But when you are with her, you scowl and frown and seem very fierce—'

'If I scowl, it's because I hate the thought that she is self-conscious about it,' Angelos bit out. 'That she is ashamed. She has no reason to be. None. If anyone does, it is me.'

'What do you mean by that?' Talia asked. 'Why should you be ashamed, Angelos? What is it that keeps you—?'

'I failed her,' he said flatly. 'In the fire.'

'Because you couldn't protect her from getting hurt?' Talia surmised. 'But it wasn't your fault—'

'Actually, it was. But we will not discuss it.'

'Maybe you need to discuss it—'

'Did you not understand what I said to you before?' Angelos cut across her, his voice hard and flat. 'You are taking liberties, Miss Di Sione.'

'Don't "Miss Di Sione" me,' Talia snapped. She hated how Angelos hid behind cold formality. She *knew* he was hurting and afraid, but there was absolutely nothing she could do about it. She wouldn't humiliate herself again by insisting he really cared about her, or begging him to unburden himself to her. 'Just think about what I said.

And maybe ask Sofia if she would like to go to school on Naxos.'

Not trusting herself to say anything more or to keep herself from breaking down, Talia strode from the room, slamming the door with satisfying force behind her.

CHAPTER THIRTEEN

ANGELOS REMAINED WHERE he stood, the echo of Talia's slamming the door reverberating through the room.

Was she right? Could Sofia possibly think that he was ashamed of her? In his letter he'd taken pains to tell her how proud he was of her, how beautiful he thought her. But maybe letters weren't enough. Maybe the way he acted when he was with her spoke louder than his cowardly written words. Because the truth was, looking at his daughter hurt *him*, because it reminded him of his own failures. But the possibility that it was hurting *her* was agony. Torture. He'd spent the last seven years trying to atone for his sins, working hard to keep Sofia feeling safe and protected. The idea that he'd failed utterly in his goal possessed the power to fell him. What if he, in his ineptitude and fear, had made things *worse*?

And Talia had had the courage to confront him about it, knowing he would be angry, that he would drive her away, just as he had done. She really was brave.

Sighing, Angelos sank into his chair. First he needed to talk to Sofia. He could deal with Talia later.

When Angelos came in that evening before bed to talk to Sofia, his expression serious, Talia's heart lifted even as her insides quailed with trepidation. She quietly excused herself and when she returned an hour later, having heard Angelos's slow, heavy tread down the stairs, Sofia had already fallen asleep.

Leaning close, Talia had been able to see the tracks of tears on the girl's face and she'd bitten her lip, wondering how the conversation between father and daughter had gone. Angelos had made it abundantly clear that it was not her place to ask.

She went back to her bedroom and watched the moon rise above the sea, trying to enjoy the moment for what it was. In two weeks she'd leave Kallos, leave Angelos and Sofia behind for ever. But she hoped the things she'd experienced here, the lessons she'd learned, would equip her to face her own future with more courage.

And what about Giovanni's book? Sighing, Talia sat on her bed, wrapping her arms around her knees and resting her chin on top. She hated admitting her failure to her grandfather, but what else could she do? At this point she doubted Angelos even had the book. He'd certainly expressed no interest in poetry.

But then she hadn't tried very hard at all. The least her grandfather deserved was for her to make a proper attempt. And she didn't really have anything left to lose when it came to her relationship, or lack of it, with Angelos.

Before she left, Talia promised herself, she'd ask him straight out. At least then she could go back to Giovanni with a clear conscience and a conviction that she'd done the best she could.

She only wished she felt that way about her relationship with Angelos and Sofia. What if she'd made things worse, by telling Angelos her fears about Sofia's feelings? What if too much honesty had damaged their fragile father-daughter relationship?

Restless now, she rose from the bed and went downstairs, intending to take a walk on the beach to clear her head. The light filtering under Angelos's study door made her pause on the bottom stair, wondering if she dared go in and ask him how his conversation with Sofia had gone.

The thought of facing his stony-faced fury a second time made her falter, and after another second's hesitation she continued on to the front door. She'd just put a hand on the latch when she heard a sound coming from Angelos's study—something between a moan and a sob—and then the shattering of glass.

Her breath catching in her throat, her heart beating hard, Talia turned back to his study. She could not ignore those sounds of grief and despair, yet she also cringed at the thought of Angelos's rage. Hesitantly she tapped on the door and when there was no answer, she turned the handle and pushed the door open with her fingertips.

Angelos sat sprawled in a chair by the fireplace, shattered glass sprinkling the hearth and the strong anise smell of ouzo permeating the air.

'Angelos…'

He glanced up at her, his hair rumpled, the buttons of his shirt half undone, his gaze bleary. 'I'm not drunk, if that's what you're afraid of,' he said. 'I haven't had so much as a sip.'

'I suppose that accounts for the smell and the broken glass,' Talia said as she closed the door.

Angelos glanced indifferently at the shards of glass surrounding him. 'I suppose it does.'

'No point in cutting yourself,' Talia said, and bent to pick up the larger pieces. She swept them into her hand and then looked around for the bin.

'Beneath the desk.' Angelos's eyes were closed, his face a ravaged mask of pain. 'Thank you.'

She got rid of the glass and then sat gingerly in the chair opposite him. 'Do you want to talk about it?'

'No.'

'That's not actually a surprise.'

He cracked open an eye and stared at her. 'You can joke?'

'I don't know what to do,' Talia admitted. 'Let me help you, Angelos. I can tell you're hurting.'

He closed his eyes again. 'You have no idea.'

'I know I don't. So tell me.' He just shook his head and she expelled an impatient breath. 'You are the most stubborn, mule-headed man I've ever met!'

He smiled faintly at that, the barest quirk of his lips, but at least it was a reaction. 'I must be.'

'It's as if you *want* to be miserable—'

He opened an eye, arched an eyebrow. 'A glutton for punishment?'

'It appears we both are,' Talia answered, a flush touching her cheeks as she remembered how she'd practically begged for Angelos to care about her. The memory was enough to make her admit defeat. 'Fine. You know what, Angelos? You can stew here for as long as you like. Drown in ouzo if you want to.' She took a trembling breath. 'You gave me the courage to face my fears but it seems I am not able to give you the same. So I give up.' She turned towards the door, blinking back tears, hating how much this man affected her. How much she wanted to help him and couldn't.

'Talia.' Her name was a whisper as she put her hand on the doorknob. 'Don't go.'

Slowly Talia turned around. 'Do you mean that?'

His eyes were closed, his expression bleak. The word, when it came, was barely audible. 'Yes.'

Silently she returned to her chair, and then sat down and waited, her hands clenched in her lap, her heart beating hard.

Angelos let out a long, low breath and opened his eyes. 'I spoke to Sofia tonight, as you know. She told me…she told me the same thing you had told me. That she thought I was ashamed of her. That I kept her on this island to hide her from people, because I didn't want anyone to see her scar.' He scrubbed his face with his hands. 'If I'd known that she would think that…the damage I would cause, on top of everything else…' He shook his head. 'I am the one who is ashamed. Of so much.'

'What are you ashamed of?' Talia asked softly.

She didn't think Angelos was going to answer. He remained silent for a long time, his hands still covering his face, and then he slowly dropped them and stared at her. Talia nearly gasped at the utter bleakness she saw there.

'Because,' Angelos said heavily, 'it was my fault that there was a fire.' Talia knew instinctively there was more, and so she remained silent, waiting and alert. After an endless moment Angelos continued. 'I was working downstairs. It had been a hard week, sleepless nights… Sofia was teething.' He let out a sound that he choked off as soon as it came out of him, pressing the back of his hand to his mouth. 'She was such a sweet baby. So good-natured. Xanthe and I were so blessed. I'd never thought to have a wife, a family. Me, a gutter rat from the docks.' He shook his head, lost in memory, awash in grief.

'What happened, Angelos?' Talia asked quietly. 'That night?'

'Xanthe was upstairs with Sofia. She was rocking her in the nursery. We lived in Athens at the time, a town house in Kolonaki. An old building, with leaky pipes and faulty wires…'

'It was an electrical fire?' Talia guessed, and Angelos nodded, his face twisted in regret.

'I always meant to have the building inspected. I knew it was old—I picked it up for a song…'

'You can't blame yourself for that,' Talia protested. 'An electrical fire could happen to anyone, anywhere…'

'It wasn't just that.' He drove his fingers through his hair, his head bowed. 'I'd been drinking. A couple of glasses of ouzo, while I worked on reports. But I was tired and it must have affected me more than I'd thought because I was so slow.' He dropped his hands and looked at her openly then, his pain naked, his face screwed up in anguish. 'Talia, I was too *slow*.'

'Oh, Angelos.' His name caught in her throat and she blinked back tears as she realised the depth of the agony he'd endured then, and in the seven years since. Unthinkingly she dropped to her knees in front of him and took his hands in hers. 'Tell me,' she whispered.

'It started in the nursery.' He bowed his head, his hands clenched in hers. 'The door was shut, and Xanthe had fallen asleep in the rocker with Sofia. By the time the alarm went off and I smelled the smoke, the fire was already raging. Xanthe was screaming, *screaming*…she couldn't get the door open. The heat had swollen it shut. I tried to kick it down, I shoved my whole body against it over and over again, but I couldn't. And the fire brigade was taking so *long*…' His hands tightened on hers, hard enough to make Talia wince, but nothing would make her let go of Angelos now. 'Xanthe told me to leave. She knew…she knew she couldn't get out, but she wanted to save Sofia. She told me to go downstairs and she would throw her to me.'

'Oh, Angelos…'

'I refused. I refused, Talia, because I still wanted to save my wife. By the time I finally realised I couldn't and ran downstairs, Sofia had already been burned. If I'd only listened…if I'd have acted faster…' He shook his head. 'Xanthe threw her down to me, and as I held our daughter, the flames engulfed her.' A tear splashed onto her hand and wordlessly Talia put her arms around Angelos. He pressed his head against her chest, seeking comfort.

'The fire brigade came then,' he continued in a choked voice. 'Too late. Too damned late. And Sofia's face was badly burned, and parts of her body…she was so *little*. She spent six months in hospital, having to have skin grafts and surgeries. It was hell for both of us. She was in terrible pain and she missed her mother. She cried constantly— she didn't want me, not even to hold her. She didn't understand any of what had happened and I was so useless…' He let out a choked sob and shook his head. 'So useless, in so many ways.'

'Oh, Angelos,' Talia whispered as she stroked his hair. 'How terrible for both of you. I'm so, so sorry.'

Neither of them spoke for a long moment and then finally Angelos eased away, his head still lowered. 'It was easier to keep my distance from her afterwards. I bought Kallos and employed a nanny who could give her the care I never could. I thought I was doing the right thing, the best thing, for Sofia. But maybe I was just being selfish, keeping my distance because I couldn't bear to be reminded of my own failings.' He shook his head. 'And I just made things worse.'

'But you can make them better now,' Talia insisted. 'Sofia is only nine, and she needs you. She loves you. Make things better now, and love her back.'

'I do love her—'

'Spend time with her. Live on Kallos, or bring her to Athens with you. Show her and the world that you're not ashamed of her.'

Angelos lifted his head and gazed at her, his brown

eyes damp, his thick, dark lashes spiky. 'How did a young woman like you become so wise?'

Talia let out a self-conscious laugh. 'Am I really so wise? I've hidden away for the last seven years rather than face reality or try to conquer my anxiety. It's easy to speak to someone else's situation.'

'But you conquered your anxiety in coming here.'

'Yes.' Her throat dried at the intent look in Angelos's eyes, the realisation of how close his face was to hers. 'And for that I am truly thankful,' she managed to continue, 'to you.'

'You have nothing to thank me for.'

'I do—'

'I was a right bastard to you when you arrived.'

'Well, maybe,' she allowed with a little laugh. 'But I've seen how kind you are.' She tried for a playful smile. 'Your secret is out, Angelos.'

'Is it?' he asked, his voice low and aching, and Talia's heart gave a hopeful thump, like the tail wagging on a dog.

'I think so…' she murmured, and her mouth was so dry she touched her tongue to her lips, eliciting a groan from Angelos.

'Talia…' He wrapped one hand around the back of her neck, his fingers warm and strong and sure. 'Talia, you drive me crazy…'

'Do I?' she whispered, and then he was pulling her towards him and his lips were on hers, seeking and finding her as she'd wanted for so long, since the last time he'd kissed her.

Talia reached up and tangled her hands in his hair, anchoring his mouth more firmly to hers. She couldn't get enough of him, of the taste and feel and sheer beauty of him as he slid his hands from her neck to her shoulders, pulling her from her kneeling position to sprawl on his lap as his mouth plundered hers.

Her heart raced as sensations exploded in her like fireworks, each one more intense than the last. Angelos's hand sliding under her shirt, his palm flat on her belly, and then moving upwards, cupping the warm fullness of her breast, his thumb brushing its aching peak…

How did anyone survive this? she wondered hazily as she kissed him back with untutored enthusiasm and passion. How did anyone feel this way and live?

Then Angelos tore his mouth from hers, his breath coming out in a gasp. 'We shouldn't…'

'We should,' Talia insisted. She would not be put off a second time. 'Angelos, I—' *I love you* bubbled on her lips but she swallowed the words down. He didn't want to hear that. Not yet, and probably not ever. 'I want you,' she said instead, and his expression darkened, his pupils dilating.

'I want you too. Very much so.'

'Then why not?'

'It will complicate things—'

She glanced down at her rucked-up shirt, her legs sprawled across his lap, the hard and intriguing bulge of his arousal against her calf. 'Things are already pretty complicated.'

Angelos let out a groan and leaned his head back against the chair. 'Talia, you're going to kill me.'

'Then surely it will be a pleasant death?' Some inner vixen emboldened her to press her palms against his chest, stroking the hard planes of muscles, teasing his nipples. She ached to touch him, and the evidence of his response as he groaned again and his body stirred was utterly thrilling. She leaned forward, her hair brushing his cheek, and pressed a kiss to his lips. 'Please, Angelos,' she whispered, 'don't make me beg.'

He caught her face in his hands and forced her to meet his fierce gaze. 'If you're sure?'

'Of course I'm sure.'

Angelos stared at her for a long, hard moment and then he nodded. 'All right, then. Come with me,' he said, and in one fluid movement he caught her up in his arms and strode from the study, up the stairs and to his bedroom.

CHAPTER FOURTEEN

ANTICIPATION RACED THROUGH Talia as she hooked her arms around Angelos's neck and held on. He entered his bedroom, kicking the door closed behind him, before he deposited Talia on the huge bed, its dark silken sheets slippery beneath her.

She stared up at him, her eyes wide as he began to unbutton his shirt. She'd seen his bare chest before when they'd gone swimming but she'd never seen him like this—eyes dark, liquid and burning with intensity, his long, elegant fingers slipping his buttons out of their holes, his gaze never leaving hers.

She let out her breath in a shaky rush and wondered if she should tell him how untouched she was. But surely he knew? Since she'd confessed to living like a hermit for seven years?

'You're not having second thoughts?' Angelos asked in a low voice.

'No, of course not.' Her whole body throbbed and ached with the need to feel him again. Touch him again.

'I don't have any birth control,' he told her, his hands stilling on his shirt as his gaze widened in realisation. 'I've never…' Talia gaped in astonishment as a light blush touched his cheekbones. 'I haven't needed any here.'

'I'm on the pill,' Talia assured him. She'd been on it

since she was sixteen, to regulate her heavy periods. 'And as for…other stuff, I'm not…that is, I'm…' She was trying to tell him she was a virgin, but Angelos cut her off with a nod.

'So am I.' Somehow she didn't think he was talking about virginity. 'Clear,' he clarified, and she realised she must have been looking blank.

'Oh. Right. Well, then…' The moment for telling Angelos she was a virgin had passed. Talia didn't want to ruin the mood, and he seemed like the kind of man who might scruple at taking a woman's virginity.

'It's all good,' he said, his smile turning wolfish as he finished unbuttoning his shirt and shrugged the crisp white cotton from his glorious shoulders. Talia was glad not to have to explain, especially since she seemed to have lost the ability to speak or even to think. Angelos, with his hair rumpled, his eyes burning and his chest bare, was an utterly magnificent sight.

She watched, her mouth dry and her heart pounding, as his hands went to his belt buckle, and then stopped.

'Don't…' she breathed, and he frowned.

'Don't what?'

'Don't stop,' she clarified on a groan and, amazed at her own audacity, she reached for him, her fingers sliding around his belt buckle so she could tug him towards her.

He put one arm out to brace his fall, landing beside her on the bed, his body lean and hard, hot and bare. Gently Talia skimmed her fingers along his chest, her fingers brushing the crisp dark hair, teasing, questing.

'I've been wanting to do this for a while,' she admitted on a laugh, and then because she couldn't keep herself from it, she pressed a kiss to his chest. Angelos groaned and rolled onto his back, taking her with him.

'You are so very sweet.'

'I'm… I'm not sure I'm very good at this,' she confessed, which was as close as she was willing to come to
admitting she was completely inexperienced.

'Trust me, you are very good at this,' Angelos said.
He slid his hands under her T-shirt, his palms exquisitely
rough against the smooth skin of her back. With one swift
tug he had the shirt up and over her head and she struggled
to pull it off, laughing breathlessly until her naked breasts
came into contact with his chest and then she gasped in
the sheer pleasure of the sensation.

'*Oh*…that feels good.'

Angelos grinned up at her as he started to tug off her
shorts. 'We're just beginning.'

Another tug and her shorts were gone, and she lay before
him completely naked, utterly exposed, and yet she felt no
nervousness or vulnerability. She basked in his appreciative
stare, the way his pupils flared as his gaze roved over her.

He reached out and cupped her breast, his thumb moving slowly over the peak. Talia arched up helplessly to
meet his hand.

'You are so beautiful,' Angelos rasped, his eyes dark
with desire.

'*You're* beautiful,' she answered on a gasp, and he
laughed softly before he put his mouth to her breast and
Talia gasped again, her hands fisting in his hair, as pleasure rippled through her in exquisite shocks. '*Oh*…' She
sucked in a hard breath as he moved his mouth to her other
breast. 'Oh, I didn't *know*…'

He lifted his head to glance at her, lazily amused.
'Didn't know what?'

'That you could feel…' She trailed off, overcome, because Angelos was giving her so much, showing her so
much. *If she hadn't come to Greece…if she hadn't been
able to feel this way, to know you could feel this way…*

It didn't matter that it would end in a few weeks or even that night, Talia told herself fiercely. It didn't matter if she left Greece heartbroken and alone. She had this, and it would be enough. She would never regret it.

'Talia…' Angelos propped himself up one elbow as he looked down at her, his smile soft, his expression unbearably tender. 'Talia, are you all right?'

She realised how close she was to weeping, not with sorrow, but with sheer emotion. With joy. 'I'm fine,' she assured him, and kissed him hard, wrapping her arms around him, pressing her naked body to his. 'I'm completely and utterly wonderful.'

Angelos caught her up in the kiss, his tongue tangling with hers as his arms came around her, clasping her to him.

He flipped her onto her back, making her let out a sudden laugh of surprise, and then slowly he slid his hand down her body, savouring each dip and curve before he pressed his palm to the juncture of her thighs.

Talia let out a little yelp of shock and Angelos glanced at her, one eyebrow quirked in question.

'That feels…'

'Good?' he finished as his fingers touched her more intimately than she'd ever imagined.

'Yes,' she gasped as her hips arched instinctively. 'Yes…'

She felt her body convulse as pleasure ripped through her in deepening waves, so an instinct she hadn't even known she'd possessed took over, driving her forward. She grabbed Angelos's hand with both of her own, and he gave a low laugh as his fingers worked their deft magic.

'I'm not going anywhere,' he assured her.

'You'd better not,' she breathed, and then pleasure gripped her like a vice before releasing her in a breathless daze. 'Oh…'

In one fluid movement Angelos rolled over her before he slid smoothly inside, only to stop before he'd barely begun, shock turning his body rigid. 'Talia…'

She blinked, surprised and a little alarmed at how…*full* it felt. 'I'm okay,' she said.

Angelos's jaw was clenched as he struggled to keep himself still inside her body. 'But—'

'I'm okay,' she insisted, and she angled her hips upwards to take him more fully into her body. It hurt; not a sudden, sharp pain, but more of a deep ache of adjustment.

Angelos's face was etched with lines of restraint and regret. 'I didn't…'

'No, don't, please.' She pressed her fingers against her lips. 'This is what I wanted.' She shifted beneath him, felt her body expand to accommodate him. 'This is good.'

'Tell me if—'

'It doesn't hurt, I promise.'

Angelos started to move, a groan escaping him as he braced himself on his forearms and after a few seconds Talia sought to match each smooth stroke. And with each stroke she felt the embers of pleasure rekindle, and then her body found a rhythm of its own. She clutched at his shoulders, meeting each thrust, gasping as it stoked the fire inside her higher and higher, until finally it exploded in a rush of sensation that left her boneless and trembling, tears leaking from beneath her closed lids.

'Talia,' Angelos said brokenly as he kissed the tears away from her cheeks. 'Please don't cry.'

'It's only because I'm so happy.' She opened her eyes, giving him a watery smile. She still felt as if she could burst into tears, but not in a bad way. 'That was…amazing. Overwhelming. I didn't know…'

'Why didn't you tell me you didn't know?' Angelos asked. He'd rolled over onto his side, his skin glistening with a faint sheen of sweat, his eyes dark and fierce. 'How much you didn't know?'

'I was afraid you wouldn't want to go through with it,' Talia confessed.

'You should have told me,' Angelos insisted as he brushed away a strand of hair from her cheek, tucking it gently behind her ear. 'I would have done things differently.'

'I didn't want things done differently. And actually, I thought you might already guess... I told you how limited my life was.'

'Yes, but...' Angelos shrugged. 'You're a beautiful young woman. I thought you must have still had opportunities.'

Talia shook her head ruefully. 'I dated a boy when I was seventeen, and we kissed a couple of times. That's all.'

Angelos's eyebrows rose almost comically. 'That's all? But then you were completely untouched.'

'I wasn't all that interested in boys to be honest,' Talia told him. 'I wanted adventure of a different kind. Seeing the world, painting pictures...that was what interested me.'

'Which makes it all the more tragic that you hid yourself away for so long.'

'I'm not going to hide away any more,' Talia promised. 'No matter what happens. I want to live life properly now.' Angelos frowned and she hastened to add, 'I'm not expecting... I know we haven't made any...' A flush rose to her skin and since she was naked Angelos could see how she blushed everywhere. She let out a groan of embarrassment as she closed her eyes.

'Haven't made any what, Talia?' Angelos asked, and she couldn't tell if he was amused or annoyed.

'Commitments. I just wanted to assure you I didn't expect any kind of...' Again words failed her. 'You know.'

'I'm not sure I do know,' Angelos answered. He cupped her cheek, his thumb resting on her lips, and Talia opened her eyes. 'You know, you're the first woman I've been with since my wife.'

'What?' Talia stared at him in shock. 'I know you said you hadn't recently, but it's been seven years…'

'Trust me, I know. A very long seven years, at least in that regard.'

'Why haven't you…? I mean, there must have been women in Athens.' Her mouth curved in a playful smile that he traced with the pad of his thumb. 'And what about all those nannies who crawled into your bed? Maria told me about them.'

Angelos gave a mock shudder. 'I did not want any of them. They were brazen, grasping. But the truth is…' He let out a sigh. 'I had no desire for a woman, or for any of life's pleasures. I felt numb…frozen even, after all the fire and then its aftermath. Survival was all I could manage. And like you, I hid away from life.' He grimaced. 'And now I have realised that Sofia paid the price.'

'And, like me, you won't hide away any more,' Talia said softly. 'Will you?'

'No. For Sofia's sake I will allow her to go to school on Naxos, and come to Athens with me on business trips. I decided that tonight. I'm not ashamed of my daughter, Talia.'

'I know you're not.' Fresh tears shimmered on her lashes and she blinked them away. 'You're a good man, Angelos, even if you haven't believed you are. I know you did everything you could the night of the fire, even if you refused to believe it. You couldn't have saved them both. You *couldn't* have.'

Angelos's face contorted for a second and then he threw his arm over his face as he took a few deep breaths. 'I know you believe that…' he began, and Talia pulled at his arm, needing to look at him, to have him see her and how serious she was.

'*You* need to believe it,' she said. 'For Sofia's sake as well as your own.'

'I'm not sure I can.'

She pressed her palm on his chest, felt the steady thud of his heart underneath. 'In time, then,' she said softly. 'I know it isn't easy. One boat ride doesn't cure my claustrophobia, and living life outside the walls of my grandfather's estate isn't going to be easy. But with time, all things are possible.'

'You believe that?'

'I need to. And so do you.'

He let out a sigh and then gathered her into his arms, resting his chin on top of her head. 'Thank you,' he whispered. 'For giving me a second chance at life.'

'You deserve one.' They lay there quietly for a moment, their arms around each other, and Talia wondered if she would ever possess the courage to say all the things in her heart. That she loved him. That she didn't want this to be some kind of fling. That she was already dreaming of for ever with this man, even though she knew it was crazy and unrealistic and maybe even impossible.

But what if it wasn't?

What if they could have a love that healed their old hurts and brought them both a second chance at life, made them into the family Sofia needed, that they needed? *What if?*

In that moment, with Angelos's arms around her so securely, it all seemed possible, like a promise shimmering on the horizon, almost able to be grasped if she just dared to reach for it. If they both did.

Angelos stroked her hair and she snuggled against him, contentment vibrating through her bones, sleep beginning to settle over her.

Her eyes were starting to drift closed when her gaze settled on the book lying on the bedside table. A slender, leather-bound tome with hand-tooled engraving. Giovanni's book.

Her gaze snapped open and every nerve twanged with realisation as she struggled out of Angelos's embrace.

'Talia…' His voice was fuzzy with sleep. 'What…'

'The book,' she said, the words spilling from her. 'You really do have the book.'

She felt Angelos's body stiffen in surprise and he propped himself up one arm. 'Book? What book?'

'This…' Reverently Talia reached for the book of poetry. The leather was butter-soft and worn. She flipped the book open and let out a gasp of both surprise and satisfaction at the sight of the inscription, which she read aloud: '"Dearest Lucia, For ever in my heart, always. B.A."' She smiled, feeling emotional all over again. 'Just like he told me.'

Belatedly Talia registered the tension emanating from Angelos's body. He withdrew from her, sitting up, his arms folded across his chest. 'Just like *who* told you, Talia? And how the *hell* do you know about my wife's book?'

CHAPTER FIFTEEN

ANGELOS WATCHED AS Talia slowly closed the book and turned to him, her smile sliding off her face, her eyes shadowing, her shoulders starting to hunch. Guilt. That was what was written on her face, all over her body, in bold, stark letters. *Guilt.*

'Well?' he bit out. 'Do you have an answer?' He didn't even know what to think, how to process what she had said. How could Talia possibly know about Xanthe's precious book? And what on earth had she meant, he really did have it? Suspicions formed on the horizon of his mind, a boiling black cloud of fear and anger that was moving closer, drowning out all rational thought. 'Why can't you explain it to me?'

'I can,' she said. Her voice sounded small and she was clutching the book to her chest.

'Put down the book,' Angelos barked out, driven by a deep and overwhelming emotion he couldn't name; he only felt himself trapped in its clutches. 'Don't you dare touch it.'

Talia's gaze widened and carefully she returned the book to his bedside table. 'I'm sorry.'

'So am I.' Angelos rolled out of bed, swearing under his breath as he reached for his clothes.

'Angelos, please. Don't…'

'Don't what? Ask questions? Demand answers? Why do I feel like there is something you are not telling me? Something big?'

'There is,' she admitted, and her words were like a hammer blow to his fragile, taped-together heart. Everything inside him shattered. She leaned forward, kneading the sheet between her fingers, her golden-brown hair falling over her freckled shoulders, making him desire her even now, a realisation that sent disgust following hard after. 'But, Angelos, please,' she said. 'It doesn't *have* to be big.'

'Why don't you let me be the judge of that,' he snapped, and yanked on his trousers.

'Please,' she whispered. 'If you could just see…'

'See what? That you lied to me?' He grabbed his shirt and thrust his arms through the sleeves. 'Because that's what you did, isn't it?' He pointed to the book lying on the bedside table, the book his wife had cherished. 'How did you know about that book?'

Talia swallowed hard, the muscles jerking in her slender throat. 'My grandfather once owned it. It was a treasured possession of his.'

'Another lie,' Angelos dismissed. 'That book has been in my wife's family for generations.' She paled at that and he gave a hard, derisive laugh. 'So what is it really, Talia? Are you after the book because it's valuable?'

She drew back in shock. 'Valuable? You think I'm after your *money*?'

'The book has been valued at fifty thousand pounds. It's an extremely rare edition.'

'I don't want or need your money,' she spat. 'My grandfather is Giovanni Di Sione, of Di Sione Shipping—'

'Impressive,' Angelos cut across her, his voice a furious drawl. 'Other things you didn't feel you needed to tell me.'

'You didn't ask,' Talia protested. 'I mentioned my grandfather's estate…'

Of course she had. And looking back, Angelos realised he'd known she was from money. The clues she'd dropped about the estate, her studio, the travelling she'd done. Of course she was rich.

'It doesn't matter,' he stated flatly. 'I don't care about your grandfather or his estate.'

'But it's because of my grandfather that I was looking for that book,' Talia said quietly. She was clutching handfuls of sheet in her fists, her knuckles as blazing white against the dark silk. 'It did belong to him, Angelos, a long time ago. It was very precious to him.'

'The book belonged to my wife's grandmother,' Angelos told her. 'She was a lady's maid for a duchess on Isola d'Oro. The duchess gave it to her as a parting gift.'

Talia frowned, shaking her head slowly. 'I don't understand. My grandfather is from Italy. But I know it was his. He told me about the inscription on the front page.'

'"Dearest Lucia, For ever in my heart, always. B.A."' Angelos turned away abruptly, not wanting Talia to see the expression on his face. Not wanting to feel the pain that rose up in him. He and Xanthe had said the same thing to each other. *For ever in our hearts, always.* 'My wife loved that book,' he said tonelessly. 'It was her prized possession. She kept it on her bedside table. It was the only thing saved from the fire, and that only because I'd had it in the safe in my office. I'd just had it valued for insurance. I was going to return it to Xanthe that night.' Talia made a small, abject sound, and feeling cold and emotionless now, Angelos turned around. 'And you want to what? Buy it off me?'

'My grandfather asked me to find it for him,' Talia

said in a small voice. 'I didn't realise how important it was to you…'

'How did you trace it to me?' Angelos asked. 'Out of interest?'

'I found a website dealing in finding rare books. Someone from Mena Consultancy had put a query forth about other books by the same poet.'

'Ah, yes.' His gut soured as he remembered. 'I tried to find a second book for my wife's birthday, years ago.' He shook his head. 'And you came all the way here for that.'

'Yes…'

'That's why you were in my office in the first place,' he surmised. Realisation after realisation thudded sickly through him. 'Not to apply for the nanny position as I'd assumed.'

'No, but—'

'And you didn't see fit to tell me? You could have cleared up my misunderstanding in minutes. In *seconds*.'

'I know, but it was difficult. I was tired and overwhelmed by travelling all that way, and then when I realised I could help Sofia…'

'And snoop around for the book as well, no doubt.'

Talia swallowed, a gulping motion. 'Not snoop, but yes, I thought I'd be able to look…'

'That's why you asked me about poetry on the boat, isn't it?' Angelos said with a disgusted shake of his head. 'I thought it an odd question, but I believed you were just trying to get to know me.' The exposure that admission caused, the realisation that he'd *wanted* her to get to know him, had him turning away.

'I *was* trying to get to know you,' Talia whispered. 'I wanted—'

'Enough.' Angelos slashed his hand through the air. '*Enough.* I can't bear to hear any more of your pathetic excuses. Leave me.' He turned around, watched as tears filled her eyes and her fingers trembled on the sheet.

'Angelos, please. I know I should have said something earlier, but I was starting to care about Sofia, about you, and it seemed so difficult to admit—'

'*Go,*' Angelos roared, and he turned around, unable to face her. He heard her rise from the bed and scramble for her clothes, and then the soft, quick tread of her feet and the click of the door closing.

He let out a shuddering sigh and raked his hands through his hair, grief and guilt and deep, deep regret coursing through him in an unbearable torrent. He'd *trusted* her. He'd told her more than he'd told anyone, even Xanthe. Xanthe hadn't wanted to know about his deprived childhood, the hard lessons he'd learned. Yet Talia had seemed interested, sympathetic, kind. All of it an act to get what she wanted.

A remote part of him insisted he was being unfair, judging Talia so harshly. He could understand why she'd be reluctant to speak up, and yet…

She'd lied. And she would be leaving anyway. The night they'd shared together, and so much more than a single, simple night, had been a mistake. That much Angelos knew with leaden certainty.

Talia crept into her bed and lay there shivering despite the sultry night air. She'd ruined everything by not coming clean to Angelos. Why hadn't she told him about her grandfather and the wretched book earlier? The answer was depressingly obvious. Because she'd been afraid. Afraid of Angelos's anger, of losing what they had together. And so she'd waited, and now she'd lost so much more.

But perhaps she'd never had it to begin with. She

thought of the grief and pain she'd seen so nakedly on Angelos's face. He'd loved his wife. Perhaps he still loved her. Perhaps she and Angelos had never had even a whisper of a chance of a future together.

Eventually Talia drifted into a restless doze, only to wake as dawn's pale grey light filtered through the shutters. She listened to the birdsong and the gentle shooshing of the waves on the beach and knew she had only one choice. She'd have to leave. Better to leave than be fired, which Angelos surely intended to do, and she couldn't endure another week of being with Angelos and having him hate her. Knowing she'd wrecked any hope of a future together.

Sofia's new nanny would arrive in a matter of days, and Talia knew she would be leaving the girl in good hands. Perhaps Angelos could have a few days alone with his daughter, or Maria could manage. She wouldn't be leaving anyone in the lurch if she went now, a thought that still managed to hurt her. She wasn't needed, not really.

With a leaden heart she showered and dressed and then packed her few possessions. The lovely silk Angelos had bought on Naxos she left, still in its paper wrappings. Perhaps he could have a dress made for Sofia.

Downstairs she went directly to Angelos's study and knocked on the door. His terse, 'Enter,' had her insides trembling but she lifted her chin, opened the door and walked in.

'Yes?' Angelos's cold stare was unwelcoming, his lips compressed into a hard line. It seemed incredible to Talia that last night he'd held her in his arms, she'd drawn him into her body. She'd been happier than she'd ever been before.

She blinked the images away and forced herself to

speak. 'I thought it best if I leave. Your new nanny is coming soon anyway, and I'm sure Maria can manage on her own for a little while, or perhaps you and Sofia can spend some more time together. But I think I'll just be… in the way.'

Angelos didn't answer and Talia forced herself not to look away from the cold, assessing stare that reminded her so painfully of the man she'd first met, back in Athens.

'Very well,' he finally answered tonelessly. 'I will arrange for the helicopter to pick you up this afternoon.'

'Thank you,' she whispered.

'You will manage?' Angelos asked. 'In the helicopter?'

'Yes, I think so.' Tears sprang to her eyes at the realisation that even now Angelos was concerned for her. It almost made her want to stay, to *try*… 'Angelos…' she began, and he looked up from his laptop screen.

'There is nothing more to say.' He cut her off in a clipped voice. 'You may say your goodbyes to Sofia.'

Swallowing hard she nodded and turned from the room.

Her farewell to Sofia was awful, worse than anything Talia could have imagined.

'But you *stay*,' Sofia exclaimed as tears started in her eyes. 'Stay. *Parakalo*.' Not having the English to say more, the little girl simply stared at Talia, imploring her with her eyes just as she had back in Athens. This time Talia had to refuse.

'I can write,' she said, miming the action. 'Emails and letters.' Although she wondered if Angelos would allow it. 'Take care, Sofia. *S'agapo*.'

'I love you too,' Sofia answered in English, and then broke down into noisy tears.

Two hours later Talia walked alone from the villa, her suitcase in hand, to the waiting helicopter. She felt emotionless and empty now, and she clambered up into the helicopter without so much as a twinge of fear.

Heartbreak trumped claustrophobia perhaps, she acknowledged as she sat down and buckled herself in. The helicopter lifted off, and no one came to a window or door to say goodbye. Talia watched the island of Kallos grow smaller and smaller and finally disappear over the endless blue horizon.

Twenty-four hours later she was back on her grandfather's estate, the muggy warmth of a mid-August afternoon oppressive after Kallos's dry heat and sea breezes.

The house was quiet as she entered, the rooms seeming to echo with silence all around her. She let out a long sigh, feeling both emotional and physical exhaustion in every muscle and sinew.

'Miss Talia!' Alma, her grandfather's housekeeper, came bustling towards her. 'You're back. You sent no word.'

'I'm sorry. I didn't have time.'

'It's all right, of course,' Alma assured her. 'Your grandfather will be so pleased to have you back home.'

'How is he?' Talia asked. She'd been in regular email contact with Giovanni, but she knew he would never mention any health concerns to her, especially when she was so far away.

'Tired,' Alma said with a small, sad smile. 'But in good spirits. He's upstairs in his usual room. He's just woken up, if you'd like to see him. Dante and Willow are here as well.'

Talia knew she'd have to tell Giovanni that she had been unsuccessful in retrieving his book, and she decided it would be better to get it over with sooner rather than later, and so with a nod she headed upstairs.

Giovanni was in a small sitting room that adjoined his bedroom, a blanket over his legs despite the heat, frowning as he clicked the remote control of the TV.

He glanced over as she opened the door, his wrinkled face breaking into a huge smile as he caught sight of her. 'Talia, *cara*! You have returned.' He held out his arms and Talia went to him, kissing his withered cheek and embracing him lightly before she sat down across from his chair. 'You do not look happy, *cara*,' Giovanni said. 'What has happened?'

'I wasn't able to get your book, Nonno. I'm sorry.'

Giovanni didn't answer for a moment; he simply stared at her, his gaze almost as assessing as Angelos's had been. 'But you tried, yes?' he finally said, and she nodded.

'Yes. And I did find it. But the book is very special to its current owner. It belonged to his late wife.'

'Did it?' Giovanni nodded slowly and leaned back in his chair.

'Apparently her grandmother was a lady's maid to a duchess on some island. The duchess gave it to her as a parting gift.'

'Ah. I see.' Giovanni closed his eyes briefly, and Talia wondered what he wasn't saying. 'I'm sorry,' she said again.

'It is no matter, Talia. But I don't think this unhappiness I see in you comes simply from not being successful in the task I set you.' He opened his eyes and gazed at her with kind shrewdness. 'Does it?'

'No,' she confessed, and couldn't manage any more. Her throat had gone tight and she blinked rapidly.

'Ah, Talia. I wanted you to see more of the world, to kindle the spark I know still lives in you for adventure, for life. But I fear I quenched it instead.'

'You didn't, Nonno,' Talia assured him. 'It's only…

living is hard sometimes. Feeling everything so much. You know?'

'Yes.' He smiled at her sadly and then reached out to clasp her hand. 'I know.'

Days passed by and Talia didn't leave the estate. She walked its manicured grounds, reacquainting herself with its beauty even as she yearned for the rocky hills and white sand beaches of Kallos. She missed Angelos and Sofia with an intensity that was like a physical pain; it kept her from eating and sleeping, leaving her hollow-eyed and gaunt.

Alma scolded her and tried to ply her with food and Talia attempted a few meals to appease the concerned housekeeper, but she couldn't stave off the sorrow that swamped her soul.

Finally, at the end of August, Giovanni confronted her. It had been two long weeks since she'd left Kallos, and she'd done no more than drag herself through each day.

'Cara, I can tell you are hurting,' Giovanni said without preamble. 'And I recognise the hurt it is. You are heart-broken.'

Talia managed a wobbly smile at her grandfather's astuteness. 'Maybe. I've never known what that feels like before.'

'I did not send you away to break your heart,' Giovanni said sternly. 'I sent you away to discover it again. This will not do, Talia. You must live—and love—once more.'

Talia nodded wearily. 'I want to, Nonno, but…'

'But nothing. I have arranged for a local gallery to showcase your work in two weeks' time.'

Talia's mouth dropped open. 'What…'

'I know you have resisted such public appearances before, but you know very well that many galleries have clamoured for your work. Every year they ask. It is time for you to appease them, Talia. It is time for you to show yourself to the world.'

CHAPTER SIXTEEN

'YOU'RE NOT WEARING THAT, surely?'

'What?' Talia looked down at her plain mint-green shift. It was the morning of her exhibition, and she'd taken care with her appearance, or at least she'd thought she had. 'This is one of my best dresses,' she told Willow, the fiancée of her brother Dante. They'd arrived a few days ago, as had many of her siblings, for her gallery exhibition today, but beyond a few conversations she hadn't seen much of either Willow or Dante, secluded as they were on one of the estate's private cottages.

Nerves fluttered in her stomach as she thought about what she was going to do this afternoon. Show her artwork to the world, rather than keep to private portraits. Circulate among the crowds, conquer her anxiety and claustrophobia. Hopefully.

Since her grandfather's pep talk Talia had realised she wanted to move on, even though it was hard, and maybe even impossible. She'd selected the paintings she was proudest of for the exhibition, excitement and anxiety coursing through her at the thought of showing them to the world. But the artwork she was most proud of was one that wouldn't be on display; it was a sketch of Angelos and Sofia that she had, after much deliberation, sent to him on Kallos.

It had been amazingly easy to draw them both from

memory. She'd sketched them on the beach, building a sandcastle as they had on that first outing on Kallos. She'd drawn Angelos's face suffused with love, and Sofia's with wonder, both of them working together, drawing pleasure from each other's company. It had felt like a healing, the lancing of a wound, to draw them. Each pencil stroke had been a blessing, and she hoped Angelos would keep the drawing, and see in it the esteem and affection she held for them both.

'So what's wrong with this dress?' she asked Willow, who was moving around her, clucking her tongue.

'Honestly? It looks like a green bin bag,' Willow said frankly, and Talia let out a reluctant laugh. She couldn't help but admire her brother's fiancée's plain speaking. 'Admittedly, a very nice shade of green,' Willow added generously, 'but still.' She shook her head, eyes dancing. 'You have a knockout figure and gorgeous hair, and you don't do much with either.'

'I've never had to,' Talia admitted. Living like a hermit precluded fancy hair, make-up or clothes.

'But today is different, isn't it?' Willow asked. 'It's meant to be special.'

'Yes...'

Willow glanced at the clock on the mantelpiece. 'We have a few hours before the exhibition. Will you let me give you a bit of a makeover? Only if you want to, of course.'

'A makeover?' Talia started to shake her head, inherently resisting the idea, before she paused. Why shouldn't she have a makeover? This was her new start, after all. She wanted to move on. Desperately. 'Sure,' she said, and smiled at Willow. 'Why not?'

He wasn't going to open it. Angelos stared at the plain brown manila envelope postmarked from America and scowled. He didn't want to know what Talia had sent. He didn't care.

It was a lie that was becoming harder and harder to believe, especially considering how much time he'd spent and sleep he'd lost thinking about Talia.

It had been a month since she'd left, an utterly endless thirty days of misery. The new nanny had arrived, and she was just what Angelos had wanted. Once. She was cool and capable and a little bit remote, and while her attention to Sofia was faultless, neither Angelos nor Sofia had been able to warm to her. Her laughter didn't ring through the rooms of the villa; she didn't speak in clumsy, pidgin Greek; she didn't have freckles on her shoulders and sunlight in her hair. She wasn't Talia.

He knew he should forget Talia. She'd lied to him, after all. In the month since she'd left Angelos had vacillated between regret at treating her so harshly and certainty that he'd done the right thing, the only thing. They had no future.

Expelling a low, frustrated breath, Angelos stared at the unopened parcel before him and then, his mouth in a hard line, he slit the envelope.

The paper he drew out was not the letter he'd been expecting. It was a drawing, and when he saw it for what it was his heart clenched hard inside him. He didn't need to see the initials 'TD' in the corner to know it was Talia's work.

Yet what humbled and amazed him was how she'd drawn him. He looked so…loving. Gentle and tender, like the best version of himself, a version he hadn't believed existed before Talia had come into his life. And she'd drawn Sofia with her face alight, her eyes bright with happiness. A slip of paper fell out of the envelope, and frowning, Angelos picked it up. His heart clenched again at the words Talia had written:

I drew what I saw.
This is who you really are.
—Talia

Angelos closed his eyes against the wave of regret that crashed over him. Talia had seen more in him, more hope and love and gentleness, than he'd ever shown her. How was that possible? And what could he do about it now?

He opened his eyes and gazed at the sketch once more, a lump forming in his throat, and then, swallowing it down, he put the drawing back in the envelope and rose from his desk.

'Almost ready.' Willow brushed Talia's face with loose powder before stepping back and examining her handiwork critically, her hands on her hips. 'I think you'll do,' she said with a wink, and Talia lifted one shaky hand to her hair that Willow had subdued into glossy perfection.

'I'm almost afraid to look.'

'And I'm almost insulted by that,' Willow teased. 'Look in the mirror.'

'Okay.' Taking a deep breath, Talia swivelled around in her chair to face the full-length mirror. And gasped in shock. Her usual tangle of golden-brown waves had been pulled into an elegant, smooth chignon. Her figure, usually shrouded by shapeless T-shirts and shorts, was encased in an ice-blue halter-top dress that clung to every slender curve. Matching high-heeled strappy sandals completed the outfit.

'Oh, my goodness,' she whispered. 'I don't think I've ever looked so...'

'Beautiful?' Willow filled in, and Talia let out an uncertain laugh.

'So glamorous. So on display.' She had, she realised,

hidden herself in more ways than one: both on the estate and in shapeless clothes. But she wanted to be different now. She would be different.

She smoothed her hands down the shiny satin of her dress before turning to Willow. 'Thank you. I feel great.'

'And you look great,' Willow said as she kissed her cheek. 'Don't forget it.'

'I won't.'

Most of her family had come for the gallery exhibition, and Talia was both humbled and amazed by their encouragement. She knew how busy everyone was, with her brothers and sisters all involved in some aspect of the Di Sione corporation. She appreciated them taking the time to come and show their support.

She rode to the gallery in her grandfather's limo; Giovanni sat next to her, looking more alert and refreshed than he had in a long time.

'I'm so pleased for you, *cara*,' he said, and patted her knee. Talia smiled back at him.

The gallery was housed in a shingle-roofed cottage by the beach, one wall made entirely of glass overlooking Long Island Sound.

The curator of the exhibit had done a fantastic job hanging her pictures, making the best use of the natural light and airy space. Waiters circulated with trays of canapés and flutes of champagne, and guests, including most of her family, had already arrived.

'Talia!' Her sister Bianca came towards her, arms outstretched.

'Bianca.' Talia hugged her sister; they'd always been close, separated only by a year. 'It's been too long.'

'I know, I know.' Bianca shook her head, blushing, her gaze moving from Talia to a rugged-looking man with sandy hair and ice-grey eyes. 'Liev,' she murmured. 'My fiancé.'

'I can't believe it,' Talia murmured as she hugged her sister again. Bianca let out a shaky laugh and hugged her back. 'I think there's a story behind this,' Talia said, and she laughed again.

'There is. But I'm not going to tell it now.'

'I'll be waiting.' Talia loved seeing her sister looking so happy; joy radiated from her in a way Talia knew she'd felt once, in Angelos's arms. 'I'm so glad you're happy, Bianca,' she said. 'I can tell how much you love him.'

'And he loves me,' Bianca answered. 'Which is amazing in itself—I remember finding a love letter once, between the pages of a book in the library, from someone named Lucia. I don't know who she was, or whom she was writing to, but reading that letter made me wonder what it would feel like to be loved so much. And now I know.'

'Lucia,' Talia repeated in surprise as she thought of the inscription in *Il Libro d'Amore*. 'Do you think…do you think she had something to do with Grandfather?'

'I don't know. He's never told us the real story behind the Lost Mistresses, has he?'

Talia glanced at her grandfather; he was chatting with her brother Matteo, smiling and nodding, and even though he looked better than he had in a long time, he was still tired and frail. 'I hope he tells us sometime,' she said quietly.

Talia continued to circulate among her guests, chatting to her brothers and sisters, enjoying their encouragement and praise. She noticed her half-brother, Nate, standing by a wall, holding a glass of champagne, and she approached him with a hesitant smile.

'Nate, it's been such a long time.'

'It always is,' Nate said with an answering smile and veiled eyes.

'You know you're the only brother I have whose portrait I haven't painted?'

'Half-brother.'

'I don't count by halves.'

His smile deepened and the darkness in his eyes lifted a little. 'I'm glad of that, Talia.'

'Will you sit for me? Please?'

'At the estate?'

'Does that bother you?'

He rubbed his jaw. 'I don't know.'

'Nate...' Talia put a hand on his sleeve. 'You should talk to him,' she said softly, for she'd seen that her brother's gaze had drifted to Giovanni and Matteo talking. 'He doesn't have long, you know. You should reconcile while you can.'

'Maybe,' Nate answered, but he didn't sound convinced.

'He asks after you sometimes,' Talia told him. 'Did you know that?'

Nate's gaze had darkened again and he shook his head. 'No, I didn't.'

'Talk to him,' Talia urged again. She was just turning away to greet another person when she caught a familiar figure in her peripheral vision. Even though she couldn't actually see the person, her body prickled in instinctive awareness and her heart began to beat hard.

Slowly she turned and looked towards the doorway of the gallery, where Angelos stood, his gaze burning into hers.

CHAPTER SEVENTEEN

'ANGELOS...' HIS NAME slipped from her lips, and she nearly swayed. Angelos strode towards her, the crowds parting before him, and then he was right there in front of her, looking tall and strong and as devastatingly attractive as ever.

'Talia, I'm sorry.'

'No, I'm sorry,' she blurted. 'For not telling you about the book. For leaving the way I did...'

'I let you leave. And I overreacted about the book.' He glanced around the room, every single person's speculative gaze swivelled towards them. 'May we talk in private? For a moment? And then I want to look at all these fabulous portraits, although I think I have the best one by far, back in Kallos.'

'You received the sketch?'

'Yes, and it made me realise how much I'd wilfully threw away. How stupid I was—' He broke off and reached for her hand. 'But let me tell you in private.'

Talia let him lead her outside, down to the beach that wasn't nearly as soft and white as the sand on Kallos, but she didn't care where she was, as long as she was with Angelos.

'Well?' she said, her voice wobbling a bit in trepidation, because even now she wasn't sure what he was going to say. She was afraid to hope, to *believe*... 'Why did you come all the way to New York?'

'To tell you I love you. And I'm sorry for the way I acted over that book.'

'You love me?' An incredulous smile bloomed across her face. 'Really?'

'I think I fell in love with you the first time you stormed into my office and demanded I spend more time with Sofia.'

'You seemed infuriated at the time—'

'I was,' Angelos admitted with a laugh. 'But I admired your strength and courage, and I knew you wanted to do right by my daughter.' He sat down on the sand, tugging her down with him. Talia went, heedless of her satin dress. They sat side by side in the sand, hands linked, savouring being together, before Angelos spoke again. 'I've been afraid, Talia,' he said quietly. 'Afraid of loving someone again, of giving my heart and then getting hurt.' His grip tightened on her fingers. 'I shut Sofia out for that reason, although I convinced myself it was for her benefit. Seeing your sketch of us made me realise how much I've missed, how much I haven't let myself feel. I thought it was because I couldn't, and I told myself I was staying away for Sofia's sake. But the truth is it was for my own. It's easier to build a shell around yourself than let yourself be hurt. I couldn't bear the thought of losing someone again.'

'I know you loved your wife very much, Angelos—'

'I did, but it doesn't mean I can't love again.'

'But when I told you about the book…' Talia swallowed hard. 'I left, at least in part, because I felt like I could never be first in your heart. The way you talked about your wife and the inscription in the book that you shared… I thought there was no way we could have that together.'

'We'll have something different,' Angelos answered, 'and every bit as strong and good. You're different than Xanthe, Talia. You reached me in a way she never did, as much as we loved each other.'

Talia frowned in confusion. 'What do you mean?'

'Xanthe never wanted to hear about my childhood. She wanted to pretend I'd been born a billionaire—I think she was ashamed of my humble roots.'

'But her grandmother was a lady's maid!'

'To a duchess,' Angelos reminded her. 'Everyone has a weakness, and perhaps that was hers. We loved each other, and it was a good marriage, but I am ready to move on. I know I need to, and I want to, with you.' His dark gaze met hers, and Talia ached see the touching uncertainty in his eyes. 'If you'll still have me.'

'Oh, Angelos, of course I will,' she exclaimed, her voice choking. 'I'm the one who should be sorry. I handled the whole thing with the book so wrong. I know I should have told you earlier. You said it's easier to build a shell around your heart—in my case, it was easier simply to run away. You helped me to face my fears but they still defeated me in the last moment. I left because I was hurting and scared, and I couldn't bear being around you while you shut me out. I should have stayed and battled it out.'

'Perhaps we needed some time apart,' Angelos allowed, 'as long as we don't have any more.'

'Never,' Talia agreed, and then to both her relief and joy, he slid his hands to frame her face and kissed her.

The touch of Angelos's lips to her own was a balm to her soul and sent sparks showering through her body. She deepened the kiss, every part of her yearning for him, and Angelos responded in kind. In moments they were both lying on the sand, limbs tangled together as their hands roved and their mouths fused.

Finally Angelos broke apart from her with a shaky laugh. 'I do not want to embarrass myself,' he said, running a hand through his hair as Talia tried to straighten her clothes. 'And I wanted to give you this.' He withdrew a familiar, slim volume from the inside of his jacket and Talia gasped in surprise.

'*Il Libro d'Amore*…but it's so precious to you…'

'And precious to your grandfather, I think, if he wanted it so much.'

'I don't fully understand why,' Talia answered. 'But I think there are many things my grandfather hasn't told me.' She took the book, running her hand along the butter-soft cover. 'But are you sure? I know how much this means to you.'

'You mean more to me, Talia,' Angelos said. 'I want you to give the book to your grandfather. He has only memories left. We have a future, together.'

'Then let's give it to him together,' Talia said, and Angelos smiled ruefully.

'I have not even met him or any of your family yet.'

'I'll introduce you,' she said. 'And then we can give the book to my grandfather. He'll be so pleased, not just to get the book, but to know I am happy with you. He could tell how miserable I was these last few weeks.'

'And so could Sofia with me,' Angelos admitted. 'Maria told me she'd never seen me so grumpy.'

'Now that's saying something,' Talia teased, and with her heart full and singing, she pulled him up from the sand and led him back to the gallery, where the rest of her life waited, ready to unfold.

* * * * *

Want even more
ROMANCE?

Join our bookclub today!

LET'S TALK
Romance

For exclusive extracts, competitions
and special offers, find us online:

 facebook.com/millsandboon

 @MillsandBoon

@MillsandBoonUK

Get in touch on 01413 063232

For all the latest titles coming soon, visit
millsandboon.co.uk/nextmonth